TYCOON PROTECTOR

"I need you, Ysabel."

More than I ever thought possible. "And you owe me a two-week notice."

"Does everything have to be on your terms?"

"Damn right." She had him tied in a knot so tight he couldn't remember how to breathe. His hand curled around the back of her neck, feathering through the silky smooth hair falling down to her waist.

"Someone needs to teach you a lesson on compromise." Her own arms twined around his neck and she brought his mouth closer to hers.

He stopped a breath away from her lips. "And I know just the one who can do it." Then his lips closed over hers.

Two months hadn't been nearly long enough to erase Ysabel from his mind, hadn't been long enough to make him forget how she felt against him.

And his body remembered.

First published in Great Britain 2010
Harlequin Mills & Boon Limited,
Eton House, 18-24 Paradise Road, Richmond, Surrey TW9 1SR

ISBN: 978 0 263 88239 1

46-0710

Harlequin Mills & Boon policy is to use papers that are natural, renewable and recyclable products and made from wood grown in sustainable forests. The logging and manufacturing processes conform to the legal environmental regulations of the country of origin.

Printed and bound in Spain
by Litografia Rosés S.A., Barcelona

MANHUNT IN THE WILD WEST

BY

JESSICA ANDERSEN

TYCOON PROTECTOR

BY

ELLE JAMES

MILLS & BOON

MANHUNT IN THE WILD WEST

BY
JESSICA ANDERSEN

Though she's tried out professions ranging from cleaning sea lion cages to cloning glaucoma genes, from patent law to training horses, **Jessica Andersen** is happiest when she's combining all these interests with her first love: writing romances. These days she's delighted to be writing full-time on a farm in rural Connecticut that she shares with a small menagerie and a hero named Brian. She hopes you'll visit her at

www.JessicaAndersen.com for info on upcoming books, contests and to say "hi!"

Chapter One

WWJBD? Chelsea Swan asked herself as she headed out to the loading dock of the medical examiner's office of Bear Claw, Colorado. The e-speak stood for *What Would James Bond Do?* and served as her mantra, though some days she replaced 007's name with some of her other favorite fictional spies: Jason Bourne, Ethan Hunt, Jack Bauer and the like.

Regardless of who she was trying to channel on a given day, the mantra meant one thing: don't be a wuss. On the scale of fight or flight, Chelsea fell squarely in the "flight" category, which wouldn't be such a big deal if another part of her didn't long for adventure, for the sort of danger she read about and watched on TV, and experienced secondhand through her bevy of cop friends.

She'd gone into pathology because she'd wanted to be near police work without actually carrying a gun, and because she liked medicine, but didn't want to be responsible for another human being's life. She was good at fitting together the clues she found during an autopsy, and turning them into a cause of death. She liked the puzzles, and the knowledge that her work sometimes helped the families understand why and how their loved one had died. Occasionally she'd even even assisted the Bear Claw Creek Police Department in finding a killer, and the success had given her a serious buzz.

Most days the job was rewarding without being actively frightening. Then there were days like today, when even James Bond might've hesitated. Chelsea figured she was entitled to some nerves, though, because while she was certainly no stranger to death, today was different. The dead were different.

The four incoming bodies belonged to terrorists, mass murderers who'd been incarcerated in the ARX Supermax prison two hours north of Bear Claw, and who'd died there under suspicious circumstances. The knowledge that she'd be autopsying their bodies in under an hour gave Chelsea a serious case of the willies as she headed out to meet the prison transport van. No matter how many times she told herself the dead deserved justice, she couldn't talk herself into believing it in this case.

Besides, the bodies came with major political baggage, which meant the ME's office would be under microscopic scrutiny.

Unfortunately, they didn't have a choice in the matter.

Three of the men, who went by the names of al-Jihad, Muhammad Feyd and Lee Mawadi, were international-level terrorists who'd been convicted of the Santa Bombings that had rocked the Bear Claw region three years earlier. The fourth, Jonah Fairfax, had tortured and murdered two federal agents in the days leading up to a bloody government raid on a militant anarchists' compound up in northern Montana, and had apparently hooked up with the terrorists inside the prison, despite being in 24/7 solitary confinement. The four were seriously bad news.

Chelsea, who usually managed to find the upside of any situation, wished the prison had stuck to its standard procedure of handling everything internally, including autopsies. Unfortunately, budget cuts had forced Warden Pollard to pare back his medical staff. When the four prisoners had died of unknown causes within an hour of one another, Pollard had requested an outside autopsy and the state had turfed the bodies to Bear Claw.

"Lucky us," Chelsea muttered as she pushed through the doors leading to the loading dock, which opened onto a narrow alley separating the two big buildings that housed the ME's office and the main station house of the Bear Claw Creek Police Department.

Two other members of the ME's office were already waiting on the loading ramp: Chelsea's boss and friend, Chief Medical Examiner Sara Whitney, and their newly hired assistant, Jerry Osage. Under normal circumstances there wouldn't have been a welcoming committee for the bodies, but these were far from normal circumstances. The deaths had gained national media attention at a time the ME's office would've strongly preferred otherwise.

That worry was in Sara's eyes as she turned to Chelsea, but her voice held its normal brisk, businesslike tone when she said, "I'm glad you're here. Chief Mendoza wants me to come out front and say a few words for the cameras so we can sneak the van in the back way while the newsies are distracted." Sara slipped out of her fall-weight wool jacket and held it out, revealing a jade-toned skirt suit that perfectly complemented her shoulder-length, honey-colored hair and arresting amber eyes. "Take this in case you're waiting long."

The mid-October day was unusually cool, thanks to

a sharp breeze that brought frigid air down from the snow-covered Rockies. It was just another change in the unusually unpredictable weather they'd been having lately. The mix of snow squalls and torrential downpours had triggered landslides in Bear Claw Canyon as well as the hills west of the city, taking out roads and at one point even prompting evacuation of the Bear Claw Ski Resort, which was just starting to gear up for the winter season.

For the moment, though, the skies were clear, the wind sharp. The Rocky Mountains were a dark blur on the horizon, well beyond the huge wilderness of Bear Claw Canyon State Park, which formed an unpopulated buffer between the city suburbs and the ARX Supermax prison.

Chelsea shivered involuntarily, though she couldn't have said whether the chill came from the wind biting through the thin scrubs she wore over her casual slacks and shirt, or the thought of how little actually separated them from an enclosure housing two thousand or so of the worst criminals in the country.

She took Sara's coat and drew it over her shoulders. "Thanks."

The garment was too long everywhere and she didn't have a prayer of buttoning it across the front, mute testimony that Sara was tall and lean and willowy, whereas Chelsea was none of those things.

Five-five if she stretched it, tending way more toward curvy than willowy, Chelsea wore her dark, chestnut-highlighted hair in a sassy bob that brushed her chin, used a daily layer of mascara to emphasize the long eyelashes that framed her brown eyes, and considered her smile to be her best feature. If life were a movie, she would probably play the best friend's supporting role to Sara's elegant lead, and that was okay with her.

Some people were destined to do great things, others small ones. That was just the way it was.

Within the ME's office, Chelsea was good at the small things. She was the best of them at dealing with the families of the dead, mainly because she genuinely liked people. She enjoyed meeting them and learning about them, and she liked knowing that the information she gave them often helped ease the passing of their loved ones. She might not be saving the world, but she was, she hoped, making the natural process of death a bit easier, one family at a time.

At the moment, though, she didn't particularly care if the incoming bodies were tied to people who had loved them and wanted answers. As far as she was concerned, monsters like the four dead men didn't deserve autopsies or answers. They deserved deep, unmarked graves and justice in the afterlife.

"I wish the prison had kept the bodies," Sara grumbled, her thoughts paralleling Chelsea's. Then she sighed, clearly not looking forward to the impromptu press conference. "Okay, I'll go do the song and dance and leave you guys to the real work."

The snippiness implied by her words was more self-directed than anything—as the youngest chief medical examiner in city history, and a woman to boot, she'd found herself doing far more politicking and crisis management than she'd expected, when Chelsea knew she'd rather be in the morgue, doing the work she'd trained for.

The two women had only met the year before, when Sara had pulled Chelsea's résumé out of a stack of better-qualified applicants because she'd been looking to build a young, cutting-edge team that combined empathy with hard science and innovation. That had been great until six months later, when the young, aggressive mayor who'd recruited Sara had stepped down in the wake of an embezzlement scandal, and his old-guard deputy mayor had taken over and promptly started undoing a large chunk of his predecessor's work.

Acting Mayor Proudfoot hadn't yet managed to disassemble the ME's office, but he was trying. That had Sara, Chelsea and the others watching their backs at every turn these days.

"We've got this," Chelsea assured her boss. "You go make us look good, okay?"

Sara shot her a grateful smile and headed inside. When the door shut at her back, Chelsea glanced at Jerry. She grinned at the sight of the assistant's obvious discomfort in the sharp air. "Dude, your nose is turning blue."

Dark-haired and brown-eyed, the twenty-something Florida native was having a tough time adjusting to his first cold snap, having moved to Bear Claw just that summer to be with his park-ranger girlfriend. But Jerry was a hard worker and an asset to the team. He didn't accept her invitation to bitch about the cold, instead saying, "The van's late. Wonder if the driver got lost or stuck in the media circus or something."

Chelsea pulled out her cell and checked the time display, frowning when she saw that he was right, the transpo coming from the prison was a good fifteen minutes overdue. "Maybe I should call the prison dispatcher and see if there's been a delay."

"Never mind. I think I see them."

Sure enough, a plain-looking van nosed its way into the alley, then spun away from them and started backing toward the cement loading dock, its brake lights flashing as the driver struggled to navigate the tight, unfamiliar alley, which was made even tighter by an obstacle course of trash bins and parked vehicles.

Unmarked and unremarkable, the van looked like nothing special on first glance, but a closer inspection revealed that it was reinforced throughout, with mesh on the small back windows.

Through the mesh, Chelsea could see one of the guards' faces. His eyes were a clear, piercing blue, and a thin scar ran through one of his dark eyebrows, probably tangible evidence of the dangers that came from working within the ARX Supermax.

As the van's rear bumper kissed the rubber-padded lip of the dock, the guard's eyes locked on Chelsea and another shiver tried to work its way through her. This one didn't come from the cold or unease about the prisoners' bodies, though; it was a sensual tremor, one that tempted her to rethink the "career first" vow she'd made in the wake of yet another near-miss of a relationship.

The guard's eyes hadn't changed and he hadn't moved, but suddenly her breath came thin in her lungs and she had to lock her legs against a wash of heat and weakness, and an almost overwhelming urge to see the rest of him. In private.

"Wow," she said aloud. "Note to self: take Sara up on her offer to bring her brother around for a look-see." Chelsea might've sworn off serious relationships, but there was no doubt her body was telling her that it was time for some recreational dating.

"'Scuse me?" asked Jerry, who looked confused.

"Just talking to myself," Chelsea said as the van came to a stop and the guard disappeared from the window.

She felt a little spurt of disappointment to have their shared look broken off, followed by a kick of nerves that she'd see the rest of him in a moment. Not that she was likely to follow up on the attraction, if it was even reciprocated. His direct, challenging stare warned that he'd probably be too intense for her, too unnerving.

She liked her guys the same way she preferred her Tex-Mex and curry: a little on the mild side, satisfying yet undemanding. She might be drawn to the other kind of guy, the tough, challenging sort she liked in her books and movies, but that was where her inner wimp kicked in. She didn't want to date a guy she couldn't keep up with.

And that was so not what she was supposed to be focusing on right now, she lectured herself as the driver killed the engine and emerged from the vehicle, carrying the requisite paperwork. Moments later, the back doors swung open and two other guys jumped down and started readying the body bags for transfer into the morgue. The men were wearing drab uniforms with weapon belts, and hats pulled low over their brows, making them blend into a certain sort of sameness…except for the blue-eyed guard, who Chelsea recognized immediately, even from the back.

He was maybe five-ten or so, with wide shoulders and ropy muscles that strained the fabric of his uniform, as though he'd bulked up recently and hadn't yet replaced his clothes. His hips were narrow, his legs powerful, and though she'd never really gone for the uniform look before—she was surrounded by cops on a daily basis, so there wasn't much novelty in it—the dark material of his pants did seriously interesting things to his backside when he bent over and fiddled with one of the gurneys, unlocking it from the fasteners that had kept it in place during transport.

As far as she could tell, two of the bodies were on gurneys, two on the floor of the van. Normally she would've been annoyed by the lack of respect for the dead. Not this time, though.

When the driver moved to hand the paperwork to Jerry, the assistant waved it off and pointed at Chelsea. "She's in charge. I'm just the muscle."

She tore herself away from ogling the guard to reach for the clipboard. "I'll take the paperwork. Jerry can help you unload and show you where the bodies go."

The driver frowned. "I thought a guy was supposed to sign off on the delivery. Rickey Charles."

Chelsea flipped through the pages, nodding when everything looked good. Once all the bags were inside the morgue, she would open them up and inspect the bodies, making sure the info matched. Then, and only then, would she sign the papers indicating that she'd accepted the delivery, freeing the guards to make the return trip to the prison.

Not paying full attention to the driver, she said, "Rickey got held up this morning. I'm covering."

Actually, her fellow medical examiner was in lockup, sleeping it off after being arrested on his third DUI, but she wasn't about to advertise the fact. Sara had made a monumental mistake hiring the charismatic young pathologist in the first place, but he was related to one of her higher-ups, and he'd fit the "young and innovative" stamp she'd been trying to put on the ME's office, so she'd given him a chance despite his less-than-stellar recommendations.

That'd come back to bite Sara, but Chelsea knew her

friend would handle it quietly. There was no need to gossip.

Noticing that the driver had started to fidget, she said, "Don't stress. It'll just take a few minutes."

He mumbled something, grabbed the clipboard and turned away, heading back for the van.

"Hey!" she called, starting after him. "I haven't signed off yet."

Just then, Jerry started pushing the first gurney toward the morgue, and she saw that he'd acquired a smear of red on the front of his scrubs.

"Jerry, stop," Chelsea said quickly as a twist of worry locked in her stomach. She crossed to the blue-eyed guard, who was facing away from her, prepping the second bag for transport. She tapped him on the shoulder. "Weren't these body bags surface-cleaned back at the prison?"

They certainly should've been. Not only was it standard protocol, but it was also doubly important in this case, given that they didn't yet know why or how the prisoners had died.

Her guard turned—that was how she found herself thinking of him, as "her guard," though that was silly—and she got the full-on gut punch of his charisma. His features were lean, his skin drawn and pale, and he didn't look like he smiled much. And those eyes…up close they were even more magnetic than she'd thought them from afar, ice blue and arresting, and holding a level of intensity that reached inside her and grabbed on, kindling a curl of heat in her belly.

He looked more like a grown-up than most of the thirty-somethings she knew. He looked like a leader, like someone who would take charge of any situation.

"We're just the transporters," he said, his voice a rough rasp that slid along her nerve endings and left tiny shivers behind. "We're running late, so it'd be best if you signed off on the delivery so we can be on our way." Something moved in his expression, there and gone so quickly she almost missed it, but leaving the impression that his words were more an order than a suggestion.

Nerves fired through her, warning that something wasn't right.

Not liking the feeling, or the strange effect the guard had on her, Chelsea backpedaled a step. But she stuck to operating procedures, saying, "I'm not signing anything if there's blood on the bags. You have no idea what killed these men. For all we know, it could be an infectious agent." She gestured for Jerry to step away from the gurney, and reached for her cell phone. "Leave everything right where it is. I'm calling my boss."

This is so not what Sara needs right now, she thought, but protocol was protocol, and if the medical staff at the ARX Supermax had been so sloppy as to allow the bodies to be shipped without the bags being disinfected first, who knew what other safety precaution they might've skipped?

"Wait," the blue-eyed guard said, holding up a hand. At that same moment, the guard behind him spun and grabbed for something on his belt. A gun.

Chelsea's eyes locked on the weapon, and she froze.

Jerry's head jerked up and his mouth went slack, his eyes locking on the other guard. "Hey, aren't you—"

The man shot him where he stood.

Jerry jerked spasmodically as blood bloomed in the center of his forehead. Then he went limp and fell, his eyes glazing as he dropped, his mouth open in an "O" of surprise.

To Chelsea, the world seemed to slow down, his body collapsing at half-speed. She sucked in a breath to scream, but before she could make a sound, something slammed into her temple, dazing her.

She staggered, only just beginning to realize that the guards weren't guards at all. They were convicts wearing the clothing of the guards who were no doubt filling the body bags in the van. Somehow the prisoners had played dead and then pulled a switch en route.

Heart drumming as her consciousness dimmed, Chelsea fumbled for her phone, and watched it spin out of her grasp and clatter to the ground, which pitched and heaved beneath her. The blue-eyed guard caught her as she fell, supporting her in his strong, steady arms, in a grip that shouldn't have felt as good as it did.

The last thing she comprehended before she passed out was a piercing sense of disappointment that somehow existed alongside the terror. Of course he was trouble; she'd never been truly attracted to any other kind of man. Sara had even joked one time that Chelsea's taste in men was going to be the death of her.

What if she'd been right?

Chapter Two

Jonah Fairfax hadn't touched a woman in nearly nine months, and this was *not* how he'd pictured ending the drought.

When Fax had imagined his reintroduction to feminine companionship from the sterile gloom of his six-by-ten cell, he'd figured on candlelight, good food and soft music, and either a paid escort or a sympathetic friend of a friend. Or, hell, even his handler and sometimes lover, who called herself Jane Doe even in bed.

The woman's identity hadn't been particularly important to his sexual fantasy. What had mattered were the trappings of civilization, the colors and smells, and the textures of real life.

However, that fantasy most definitely hadn't involved a prison meat wagon backed up to the morgue where they'd been stood up by Rickey Charles, the contact who was the key to the next stage in their getaway. And it definitely hadn't starred a pistol-whipped woman hanging limply in his arms…and three seriously nasty terrorists glaring at him like they already regretted involving him in their jailbreak.

Not that they'd had a choice. He'd made damn sure of

that, with help from Jane and some of the other agents working underneath her. She headed up a national security agency so secret it didn't even have a name, one that was organized along the lines of the very terror networks it hunted, with each agent functioning as a separate cell, not knowing who else might be involved, or how.

For this particular op, Jane had gotten Fax arrested for murder, constructing such a deep, seamless cover that even his mother and brothers had written him off. That had been the only way to make him useful to al-Jihad, just as orchestrating an escape had been the only way they could come up with to flush out the high-level terrorist's suspected contacts within Homeland Security itself.

The deaths of the prison guards and the morgue attendant were regrettable, but Jane had chosen Fax for the op because she knew he could function in the bloodiest situations and deal with an acceptable level of collateral damage—and innocent lives lost—if it meant getting the job done. It was cold, yes, but necessary.

Jane had honed that level of detachment, perhaps, but he could thank his wife, Abby, for setting him on the path. She'd been dead five years now, and he thought she would've hated what he'd become. No way she would've accepted the part her betrayal had played—she'd never been big on personal accountability. But even as he thought that, Fax was mildly surprised to realize it'd been some time since he'd last thought of the woman who'd been his high-school sweetheart, and later his wife. In the past, her memory had driven him, haunted him, made him into the bloodless man he'd become, the one Jane had needed and wanted.

Now, it seemed, even the warmth of anger was fading, leaving him colder still.

"You gonna kill the bitch or dance with her first?" Lee Mawadi asked, nodding to the woman in Fax's arms with a sneer.

Then again, Lee seemed to do pretty much everything with a sneer. Fax was pretty sure it covered some major insecurities.

Fax didn't know any of his fellow escapees well, because the 24/7 solitary confinement at the ARX Supermax tended to cut down on social discourse. He'd met the three terrorists in person for the first time just an hour earlier, when they'd awoken from the drugs Jane had smuggled to him, which had mimicked death close enough to pass inspection for twelve hours.

Almost immediately upon awakening, Fax had pegged the thirtysomething, blond Lee Mawadi as a wannabe, a follower. Lee had grown up a rich, pampered American, but had developed a love of violence along the way, a desire to kill, and be part of a killing squad. He'd hooked up with al-Jihad and had found the leader he'd been seeking. He'd played the part of a businessman, married a photographer and lived the American dream, all while working as a member of al-Jihad's crew, following orders without question.

Lee was a lemming, but Fax suspected he was a nasty critter, the sort that would bite you before it ran off the cliff in pursuit of its leader.

"No need to kill her," Fax said in answer to Lee's question. "She's out cold." He shifted the woman's deadweight, figuring on dumping her off to the side, out of harm's way. The younger, male morgue attendant was beyond help, but if Fax played it right, he could probably leave the woman alive without attracting too much suspicion. Motioning to the van with his chin, he raised his voice and called to the other members of the small group, "Let's get out of here. Our cover's blown to hell thanks to Lee's itchy trigger finger."

As planned, they'd come out of the coma-inducing meds mid-transpo. Fax had suffered a moment of atavistic terror at finding himself zipped inside a body bag, but al-Jihad had come through as promised. The bag was taped shut rather than zippered, and one of the four guards had distracted the others long enough for the prisoners to emerge from their bags and get into position. Then they'd killed all four guards—including their accomplice, whom al-Jihad didn't trust to stay bought—by breaking their necks, so as to keep their uniforms unbloodied. Then they'd switched places, four for four. Fax didn't know what the death-mimicking meds had contained, but they'd left him with a nasty hangover and occasional double vision. That didn't matter, though. He was still alive, his cover intact. His job was to keep it that way until he figured out who al-Jihad was working with, and what they planned to do next.

With fanatical monsters like him it wasn't a case of if; it was a case of when and where.

"Hey!" Slow to catch the insult, Lee spun in the midst of dragging the younger man's body into the van. "The guy recognized me. I had no choice!"

"Maybe," Fax retorted, propping the woman up against the cold cement wall, partially hidden behind a Dumpster. "Maybe not."

Knowing he was pushing it, he slid a look at the other two men, who as far as he was concerned were far more dangerous than Lee Mawadi.

Muhammad Feyd's dossier pegged the dark-eyed, dark-haired man at thirty-eight, a fanatic among fanatics who'd left al Qaeda in search of a more proactive group of anti-Western terrorists. He'd found exactly that in the man seated in the passenger's seat of the prison transpo van…a man known simply as al-Jihad.

The terrorist leader's dossier was thin, devoid of any information predating the new millennium. He'd appeared on the world stage just before the September 11th terror attacks, had slipped out of the country immediately thereafter, and had played tag with Homeland Security for the next several years. Federal law enforcement suspected that he'd been the mastermind behind numerous bombings and other atrocities, but had never managed to concretely tie him to any of the attacks until he'd finally been tried and convicted for the Santa Bombings that had occurred in several major Colorado cities a few years earlier.

Targeting six shopping malls all owned by the American Mall group, the bombings had been planned to coincide with the ceremonial arrival of the mall Santas to their decorated thrones. All six of the Santas had died…along with the parents and children who'd been lined up, eagerly awaiting the kickoff to the holiday season.

It had been terrorism at its most horrible, and local and federal law enforcement had worked around the clock to indict and convict al-Jihad and his henchmen. They had succeeded, but the evidence had been more circumstantial than proof-positive. The terrorists' high-powered defense attorney had lodged appeal after appeal, but the filings had wound up logjammed in the legal system, which Fax figured was no accident. The courts had no love of terrorists.

The delay had given Jane time to formulate Fax's cover and arrange to have him locked up in the same prison as the terrorist leader and his two lieutenants. She'd turned Fax's honorable military discharge into a dishonorable ousting, cast him in the role of anarchist, invoked the USA PATRIOT Act and held him without trial, making him that much more attractive to an anti-American bastard like al-Jihad.

And thus, an unholy alliance had been born, right on schedule.

In person, the terrorist leader was tall, thin and angular, and graceful enough in his movements that he almost appeared effete…except for his eyes, which were those of a killer.

From reading the available reports, Fax had known that al-Jihad would be a smart, driven, dangerous man. Meeting him in the flesh had reinforced that impression and added a new realization: the bastard wasn't just dangerous; he was completely without a conscience when it came to killing Americans. Worse, he enjoyed the hell out of it.

That put Fax in an even more tenuous position than he'd anticipated, making it a seriously bad idea to draw attention. Yet that was just what he was risking if he fought too hard to save the pretty medical examiner from becoming part of the collateral damage.

"Boss?" Lee said plaintively, looking at the passenger's seat of the van, where al-Jihad sat silent and square-shouldered.

The terrorist leader sent his follower a dark look that all but said "get a spine," yet he said nothing.

Muhammad aimed a kick at Lee and growled, "Get in the damn van." He jerked his chin at Fax. "You, too. And bring the woman. We'll need a hostage if things get sticky on the way out."

The original plan had been for Rickey Charles—whom al-Jihad had somehow contacted and bribed—to cover the switch for as long as possible, giving them time to get well away. In the absence of that help, their window of opportunity to escape cleanly was closing fast.

"But—" Fax bit off the protest, knowing he was already on tenuous footing with the terrorists.

The only reason he was there at all was because he'd developed the contact for the death-mimicking drugs they'd needed to get on the meat wagon. He'd contacted al-Jihad through a Byzantine trail of notes hidden in the few common areas the prisoners were given access to, one at a time. He'd offered the drug in exchange for a place within al-Jihad's terror cell, and the plan had been born.

Frankly, he was somewhat surprised they hadn't tried to kill him yet, now that they were outside the prison walls. That they hadn't tried to off him indicated that they still had some use for him, but he had a feeling that amnesty wouldn't last long if he started arguing orders.

She's acceptable collateral damage, he told himself, and went back for the woman.

Damned if she didn't stir a little and curl into him when he picked her up and held her against his chest. Surprised, he looked down.

She had dark, chestnut-highlighted hair and faint freckles visible through a fading summer tan. Her cheeks and lips were full, her chin softly rounded, and her nose turned up slightly at the end, giving her an almost childlike, vulnerable air. But there was nothing childlike about the curves that pressed against him, and there was sure as hell nothing juvenile about the unexpected surge of lust that slammed into him when she shifted and turned her face into his neck, so her hair tickled the edge of his ear and feathered across the sensitive skin beneath his jaw.

"Move your ass," Lee snapped from inside the van.

Muhammad finished disabling the vehicle's state-issued GPS locator and got in the driver's seat, then gunned the engine to warn Fax that he was running out of time.

Sometimes it's necessary to sacrifice a few to save the rest, Fax reminded himself. Still, his stomach twisted in a sick ball as he slung the woman through the side door of the vehicle, so she landed near her dead friend, whose corpse was stacked with two of the guards' bodies. The other two bodies were still on the gurneys, one of which was jammed in at an angle where Lee had shoved it in after their escape plan had blown up in their faces.

Even without Rickey Charles, they might've bluffed their way through the body transfer and talked the woman into signing off without confirming the identities of the corpses, but once Lee killed the morgue attendant, even that slim chance had disappeared.

Their escape could get real messy real quick, Fax knew. Problem was, he needed them to get free so the terrorists would reach out to their contacts and plan their next move.

Which meant the woman's life—and his own, for that matter—were expendable in the grand scheme of things.

Hating the necessity more than he would've expected to, he jumped into the van and rolled the side door closed just as Muhammad hit the gas and the van peeled away from the ME's office.

The four men braced to hear the alarm raised any second, to see pursuit behind them. But there was no alarm, no pursuit as al-Jihad's second in command navigated the city streets of Bear Claw.

Fax noted that they were heading roughly northward, back in the direction of the prison rather than away, but he didn't ask why, didn't even let on that he'd noticed or even cared. He simply filed the information, and hoped like hell he'd have a chance to get it to Jane before al-Jihad and the others decided he'd outlived his usefulness.

Maybe five miles outside the city limits, well down a deserted road that wound through the state forest, Muhammad pulled off into a small parking lot that served a trailhead leading into the wilderness.

Al-Jihad, who was still riding shotgun, turned to Lee and Fax, and said in his dead, inflectionless voice, "Kill the woman and dump all of the bodies in the canyon. We won't need them where we're going."

Which is where? Fax wanted to ask but didn't because he knew the game too well. The more he followed orders without question, the longer he would live, and the more information he'd gain about the structure of al-Jihad's network inside the U.S.

So instead of asking the questions he wanted answered, he nodded and rolled open the side door, then waited while Lee climbed out. When the other man turned back, Fax shoved one of the body bags at him.

Lee caught the dead guard and nearly went down. "Watch it!" he snapped, glaring at Fax.

"Sorry," Fax said with little remorse, having already figured out that al-Jihad and Muhammad liked the fact that he didn't let the lemming push him around. Jerking his chin in the direction of the trailhead, he said, "I'll be right behind you."

Lee muttered something under his breath, but slung the body bag over his shoulder in a fireman's carry, and headed off into the woods, struggling only slightly under his burden.

Hyperaware of the scrutiny he was receiving from the two men in the front of the van, Fax reached down for the woman, his mind spinning as he desperately tried to figure out a way to keep her alive while protecting his cover.

He didn't know her name, but somehow she'd become the symbol of all the warm, civilized things he'd dreamed of from the confines of his cell, all the beauty and laughter he lived in the darkness to protect.

Jane might be his boss and sometimes lover, but the pretty medical examiner was a real person, one who belonged in the sunlight, not the shadows.

Hefting her over his shoulder, he turned and headed into the forest in Lee's wake. Once he was out of earshot, he said under his breath, "I know you're awake. Don't do anything stupid and you might live to see our backs."

CHELSEA STIFFENED at the sound of his voice, but was too terrified to process his words. The only reason she wasn't already screaming was because she was too damn scared to breathe. That, and she was pretty sure there was nobody nearby to hear except the escaped convicts, who would probably enjoy her terror. So she kept the panic inside, save for the tears that leaked from beneath her screwed-shut eyelids.

She couldn't believe she'd been kidnapped, couldn't believe that the blue-eyed guard—or rather, the blue-eyed *escaped convict*—she'd been ogling on the loading dock was carrying her into the state forest, acting on a terrorist's orders to kill her and dump her in Bear Claw Canyon.

Things like that just didn't happen to small-scale people like her.

She would've thought it was all a dream, a nightmare, except that the sensations were too real: her head pounded from the blow that'd knocked her unconscious, her tears were cool on her cheeks, and the man's shoulder dug into her belly as he carried her along the path. Opening her eyes, she saw that what she'd figured were signs of recent muscle gain were actually places where his uniform didn't fit; the material gapped at the small of his back, where he'd tucked the guard's weapon into his belt.

WWJBD? She knew she should struggle, she should try to escape, but when? Now or after they reached their destination? What were the chances she could grab that gun and turn the tables?

"Don't," he warned in a low voice.

Before she could respond, or act, or do anything, really, she heard another man's voice from up ahead, saying, "I found a cave. Dump her and put a bullet in her. I'll go get another load."

The man's voice was casual, careless, like he was talking about things rather than people. But to him she and the others *were* things, she realized. They were Americans. The enemy. Yet the speaker was blond, and his voice carried a trace of a Boston accent. She would've passed him on the street and never once thought to wonder about him.

Vaguely, she remembered a snippet of newscast that'd said one of the three escapees, Lee Mawadi, was a homegrown terrorist who'd hooked up with al-Jihad for the Santa Bombings.

Back then, sitting safe in her living room, terrorism had been an abstract concept, something she saw on TV and exclaimed over while secretly thinking that such things would never happen to her. She hadn't even been in Colorado during the Santa Bombings; she'd been finishing a nice, safe rotation in a private practice outside Chicago, reveling in the early stages of a relationship she'd thought was The One, but had turned out to be another Not Quite.

Now, though, she was all alone, with terror her only companion.

"Sounds good to me," the man carrying her said, his voice easy as he agreed to the plan of shooting her and dumping her in the cave.

But his touch, while firm, was disconcertingly gentle and he'd hinted at the possibility that she might live. Did that mean he had a soft spot for her because of their shared look out by the loading dock? Would he somehow prove to be an ally?

Get a grip, her inner voice of practicality snapped. *He's a murderer.*

If the other speaker was Lee Mawadi, then the blue-eyed man she'd shared a long look with must be Jonah Fairfax. That meant he hadn't been part of the Santa Bombings, but it didn't make him innocent or safe. The ARX Supermax didn't cater to white-collar criminals, and Fairfax had been jailed for torturing and murdering two of the FBI agents sent to infiltrate the anarchist camp he'd been a member of.

Yet he'd made it sound like he wanted to save her somehow. It made no sense.

When footsteps warned that the other man—Lee Mawadi—was passing them on the trail, Chelsea screwed her eyes shut. Moments later, the sunlight beyond her eyelids cut to black and the echoes told her that they'd entered the cave he'd spoken of.

The blue-eyed man—Fairfax—flipped her off his shoulder without warning, then caught her before she could slam to the ground. She kept her eyes shut as he lowered her so she was half propped up against a rock wall. She could feel him crouch over her, leaning close and blocking any hope of escape.

"I need you to stop playing dead and listen very carefully," he said, his voice low and urgent. "I think I can get you out of this, but you're going to have to trust me."

She opened her eyes at that, and nearly screamed when she saw that he'd put her down right next to one of the body bags. Worse, it was open, revealing one of the dead guards, shirtless, his eyes open and staring in death.

She held in the scream, but plastered herself against the rock wall, her quick, panicked breaths rattling in her lungs.

"Look at me." The blue-eyed man touched her chin and turned her head toward him. "Don't scream and don't move. Lee is going to be back in a minute, so we've got to work fast." He paused as though gauging her. "I need to get something out of my shoe. Can I trust you not to try to run?"

She nodded quickly, though she didn't mean it. The second an opportunity presented, she was so out of there.

He gave her another, longer look. "Yeah. That's what I thought." As though he'd read her mind, he stayed between her and the mouth of the cave, which was little more than a crevice in the rock, probably part of the canyon that'd been pushed up and over ground level by a long-ago glacier or earth shift, or maybe even one of the recent landslides.

Fairfax worked at his right shoe for a moment and came up with a small ampoule of pale yellow liquid. He crowded close to her, leaving no room for retreat or escape. "This is going to knock you out and depress your vitals so far that it'll look like you're dead, but you won't be. You'll come around in twelve hours or so, and we'll be long gone."

Then, before she could react, before she could protest, or scream, or any of the other things she knew she damn well ought to do, he'd broken off the tip of the ampoule, jammed the needle-point end into her upper arm, and squeezed the yellow liquid into her.

Pain flared at the injection site, hard and hot.

She opened her mouth to scream but nothing came out. She struggled to stand up and run, but her legs wouldn't obey. Her muscles turned to gelatin and she started sliding sideways, and this time Fairfax didn't catch her or break her fall.

She heard him stand, heard a weapon's action being racked in preparation for firing. Then there was a single gunshot.

Then nothing.

FAX KNEW HE didn't have much time, if any. He went to his knees beside the body bag containing the dead guard, whom he'd just shot. Pressing his hand against the wound, he got as much cool blood as he could from the dead man, and slathered it across the unconscious woman's face, concentrating on the hair above her temple.

When he heard footsteps at the entrance to the cave, he readjusted the body bag and wiped off his hands on part of the woman's coat, then tucked the stained section beneath her before he stood.

Feigning nonchalance, he put the safety on his gun and stuck the weapon in his waistband before he turned toward Lee, hoping like hell the lemming wouldn't notice that the blood on the woman wasn't exactly fresh.

Only the newcomer wasn't Lee. It was al-Jihad himself.

The terrorist leader stood silhouetted at the cave mouth, a lean, dark figure whose presence was significantly larger than his physical self.

A shiver tried to crawl down the back of Fax's neck but he held it off, determined to brazen out the situation and keep himself in the killer's good graces. Gesturing casually toward the woman, he said, "She's all set. Want me to go help Lee with the other guards?"

Al-Jihad moved past him without a word, gliding almost silently, seeming incorporeal, like the demon he was. Crouching down beside the woman's motionless, blood-spattered body, he touched her cheek, then her throat, checking for a pulse.

Fax forced himself not to tense up, reminded himself to breathe, to act like the cold, jaded killer Abby's betrayal had made him into. Only the thing was, something had changed inside him. He'd been playing the role of convict for so long it'd become second nature to hold the persona within the prison, but he found he was in danger of slipping now that they were outside those too-familiar walls.

Hell, face it; he'd already slipped. There was no rational reason for him to jeopardize his position by faking the woman's murder. The ampoule of the death-mimicking meds he'd tucked into a false, X-ray-safe compartment inside one of his not-quite-prison-issue shoes was supposed to be a safety net, a way for him to fake his own death if the need arose. Similarly, the GPS homing device he'd activated and placed in her coat pocket was supposed to be used only if he thought he was in imminent danger of being killed, and wanted to make sure Jane could find his body.

Sure, he'd also planted a message on the woman, information he needed to get to Jane. But he could've gotten the info to her in other ways, ones that wouldn't have used up so much of his dwindling bag of tricks.

So why had he gone all out to save a woman whose name he knew only because he'd palmed the ID tag off her scrubs?

Reaching into his pocket to touch the plastic tag, which read *Chelsea Swan*—a lovely name for a lovely woman—he thought he knew why he'd endangered himself and his mission for her. It was the freckles. Abby had had freckles like that, back when they'd been high-school sweethearts, before he'd done his stint in the military, blithely assuming things would stay the same while he was gone.

Back when Abby'd had freckles, their biggest problems had been arguments over which movie to see, or which radio station to play as they'd tooled around town in his beat-up Wrangler with the soft top down. Eventually, though, she'd outgrown her freckles…and him.

Chelsea Swan reminded him of those earlier times. Good times. Times that might as well have happened to someone else. But because they hadn't, and because she looked like the sort of person who ought to have more good times ahead of her, he'd dabbed blood over her scalp and face to simulate a head wound, and he'd used his meds to make her body play dead.

Question was, would it be enough to save her?

Al-Jihad stood without a word, and gestured for Fax to return to the vehicle. "Go help Lee."

Fax stayed tense as he followed orders, fearing that

al-Jihad was playing him, that the bastard knew what he'd done and was teasing him with the illusion of success. But the terrorist leader returned to the van a few minutes later, and on Fax's next trip into the cave, he saw that Chelsea remained just as he'd left her.

He and Lee finished unloading the other bodies, opening up each of the bags so the scent would attract scavengers, in hopes that they'd deface the bodies, further complicating forensic analysis when the dump site was eventually found. At least that was the terrorists' theory. In reality, the homing beacon would have Jane's people on-site in a few hours.

Once the job was done, Fax hung back in the cave.

"Move it," Lee snapped when they both heard an impatient horn beep from the direction of the road. "The cops'll get the roadblocks up soon."

"I'm right behind you," Fax said. But as the other man hustled down the trail, Fax stayed put.

Moving fast, he pulled the jacket and heavy sweatshirt off the dead morgue attendant, and packed them around Chelsea's limp body. When that didn't look like it'd be enough, he whispered, "Sorry," and pulled the attendant's still-warm corpse over her as added insulation. It was too cold and her vitals were too depressed for him to worry about niceties. If Jane took too long to respond, Chelsea could freeze to death.

Hopefully, though, Jane would send someone right away. The responding agent could then administer the counteragent to the death-mimicking drug, collect the GPS beacon and info pellet Fax had planted on Chelsea, and phone in an untraceable tip that would lead the locals to the location. The agent would undoubtedly also reset the scene, making it look as though her survival had been accidental rather than intentional.

With no way of knowing where al-Jihad had eyes and ears, they had to be careful not to make it obvious that the terrorist had a traitor among his small crew.

"Just hang on for a few hours, Chelsea," Fax said quietly, his words echoing in the cave. "Help should be on its way soon."

Then, knowing he'd done the best he could for her, he paused at the cave mouth and looked back at the six bloodied bodies, five of which weren't going to wake up ever again.

"Collateral damage," he murmured. Uncharacteristically, he found himself regretting that he couldn't have saved the others, hadn't even tried. And, as he walked into the sunlight, he found himself wishing that he believed he was going to live long enough to see pretty Chelsea Swan again, under better circumstances.

But as soon as he caught himself thinking along those lines, he squelched the emotions.

There was no room for softness around men like al-Jihad, and Fax had a job to do. That took priority, period.

Chapter Three

"She's coming around." Chelsea felt a couple of light taps on her face, and heard a babble of voices close by, but she couldn't quite grasp what any of it meant.

Reality and recognition were distant strangers. Cocooned in a warm lassitude, she felt too lazy to move, too tired to care that moving was impossible.

"Are you sure none of this is her blood?" a second voice asked, this one female.

"Positive," the first voice answered. "She doesn't have a single laceration on her, just the bump on the back of her head."

"Then where'd the blood come from?"

"From one of the others, looks like." Another series of taps on her face. "Chelsea? Can you hear me?"

She moaned and swatted at the hand that was gently slapping her. At least she tried to swat. She failed, though, because her arms didn't move.

"Here she comes," the first voice said, sounding pleased. "Okay, kiddo. I need you to open your eyes now. Can you do that for me?"

Chelsea did as she was told, squinting into the fading light of dusk, which showed that she was inside a cave of sorts. The details were lost to the shadows and the glare of handheld lights, but she was aware of numerous people inside the small space, most of them cops.

A paramedic was crouched over her. Behind a plastic face shield, his brown eyes were dark with concern. It wasn't the concern that confused her though; it was her sudden, utter conviction that his eyes were the wrong color. They weren't supposed to be brown; they were supposed to be…

Blue, she remembered. Ice-cold blue.

The memory of the man's eyes unlocked a flood of other recollections. She gasped as the memories swamped her, slapping her with terror and confusion, and the unbelievable realization that Jonah Fairfax, double murderer, had done exactly as he'd promised. He'd saved her.

But as the pieces lined up in her brain—sort of—they didn't click. He'd said the drug would take twelve hours to wear off, and she'd been abducted near lunchtime, yet she could see dusk outside.

"What day is it?" she asked, her voice cracking from disuse and whatever drug he'd stuck in her system.

The paramedic said, "Tuesday. Why?"

Which meant she'd only been out for a few hours. "How did you find me?"

"Anonymous tip," he said, looking past her to confer with someone outside her line of vision.

Her brain jammed on the information, which didn't make sense. Fairfax had said something about the escapees being well away by the time she came around, but she'd only been out for a few hours. Had he changed his mind and made the call himself? Had—

The spiraling questions bounced off each other inside

her throbbing skull and logjammed, and a sudden shiver wracked her body. "I'm f-freezing," she managed between chattering teeth.

"We're working on that," the paramedic replied. "We'll have you out of here in a jiff."

It wasn't until he and his partner lifted her that she realized she was on a stretcher, swathed in blankets and strapped down, which explained the feeling of immobility.

She was aware of commotion around her as she was carried out of the cave and back along the wooded trail. She caught glimpses of concerned faces, many of them belonging to cops she saw in the ME's office on a regular basis. She wanted to stop and talk to them, wanted to tell them what had happened to her, but her lips didn't work right and the light was all funny, going from the blue of dusk to a strange grayish-brown and back again.

When they reached the ambulance, Sara was there waiting, tears coursing down her cheeks when she saw Chelsea. Her lips moved; the words didn't make any sense but Chelsea knew her friend well enough to guess Sara was apologizing for leaving her out on the loading dock.

It wasn't your fault, Chelsea tried to say. *Don't blame yourself. I'll be okay—Fairfax saved me.* But the words didn't come out. She couldn't move, couldn't speak, couldn't do anything but let the world slip away as the paramedics loaded her into the waiting ambulance.

Everything faded to the gray-brown of unconsciousness.

She surfaced a few times after that—once as she was being wheeled through the hospital corridors, the fluorescent lights flashing brightly overhead, and once again during some sort of exam, when she heard doctors' and nurses' voices saying things like, "That doesn't make any sense" and "Check it again."

She didn't come around fully until early the next morning. She knew it was morning because of the way the light of dawn bled pale lavender through the slatted blinds that covered the room's single window, and the way her body was suddenly clamoring for breakfast and coffee, not necessarily in that order.

A quick look around confirmed that she was, indeed, in the hospital, and added the information that homicide detective Tucker McDermott was fast asleep in the chair beside her bed.

The realization warmed her with the knowledge that her friends had closed ranks around her already.

She knew Tucker through the ME's office, and more importantly through his wife, Alyssa, who was a good friend. Alyssa, a forensics specialist within the BCCPD, was quick-tempered and always on the go. In contrast, Tucker was a rock, steady and dependable. He might've had a flighty playboy's reputation a few years back, but marriage had settled him to the point that he'd become the go-to guy in their circle, the one who was always level in a crisis, always ready to listen or offer a shoulder to lean on.

He made her wimpy side feel safe.

She must've moved or made some sound indicating that she'd awakened, because he opened his eyes, blinked a couple of times, then smiled. "Hey. How are you feeling?"

"I'm—" She paused, confused. "That's weird. I feel fine. Better than fine, actually. I feel really good." Energy coursed through her alongside the gnawing hunger, but there were none of the lingering aches she would've expected from her ordeal. Lifting a hand, which didn't bear an IV or any monitoring lines, she probed the back of her head and found a bruised lump, but little residual pain. Oddly, though, she didn't feel the brain fuzz of prescription-strength painkillers. "What did the doctors give me?"

Tucker shook his head. "Nothing. By the time you arrived, your core temp was coming back up and your vitals were stabilizing. They decided to let you sleep it off and see how you felt when you woke up."

"I'm okay," she said weakly, her brain churning. "Okay" wasn't entirely accurate, though, because the more she thought about her ordeal the more scared and confused she became, as terrifying images mixed with the memory of the convict who'd saved her life, and the coworker who'd lost his.

"Jerry's dead, isn't he?" she asked softly.

She remembered the gunshot, remembered him falling, even remembered him lying in the van, limp in death, but a piece of her didn't want to accept that he was gone. She wanted to believe he'd been stunned like she'd been. Not dead. Not Jerry, with his cold nose and ski-bunny girlfriend.

But Tucker shook his head, expression full of remorse. "I'm sorry."

Chelsea closed her eyes, grief beating at her alongside guilt. She should've done something different. If she hadn't been staring at Fairfax, she might've been quicker to recognize that there was a problem with the delivery. She might've been able to—

"Don't," Tucker said. "You'll only make yourself crazy trying to 'what if' this. If you'd done something different, they probably would've killed you, too."

"They did, sort of," Chelsea whispered, her breath burning her throat with unshed tears.

Tucker shifted, pulled out his handheld, which acted as both computer and cell phone. "You okay if I record this?"

She nodded. "Of course." No doubt she'd have to go through her statement over and over again with a variety of cops and agents, but this first time she'd rather talk to Tucker than anyone else.

Haltingly at first, she told him what had happened, her words coming easier once she got started, then flowing torrentlike when she described waking up in the van and realizing she'd been kidnapped by the escapees, followed by Fairfax's strange actions. She kept it facts only, reporting what he'd done and said, and figuring she'd leave it to Tucker and the others to draw their own conclusions.

When she was done, she glanced at Tucker and was unsurprised to see a concerned frown on his face.

"That sounds…"

"Bizarre," she filled in for him. "Like something from a not-very-believable action movie. I know. But that's what happened."

He nodded, but she could tell he didn't believe her. Or rather, he probably believed that *she* believed what she was saying, but thought her so-called memories were more along the lines of drug-induced hallucinations shaped by her penchant for spy movies that always included at least one double agent and a couple of twists.

Then again, she thought with a start, what if he was right? She felt terrible that she'd been paying more attention to Fairfax's butt than to her job and the potential security risks, opening the way for Jerry's murder. What if her subconscious had taken that guilt and woven a fantasy that cast the object of her attraction as a hero, making her lapse, if not acceptable, then at least less reprehensible?

"Maybe I'm not remembering correctly," she said after a moment.

"The info about Rickey Charles fits," Tucker said, though he still sounded pretty dubious. "He was found dead in his holding cell this morning."

Chelsea sat up so fast her head spun. "He what?"

Tucker winced. "I should've phrased that better. Sorry, I went into cop-talking-to-ME mode and forgot you knew him."

"What did he—" Chelsea broke off, not sure how she was supposed to feel. She hadn't cared for Rickey and couldn't forgive that he'd apparently made some sort of deal with the escapees, but she wouldn't have wished him dead under any circumstance.

"It was murder concocted to look like a suicide," Tucker said succinctly. "I guess, based on what you just told me about what the driver said to you out on the loading dock, that Rickey was supposed to have signed off on the bodies, delaying discovery of the switch. When he turned up in the holding cell instead, someone working for al-Jihad killed him either to punish him or to shut him up, or both."

Which would mean that someone in the PD—or at least someone with access to the overnight holding cells—was on the terrorists' payroll, Chelsea thought. She didn't say it aloud, though, because the possibility was too awful to speak.

Tucker nodded, though. "Yeah. Big problem. That's why I'm here."

He hadn't stayed with her strictly to keep her company, she realized. He'd stayed because the BCCPD had figured it might not be a coincidence that the ME who'd missed his shift that morning had wound up dead. Tucker's bosses—and her own—thought she might be at risk, that whoever had killed Rickey might go after her next, looking to silence her before she told the cops anything that might help lead them to the escapees.

Except she didn't know anything that would help, did she?

"Don't worry," Tucker said, correctly interpreting her fears. "We're keeping the story as quiet as possible, and letting the media think you're dead, too. If the escapees are following the news, they have no reason to think you're alive."

Unless Fairfax had told them for some reason. But why would he, when he'd been the one to save her?

She didn't know who to trust, or what to believe, and the confusion made her head spin.

She sank back against the thin hospital pillow, noticing for the first time that she was wearing nothing but a hospital johnnie and a layer of bedclothes. "Can I—" she faltered as the world she knew seemed to skew beneath her, tilting precariously. "Can I get dressed and get out of here?"

His expression went sympathetic. "Yeah, you're cleared…medically, anyway. Since your purse was still at the office, Sara used your key to grab clothes, shoes and a jacket for you, along with a few toiletries." He gestured. "They're in the bathroom, along with your purse. The keys are in it."

He didn't offer to help her, which told her it was a test: if she couldn't make it to the bathroom and get herself dressed unassisted, she was staying in the hospital until she could.

She'd been telling the truth, though. She felt fantastic—physically, anyway—and was able to make it to the small restroom and get dressed without any trouble.

In the midst of pulling on her shirt, she paused and frowned in confusion when she saw that there wasn't any discernible mark where the injection had gone into her arm. He'd jammed the tip of that ampoule in hard enough that it should've left a mark. Did that mean it hadn't happened the way she remembered?

It didn't take too many minutes of staring at her own reflection in the mirror for her to conclude that she didn't know, and she wasn't going to figure it out standing in a hospital bathroom. She emerged to find Tucker waiting for her, with his cell phone pressed to his ear.

"You shouldn't be on that thing in here," she said automatically, her med-school training kicking in even though the actual risk was relatively minor.

"I'm off," he said, flipping the phone shut and dropping it in his pocket. "You ready to go?" He indicated the door with a sweep of his hand.

He didn't offer to let her in on the phone call that'd been so important he'd broken hospital rules to take it, but his eyes suggested it was something about her, or the escapees.

Have you caught them? she wanted to ask, but didn't because she feared it would come out sounding as though she hoped the men were still at large. Not that she did—her terrifying ordeal had more than convinced her that al-Jihad, Muhammad Feyd and Lee Mawadi were monsters who didn't even deserve the benefit of an autopsy.

"The man who helped me, or who I think helped me, anyway…that was Jonah Fairfax, right?" she couldn't help asking.

She hadn't wanted to say too much about him, lest Tucker read too much into her words. But it wasn't like she was going to be able to ask anyone else either.

After a long moment, he inclined his head. "Yeah. The description fits."

"Have they been caught yet?"

"No." Tucker paused. "Maybe it'd be better for you to stay in the hospital a little longer, for observation."

Translation: I think you should go upstairs to the psych ward and have a nice chat with a professional about the definition of Stockholm syndrome.

"That's not necessary," she said quickly. "I'm feeling fine. Hungry, but otherwise fine."

"Are you sure?"

"Don't worry about me," she said, summoning a smile. "I'm not confused about Fairfax, and I'm ready to do the debriefing thing. I figure I might as well get it over with." She took a deep breath and beat back her nerves. "I promise I'll hold it together."

And she did. She held it together while they returned to the BCCPD by way of a breakfast sandwich to soothe her hunger pangs. Once she was at the PD, she held it together through several more rounds of questioning. The worst of it came from Romo Sampson, a dark-haired, dark-eyed suit from the Internal Affairs Department, but she stayed strong and answered his questions fully on everything except the way her heart had bumped when she first saw Fairfax. That much she kept to herself.

After the questioning, Chelsea also held it together—more or less—through a tearful reunion with Sara and her other coworkers, and a trip down to the morgue to say goodbye to Jerry. She held it together through a phone call to Jerry's devastated girlfriend, and then through calls to her own parents and sister. Each person she spoke to or saw was cautioned to pretend they hadn't heard from her if asked; her survival was being kept very quiet because the escapees—three of them, anyway—thought she was dead. The fourth was still an enigma.

Once she was off the phone with her mother, Chelsea thought about calling her father, but didn't. Despite her mother's best efforts to keep the family together, her parents had divorced when she was in her early teens. Her boat-captain father, a charismatic man with a wandering heart, had called and visited a few times a year for the first few years after the divorce, but that had dwindled and eventually stopped. Last Chelsea had heard, he was living with a woman twenty years his junior, running charters off the Florida Keys. He didn't have a TV, and if he happened to hear about the escape, he probably wouldn't even remember she lived in Bear Claw.

Besides, she figured he'd lost the right to worry about her, in the process teaching her a valuable lesson that had only been reinforced in the years since: men who seemed larger than life usually cared more about that life than they did the people around them.

Chelsea, on the other hand, cared very deeply about her mother and sister, and the friends who had become her extended family in Bear Claw.

Just because she cared, though, didn't mean she was going to let them run her life; she stood her ground when it was time for her to go home, and each of her friends had a different theory on where she should stay, none of the answers being "at home," which was where she wanted to be.

Mindful that Tucker was still watching her for signs

of collapse—or Stockholm syndrome—she held it together through the arguments that ensued when she insisted on going home that night, and refused to let any of her friends stay over.

She loved them, she really did, but her self-control was starting to wear seriously thin. She just wanted some alone time, some space to fall apart. Permission to be a wimp.

"Seriously," Sara persisted, "I don't mind."

You might not, but I do, Chelsea thought, her temper starting to fray. She just wanted to go home and cry. "I'll be fine," she said, pulling on her coat. "I'll be under police protection, for heaven's sake." Tucker had arranged to have a patrol car watch from out front of her place, just in case. She shook her head and said, "Honestly, what can you do that the cops can't?" Like her, Sara was an ME. They didn't carry guns, didn't live in the line of fire.

Not usually, anyway.

"I'll listen if you want to talk," Sara said softly, quick hurt flashing in her eyes.

"I'm all talked out," Chelsea said firmly. But she leaned forward and pressed her cheek to Sara's. "I'll call you if that changes, I promise."

She held her spine straight as she marched out of the ME's office, and made herself stay strong as she drove home in her cute little VW Bug, hyperaware of the Crown Vic following close behind her, carrying the surveillance team.

After an uneventful commute, made unusual only by the fact that she couldn't turn on the radio without hearing some mention of the jailbreak and her own supposed death, she pulled her cherry-red Bug into her driveway.

The small, cottagelike house faced a side road and had large-lot neighbors on either side, with a finger of Bear Claw Canyon State Park stretching across her back boundary. The rent was on the high side, but she liked the feeling of space and isolation. At least she usually liked it. Given the events of the day, she wondered whether she might've been better off in a hotel for the night.

No, she decided. She wanted to be in her own space, surrounded by familiar things. Besides, she'd be safe. The cops would see to it.

The Crown Vic pulled in behind her car and two officers got out; one stayed with her while the other went into the house first and looked around to make sure she was safe and alone.

Wrapping her arms around herself, she waited, shivering slightly even though the car's heater was going full blast. Then again, why shouldn't she shiver? She'd been kidnapped and nearly killed, and had gotten away only by the grace of God and the unexpected help she'd received from the fourth escapee. Or so she thought.

Fairfax was as much of a monster as the others he'd been caged with, Tucker had told her pointedly earlier in the day, and Chelsea knew he was right. She also knew he'd been warning her not to romanticize, as though he'd picked up on the fact that she kept thinking about the man who'd protected her, even though she knew she shouldn't.

Fairfax's angular face was fixed in her mind, and the sound of his voice reverberated in her bones. She couldn't help thinking that if they'd met under different circumstances she would've found him handsome. Heck, even under the current circumstances, she was having serious trouble reconciling the facts with her perception of the man.

Then again, she'd never had very good instincts when it came to guys. Or rather, her instincts were okay; she just tended to ignore them. She'd seen what her mother had gone through with her father. And she'd been through a couple of near-miss relationships that had only reconfirmed that she needed to find herself a guy who might not be all that exciting, but was loyal and relationship-focused.

Yet here she was, practically fantasizing about an escaped double murderer. Maybe she *should* be checking out the hospital's psych ward.

The cop who'd stood guard by her car knocked on the window, making Chelsea jump.

"Sorry," he said when she opened the door, "didn't mean to startle you."

She shook her head. "It's not your fault. I was spacing out." She glanced at the front door, and saw his partner waiting there. "The house is all clear?"

"I'll walk you up." He escorted her to the front door, where he and his partner turned down her offers of coffee, food or a restroom, and then left her to return to their vehicle, where they would spend the night, making regular patrols to ensure that the escapees didn't try to contact her, or worse.

When the cops were gone, Chelsea shut the front door, and locked and deadbolted it for good measure.

Then she turned, leaned back against the panel, and burst into tears.

She'd held it together like she'd promised Tucker she would. Now that she was alone, she gave herself permission to fall apart.

Sinking down until she was sitting on the floor with

her spine pressed up against the entryway wall, she cried for Jerry and his girlfriend, and for Rickey, even though he didn't deserve her tears. She cried for the four dead guards laid out in the morgue, two of whom had been a father and son working together. And she cried for herself—for the fear and confusion of being abducted and then rescued by a man she'd been attracted to, a man who'd been called a monster by people she trusted.

Above all, she cried because when it came down to it, she'd frozen. She hadn't struggled or fought, had only survived because of a series of events she didn't understand. She hadn't saved herself. She'd just curled into a little ball and let bad things happen.

It didn't matter what 007 or any of the others would've done. She'd done nothing.

A long time passed before her tears dried up, but eventually they did.

When that happened she swiped her hands across her eyes and drew a deep breath. "You're okay," she told herself. "You're going to be okay."

Thinking things might look a little less grim if she ate something—the breakfast sandwich she'd had seemed aeons in the past—she stood and headed for the kitchen.

She was almost there when a man stepped into the kitchen doorway. She saw his silhouette first, big and muscular, then his dark hair, the lines that cut beside his mouth, and piercing blue eyes that seemed to bore into hers. He was wearing tough-looking black cargo pants and heavy boots, along with a thick sweater and scarred leather jacket, rather than the guard's uniform from before, but she recognized him instantly.

Fairfax.

Heart jolting into her throat, Chelsea screamed. At least she tried to. But he moved too quickly, getting an arm across her collarbones and pressing lightly on her throat while he clapped a hand across her mouth, holding her body motionless as effectively as he trapped the scream in her lungs.

"Don't," he ordered. "I won't hurt you."

Rationality said she should fight, but she hesitated instead, still caught up inside her own skull, torn between attraction and logic, between gratitude and fear.

When she stilled, his grip loosened a fraction. "Good girl," he said, which was patronizing yet somehow soothed her, for reasons she promised herself she'd analyze later. "You going to behave if I let you go?"

She nodded as her pulse hammered in her veins.

"Okay. Here goes." He let his hands fall away, and stepped back.

Chelsea bolted for the front door, screaming, "Help! Help me!"

She heard his bitter curse, heard his footsteps too close behind as she grabbed the knob and twisted. Before she could get the door open, she found herself hanging midair, suspended by her belt and the back of her shirt.

"Damn it." He half hauled, half carried her into the living room, where he tossed her on the sofa. Then he loomed over her, cold blue eyes snapping with temper. "I said I'm not going to hurt you. Settle down!"

She glared back. "Why should I do anything you say?"

"I—" He snapped his jaw shut and exhaled. "Because you owe me one. I saved your life."

Of all the things for her to feel at that moment, disappointment probably wasn't the most logical. But that was what flooded through her, alongside a flare of anger and disillusionment at the realization that he was no different from the others, after all. He hadn't saved her because she'd aroused some soft emotion in him. He'd saved her so he could use her.

"You want me to help you escape," she said, voice flat with anger.

"I managed that one on my own, thanks."

"Then what—" She thought of Rickey's body and shuddered. "You're going to kill me after all."

He shook his head, managing to look both frustrated and vaguely insulted without a change in his cool blue eyes. "No, I'm not going to kill you. I need you to sneak me inside the ME's office."

That confused her enough to dampen some of her panic, especially given that he hadn't made a move in her direction since tossing her on the couch. He was keeping half his attention on the windows—being careful not to cross between them and the light—and the other half on their conversation. He wasn't concentrating on her, wasn't making her feel any immediate menace.

He was treating her like a means to an end, nothing more. Like the way one of her fictional spy heroes would treat an asset.

"Why do you want to break into the ME's office?" she asked, not sure if she'd stopped trying to escape because she was frozen in shock, or if it was because of the way the inexplicable events of the day were realigning themselves in her head, shaping themselves into an impossible hypothesis.

"I need information on Rickey Charles's murder."

Which either meant that Rickey hadn't been killed on al-Jihad's order…or Fairfax was clandestinely working against the terrorists somehow.

That might explain why he'd been unable to kill her in cold blood, and why he'd had a death-mimicking drug hidden in the heel of his shoe, one that hadn't shown up on any of the tests the doctors had run, and had left her feeling energized rather than half-dead. It was a high-tech, classified drug of some sort, one that—

She stalled her train of thought before it went off the rails, because the scenario was too Hollywood to be real.

Still, she couldn't help asking, "Who…who do you work for?"

Surprise flashed in his eyes, one of the few emotions she'd been able to read there during her brief association with the escaped convict—or whatever he really was.

"The group doesn't have a name," he said carefully.

She felt a spurt of something that shouldn't have seemed like excitement. "Who signs your checks?"

"No checks. I'm paid in wire transfers from shell companies held by other shell companies." But he knew what she was asking, and finally said, "If you go deep enough, the money comes from the U.S. government."

"You're undercover."

He nodded to the bookshelves that lined most of one wall of her living room. They were filled with paperbacks and DVDs. "You read too many spy novels."

"You're telling me I'm wrong?"

"No, just that you shouldn't confuse fiction with reality."

"Did you kill those FBI agents? The ones in Montana?"

He shook his head. "No. That was part of the cover."

"But you *have* killed people."

"Yes," he said calmly. "But right now I'm not looking to kill anyone. I need to get into the ME's office, and I need someone to translate Ricky Charles's autopsy findings into lay English for me." He paused, and seemed reluctant to admit, "You're right, I'm one of the good guys, more or less. I'm part of a unit that's so secure we don't even know each other. We only know our handler, who goes by the name Jane Doe, and doesn't appear in any government database that I've ever accessed. Anyway, I haven't been able to get in touch with Jane since late last night, which means I'm low on options here. I'm asking for your help."

"Why can't you reach her?"

"My guess? Because she's dead."

Chapter Four

Chelsea thought she heard something in his voice—pain, maybe, and anger—but she couldn't be sure. He was so brutally controlled that very little broke through.

"I'm sorry," she said, and there was a serious quaver in her voice, because the whole conversation seemed patently unbelievable. Handsome undercover operatives just didn't break into the homes of people like her and ask them for help. They just didn't.

Then again, people like her didn't normally get kidnapped, drugged and rescued either.

"Will you help?" he asked, holding her eyes with his.

"Why me?" she managed to ask, her voiee sounding thin and strange. "How did you find me? How did you get in here?"

They weren't the most important questions, but they were the only ones she could manage right then, as a whirl of thoughts jammed her brain and her inner wimp told her to stay the hell away from Fairfax, while her spy-loving self wanted to know more, wanted to know everything.

"The first two questions have the same answer," he said. He reached into his pocket and withdrew a flat plastic square, and flipped it to her.

She caught it on the fly. "My name tag. Which answers how you found me—I'm in the phone book, on Google, however you want to look me up. But it doesn't explain why you came to me."

"Because you work in the ME's office."

"Oh. Right. And that was the only reason?" She knew it was stupid of her to ask, and even stupider to feel a spurt of disappointment.

"The only one I'm admitting to." His lips tipped up in a faint, sad smile, there and gone so quickly she might've thought she'd imagined it if she hadn't seen the unexpected hint of a dimple on one cheek. It didn't exactly make him look boyish and approachable—she had a strong feeling he didn't do boyish or approachable very well—but it definitely stirred her juices, bringing a flare of warmth where such a thing should never have existed.

At best, he was an undercover fed with so few outside ties that he'd willingly gone to jail for an op. At worst, he was lying through his teeth, and really was a murderer, and an escapee.

She knew she should run far and fast. Somehow, though, she couldn't. Instead, she stood and crossed to him, stopping just short of where he stood in the shadows cast by the single lamp that lit the living room. "What, exactly, do you want me to do?"

He glanced at her TV, where the digital display on the cable box showed that it was nearly 7:00 p.m. He muttered a curse. "I don't have time tonight. I've stretched the supply run as long as I can. They'll be expecting me back soon."

At the mention of the others, she looked around in sudden panic, locking on the woods beyond her yard.

"Where are they?" Images of al-Jihad and the others crowded her brain. "Are they out there?"

"No." But he didn't elaborate. "Will you help me?"

"Why are you protecting them? Why not tell the cops where they are?"

"Because I'm the one who helped them escape, remember? Why else do you think I had the knockout drops?"

"You—" She broke off as a sinking sensation warned her that she was way out of her depth. Making a sudden decision, she said, "I can't deal with this." She turned for the door. "You have until the count of ten to get the hell out of here. When I hit ten, I'm opening the front door and screaming bloody murder."

This time he didn't try to stop her physically. Instead, he said, "Didn't you wonder why you recovered from the drug so fast and why the doctors couldn't find any trace of it in your blood? Didn't you wonder who called in the nine-one-one and gave the cops your location?"

She stopped, but didn't turn around. "I suppose you can explain that?" She cursed herself for giving him the opening, but he'd nailed the questions she'd been asking herself all day.

"Look at me."

Still cursing herself for a fool, she did exactly that, only to find that he'd moved, so silently she hadn't known he was coming until he was inside her space the way she'd been inside his only moments earlier.

She wanted to back away, but something told her now was not the time to let him know exactly how much his physical presence—and the feelings he kindled inside her—intimidated her. So instead of retreating, she stood her ground and lifted her chin. "Well?"

He leaned in, until their faces were too close together and his breath feathered across her skin. "I planted a homing device on you, along with a data pellet. Jane—or more likely, one of her people—retrieved the information and the bug, gave you the antidote to the injection, and rearranged the scene a little before calling it in."

Her mouth had gone dry during his recitation, which was too far-out to be true, too consistent with the evidence to be a lie. Heart drumming against her ribs, she said, "If you've got other people on your team, why do you need me?"

His voice was flat when he said, "I only know how to contact Jane. It's safer that way."

Until she gets knocked out of the picture, at which point you're on your own, Chelsea thought, but didn't say. It seemed like a very lonely way to live, and was the sort of detail the movies skimmed over in order to hit the action and danger.

"You've got to have some sort of backup plan, right?"

"Wrong."

Chelsea exhaled a frustrated breath. "There's nobody who can confirm your story?"

"Nobody I trust."

She got the feeling the number of people he trusted could be counted on one finger, and that person was out of commission either temporarily or permanently.

"Why not turn them in?" she asked again. "If you're cut off, then your plan's already shot, right? There's no need to keep going. If you help recapture the escapees, then—"

But he was already shaking his head. "Even in captivity, al-Jihad is threatening this country. He's got people inside Homeland Security. He got to people inside your office. We suspect his network extends much farther than we ever guessed, which is why I had to break him out. He'll make contact with his conspirators now, and he'll be planning something big. I can guarantee that much." His expression went grim and determined. "When those plans are in place, we'll bring down his whole godforsaken network, not just a few players."

"But who is 'we'?" she protested. "You just said you're on your own. If you don't have anyone else you can trust—"

"That's not your concern."

Chilled by his flat pronouncement, Chelsea wrapped her arms around herself. "What about me?"

She didn't know what she wanted him to say, didn't know that anything could possibly make this entire conversation any less unreal than it felt at that moment.

"I saved you," he said flatly. "Now I need your help. Tomorrow, I want you to ensure that the office will be deserted and the security off-line after hours."

Chelsea couldn't figure out which was worse: that he was asking her to betray Sara and the others by breaking more laws than she could immediately name…or that she was actually considering doing it.

What was wrong with her? She had no proof he was who he said. In fact, logic said he was a criminal and a liar.

"If you were really an undercover agent working for the U.S. government," she said, her voice barely above a whisper, "then I can't imagine you'd come here and tell me that to my face." She looked up at him, baffled, wanting to believe him, but not sure she dared. "You haven't even sworn me to secrecy or anything."

The corners of his mouth twitched, the almost-dimple making it seem as though there was a younger, happier man trapped inside his unemotional shell. "Go ahead and tell your friends about this," he said, daring her. "You don't believe me and you're standing here. What do you think they'll do?"

"Put me on the head-shrink express," she said. "Damn it." He was right. She couldn't tell. Not unless she had proof, and there was only one way to get that proof. She tilted her head, shot him a look from beneath her lashes, and felt her heart begin to pound with fear, with excitement. "Tomorrow night, you said?"

His look was long and slow, until finally he nodded. "Tomorrow. Make sure the place is going to be clear."

"I can do that."

"Yes, but will you?" It was a direct challenge.

She met his eyes, and nodded, unspeaking.

"Good." He moved, but instead of moving away from her, as she might have expected once he'd gotten his way, he moved in, closing the gap between them. "You wanted to know why you." It wasn't a question.

Her blood sped in her veins, and prickles of awareness shimmered to life. "Yes." The word was barely a breath, more an invitation than a question as the attraction that she'd felt earlier in the day, when their eyes had connected through a pane of tempered and meshed glass, sprang to life full-blown, even stronger now, and with no glass separating them.

"Yeah," he said, as though she'd answered him far more fully than she'd intended to. "That's why."

Then he leaned in and kissed her, and although she'd seen it coming, knew what he'd intended, she didn't move away, didn't stop him cold. Instead, she uncrossed her arms and flattened her palms on his chest, not to push him away, but to draw him close, her fingers twining in the material of his shirt and holding him fast.

And, even though she knew better, damn it…she kissed him back.

TEMPORARY INSANITY. That was Fax's only excuse for initiating the kiss, and it wasn't much of an excuse to begin with. Then, about three seconds after he'd lost his mind and gone in for a taste of her lips, those very same lips parted and a soft sound escaped her, and she started kissing him back.

After that, there was no excuse. There was only insanity.

She tasted of sweetness, sunshine and laughter, and so many other things he hadn't known in a very long time. Her skin was soft beneath his fingertips when he raised his hands to frame her face, to touch her neck and hair, relearning feelings he'd left behind.

Heat came, and lust. But even the lust was tempered with sweetness. It stole inside him and buoyed his heart, making him feel light and free, while the heat warmed him from within, thawing parts of him that had been cold for so long.

Which wasn't a good thing, he realized with a sudden dash of icy reality. Not where he was going.

"Wait." He broke the kiss, only then realizing that he'd moved in very close to her, that they were plastered together against the living-room wall, his body pressed against hers, hard and needy.

Her face was upturned to his, her lips parted and moist, her eyes bright with arousal and self-awareness, letting him know she knew what he was—or thought she did—and she'd kissed him back anyway.

He forced himself to let her go and move away, remembering to stay out of the window lines, but only barely. His head was spinning, his blood pounding an up-tempo number in his veins, and pretty much everything inside him was clamoring for him to go to her, kiss her again, take whatever she was willing to give.

What was going on with him? He wasn't the kind of guy who lost himself in a kiss, wasn't the type to forget reality in a moment of lust.

Only that was what had just happened, and it'd happened with a woman who was so far out of his present sphere that she might as well have been from another universe entirely. She was the sort of person he was trying to protect—in a general sense—when he did what he did. She was sunlight and family; he was alone in the darkness, and needed to keep it that way.

She was attracted to him, he knew, had been from the first moment they locked eyes. It wouldn't take much for him to get her to take it further, especially after all they'd been through together in the past couple of days. She'd said it herself, she owed him her life. He could lean on that, use it to get what he wanted, what his body was demanding he take, hard and hot and fast.

And that, he thought bitterly, *is the convict talking.*

He'd been playing the scumbag role for so long, through a string of assignments even before the al-Jihad op, that he honestly wasn't sure it was a role anymore. His mother used to warn him and his brothers that if they made faces too often, they'd get stuck that way.

Well, somewhere along the line he'd gotten stuck. He'd not only lost his family, he'd lost most of himself. Worse, he wasn't really sure he minded.

He did, however, mind the idea of using someone

like Chelsea for sex when he could offer nothing else but his body.

"Bad idea," he said, voice rough. He jammed his hands in his pockets when they wanted to reach for her, and forced his feet to stay put when they wanted to move. "I don't think—"

A knock at the door had him breaking off with a vicious curse. He'd way overstayed his limit, and was seconds away from being busted.

Eyes locked with his, Chelsea raised her voice and called, "Just a minute." She pushed him toward the kitchen, lowering her voice to whisper, "Go. Meet me here tomorrow, and I'll get you into the ME's office."

She didn't say anything about the kiss, but it buzzed between them like a living, tempting thing.

He hesitated, wanting to tell her to forget about tomorrow night, to say there was another way. But there wasn't. He'd already gone over all his options. Without Jane he had no backup—and the very fact that she'd dropped off the grid was a very bad sign. It suggested that al-Jihad's conspirators had shut her down, maybe even killed her, as he'd said to Chelsea.

What he hadn't said was that if Jane was gone, he was locked in a deadly race. He needed to find the traitors and figure out who he could trust to take them down, before they found and dealt with him. And now he was adding another layer of complication: he had to keep Chelsea safe.

He'd kissed her. There was no way he could consider her collateral damage now. He was a cold bastard, yes, but he wasn't completely bloodless.

Unfortunately, that didn't change the fact that he needed her help.

Making the only decision he could under the circumstances, he nodded and headed for the kitchen door, and the shadows beyond. He trusted his training and instincts to get him out even if the second cop had gone around to the back of the house. With the state forest so close to the back door, it would be easy—too easy if you asked him—for him to slip away, unseen.

He turned in the kitchen doorway. Chelsea's eyes met his, and when they did he felt a punch of heat that was sharper, edgier than it'd been when they kissed. This heat was less about lust and more about territoriality and protectiveness, which were two things he absolutely couldn't afford on this mission.

"See you tomorrow," he said softly. And left.

But no matter how fast he slipped through the shadows and away, no matter how fast he drove the car he'd boosted and filled with stolen provisions, he couldn't escape the knowledge that he'd just made this operation far more complicated than it had been, far more complicated than it ought to be.

He only hoped he could pull it off, because if he couldn't, if al-Jihad succeeded in gathering his forces and launching another terror attack, Fax knew the deaths would be on him.

BY THE TIME Chelsea arrived at work after a mostly sleepless night, with her police detail shadowing her until she was safely inside, she had pretty much convinced herself she'd gone a little crazy the night before.

She'd allowed Fax to enter her house and escape again, even though he was a wanted felon. She'd agreed to help him in an investigation that might or might not be legitimate. She'd kissed him and would've offered more than a kiss. But the surveillance team had interrupted to check that she was okay, having thought they'd seen a man's shadow in one of the windows.

She'd definitely lost it.

After dumping her coat and bag in her small cubbyhole of an office and pulling fresh scrubs on over her street clothes for the day ahead, Chelsea went in search of her boss. If anyone would have a levelheaded perspective on the situation, it'd be Sara.

Sara was in her larger, windowed office, frowning over a mountain of paperwork. But when Chelsea knocked on the door frame, she looked up and smiled, her expression tinged with concern. "You're here!"

Chelsea frowned. "Shouldn't I be?"

"Of course, I just—" Sara broke off, shaking her head. "Never mind. You're right. I wouldn't want to be sitting home alone after what you went through. Better for you to be here, working. Keeping your mind off things."

"Exactly," Chelsea said. But the strange thing was, she realized, she didn't totally *want* to keep her mind off what had happened. She wanted to really think about everything that'd happened, dissecting the memories not just for the flush of heat brought by thoughts of Fax, but also so that she could think about what the other men had said and done during her abduction, and what it might mean.

Fax had said al-Jihad had people inside federal law enforcement. What if she could actually do something to help identify the traitors, and prevent al-Jihad from launching the terror attack that Fax seemed convinced was on the horizon?

Or conversely, what if none of that existed and he was just using her for some other purpose? Horror spurted through her veins at the sudden thought that he could be somehow using her to plan the very terror attack he was claiming to want to foil.

But how could she know which was the truth when there was nobody she could ask?

"Chelsea?" Sara leaned forward in her desk chair, looking concerned. "Are you sure you should be here? Your color's off."

To be honest, she was dizzy and on the brink of nausea, but she wasn't going to admit that to her boss, who would send her home, or, worse, to the hospital. That was probably where she should be, only she couldn't bring herself to believe she'd been suckered. She had to believe what Fax had told her, not the least because his explanation fit perfectly with her rescue from the cave. Surely that was evidence that Fax and Jane Doe were real?

Maybe, maybe not. But if what he'd told her was true, then it was her responsibility to help, even though her inner wimp wanted to run and hide.

She took a deep breath and forced her voice steady when she said, "I'm fine, really. What's on the docket for today?"

Sara gave her a long up-and-down look, but eventually nodded, seeming to accept her decision. She ran down the day's pending autopsies, all of which sounded fairly routine.

Chelsea frowned. "What about Jerry and the guards?"

The very thought of cutting into a friend made the nausea spike hard, but she didn't want to be shut out of the investigation because Sara and the others thought she couldn't handle it. She'd find a way to deal.

"They're being taken care of," Sara said tightly, her expression a mix of irritation and sorrow.

"They were turfed somewhere else?" Chelsea supposed it made sense, given that the Bear Claw ME's office was directly involved in the crime. She could see that the decision had wounded Sara, though her friend's expression made her suspect there was more to it than just the autopsies being sent elsewhere.

Something bad was going on behind the scenes. But what? Chelsea wondered. Did Sara know something more about Rickey's involvement? Was she somehow involved in—

Stop it, Chelsea told herself sternly. *Just stop it now.* There was no way Sara was involved with terrorists. Absolutely not.

"The bodies were kicked up a level to the feds," Sara said with a grimace. "The good news is that Seth got permission to sit in on the autopsies, so we'll have some information flow."

FBI evidence specialist Seth Varitek was married to another of Bear Claw's finest, forensic evidence specialist Cassie Dumont-Varitek. Although Chelsea wasn't as close to the couple as she was to Alyssa and Tucker, she knew and trusted Seth. That meant she could add another name to the list of trusted people who were involved in the investigation.

Which got her wondering whether Fax would take her word on that and let her involve a few other people in his investigation. He'd have to believe that there wouldn't be any leaks, but added cops would spread out the work and the risk, and exponentially increase their chances of success.

It would also mean she wouldn't have to lie to her closest friends.

Chelsea decided she'd talk to Fax about the idea that

night. Which, she realized, meant that she'd fully committed inwardly to meeting him and sneaking him into the office, despite her myriad misgivings.

Not wishing to examine that decision—or the reasons behind it—too closely, Chelsea said, "How is the acting mayor handling the situation?"

Sara made a face. "About how you'd expect. Proudfoot is launching a media blitz designed to convince the locals and tourists that it's safe to come to Bear Claw for the big party on Sunday."

Chelsea frowned. "Party? What's— Oh, right. The parade." Each year, Bear Claw hosted its own take on Oktoberfest, designed to kick off the ski season. "I forgot."

"You've had a few other things on your mind," Sara said wryly, then continued, "In addition to his media campaign, Proudfoot is also doing a Riverdance-worthy two-step, simultaneously taking credit for our successes, while making sure everyone knows it was the former mayor's hires who either messed up or were actively engaged in criminal behavior."

"What a prince."

"Yeah, well." Sara's shoulders slumped. "Unfortunately in this case he's not the only one thinking along those lines. I'm expecting another invasion from Infernal Affairs any minute."

Taking that as a hint, Chelsea said, "I'll go look busy, then. Catch you later, and don't let IA get you down."

She had a feeling that it wasn't IA in general, but rather one particular internal investigator who got on Sara's nerves, but she'd learned early on not to ask about Sara's combative relationship with Romo Sampson. That was one of the few topics pretty much guaranteed to put her friend in a bad mood.

It took a while, but eventually Chelsea managed to get back into the swing of her work. She cranked through several routine cases with minimal fuss, labeling and packaging the samples that would be sent out to an off-site lab for testing, and preparing the bodies for release to their families.

She worked efficiently, but compassionately, handling the dead with as much respect as possible under the circumstances, knowing that her work helped bring closure, if not always comfort.

All the while, she was thinking about what had happened two days earlier and the night before. She was definitely feeling more settled than she had the previous afternoon; it helped immeasurably to know—or to at least think she knew—that Fax wasn't the sort of man the media had portrayed him to be.

She wasn't naive enough to think he wasn't capable of doing what they said he had. He was capable of all that and more. But her instincts said he'd been telling the truth about Jane Doe, his allegiance to the U.S. and his hatred of terrorists.

After so many years of reading about them, she'd finally met an actual spy. Under the circumstances, it seemed silly to find that exciting, yet her excitement built through the course of the day, thinking of him and of the kiss they'd shared.

Then it came to quitting time and reality returned with a crash, warning her that the excitement had been nothing more than her mind's way of not dealing with the fear, of not thinking about what she planned to do that night.

She was putting her career on the line for a guy who'd escaped from the ARX Supermax and taken three convicted terrorists with him. A man who claimed to be one of the good guys, but didn't have a damn thing he could show her to back it up.

Suddenly, the psych ward didn't seem like such a bad idea after all.

Dressed in another snazzy wool coat—this one a deep burgundy that flared at the hem—Sara paused outside Chelsea's cubbyhole office and said, "You want to get something to eat, maybe hang out for a while?"

Nerves skimmed just beneath the surface, flowing alongside guilt at lying to a friend, but even in her preoccupied state, Chelsea could see that Sara looked done-in. She shook her head. "We both know you're hoping I'll say 'no thanks, I'm good.' So I'll say it. No thanks, I'm good."

Sara scrubbed a hand across her face. "It's that obvious? Sorry."

"You've had a rough few days. We all have. It's only natural to want some alone time when you've got half the city breathing down your neck."

"I'm here if you need me, though."

"I know." Chelsea rose and moved around the desk so she could press her cheek to Sara's. "Same goes."

After Sara left, Chelsea fiddled around for a few minutes longer, then started closing up the morgue for the night, powering down the computers and lights, and the nonessential machines. When she set the security system, though, she deliberately took the back door offline, so her reentry later wouldn't alert the officer on duty at the main desk of the PD, which had a hardwired feed from the security system at the ME's office.

Deliberately rigging the security system gave Chelsea serious queasiness. If—or rather *when*—IA figured out that someone had been inside the morgue after hours, it would be ridiculously easy for the investigators to figure out that she'd been the inside woman. But that didn't stop her. She had to believe she was doing the right thing, even if it might not look that way to the people who knew her best.

If everything went right, she'd be a hero. If not, she'd be unemployed and unemployable. It was her call, her choice.

Stifling the little voice that said she should go straight to Seth and Tucker and tell them about Fax's visit to her house, she collected her police escort and headed home. After the two cops checked out her house and refused her offer of coffee, they left her and went across the street to their cruiser, considering her tucked in safely for the night.

In reality, she was waiting. And jittering.

Amped up, both by the risk she was about to take and by the promise of seeing Fax again, knowing now how he tasted and how his body felt against hers, she moved from one room to the next, unable to settle. Having seen him do it the night before, she avoided the windows, not wanting the cops to see her pacing one minute, gone the next. She tried to copy his movements, too—the way his footsteps had been almost silent, and how he had seemed perfectly balanced, ready to fight or flee at a moment's notice.

Or rather, ready to fight, not flee. He wasn't the sort to back down from any challenge.

Stop it, she told herself. *He's not a character from some book or movie that you're free to have a crush on. He's a real guy, and he's not yours.* Which was true, she knew. Fax might have asked for her help because he had nowhere else to turn, and he might want her physically, but he'd never stick around or ask her to come away with him. She knew that like she knew her own name, her own weaknesses.

That didn't mean she couldn't indulge for the duration, though, she thought, imagining him naked, remembering the taste and feel of him, the—

"Chelsea."

She gasped and spun, and there he was, standing in her darkened kitchen doorway with the night at his back. He was wearing dark jeans that fit like they'd been made for him, along with heavy hiking boots and a sweater the same blue as his eyes. He wore the lined leather jacket he'd had on the night before, along with black gloves because the night was crisp, the air hinting at more rain, or maybe wet snow.

She imagined he had his gun tucked at the small of his back, and found that dangerous detail to be staggeringly sexual.

His eyes locked on her and went hot for a second, flaring with the same heat that slammed through her, warning that the rest of it was all rationalization, that her first and best reason for doing what she was about to do was because he'd asked. Because she wanted him.

The kiss they'd shared the night before resonated in the air between them, almost a tangible thing. Electricity sparked, sizzling a wordless question of what they were going to do about it, where they would go from there.

Then his eyes blanked back to icy cool, and he said only, "You ready to go?"

She took a deep breath and nodded, and when he turned and glided out into the night, she followed him into the forest behind her house and didn't look back.

Chapter Five

Fax cursed himself inwardly as he led Chelsea along a short loop through the woods to where he'd stashed the nonstolen, properly registered car that al-Jihad had procured through his network of area contacts, none of whom Fax had met yet.

This is a really bad idea, he thought. He should've stayed back at the hideout, working on getting Muhammad to trust him. Instead, he was following a lead he didn't have nearly enough manpower to do justice to, one that would most likely threaten Chelsea's job, if not her life.

He'd tried to talk himself out of the plan a few times over the course of the day. Okay, more like once every ten minutes or so, which was about how often he'd thought about her.

He'd thought of how it had felt to kiss her the night before, and he'd thought of doing it again, of working his way down her body, tasting every inch of creamy skin. Of losing himself inside her.

He'd thought of her as he'd helped Lee and Muhammad set up the small cabin they were using, located high on a ridge that overlooked Bear Claw Canyon and led up to the mountain used by the city's main ski resort. They'd outfitted the cottage with the supplies he'd stolen, along with boxes of other essentials that'd appeared out of nowhere, reconfirming that al-Jihad's reach remained long, his subjects loyal.

And he'd thought of her as he'd looked in the terrorist leader's eyes and seen the cold sanity there, the murderous rage, the desire to kill the whole country, and the American way of life.

This was far too dangerous a situation for Chelsea. It was too much to ask of anyone, never mind someone like her. She was sweetness and innocence, America and apple pie. She was all the things people like al-Jihad wanted to wipe from the face of the earth.

It wasn't right. Unfortunately, he still hadn't been able to reach Jane—the lines of communication had gone dead, and the very nature of his cover meant that he didn't have access to the information he'd once had at his fingertips. He was going to have to do things the old-fashioned way, through hands-on investigation.

Even worse, based on a few things Muhammad had let slip, he suspected that they didn't have much time left. Whatever al-Jihad was planning, it was going to happen Sunday morning, which was less than seventy-two hours away.

If Fax thought there was a chance that turning himself in and leading the authorities to the escapees' hideout would prevent an attack, he would've done just that. But logic and experience said that the plan was already in place, and the underlings had their orders. Even if al-Jihad and the others were back in custody, the attack would be carried out on schedule.

Fax needed to know who else was involved. He

needed to take them down all at once. That was the only way he was going to save lives. And for that, he needed more information on Rickey Charles. Which meant he needed Chelsea.

When they reached the dark bulk of the car, he used the keyless remote to pop the locks and got her door open for her.

He caught the flash of surprise in her eyes. "Thanks."

"My mother taught me well."

Once he was in the driver's seat and they were headed down the road into town, she said, "Does she know… you know. What you're doing?"

"She knows I'm in jail for murder," he said shortly, wishing he'd never mentioned her. This wasn't the time or place for getting-to-know-you chitchat.

The slip was just another sign of how Chelsea's involvement was messing him up, blurring the line between the man he'd been and the one he had to be now.

He glanced over and caught her looking at his profile.

When their eyes met, she looked away. "In other words, you don't want to talk about your family."

"What's the point?" When that came out sounding far harsher than he'd intended, he muttered a curse, took a breath, and forced himself to back it down a notch. "I'm sorry, I don't mean to be a jerk. It's just I don't want—" He broke off, not sure anymore what he did and didn't want. "Damn it."

"I'm the one who should be sorry." She looked away, so her voice was slightly muffled when she said, "This isn't a date. There's no reason for us to get to know each other better. I'm just…" She shrugged. "I was just trying to make it seem a little more normal, I guess. Which is silly, really, because this is anything but normal."

"You can say that again," he said, and let the conversation lag as he sent the car through the twisty streets of Bear Claw, headed back to the loading dock where they'd met.

Strange thing was, part of him wanted to do the small-talk thing, wanted to get to know her better. The urge was separate from the attraction, too, like he was looking to take a piece of her sweetness for himself by pretending he was the sort of man she'd be with if she'd had a choice in the matter.

Because really, he was under no illusions on that front. Once upon a time he'd been the sort of guy nice girls went for, but those days were long gone.

"We're here," he said as he pulled up to the back dock of the ME's office, then winced and said, "Sorry. You knew that."

She looked over at him. Her chocolate-brown eyes were very serious, but her full lips twitched at the corners, turning up in a half smile that held more resignation than humor. "Let's agree to stop apologizing, okay? This is weird for both of us."

He nodded. "Thank you. For doing this, I mean. And I promise I'll do my best to keep you safe."

"I know." She stared at the doors leading to the morgue, and he could tell she was thinking about what'd happened there two days earlier, about her friend who'd been killed. About what might've happened to her, what would've happened if she hadn't lucked into the middle of an undercover op.

"You want to bail out on this?" he asked.

"Of course I do." But she popped open the door and unhooked her seat belt. "I'd be stupid if I didn't. But you need help."

She got out of the car before he could follow his impulse to call her back, to call it off and come up with another plan.

Only there was no other plan. And they had less than three days to root out al-Jihad's conspirators and prevent what he feared would be a major terror attack.

CHELSEA HAD WORKED odd hours in the morgue before, during crisis situations and high-priority cases, when the cops needed answers pronto. She'd stayed late a night or two doing paperwork as well. But she'd never come back in after hours and been the only one there.

Even the cleaning crews were gone for the night—which, of course, was why they'd waited until so late to come. But the silence was creepy, the dim lights even worse.

For the first time, her job seemed less about compassion and more about corpses. Her imagination started playing tricks on her, showing flickers of motion at the edges of her peripheral vision, and sending the sly scrape of a footstep to her ears, just below the threshold of hearing.

Then a hand grabbed on to her arm, and she jumped a mile, giving a little squeak of fear.

"Shh," Fax ordered. "It's me." He shook her arm. "Hold it together, okay?"

She concentrated on the feel of his touch, the strength of his fingers, firm yet gentle on her flesh, and warm even through her shirt and light jacket. Using those sensations to steady herself, to anchor herself, she nodded. "I'm okay. What do you want to see first?"

"Did Rickey Charles have a computer station of his own? An office, or a cube or something?"

"This way." She led him down a short corridor, gesturing to doors as they passed. "This is Sara's office. Mine." She stopped outside the next door down. "Rickey's."

Fax paused. "Have the crime scene techs been here already?"

She frowned. "You know, I'm not sure. Sara said something about them being delayed."

"Big surprise," he muttered. "Al-Jihad has friends everywhere, it seems." He glanced at her. "You got any nonpowdered latex gloves?"

"Of course." She went and grabbed a handful from the morgue, feeling strange and ill at ease in her own space.

Fax was waiting for her in the hallway when she returned. She practically shoved the gloves at him. "Here. Let's hurry."

He didn't say anything, just looked at her, and his icy reserve softened just the barest hint around the edges. "I know we said no more apologies, but I really am sorry I dragged you into this."

"Didn't stop you from doing it, though, did it?" She pushed at his shoulder, aiming him at the door. "Just do whatever you need to do."

"I'll be quick."

And he *was* quick, she realized over the next forty minutes as she watched him go through Rickey's work life inside and out, and then turn his attention to Sara and Jerry. He even went through the desk of their forty-something clerical assistant, Della Jones. She was a divorced mother of two who sometimes dated their thirty-something meat wagon driver, Bradley.

She was definitely *not* a terrorist.

Then again, what do I know about terrorists? Chelsea thought as she hovered over Fax's shoulder, her stomach in knots, half afraid he wouldn't find anything, half afraid that he would.

When he bypassed her office and headed for the morgue itself, she said, "You don't want to toss my office?"

He stopped and turned, his strong body silhouetted in the dim emergency lights that were the only thing illuminating the hallways so late at night. "Why?" His voice seemed almost disembodied. "Should I be worried about you?"

"You seem to be worried about everybody else." Her voice was sharper than she'd intended, the irritation closer to the surface than she'd realized. "I told you Jerry was harmless. And Sara's my friend. She wouldn't ever in a million years do something like this. Never mind Della, who wouldn't hurt a flea."

He approached her, his footsteps nearly silent on the marble tiles lining the hallway. Stopping very near her, he leaned down and whispered, "It's my job to be worried about everyone and everything. If I stop worrying, then I stop breathing."

For a second his lips hovered above hers and she thought he was going to kiss her. She felt the zip of heat in a time and place it shouldn't have existed.

Then he moved away, turned on his heel, and headed for the autopsy theater. "Show me the computers in here, and how to hack in. I need to see the guards' autopsies."

"You were there when they died. What will the autopsies tell you that you don't already know?" Her voice was starting to crack around the edges from the strain of the past few days. She was getting ragged, beginning to think she'd made a mistake.

He was investigating her coworkers, her friends. And she was helping him.

He might be looking for a traitor, but she already was one.

"Chelsea." He was near her again without her having been aware that he'd moved. He touched a finger beneath her chin and used it to tip her face up to his, not for a kiss, but so that she was looking into his eyes when he said, "This is necessary. I swear it."

The thing was, she believed him. Was that her instincts talking or something else?

She stepped away and nodded. "Come on. I'll get you into the files."

Five minutes later, he made a low sound of satisfaction. "Gotcha."

"What?" She crowded behind him, and leaned over his shoulder. "What do you see?"

"Here." He pointed to a line of autopsy notes. "This isn't right. I know for a fact that this guy had a bullet in him, yet the autopsy only mentions the broken neck." He glanced at her, his face too close to hers, his eyes going a little sad for her. "The autopsy was rigged. You know what that means, right?"

"That we're not your problem," she said.

He narrowed his eyes. "Excuse me?"

She gestured around the morgue. "The state made us ship out the autopsies. They said we were too close to the case, that we had to pass the bodies up the chain."

He went very still. "Who did the autopsies?"

"The FBI."

"Hell."

"Which means—" She broke off, realizing exactly what it meant, and echoed his, "Hell."

"Okay, we're done here," he said suddenly, powering down the machine. "Let's go."

She didn't even bother to ask about the rush, just followed him numbly out to the car. It wasn't until they were back on the road headed to her place that he finally said, "What's wrong?"

All of it, she wanted to say. *It's all wrong.*

"The autopsy was overseen by a friend of mine," she said softly, thinking of Cassie's husband, Seth. "Someone I trust."

"Trusted, you mean. Past tense."

She shook her head. "I don't know. None of this makes any sense." She glanced over at Fax. "I was going to ask you—beg you, really—to turn yourself in to him. I thought we could trust him, that he'd be a good guy to have on our side."

"And now?"

"Now I don't know what to think."

He reached across the distance separating them, and closed his fingers over hers. "Welcome to my world. Do yourself a favor and get out as soon as you can."

"Just tell me when and where, and I'll take a flying leap off this bus," she said, and almost meant it. But she'd seen too much death and comforted too many grieving families to walk away now, when she might be able to do something to prevent a terrorist attack and the deaths it would bring.

She sighed, realizing that her conscience could apparently override her inner wimp and almost wishing it couldn't. "What next?" she asked.

He looked at her for a moment, his eyes intent, and

something moved in their depths, making her wonder what he saw when he looked at her. A nice girl? A small life? Or something more?

But he said only, "Let's get you home before we push our luck too far."

He walked her through the woods to her back door, proving once again that her police protection was more for show than anything else.

Once she had the kitchen door open, she paused. "Do you want to come in?"

It was a foolish offer, a sign of just how confused she was inside, how much she'd blurred the lines between date and danger, adventure and stupidity. Fiction and reality.

He shook his head, his eyes holding hers. "I shouldn't."

Not *I can't,* but *I shouldn't.*

"You're probably right," she agreed, but she didn't move out of the doorway.

He stepped up onto the landing. With her standing a tread higher on the threshold, the move put them eye-to-eye.

Electricity buzzed in the air. Chemistry. Maybe it was a pointless, futureless, mad attraction, but in that moment the logic didn't seem to matter.

Only the heat mattered.

"I've gotta go," he said, but didn't.

"I know," she said, and even though it made absolutely no sense, what she really meant was, *Come inside.*

He leaned in and touched his lips to hers, a fleeting touch, there and gone so quickly that she might've imagined it, except there was no imagining the arcing shock of sensation, and the ripe, full flavor of him.

She moved to deepen the kiss.

He stepped away, shook his head. "I'm sorry."

Backing away from her, he turned and crossed her backyard, then slipped into the forest. And was gone.

AS HE RETRIEVED his vehicle and set off for the deep-woods hideout where al-Jihad and the others were hiding, Fax tried to tell himself that it'd been the right choice to reveal himself to Chelsea and recruit her help. She was a necessary asset at a time when he was cut off from his normal channels.

Despite that logic and the fact that he'd done everything he could think of to ensure her safety within the dangerous circumstances surrounding her, he couldn't outrun the growing certainty that he was playing it wrong, taking advantage of someone who deserved better, who shouldn't be part of his world.

Then again, that was part of the horror of terrorism: it brought evil into everyday life.

Unfortunately, that sometimes meant that the good guys had to bring the war into the picket-fenced backyards of America and apple pie. Fax understood the need. He'd dealt with the emotions—what few he had left—long ago, consoling himself with the knowledge that for every innocent life lost during one of his ops, several hundred other people would live on oblivious, never knowing how close they'd come to death.

Usually he neither liked nor disliked the necessity; he simply accepted it. Now, though, he was caught up in it, worried about it, thinking more about the danger to Chelsea than the menace of al-Jihad and the terrorist leader's plan, which he could sense taking shape around him but couldn't define.

He knew he had three days—*make that two and a half now,* he thought, glancing at the in-dash display, which showed that it was well past 2:00 a.m. But although he knew approximately when, he had no idea of where or how, no idea what sort of attack was being planned. Without those details, the time line was next to useless.

Complicating things even further was Jane's continued silence. He felt a pang of grief for the woman who'd given him purpose—and absolution—after Abby's death.

He knew Jane wouldn't thank him for the grief, though, so he focused on what she would've considered far more important—the information disruption caused by her disappearance and how to circumvent that limitation.

Stop stalling and come up with a plan, Fairfax, she would've said.

With her out of the loop, he didn't have the luxury of knowing a response could be up and running with the snap of a finger. Worse, he strongly suspected she'd been betrayed from within the core of the few people she trusted. She was too smart to be taken out by anything short of betrayal.

If al-Jihad's compatriots were strong enough to do that, Fax knew they were easily strong enough to make him quietly disappear if he showed up on their radar screens. Especially given that they had someone inside the FBI, as evidenced by the fudged autopsy records. All of which meant he couldn't risk contacting anyone in the federal food chain, for fear of revealing himself to one of the conspirators.

"In other words, I'm on my own," he said as he bounced his way up the narrow lane to where they'd been hiding the cars, and from there hiking up to the cabin. "As usual."

Only it wasn't business as usual, not really, because he had Chelsea on his conscience and in his head.

"You'd better focus," he warned himself as he climbed out of the car and popped the trunk to retrieve the bulging knapsack that had ostensibly been his reason for the midnight errand.

He had to get the woman out of his head, had to get himself into the game.

But as he hiked the half mile farther into the forest to the cabin, he couldn't stop thinking of Chelsea, of the way her short, chestnut-streaked hair brushed the edges of her jaw, and how her brown eyes sparked when she smiled at him, when she argued with him.

Most of all, he couldn't stop remembering the taste of her skin and mouth, the feel of her curving, feminine body pressed against him.

By the time he reached the encampment, where the plain, square cabin was covered in camo netting and pine branches, and ringed with deadly security sensors, he was more than tempted to turn the hell around and go back for her. But that was attraction talking, not logic, so he kept going, pushing through the cabin door, his senses on alert for any telltale changes, any hint that the situation he was walking into wasn't the one he'd left hours earlier.

Al-Jihad and Muhammad sat at the long table in the center of the main room, which was heaped with encrypted schematics and computer printouts, and home to four laptops run by a lean, dark-haired stranger.

Fax stopped just inside the doorway and scowled. "Who the hell is that? And where's the lemming?"

Al-Jihad glanced from Fax to the stranger and back, his expression inscrutable. "Lee is off on an errand. And this is one of my consultants." Which didn't explain a damn thing.

Fax wanted to ask more, but he also wanted to get close enough to look at those schematics, to see if he could ID the target. Problem was, he didn't know how far he could push without risking his cover. Al-Jihad and Muhammad seemed to accept his professed hatred of the establishment, and seemed to buy that he wasn't just an anarchist, he was so in love with violence that he was willing to target innocent civilians, as long as it made the government look bad. The terrorist leader and his second in command had given Fax small assignments and seemed willing to let him into their discussions, but only to a point.

He had to wonder, though, whether they were playing him just as thoroughly as he'd been playing them. What was he to them? he wondered. An asset, a tool to be used as a later distraction…or something else? Something more sinister?

Unfortunately, in the absence of other information, his best bet was to keep playing along, watching his back and gathering what information he could.

Senses humming, mind clicking over the options, he took a couple of steps toward the table. "Anything I can help with?"

Al-Jihad looked up at him, and something sparked in the depths of his dead black eyes. "Another time, perhaps."

Fax shrugged. "No biggie. I'll go unpack."

He kept his senses revved as he unloaded six-packs of beer and soda from his knapsack to the fridge. He caught a few words of the conversation, enough to realize they weren't speaking English.

When he stuck his head back through the kitchen door, the conversation cut off abruptly and the men turned to look at him.

"What do you want?" the stranger asked, not bothering to hide his irritation.

"Just checking if either of you wanted something to eat," Fax said with a hint of wary deference in his voice, playing the part of a scared lackey who knew damn well his life was subject to the whims of the terrorist leader.

"No," al-Jihad spat. "Go check the perimeter."

"Will do." Fax made a production of pulling his jacket back on as protection against the sharp wind outside and headed for the door.

On the way past, though, he managed to get a look at the papers on the table. He didn't recognize the schematics, but beneath them was a flyer of some sort, and he caught a single word.

Parade.

Chapter Six

Chelsea slept poorly and woke with a creepy feeling lodged between her shoulder blades. Then again, was there any wonder she felt unsettled? She'd broken into her own office and let a fugitive search Sara's office and scour their computer system.

Doing the wrong thing for the right reason is still doing the wrong thing, her conscience nagged as she showered and dried off, and then did her best to cover up the dark, worried circles beneath her eyes.

Her conscience was right. Unfortunately, she had no clue what the right thing to do would be. This was all so far out of her normal mode of operation, she didn't even know where to start.

The nerves stayed high as she got dressed, choosing sturdy jeans and lace-up boots because they made her feel a little armored-up, and a rust-brown turtleneck sweater that made her eyes look more caramel than brown. Feeling pretty was another layer of armor.

The thought of needing her defenses on high alert put a twist in her stomach. Then the doorbell rang, and the twist became a knot.

"Oh!" She took a couple of steps toward the door,

then stopped at the sight of a big, shadowy figure through the curtained window.

She couldn't see many details through the gauze, but immediately knew that it wasn't Fax. For one, the man was ringing at the front door rather than picking the lock on the back. For another, he was bigger than Fax, both taller and broader.

Starting to panic now, she backed up a step, trying to decide between calling for help and trying to escape on her own.

He rang the doorbell again, and knocked. Then called, "Chelsea? It's Seth Varitek."

Seth! Her breath whistled out on a gust of relief and she was halfway across the room when she stalled. Wait a minute. Seth was FBI. Someone in the FBI had falsified the report of an autopsy he'd overseen. What if he were involved?

No, she told herself. Impossible. He was Cassie's husband, part of the gang. He was a decorated expert and had worked some of the highest-profile cases in the country. There was no way he could possibly be involved with al-Jihad.

Still, she stayed in place, frozen with indecision, afraid to trust her own gut anymore.

"Chelsea?" Seth's voice had gone worried, edged with professional calm. "You've got a ten-count to answer before I come through this door."

Finally she moved, not because of the threat, but because he was Seth. A friend. She trusted him. She wasn't cold like Fax. She couldn't just turn her heart on and off.

"Hey!" She opened the door a crack and invited him inside, staying behind the panel, keeping her body shielded in case someone shot at her from the street, like her surveillance team had taught her to do.

The big man's expression cleared some when he saw her, but his eyes stayed pensive and he didn't move to come inside. "What took you so long?"

Seth was a big, dark bear of a man with brush-cut black hair and strong, almost forbidding features. He was wearing jeans and a blue sweatshirt beneath a Rockies logo jacket, suggesting he was off duty, but his holstered weapon and the badge clipped to his belt said otherwise.

"What—" Chelsea's voice faltered, but she forced the words. "What's going on?"

He gave her a long, measured look, as if to say *you tell me,* but answered simply, "Tucker asked me to pick you up. Romo Sampson wants to talk to you."

"Oh." She closed her eyes on an internal groan.

The hotshot IAD investigator was rumored to have no conscience when it came to hounding—and taking down—other cops. He also, Chelsea suspected, had a grudge against the ME's department, going back to right about the time Sara had dated and dumped him.

This wasn't going to be good.

"I could've driven myself," she said faintly, focusing on the immediate problem rather than looking ahead. "I'm not much of a flight risk."

She meant the latter as a weak joke, but even as she said it she realized it wasn't exactly true. The night before, she hadn't just strayed over the line between legal and illegal, she'd blown it up and set fire to the remains. There was no reason they shouldn't consider her a risk.

Heck, if Fax appeared in her kitchen doorway right

then and crooked a finger, she'd be sorely tempted to take off and not look back. She'd follow him into the woods…and that was where the fantasy dissolved.

She couldn't go with him to the fugitives' camp, and he had to maintain his presence there.

"It's no big deal," Seth said easily.

It took her a couple of seconds to figure out that he was talking about giving her a ride, not her relationship with a man he didn't even know she was in continued contact with. Not that there was a relationship. There was merely a wish that the situation could have been different. Then again, under other circumstances, she and Fax never would've crossed paths.

Chelsea told herself that probably would've been for the best, which made her sad.

"You ready to go?" the big FBI agent asked. Only it wasn't really a question.

"Of course." She grabbed her coat and followed him out.

Her stomach churned with nerves as she locked the door and walked with Seth to his truck. He hadn't said it, but she knew there was another reason Tucker had asked Cassie's husband to pick her up and drive her to IAD: he'd wanted her to have someone outside Bear Claw law enforcement to talk to, if she felt like she needed it.

Problem was, Seth might be outside the Bear Claw PD, but he wasn't beyond al-Jihad's reach.

As she climbed into the truck and waited for Seth to start the engine, Chelsea wrestled with herself.

She and Fax needed help, whether or not he wanted to admit it. And though it was probably the wimp talking, Chelsea readily admitted to herself that she would feel better if they could bring Seth and a handpicked few of her friends on board. It would give their investigation a sense of legitimacy, and it'd mean she wouldn't have to lie to her friends, which she hated doing.

Problem was, after last night she knew Fax would never, ever agree to bring in other people, especially not someone from the Bear Claw PD or FBI. And she didn't know him well, but she could guess that if she told them the truth and Fax found out, she'd never see him again. More importantly, she wasn't a hundred percent certain it'd be safe to involve the others.

She trusted her friends, but the evidence said she couldn't trust everyone around them. So as Seth backed out of her driveway and the surveillance vehicle fell in behind them, she tried to figure how to get the information she needed without asking questions that would reveal too much.

"Can I ask you something?" she said finally, knowing she'd have to keep it vague.

The look Seth sent in her direction warned that he wasn't fooled for a second. "Sure. Anything."

"Say someone was working undercover—and I mean deep undercover," she began, hoping she wasn't making a huge mistake. "What sort of fail-safes would there be if he lost contact with his handler?"

"What agency?"

"Any one," she said, dodging.

They drove in silence for nearly a mile before Seth muttered a curse under his breath. "What's his contact's name?"

It wasn't a promise of help or secrecy, but within their circle of friendship, that was exactly what it amounted to.

"Jane Doe," Chelsea said softly, hoping she hadn't just made the biggest mistake of her life.

THE HIDDEN CABIN hummed with activity as the plans for the terrorist attack started coming together.

At least Fax got the sense that the scheme was getting nailed down. He didn't know for certain because al-Jihad and Muhammad were keeping him as far out of the loop as possible, using him for information gathering and supply runs, and telling him almost nothing.

Not that Fax could blame them from a strategic point of view—it only made sense to give the new guy the crap jobs. But that meant he was stuck in limbo, part of the plan, yet not. It wasn't enough, damn it. He needed the names of the people on the inside who were involved.

Then and only then would he know who he could trust and who he couldn't.

Additional manpower and supplies arrived midmorning seemingly out of nowhere, which only added to Fax's frustration.

He couldn't figure out how al-Jihad was contacting his confederates, which meant he was missing a major piece of the puzzle. And if the terrorists were keeping their communication method secret from him, there was a good bet they were keeping other things hidden.

Unfortunately, he didn't dare snoop. Muhammad and al-Jihad were on high alert, as were the five other silent men who moved into and out of the cabin, casting furtive looks in Fax's direction, but not answering any of his greetings. The last member of their group—twitchy, weasely Lee Mawadi—had been growing increasingly twitchy by the hour. Worse, he'd taken to watching Fax, following him around as though the higher-ups had assigned him as a babysitter.

Fax didn't like the thought any more than he liked the man.

Were they keeping tabs on him just to be safe or did they suspect something? *Scratch that,* Fax thought to himself as he bent over his latest task of sawing foot-long pieces of pipe that he could only assume would be turned into bombs over the next two days. *Guys like these are always suspicious—that's what keeps them alive and free. Question is, what's made them extra suspicious now?*

He didn't think the authorities were anywhere close to their hiding spot—that would've brought a different kind of tension. No, this felt more like they were holding out for an answer or a piece of information that would make or break the next step in their game.

But what information? Where was it coming from? And how the hell were they getting it?

Fax wanted to shake the answers out of somebody, but he didn't dare. He could only focus on his task, too aware of the lemming sitting across from him, winding wire for a detonator coil while he divided his attention between the chatter of a daytime talk show on the small TV in the corner, and the drone of voices coming from the back of the four-room cabin.

Fax knew where each of the men were and how they were armed. He had a plan in mind if things went suddenly south—he knew what weapons he'd try for and where his escape routes were. But those were academic exercises for the most part, because experience had taught him that when things went bad, they usually spun right past contingencies and into the realm of action-reaction real fast.

So he stayed ready for action, knowing it might be

the difference between life and death—not just his own life, but those of hundreds, probably thousands of innocents who'd be planning to be part of whatever parade the terrorists targeted.

He couldn't warn the authorities yet, he knew. Not until and unless there was no possible option for apprehending al-Jihad and the others mid-crime. He did, however, fully intend to make sure Chelsea was nowhere near the planned attack.

He couldn't save everyone. But he'd damn well save her.

"Fairfax."

It wasn't until he heard Muhammad call his name from the doorway of the back room that Fax realized the air in the little cabin had changed, going from one of waiting to one of decision.

Fine tension shivered across his skin, but he played it cool, setting aside the length of pipe he'd been working on. "Yeah?"

"In here." Muhammad disappeared back into the room.

Fax found himself trading a look with Lee. If it'd been anyone other than the lemming, he might've asked whether the other man knew what was going on. But it wasn't, so he didn't. He just headed into the back room.

He was two steps in when a heavy blow came out of nowhere and struck him across the back of the head.

Fax shouted and spun, grabbing for the weapon. Al-Jihad himself wielded the short club, his dead eyes alight with killing rage as he hissed, "Traitor!" and came at Fax again.

The second blow caught him in the temple and sent him to his hands and knees, where he braced himself, retching and reeling, not able to run or fight or do anything but howl with the knowledge that his cover was somehow blown, that…

A third blow caught him below the ear and he collapsed into darkness.

He surfaced what seemed like a long time later, pulled to semiconsciousness by the sound of someone saying Chelsea's name.

He stirred and groaned when he heard her name again, and crazily wondered if she was there. But he quickly realized that it wasn't Chelsea herself. It was someone asking him about her. And that was a big problem.

Cracking open his eyes, he squinted into the too-bright light at his interrogator, and recognized Muhammad.

Rage flared when he realized the terrorists knew that he and Chelsea were connected. He was suffused with an overwhelming urge to rip into Muhammad for daring to even say her name. Moments later, though, he blearily realized that he wasn't ripping into anything any time soon. He was securely bound to a chair set in the middle of the cabin's back room. His head lolled, his consciousness was furred with drugs, and he could barely hear the questions Muhammad was firing at him.

His slurred answer was anatomically impossible.

Infuriated, Muhammad backhanded him, then spat in his face. He turned to someone out of Fax's line of sight, and said, "We learned our lesson from the traitor bitch before she died. We need leverage. Pick up the medical examiner and bring her here."

Fax roared at the confirmation of Jane's death, and the implied threat that they were going to torture Chelsea in order to force him to talk. Pushing with his legs, he lunged at the bastard, and succeeded only in toppling his chair sideways. His head slammed into the floorboards, and the world went dim for a while—a few minutes, maybe longer.

When the universe sharpened around him, he was alone.

Chelsea! Fax's heart jammed his throat and adrenaline spiked, chasing the last of the drugs from his bloodstream. He started struggling against his bonds, shouting curses and threats. But there was no answer. The men were long gone.

But how long? He didn't know, couldn't guess, could only yank against the zip ties that held him fast, knowing that he needed to get free, needed to get to Chelsea before al-Jihad and his men did.

If he didn't, she'd be dead.

THE GOOD NEWS, Chelsea realized soon after she sat down in a PD conference room opposite Romo Sampson, was that Internal Affairs apparently had no clue she'd been in the ME's office after hours the night before.

The bad news was that she'd all but confessed it to Seth on the ride over. Guilt stung at the suspicion that she should've kept her mouth shut, as she'd promised Fax she would. She trusted Seth not to say or do anything that'd get her in trouble unless he thought it was absolutely necessary, but she suspected there might be a pretty big difference between Seth's idea of "absolutely necessary" and her own.

She had to face it, she was no good at this spy stuff. She'd caved under the first real pressure she'd experienced. But then again, why should she have expected anything different? This wasn't a game, wasn't an adventure or a story. This was real life and death, a threat to her career, her own safety and that of the people she loved.

Of course she'd caved. She was a wimp.

"Do you need to take a break and get some coffee or something?" the IAD investigator said dryly, warning Chelsea that she'd zoned out on him mid-question. For all she knew, she'd been snoring.

"Sorry." She smothered a yawn. "I haven't been sleeping well." For a variety of reasons, none of which she intended to share with IAD.

Aside from her somewhat dented loyalty to Fax—and her belief that Seth was going to do right by what she'd told him—there was no way she was putting Sara and the ME's office any further under the political cross-hairs than it already was. She might be playing fast and loose with the career that had once been her life, but she wasn't going to do the same with her friends' jobs.

"So," Sampson prompted, "you were describing the van ride after your abduction."

He was a long, lean stretch of a man, with wide-palmed hands that fit with the rumor that he'd gone to college on a basketball scholarship and was headed in the direction of the NBA when a knee injury had ended the dream. His mid-brown hair was finger-tousled and in need of a trim, and his pleasant, regular features would've passed for attractive if it hadn't been for his eyes, which were a very pale hazel and seemed to stare straight through whoever he was looking at.

The effect was off-putting in the extreme. Add to that the few details Chelsea knew about the end of his and Sara's short-lived affair, plus the power he wielded through IAD, and he was downright intimidating.

At least he would've been, she realized, if she hadn't spent the past few days learning out of necessity how to stand up to Fax, who was just as intimidating and wasn't bound by the PD's code of conduct. Where Romo Sampson was civilized in his pressure, Fax was anything but.

"I've told you everything I remember," Chelsea said to Sampson now. "Twice. I'm not sure how going through it a third time is going to help."

Sampson stared at her for a long, considering moment. Then he glanced down at his notes and muttered something under his breath.

Fax did the same thing when he was annoyed with her, she realized, and couldn't help the warm little bubble that rose in her chest at the thought she was learning to recognize his mannerisms. She was trying not to count the hours until dark, until she figured there was a very good chance he'd sneak through her back door to see her.

And *hello,* she acknowledged inwardly, she had it bad. She was in full-blown crush mode for Jonah Fairfax—undercover, here-today-gone-tomorrow agent who needed her for her connections and maybe wanted her for her body, and that was it.

She'd accidentally become a Bond girl, and everybody knew they never got their man.

"Are we done here?" she blurted, interrupting Sampson mid-question.

Surprise flashed in his pale hazel eyes, followed by irritation. "We're not even close to done, and your boss assured me that you'd be cooperative."

"We both know Sara said nothing of the sort," she said, fixing him with a look that warned him she knew at least some of what had happened between him and her friend.

He scowled. "I was referring to Mayor Proudfoot."

Ouch. Chelsea winced at the direct hit, but the score didn't stop her from pushing back her chair and rising. "Look, can you honestly say I haven't cooperated? I've answered all your questions, haven't I?"

"To a point," he conceded. "But you're not telling everything, are you? Which leads me to ask myself who you're trying to protect. Is it Sara or someone else?" He leaned forward. "How well did you actually know Rickey Charles?"

She met his cool-eyed stare. "You're on the wrong track, Sampson."

"So put me on the right track."

"I'm sorry, I can't help you." She gathered her coat and bag. "You know where to find me, but don't bother unless you have something new to ask me."

Knowing she was skirting, if not actually crossing, the line career-wise, she left without waiting for his answer. Fuming, but trying not to be afraid, she headed back to the ME's office where she hoped she could find some sanity in the familiar routine of doing her job.

The bodies of the dead didn't give up their secrets easily, but at the same time, they didn't play games, not really. In contrast, she couldn't help feeling as though she'd inadvertently gotten caught up in far more contests than she'd intended to, or even been aware of. For a small person who'd always had a relatively minor impact on her corner of the world, she was suddenly playing bit parts in more dramas than she'd realized at first.

Al-Jihad and his men had used her and discarded her, thinking her dead. Fax had rescued her so he could use her to gain access to information, and as an ally, albeit one of fairly limited means. She suspected Tucker's appearance at her hospital bedside and Seth's offer of a ride that morning were more than friendly support, which suggested they knew there was something going on with her. Enter Romo Sampson, who was sure of it, but wasn't sure who was involved or how, and was convinced that Chelsea knew both. Add to that Sara, who was fighting for her department and had been subtly pressuring Chelsea to play along and not make political waves, little realizing that such a hope had long since been dashed.

On the outskirts of all that were other dramas, other bit players, like Jerry and his ski-bunny girlfriend; Rickey Charles, who'd been a snake, but hadn't deserved to die; and the four guards who'd been killed during the jailbreak.

So many people's lives were already intertwined, so many lives already lost. How many more names would be added if Fax was unable to root out the terrorist conspirators he was searching for?

Thousands, Chelsea thought, and it was enough to send her stomach up into her throat. Or maybe it'd been there for a while now, she realized, feeling nausea like an old friend, along with the relentless pound of a stress headache.

She was so far out of her element, she couldn't even see her normal life anymore. Which was why, when she reached the ME's office, she didn't go to her desk, but instead poked her head through her boss's door. "Can you cover me for the day?"

Sara looked up, her expression immediately going concerned. "Are you okay?"

"Tired, mostly," Chelsea hedged, then before Sara could ask anything else, she said, "I just got finished with Sampson."

"Him!" The word was an explosion of pent-up breath. Sara scowled. "Like there aren't enough criminals in the city that we need to go looking inside our own ranks for them? If I—" She broke off, pressing her lips together in a thin line of annoyance. "Sorry. You don't need to hear this right now."

"I just want to lie down for a while."

"You're okay to get home?"

"I'm all set," Chelsea said, letting her friend assume Seth was making the return trip, even though she was planning on catching a ride with her surveillance team. She loved her friends, and depended on them. Sometimes, though, she just needed the space inside her own head.

"Then go." Sara shooed her out the door. "Tomorrow's Saturday anyway, and I'll keep you off call. I may need you Sunday evening though, depending. The parade's going to bring out the crazies, and you know what that means."

"Busy day," Chelsea answered wanly, nodding. "I'll be here." But the parade, which had been something she'd been looking forward to only days earlier, paled when she thought about Fax and the terrorist threat to attack on—

She froze, making the connection, wondering if Fax knew about the parade yet.

"Chelsea?" Sara said. "What is it? What's wrong?"

"I've got to go." Mind racing, Chelsea rushed out of the office and found her assigned officers, and tried very, very hard not to look like a crazy person as she asked them to take her home, saying that she wasn't feeling well and needed some downtime.

She wasn't even sure why she felt like she had to hurry—Fax probably wouldn't be there until after dark either way, and she had no means to contact him and tell him to come sooner. But it suddenly seemed very important for her to be inside her own space, where he would look for her first.

When the officer pulled the cruiser up into her driveway, she would've been the first one out if she'd had a door handle in the backseat. As it was, she had to wait for the driver to let her out, and had to stay behind him as his partner checked the house. Once he'd given the all clear, she headed for her house, for her sanctuary.

She was halfway there when a shot rang out and the officer beside her crumpled and went to his knees, fumbling for his weapon.

The other cop shoved her aside and down, and went for his gun, but a second shot dropped him where he stood. Screaming, Chelsea huddled between the two of them, exposed but unable to make herself leave the fallen men.

She pressed frantically on the entrance wound in the first cop's chest while tears ran down her face and she tried to get as flat on the ground as she possibly could, knowing there had to be a third shot on the way, this one aimed at her.

Get up and run! her inner wuss screamed. *Get out of here!* But her medical training screamed louder, telling her to get in there, stay in there, keep her patients stabilized until help arrived.

Then it did.

"Goddamn it, get out of the line of fire!" Fax appeared out of nowhere, in the daylight on her front lawn, running for all he was worth, his eyes wild, his wrists lacerated and covered with blood.

He grabbed her and yanked her away from her patients just as shot number three whistled past them and nailed the corner of her house.

"No! They'll die!" She yanked away and reached back for the cops, who were bleeding out in her yard.

"So will you." Fax cursed, got her around the waist and slung her up and over his shoulder. Then he was running for the cops' cruiser, dumping her in the driver's side and shoving her over to make room.

He slammed the door, cranked the transmission and hit the gas, and they shot out of her driveway in reverse.

She lay sprawled across the bench seat, staring at her hands, which were covered in the blood of men who might not be dead yet, but would be very soon.

"Strap in," Fax ordered grimly, scooting her over to the passenger's side as he sped along the residential streets of the Bear Claw suburbs. "This is going to get bumpy."

"What?" she asked dumbly. "Why?"

He jerked his chin over his shoulder. "We've got company."

Gaping, still in shock, Chelsea looked out the back of the stolen police cruiser. Sure enough, there was a dark SUV right on their bumper.

"Down!" Fax grabbed her and dragged her head onto his lap.

Seconds later, the men in the car behind them opened fire.

Chapter Seven

Cursing a steady stream under his breath, Fax yanked the steering wheel and sent the cruiser into a controlled skid, angling them away from the gunfire as best he could while he searched frantically for an escape route.

Seeing a narrow one-lane road that claimed to lead to the highway, he thought he had it.

"Hang on!" he said to Chelsea. She braced her feet against the dash and got her seat belt on just as he overshot the turn and spun back in a cloud of burning rubber. The cruiser caromed off the curb and a street sign, and lunged onto the narrow road, where it stalled.

The dark SUV overshot, skidded, and flew into a ditch on the other side of the main road.

At Fax's shout of triumph, Chelsea straightened and looked back. Instead of whooping, she shoved at his shoulder. "Get us out of here!"

"Yes, ma'am." He cranked the engine, hit the gas and sent the cruiser hurtling along the narrow road he'd chosen, which soon opened up to a commercial district and the highway.

Once they were on the open road, he took a long look at her, reassuring himself that the blood staining her hands and clothes had come from the cops, not her. When she looked up and their eyes met, he saw fear and shock, but no pain. "What happened to you?" she asked softly.

He glanced down at his hands on the steering wheel which were streaked with blood, and his wrists, where he'd folded his sleeves up to keep them from chafing the raw marks and cuts he'd inflicted on himself while struggling to get free of his bonds. "My cover's blown," he said succinctly, "and they know about you." He cursed under his breath, still not sure where he'd gone wrong. "I don't know what happened. I thought I'd covered myself. Maybe they got something out of Jane before she died," he mused quietly, feeling a hollow ache from knowing that Muhammad had confirmed his guess. She was gone, killed by the men he'd helped escape from prison.

She'd been one of the strongest women he'd known—hell, one of the strongest people he'd known, male or female. She'd dragged him out of depression after Abby's death; she'd given him a purpose, a reason to wake up in the morning. She'd taught him that sometimes it was better and more effective not to care, and she'd given him a chance to make a difference, a role where the cold, unemotional shell he'd crawled behind after Abby's betrayal was an asset, not a liability.

She was the only person who'd ever really accepted him as he was rather than trying to fix him. And now she was gone.

She wouldn't appreciate his grief, he knew, but she had it anyway.

He was so wrapped up in those dark thoughts that it took a moment for him to realize the tense air in the cruiser had changed from fear to unease…and it wasn't coming from him.

"Chelsea?" he said quietly, concentrating on the road and calculating how far they could get before they'd have to pull over and switch vehicles. "What's wrong?"

Technically, the answer was "everything," because nothing was right, everything was wrong. But he knew that whatever was bothering her, it was very close to the surface. She wasn't the type to keep an important secret for long.

Sure enough, she looked over at him, her face stricken. "It's my fault."

Whatever he'd been expecting her to say, that wasn't it. "What was your fault?" he asked carefully, not liking the suspicion that immediately came to mind.

"Your cover being broken. My being shot at. The cops dying." Her voice dropped to a whisper. "I told, Fax. That's how they knew about us. I told."

Everything inside him froze to ice. "Who?"

"Seth Varitek." Her voice was very small.

"The FBI agent who oversaw the autopsy with the faked records?" he said, volume inching up in disbelief. "What the—" He broke off, throttling down the surge of rage, of betrayal, burying it beneath a layer of deathly cold. "Damn it, Chelsea."

He said nothing more, couldn't trust himself to say anything else on the subject, because once he started he might not be able to stop.

They drove in silence until he pulled off the highway into a commercial zone that included gas stations and used-car lots, along with a few restaurants. He pulled in at the back of one of the restaurants, where the overflow lot was half-full of cars.

When Chelsea glanced at him, he said tightly, "We need to ditch the car. It'll have a GPS tracker."

She nodded. "I know. And, Fax—"

"Not now," he interrupted. "I can't deal with this now." If he tried, he might say—or do—something he'd regret in the aftermath.

She sucked in a breath, but nodded. "I understand. You get us a car, and I'll strip this one of anything we can use." Glancing at him, she said, "Like a first-aid kit."

In other words, he wasn't hiding his injuries as well as he'd thought. His wrists were killing him, and he didn't want to look at his ankles, which had suffered similar abrasions and had all but stopped hurting—which he took as a potentially bad sign.

He nodded shortly. "It's a deal." He climbed out of the cruiser and strode off, looking for an unremarkable vehicle to boost.

It took him under a minute to settle on a late-nineties pickup truck with fat tires that'd work off-road and an oversize engine that ought to give it some pep across the pavement. Hopefully they wouldn't need pep or off-road capabilities, but he'd never bet on optimism before and sure as hell wasn't starting now.

He'd just gotten the engine started by cracking the column and stripping and crossing the relevant wires when Chelsea climbed in the passenger's side, carrying an armful of supplies along with her purse, which she'd managed to hang on to through the attack and subsequent flight.

She didn't look at him as she buckled up and pulled the door shut with a decisive thunk. "We good to go?"

"As good as we're going to get."

Fax backed the pickup out of its slot, hoping the owners didn't look out the restaurant window to see that they'd gained a cruiser and lost a pickup. Before he turned onto the road, though, he looked back at the cruiser and felt a twinge of guilt, not about stealing the vehicle, but because he hadn't gotten to Chelsea's house in time to prevent the officers from being killed.

"It's not your fault," she said, as though she was inside his head, following his thoughts. "It's mine."

He said nothing, because there was nothing to say, and because the world was starting to go fuzzy around the edges, warning him that he either had a mild concussion on top of the cuts and bruises, or the drugs Muhammad had used on him weren't totally clear of his system.

So he focused on driving, aiming for the airport, where the dozens of interchangeable chain hotels would offer them a decent shot at anonymity for a few hours at the very least.

"Pull in here," Chelsea said as they passed a rest stop.

"We don't need gas."

"No, but we do need cash." She lifted her purse. "I'm assuming we're not going to want to use my credit cards." Her eyes went sad, no doubt at the thought of her PD friends finding the downed officers and assuming the worst.

"Damn," Fax said, annoyed at himself. He should've pulled in at the first ATM they passed. Now anyone checking her account records would know what highway they'd jumped on.

Which went to show he wasn't functioning at top capacity. In fact, he thought as he pulled off the highway into the rest stop, he was working at about half-speed and falling.

Still, he was coherent enough to grab her wrist before she could climb out of the truck, and push the first-aid kit in her direction. "Wipe the blood off your hands, and see what you can do about your clothes."

She paled but did as he ordered, cleaning herself up as best she could before she headed into the food court to use the ATM. While he waited, Fax leaned back and closed his eyes, keeping his ears tuned for any hint of trouble.

At least that's what he'd intended to do. Instead, he dozed.

Chelsea's voice roused him from his stupor. "Slide over. I'm driving."

He shifted over, not arguing because he didn't particularly want to win. There had been no sign of the dark SUV since it'd gone off the road, and nobody else appeared to be following them. They'd ditched the cruiser, and his gut told him it'd be a while before the switch was noticed.

They should be okay for a few hours at least, he figured as his eyes flickered closed and the dizziness took over.

It was the last thought he had for a while.

The next thing he knew, Chelsea was shaking him awake, saying, "Wake up, Fax. There's no way I can carry you. You're going to have to walk."

"I'm up." Actually, he was surprised he'd slept. Usually he could go for days on end with no rest and not feel it until he gave himself permission to let down his vigilance. Whatever Muhammad had given him, it'd packed a heck of a delayed punch.

"Come on," Chelsea said, tugging at him. "Let's get you inside."

They were in a parking lot, he saw, and noted the airplane logos on several nearby signs. "We're at the airport?" He frowned at her because he didn't think he'd said anything about going to an airport hotel, although that had been his plan.

"It was the best I could think of," she said, her voice going faintly defensive. "I switched out the truck's license plates with ones I pulled off a minivan about twenty miles from here, and registered our room under my grandmother's maiden name, figuring anyone looking for us wouldn't go that far back."

"I wasn't complaining. You did okay," he said grudgingly. He was still mad at her for leaking information, still not sure how that was going to affect things between them going forward, but at the same time he could see how it'd happened. She wasn't a trained operative, didn't live by the same rules he did.

He could understand why she'd done what she'd done, though that didn't make it the right call. Not by a long shot.

Groaning under his breath as his body echoed with pain, he dropped down from the stolen truck, careful not to lock it before he shut the door. "Let's get ourselves a room." He wasn't listening to any discussion of one versus two rooms. He didn't give a damn about modesty, and they needed to watch each other's backs.

She didn't argue. Instead, she flashed a key card and nodded to a nearby window. "First floor, halfway between two exits. That's our window. If we have to go through it, we're practically on top of the truck."

"Okay, now you're scaring me."

"Most of it's just common sense."

"Fair enough." But he didn't move, just gave her a long up-and-down look. She'd changed in the few days they'd known each other. She was bloody and battered, as she'd been in the cave that first day, but instead of being immobilized by terror, now she was functioning. More importantly, she was thinking. "You made a hell of a mistake, talking to your friend like that," he said, "but you've got good instincts. And I don't say that lightly."

She looked away. "I read lots of spy books."

"It's more than that, and you know it."

"I'm a wimp," she said softly. "I've been terrified this whole time. And my surveillance team…" Her eyes filled with tears and she crossed her arms over herself, shivering a little.

Although he knew they should get inside, out of sight, something compelled him to say, "All of this is al-Jihad's fault, first and foremost. Nothing gives him the right to do what he does."

She glanced at him and their eyes locked. He saw her searching his face for something, and wondered what she saw, what she was looking for.

"I wanted to join the FBI right out of college," she said, seemingly out of nowhere.

"Why didn't you?"

"I told you. I'm a wimp." She turned away and headed for the hotel door, apparently not willing to discuss it any further.

As Fax followed her in, she wondered how long she'd been telling herself that and why.

The hotel room was little more than a big square with two queen-size beds, an entertainment center and a small desk. Standard, unprepossessing and safe enough for the moment as far as Fax was concerned.

He locked and chained the door and made a beeline for the nearest bed, only to be pulled up short when Chelsea grabbed him and all but force-marched him into the bathroom.

"Sit." She propelled him in the direction of the toilet. "I'll get the first-aid kit."

He did as he was told, mostly because once she flipped the harsh fluorescent lights on, he could see exactly how bad his wrists looked, all gouged and swollen and so dirty they were practically a standing invite for an infection.

Staring at them without really feeling the pain, he said, "I've had worse."

"I don't doubt it," she said, coming back into the bathroom with the small plastic box she'd retrieved from the dead cops' cruiser. "But I'm a doctor. No way I'm letting you stay like this."

Perhaps, but he suspected that it was more nervous energy that kept her going as she cleaned and bandaged the cuts at his wrists. That same nervous energy rode her as she checked the bump at the back of his head and tended to the cuts on his ankles, which weren't as bad as he'd feared.

She was moving fast, talking fast, and he didn't blame her. She'd had a terrible, wretched day full of fear and blood, danger and guilt, and she had to be feeling like it'd all catch up to her if she slowed down, even for a second.

He should know. Been there, done that. He could've told her that running didn't help, though. The memories always caught up in the end.

At the same time, he knew that wasn't what she wanted or needed to hear just now, so he let her keep going, let her check his head a second and third time, get him an aspirin, draw him a glass of tap water. She needed to be doing, he knew, and maybe a piece of him needed to be done for, just for a few minutes.

He hadn't been fussed over in a long, long time.

When she was done, when she finally ran out of frenetic energy and just sort of stalled, standing there in the bathroom, staring at the bloodstains on her sleeves, he reached out and took her hand.

It was shaking.

"Come here." He tugged and she all but collapsed, practically going to her knees on the tile. He caught her on the way down, feeling the pull of bandages as he gathered her against him, her body cradled between his knees, her head against his chest. "Hold on to me for a few minutes."

She sobbed a broken word—his name, maybe—and clung.

Then, as he'd figured she would, Chelsea burst into tears.

CHELSEA HADN'T MEANT to lose it, had been trying not to, but the moment he touched her, the moment she leaned into his warm, solid bulk and felt his arms come around her, all bets were off.

She'd been trying to be brave when she wasn't really. She was a wimp who'd gone into pathology because she couldn't deal with life-or-death situations, a poser who read about adventures and imagined herself in them, but had avoided the offers of real-life adventure that'd come her way. She'd complained about her boring, normal life sometimes, but when she came right down to it, boring was better than dangerous.

"I don't want this," she said into Fax's chest, her sobs giving way to shuddering breaths. "I thought I did, but I don't. I want to wake up and realize this was all a dream. I want my old life back."

He said nothing, simply held her, and his silence was as eloquent as a shout, one that said, *There's no going back.*

She'd broken the law, broken her friends' trust, and his. And al-Jihad wanted her dead.

"What do we do now?" she said, her voice cracking on the misery of it all.

"We rest," he said, ever practical. "We're safe enough here for the moment, and neither of us is at our best. So let's rest for a few hours, and then we'll see where we're at."

She nodded, but didn't speak, and when he rose, it was the most natural thing in the world for her to rise with him, still tangled around him.

They moved into the main room together, and there was no discussion of the second bed. Instead, they lay down together, wrapped in one another, still fully clothed. He kicked off his shoes, then used his toes to shove hers off her feet. Pulling the hotel-issue coverlet over them both, he urged her into the hollow formed by the curve of his body, and his weight on the mattress. "Get some sleep. We'll overthink the rest later."

She'd slept so little the past three nights that it was easier to comply than to argue, and besides, she didn't really want to argue. She might not want to be in the situation she was in, but that didn't change the fact that she wanted to be near Fax. She wanted to touch him, taste him, curl up with him, be with him.

There would be no future with a man like him, but foolish though it might make her, she wanted whatever the present would allow. So she cuddled up against him and laid her sore cheek against his chest. They pressed together, fitting so perfectly it made her heart ache.

The contact warmed her when she'd been so cold for too long, made her feel safe when she knew she was vulnerable. She wanted to touch him, to run her hands along his body, but she knew he was right that they needed to rest, so she let herself sink into the warmth, knowing she would be cold again all too soon come morning.

She slept, warm and secure, surfacing a few hours later, opening her eyes briefly when Fax left the bed and headed for the bathroom.

"Do I need to get up?" she asked when he returned, her voice drowsy.

"Not yet," he answered. "Go back to sleep."

The mattress dipped beneath his weight, rolling her into him. His body heat surrounded her, cocooning her in the illusion of safety. On one level, she knew she should wake up, that they needed to talk about what was happening, and what they should do next. But on another level she had no desire to do anything but sleep a little longer, put off reality for a few more hours.

So she slept.

She was awakened some time later by a sound. Through the blinded window she could see that day had gone to dark outside, making it nearly pitch inside the room. Tensing, she strained to identify the noise that had roused her.

It hadn't been a footstep or bump in the night, she realized as her mind supplied the memory. It'd been Fax's voice.

"What's wrong?" he said from very close beside her, having apparently awakened when she did.

"You were talking in your sleep."

She waited for him to deny it. Instead, after a long pause, he said simply, "Sorry. Didn't mean to wake you."

Which meant he knew what he'd said, or at least what he'd been dreaming about. She wasn't sure whether that made it better or worse, considering that the word she'd heard had been another woman's name. *Abby.*

She didn't have any right to feel hurt. But that didn't stop the emotion from coming.

"Who is she?" she asked, not really sure she wanted to know. She'd assumed all along that a man like him was alone in the world, that there was nobody waiting for his mission to end. The way he'd talked about his mother and brothers had only reinforced that impression, as had her suspicion that he and Jane had been lovers at some point.

But none of those people had been named Abby, and he hadn't spoken of them with the intensity he'd used just now, when he'd called her name.

He was silent for so long she didn't think he was going to answer. Then, finally, he exhaled a long, sighing breath and said, "She was my wife. She miscarried and bled out five years ago next month."

"Oh." That was all Chelsea could muster at first—a single syllable that didn't begin to cover her horror, both at having asked the question and having opened an obviously unhealed wound. She could hear the pain in his voice, feel the tension in his body. "I'm sorry," she said finally, though that seemed pitifully inadequate.

"I left the PD and went undercover with Jane's team six months later," he said as though that explained everything, which she supposed it did.

"You must have loved her very much," she said, empathy warring with jealousy.

Instead of answering, he leaned away from her and snapped on one of the bedside lamps, casting the two of them in warm yellow light. He stayed there at the edge of the mattress, propped up on one elbow, looking down at her with something unfathomable in his cool eyes. "Not exactly."

The doctor in her noted that he looked less tired than before, his eyes sharper, his color better. The woman in her, though, focused on his words. "You didn't love her?"

She wasn't sure which would be better, to hear that he'd loved and lost his wife or that he hadn't loved her, yet had married her and they'd started a family. And no matter how much Chelsea tried to tell herself this was none of her business, her heart said otherwise.

"I loved her," Fax said. "She was my high-school sweetheart. We stayed in touch while I was in the military, and got married once my service was up. I came home and joined the local PD. I worshipped the damn ground she walked on… Unfortunately, she didn't feel the same. Or maybe she did, once, but it didn't last." He paused, grimacing. "The baby wasn't mine. She didn't even tell me she was pregnant, which begs the question of whether she'd planned on abortion or figured I wasn't going to be part of her future plans."

"Oh," Chelsea said, taken aback. She'd assumed he was cold and hard because that was what his profession demanded. Now, she could only assume that his natural reserve had other layers to it, layers that made him even less available than she'd thought.

He nodded as though she'd asked the question aloud. "Yeah. Let's just say I'm not lining up to try the happily-ever-after thing again." Something flashed at the back of his eyes and he added, "In case you were wondering."

"I wasn't," she said faintly, lying to herself as much as him. "You woke me up talking about her. That was all."

There was a great deal more and they both knew it, but instead of hashing it out, they just stayed there, staring at each other as the small circle of yellow lamplight and the night beyond cast a layer of intimacy over the scene.

Heat kindled in her belly, so much hotter than the comforting warmth of before, a greedy fire that made her want to reach out and drag him close. She wanted to sink her fingers in his hair, in his clothes, wanted to breathe him in, inhale him whole until they were bound to one another, for the duration of the night.

There was no future for them, she knew, even less hope of it than before, now that she knew his work wasn't the only reason he held himself aloof. But if she'd learned anything from the events of the past few days, it was that things could change in the blink of an eye. They could both be dead tomorrow.

Given that, there was nothing she'd rather do than rise up on her hands and knees and cross to him on the wide mattress, watch his eyes fix on her, and see the heat flare within them.

When she did exactly that, he brought his hands up to her shoulders as if in protest. But he didn't pull her close, didn't push her away.

"Chelsea," he said, voice rasping. "Be sure this is what you want."

"I'm sure enough," she said, which was the honest truth. She wasn't positive of anything anymore, but she knew if they didn't take this moment, this chance, she would regret it for the rest of her life. Now was not the time to be a wuss.

He held her away for a long moment, until she was starting to worry that her "almost" wasn't enough, that he didn't want her enough to take the chance.

Then, when she was just about ready to draw back and stammer an apology, his fingers tightened on her shoulders and he drew her close, sliding her up his body where he lay partway propped against the headrest of the motel bed.

He held her there for a few seconds, his breath whispering against her lips, his eyes searching hers for—what? She didn't know the answer, wasn't even sure of the question. But somehow he found the reply he'd been seeking, because he whispered her name, making the two syllables sound as dear as they ever had in her entire life. *"Chelsea."*

Then he framed her face in his hands and crushed his lips to hers, and there was no more talking, no more discussion. There was only the heat they made together and the perfection that might not be forever, but was exactly what both of them needed just then.

Chapter Eight

For all the times Fax had told himself to keep his hands off Chelsea, that she deserved a man who could give her all the stability and safe adventures she deserved, when it came down to it, he was the cold, greedy bastard Abby had called him in the single fight that had marked the end of their marriage and had brought on the miscarriage that had killed her.

She'd demanded a divorce out of nowhere, or at least that was how it had seemed at the time. She'd accused him of wanting everything his way, saying that he'd chosen the military, then the police force over her. She'd claimed he'd given her no choice but to have an affair, and said he couldn't blame her for going elsewhere for the love and single-minded attention he'd been unable to give her.

Well, he damn well did blame her. But that didn't mean there wasn't a kernel of truth to what she'd said.

He wanted what he wanted and did what it took to get it.

And right now, he wanted Chelsea.

She was softness in his arms, sweet flavors in his mouth and soul as he eased her down atop him and their bodies aligned. He held on to that sense of sweetness as he kissed her, trying to give her back the humanity she gave him, fighting back the beast inside him, the cold-blooded killer who took what he wanted and to hell with the world.

One kiss spun into another as he shaped her body with his hands and lips, relearning the curves of a woman, and recognizing the ones that were hers alone.

For all the times he'd sat in the hell of solitary confinement and imagined being with someone, he'd forgotten the reality of the sensations of sex, the heat of it. Or maybe he'd remembered correctly, and Chelsea wasn't like any of the other women he'd been with before.

It was a daunting thought, and one he brushed aside almost the moment it was formed, reminding himself to stay in the here and now, because there was no guarantee of tomorrow.

He tasted that knowledge on Chelsea's lips and heard it in her soft, wanting sigh. Part of him had regretted telling her about Abby, but he realized it was all for the best, because at least it put them on level footing, with understanding and expectations—or the lack thereof—on both sides.

Then she smiled against his lips and shifted to get her hands under his shirt. Splaying her fingers over his abdomen, she murmured, "You're thinking too much. I can feel it."

"I want this," he said, uttering the words before he was really aware of thinking them.

"Me, too. So why the hesitation?"

"I don't want to take advantage."

"Of?" Her eyes held a glint of humor, a hint of impatience that made his blood burn hotter, even though that should've been impossible.

He was tempted to kiss the wickedness off her face, turning the humor to heat, but he held his baser self off a little longer, saying, "You and me. Us. The situation." He gestured to the window, not at the night, but at the figment of the cops and terrorists who were looking for them even now, and would find them before too long. "We wouldn't be together like this if it weren't for some pretty extraordinary circumstances."

Her expression saddened a little. "And we won't be together after all this is over, one way or the other," she finished for him. "Don't worry, I get it."

He cupped her face in his hands and looked deep into her eyes. "Do you really? Or is this just part of some spy fantasy, an escape from what's really going on?"

But for the first time he couldn't read her every thought from her expression, leaving him off balance when she said simply, "Does it matter?"

Before he could even think to formulate an answer, she leaned in and touched her lips to his, slipping her tongue into his mouth at the same time she slid her hands beneath his waistband.

And then he pretty much stopped thinking at all.

CHELSEA FELT THE CHANGE in him, knew the second he got out of his head and into the moment, because that was when he leaned into the kiss and opened to her, deepening and intensifying caresses that only seconds earlier had seemed hotter than was possible. Before she could brace herself, buffering against too much sensation, her body flared higher and higher still, driven by his clever touch and the raw need she tasted on his lips.

Earlier she'd been the instigator, seeking to push him past his hesitation before he talked them both out of giving in to the needs of their bodies. But now he was the one doing the pushing, heating her up and over her inner barriers before she was even aware of their existence.

Always before for her, sex had been part of a relationship, an outgrowth of love. Here, though, it was all about the physical sensations, about sex rather than love. And if a small piece of her wondered whether there might be some love on her part when there was zero expectation of that on his, the heat quickly rose up and swept away the worry, leaving nothing behind except the sensation of his lips on her skin, his body against hers.

Leaving nothing but *him.*

They stretched across the bed together, twining arms and legs and tongues until there was no clear end to one of them, no clear beginning of the other. There was only them, and the heat they made together.

His skin was a tough expanse of maleness, roughened in places with faint tracks of masculine hair. Wanting more of him, needing more, she pushed his shirt aside, rucking it up under his arms until he chuckled and eased away so he could pull it off. While they were separated, he skimmed what was left of her shirt down over her arms and off, and released the catch of her bra.

Naked from the waist up and bathed in the yellow light coming from the bedside lamp, she would've blushed and covered up if it hadn't been for the look that softened his hard blue eyes—a sort of wistfulness she hadn't seen from him before.

"You're perfect," he whispered harshly. And although he was looking at her breasts when he said it, she had a feeling he was talking about more. Then he looked at his own chest, which was sharply defined with muscle and bone, and marked with a half-dozen scars of various size and ugliness, along with a ripe bruise, no doubt acquired earlier in the day. "I'm not exactly perfect," he said ruefully before looking at her once again. "Far from it." And this time she was positive he was talking about more than just their bodies.

Emotion jammed in her throat at the suspicion that he felt things far more deeply than he let on, and that he, too, knew they'd found something together that didn't come along every day.

Rather than ruin the moment with analysis, especially when she wasn't sure she was going to like the answer she came to, she lay back on the bed and smiled an invitation, offering herself to him, no strings attached. Aware that he was watching, she shimmied out of her pants and panties, leaving herself naked beneath the soft light.

She let him look, aware that he seemed to have stopped breathing as she stretched out an arm and snagged her purse off the nightstand beside the bed. From her wallet, she pulled out a condom—one of two she kept in there as part of her "just in case" stash.

Holding it up, she tilted her head and smiled at him.

"Chelsea," he breathed, only her name, but in a tone that suggested she'd just given him a gift beyond measure.

He stood then, rising from the bed to strip out of his remaining clothes. His motions were efficient and practical, like the man himself, but the play of muscle beneath his skin was an erotic dance that made Chelsea's pulse pound a greedy beat. She'd wanted him this way since the first moment their eyes had locked. She was done with waiting for the time to be right.

The time was now, right or wrong.

"Come here," she breathed, and he made short work of donning the condom over his proud, jutting flesh. Then he joined her in the center of the bed and covered her body with his.

He might've thought to prolong the moment with another kiss or some teasing caresses, but she took that inclination away by reaching up and pressing her lips to his, pouring herself into the moment and making her urgency known.

No less urgent himself, Fax kissed her long and hard as he touched her, shaping her body with his hands, sliding his fingers along her torso and hips, then inward for a long, soft rub against her center, where she was wet and wanting already.

She arched against him and cried out, her wordless plea muffled against his lips. He heard and understood, though, and shifted to poise himself at the entrance to her body.

Then he paused, waiting.

Want spiraled to a tight core within Chelsea, centered on the empty void where her inner muscles pulsed, waiting for him.

She opened her eyes and found him braced above her, looking at her. When their eyes met and the connection clicked as it had done from the first, then and only then did he nudge his hard flesh against her, into her.

His solid length invaded her, filling her and setting off an explosion of pleasure and sensation.

Chelsea gasped and arched against him, digging her fingernails into his back and reveling in his hiss and the fine tremors she could feel in his muscles.

When he was seated to the hilt he paused again and looked at her, and this time she couldn't meet his gaze, she just couldn't. The feelings he brought out in her were too huge, too raw, so she leaned up and pressed her cheek to his, closed her eyes, and hung on for the ride as he withdrew and thrust, withdrew and thrust.

The two of them surged together, racing each other to the peak while dragging one another along at the same time. The heat built and meshed within Chelsea, a building urgency in search of an outlet, concentrating at the point of contact where he filled her and withdrew, filled and withdrew.

The orgasm slammed into her unexpectedly, a freight-train hammer of pleasure and greed that gripped her, controlled her, made her arch against him and scream his name, not Fax but Jonah. She hung on to him, used his strength as an anchor while the pleasure washed over and through her. She felt him stiffen against her, inside her, and heard him give a hoarse, wordless shout. Then they were clinging together as the passion slowed and faded, leaving them limp and breathing hard, survivors of a mad rush to the finish.

And what a finish, Chelsea thought with the few brain cells left in her head unscrambled.

Where always before she'd come on a tug and roll of pleasure, this orgasm had left her flattened and defenseless, stripped bare by feelings that were too huge to deny, too important to cope with. That, and the knowledge that the two of them were a fleeting thing, a union of flesh and convenience.

The realization chilled her and made her cling to him a little too hard. She could tell it was too much because he stiffened, then he pulled away. He pressed a kiss to her cheek, but didn't look at her as he stood and headed for the bathroom, weaving slightly on unsteady legs. He shut the door behind him, leaving her utterly alone.

Feeling utterly rejected.

FAX LEANED ON THE EDGE of the sink and closed his eyes, totally undone by what had just happened between him and Chelsea.

He'd tried to hold a piece of himself back, tried to keep hold of the shell protecting himself from the outside world and vice versa, but all of his defenses had failed in that last moment, when Chelsea had grabbed on to him and let herself go, and he'd been unable to do anything but follow where she led.

"Idiot," he muttered, glaring at himself in the mirror. Worse, he'd been irresponsible, letting down his guard way too far when neither of them could afford for him to make a mistake.

Chelsea wasn't Abby, not even close. But trusting her not to cheat wasn't the same thing as trusting her to have his back. She wasn't Jane, didn't have Jane's physical or emotional tools.

Cursing, he cleaned himself up. Then, wrapping a towel around his waist in a feeble bid for the armor of clothing, he made himself leave the bathroom and face Chelsea, knowing she was likely to be beyond furious over the way he'd boogied it out of the bed they'd shared.

"Look, I'm sorry," he began the moment he hit the main room, guilt making his tone more defensive than he'd intended. "I know that probably looked pretty bad."

"It *was* bad," she agreed levelly. She was up and dressed, and had already pulled the bed more or less back to rights, as though she was trying to remove any reminder of what they'd just done. "But I'm a big girl,

I can deal. We both needed some skin-on-skin after what we've been through together. Doesn't have to be any more than that."

Her voice sounded reasonable, but her shoulders were tight, her jaw was set, and a flush stained her cheeks and throat.

He wanted to tell her it hadn't been like that, at least not for him, but he stopped himself because what was the upside of explaining? It wasn't like things could go anywhere between them from here. It was probably better to have her mad at him, for both their sakes.

"Sorry," he said again, but didn't contradict anything she'd said.

"What now?"

It took him a second to realize she'd shifted gears, that she was asking about a plan, not a relationship. He was selfish enough to be relieved, wise enough to know that just because she wasn't talking about what had just happened between them, it didn't mean the issue was dead.

Or rather, it meant exactly that. Whatever might've been between them, it was over.

Guilt stung alongside another emotion he didn't really recognize, one that in another man might've been grief. Both were quickly gone as he put himself back in the agent's frame of mind he never should've let slip away.

She was right. They needed some sort of a plan.

He took a seat in the desk chair in the corner of the room, staying far from the beds, as though that would neutralize the hint of sex on the air. Thinking aloud, he said, "We know he's aiming for the parade, day after tomorrow, right? So tell me about it. You've been, right?" Hours earlier she'd identified the parade from the flyer he'd seen in the cabin.

"Sure, everyone in the city goes, pretty much." She perched on the edge of the far bed, the one they hadn't used, and frowned, thinking. "It's a local chamber of commerce thing that got picked up in the national media a few years ago during a slow news cycle. The idea took off after that, and it's become the Bear Claw equivalent of the Macy's Thanksgiving Day parade in New York. You know—floats, bands, balloons, lots of people lining the sidewalks."

Which was exactly the sort of target al-Jihad favored. During the Santa Bombings, his men had planted explosives in the highly decorated thrones of the Santas at a half-dozen malls all operated by the American Mall Corp. The charges had gone off thirty minutes after the Santas had arrived for the year, in the middle of the highly publicized kickoff parties that had been coordinated across all the locations owned by AMC.

The fatalities had numbered in the hundreds, the list of wounded topping a thousand. Even more devastating was the nature of the casualties—six Santas, along with mothers, fathers and dozens of children small enough to want to sit on Santa's lap and tell him their dreams.

It had been a truly disgusting attack, and al-Jihad was no doubt looking to improve upon it this time around.

Think, Fax told himself. *Focus.* What sort of target would appeal to the bastard during the parade? "Is there a place where there'll be a particularly large crowd?" he asked. "Lots of young kids, families, that sort of thing?"

She thought for a second, then a stricken look crossed her face. "There's an open-air party at the ski resort stadium where the parade winds up, followed by a concert and fireworks. It's the big finale."

"That'll be the target," Fax said, though it didn't play quite right in his head. The schematics he'd glimpsed in the terrorists' cabin—which had no doubt been evacuated by now—hadn't been for a stadium. Did that mean there was a second target? He didn't know and didn't have the tools or the resources he needed to figure it out.

"We need to tell someone," she said urgently. "Mayor Proudfoot will need to cancel the concert, if not the entire parade."

Fax shook his head, knowing the conversation had approximately two seconds left before it went downhill fast. "I can't. I'm sorry."

It took a moment for his meaning to penetrate, another for the anger to gather in her eyes and face. "You mean you want to *let* him attack the festival? You're going to use all those people as bait?" She must've seen the answer in his eyes, because she blew out a hollow, disbelieving breath and answered her own question. "You are, aren't you?"

He steeled himself against her disillusionment. "This business is about making tough choices."

"Choices like letting the guards, two of whom were father and son, die so you'd have a chance to uncover a plot that could kill many other people?" she challenged.

"Yeah," he said, thinking of the three innocent guards who'd been in the prison van during the escape, and the way two of the men had grabbed on to each other as they died, each trying to protect the other. *Father and son,* he thought, and could see the resemblance in his mind's eye. *Damn.*

When he'd first taken this job he wouldn't have cared

as long as he reached his main objective. Now he wished he'd tried to find some way to spare the guards.

Somewhere along the line his necessary detachment had started to erode, and that was a problem. It clouded his thinking and messed up his judgment.

A prime example of exactly that was the way his heart kicked when Chelsea scowled at him. "You're not doing this, Jonah. I won't let you put the people of my city in danger."

Guilt flared alongside grief, and for a change he didn't force either of them aside. Instead, he rose to his feet and crossed to her, taking her hands. She leaned away from him, still sitting at the edge of the second bed, and he kneeled at her feet, keeping his eyes on hers, wanting, needing her to believe him when he said, "I'm sorry, Chelsea."

Her eyes filled and she shook her head. "I can't let you do this. I have to call Seth and Tucker and have them pick us up."

"I know." He slid his hand up her arm in a lover's caress that stopped at the place where her neck and shoulder joined. He said, "I'm sorry," again, and pressed his thumb against the vulnerable place where the nerves ran close to the surface.

She stiffened and collapsed.

"You really are a cold bastard, Fairfax," he told himself, feeling like hell as he raided her wallet for her remaining cash, which she wouldn't be needing where he planned to stash her. "Cold, but effective."

He wasn't feeling cold or effective as he cleared their hotel room and carried her to the truck for transport, though.

He was feeling pretty much like a bastard.

CHELSEA AWOKE in the daylight, in a different hotel room, one that was seriously run-down compared to their digs at the airport. The walls were dingy, with lighter spaces where paintings had hung. There was no TV on the bureau, although there were wires where one had been, no clock on the nightstand, none of the conveniences that usually came standard.

Panic slapped at her. Confusion.

How had she ended up in what looked like an abandoned motel, wrapped in a comforter she recognized from the airport hotel?

She remembered fighting with Fax and threatening to turn him in. After that...the panic spiraled higher as she tried to remember what'd happened next and came up blank.

Bolting up in the bed, she looked around, afraid that Muhammad had found them somehow, that Fax had been captured, too, or injured...or worse.

When she moved, there was a jangle of chain.

Terror locked within her as she looked at her right wrist. What she saw confirmed her worst fears: one end of a set of handcuffs was latched around her arm, the other on to a generous length of chain that ran beneath the bed, where it was fastened to something that didn't give in the slightest when she tugged.

She was trapped.

"Help," she whispered, her heart pounding up into her throat and choking her with terror, with tears. "Fax? Are you there?" Her voice quavered, cracking on the words.

There was no answer, no sign of him when she looked around. But there was a spare blanket folded on a chair beside the bed, and a picnic cooler on the floor beside a bucket and a roll of toilet paper. The cooler proved to contain several days' worth of food and water. A small stack of paperbacks sat on the nightstand, holding down a piece of stationary bearing the airport hotel's logo.

Pulse pumping, she reached for the note as a disturbing suspicion took root in her brain. Muhammad wouldn't have left her food, a chamber pot or a note.

Fax, on the other hand, would have.

The note read:

Chelsea, I'd say I'm sorry, but we agreed not to apologize anymore. Besides, I highly doubt an apology would suffice under the circumstances. So I'll say only that this is the best way I could think of to keep you safe while I do what I need to do.

Meeting you has been the highlight of some very dark years, and I wish it could've ended differently, but I chose my path a long time ago. You, on the other hand, still have choices left, so I'll say this: you are not a wimp, Chelsea Swan. I don't know who told you that you are, or why you believed them. I only know that you're one of the bravest women I've ever met.

It wasn't signed, but she knew it was from Fax, just as she knew that he'd somehow knocked her out and brought her to some deserted motel, probably far outside the city and off the beaten track, figuring she'd be safely out of the way until after the parade.

Rage flared. Disbelief.

The son of a bitch had kidnapped her. Again.

Chapter Nine

Fax knew he'd done the right thing—his head and his heart both said so, damn it. He'd simultaneously protected both Chelsea and the job, buying himself room to do what needed to be done. But he couldn't help thinking that the right thing was feeling very wrong.

He'd left her as safe and comfortable as he'd been able to manage on short notice. What was more, back at the airport hotel, he'd used the business center computer to send a time-delayed e-mail that would go out to the Bear Claw PD if he didn't log on within six hours, bumping it back another six. The e-mail, addressed to her boss at the ME's office, with copies to Tucker McDermott of homicide and Seth Varitek of the FBI, gave her exact location up in the hills west of Bear Claw.

If anything happened to him, she'd be rescued within a few hours.

He'd done his best, it was true. But although he could justify it all he wanted, the end result was that not a half hour after losing himself inside Chelsea's body, he'd left her handcuffed to a cheap motel bed, with minimal provisions and a bucket.

That ranked pretty high on the bastard scale no matter how he looked at it.

"She'll be safe there," he told himself as he sent the stolen pickup hurtling back toward the city. "She'll be safe and you can concentrate on the job."

Which was true. But it didn't stop him from wishing there'd been another way. He'd spent too long in the hell of solitary confinement, and he was antisocial by nature. The next day or so was going to be torture for Chelsea, who needed to be surrounded with her friends and their chatter.

Brooding, Fax drove straight to the ski lodge where the parade would wind up the following day. His eyes were immediately drawn to a raised stadium, where crews were working to hang banners and prep for the next day's event.

The schematics definitely didn't match, but the sight of the raised seating—and the knowledge that all those seats would be filled the following day—kicked a shiver of unease through his gut, and a faint inner question of whether he might not be taking the idea of acceptable loss a little too far.

Maybe Chelsea had a point. Maybe it was time to turn himself in and have faith that al-Jihad's coconspirators were few and far between, that the good guys would be able to mount a workable op in the time remaining, or cancel the parade and concert, at the very least.

Problem was, even if the local authorities believed him in the absence of any evidence that he was on their side, the moment al-Jihad got wind of an official response, he and the others would go deep underground, only to reappear someplace else, someplace where they weren't expected, and where there was no possibility of preventing the attack and taking down the terrorist and his followers.

Yes, Fax was making a decision he had no official sanction to make by not warning the Bear Claw PD about the threat to the city's revelry, but he didn't see any way around it. Not if he hoped to complete his mission, which was just as vital as it had been when Jane first put him undercover.

He needed not only al-Jihad, Muhammad and the lemming in custody, he needed to ID their connections within the FBI and elsewhere.

Anything less was failure.

When he parked at the edge of the stadium lot, he saw that there were people everywhere, both workers and early-season skiers. The lot was jammed, and there were people standing around talking, or changing into and out of their gear rather than carrying it with them to the locker room up at the resort.

Given the melee, Fax figured he was probably safe taking a look around.

He donned the black cowboy hat he'd bought at a truck stop, keeping it low so it covered his ears and brow. He slouched in his heavy jacket as he exited the truck, and consciously altered his step as he headed for the stadium, on the off chance that either law enforcement or al-Jihad's people had biometrics up and running.

There was no question that the terrorists would have surveillance of some sort. It was just a question of what kind, and how long it would take them to figure out that Fax was poking around the stadium.

He would be in and out before then. He hoped.

Making a wide circuit of the stadium first, he counted the exits and tried to figure out which structural elements would matter most to the steel-and-cement building, because they would be al-Jihad's targets.

Once he had a pretty good idea what was going on outside, he headed for a quiet-looking entrance, figuring he'd grab a hammer or clipboard and look like he had someplace to be.

He was two steps in when a blur came at him from the side.

Adrenaline zinged and Fax ducked, spinning away and then coming in low, grabbing for his attacker.

Too late, he saw a second man coming in from the other side. Cursing, Fax went for his weapon, which he'd tucked at the small of his back beneath his jacket. A heavy weight slammed into him before he got the gun and his attacker bore down on his weapon hand with a shout of "Gun!"

The second guy landed on him in a bruising scrum of knees and elbows and curses, and within ten seconds, Fax found himself kissing floor with both hands behind his back and a big guy kneeling across his kidneys.

The click of handcuffs and the burr of a police dispatcher's voice on a radio nearby let him know they weren't al-Jihad's men. Then again, so did the fact that he was still alive. It was a good bet Muhammad would've shot him on sight.

Unfortunately, just because he'd been caught by the so-called good guys, didn't mean he was out of danger.

Far from it, Fax thought, fighting to slow his pulse and think rather than giving in to the urge to struggle. He might be able to take out one of the cops, but not both. He'd have to work his way out of the situation somehow.

If he didn't, al-Jihad might very well win.

"Up you go," said the guy who'd been kneeling on Fax's kidneys. He got off and hauled Fax to his feet and started reciting the Miranda warning.

Fax got a good look at the other man, who was a tall, slick-looking guy in a pale gray suit that'd barely wrinkled in the struggle. He was wearing a nine-millimeter under his arm and an FBI badge on his belt.

There was something about him that didn't ring true. Maybe it was that his suit was high-end but his dark brown hair was overgrown past an expensive-looking cut, as though something had happened recently to put this guy off his game. Or maybe it was the look of quiet desperation in the back of his hazel eyes, one that said he wasn't totally in control of the situation.

Whatever the reason, the FBI agent gave Fax a seriously bad vibe. He'd bet money that Mr. FBI was one of al-Jihad's men.

Fax's mind raced as he tried to figure out his next best step and came up pretty much blank.

"Come on," the guy behind him said, nudging Fax's heel with his toe. "Next stop, Bear Claw PD."

Question was, would the FBI agent let him make it that far, or was he planning on carrying out al-Jihad's kill order right away?

CHELSEA WORE HERSELF OUT struggling futilely against her bonds. She hated being stuck in the drab room, knowing that if Fax wasn't yet in jeopardy, he would be soon.

She let her head hang as tears stung her eyes. "Damn it, Jonah."

She'd begun the day making love with him. She hated that she was going to end the day cursing him. But what else could she do? She couldn't forgive the way he'd knocked her out, and the way he'd left her alone.

Worse, as the day dragged on, she started to wonder if he was coming back at all. What if Muhammad had caught up to him? What if he was already dead?

She tried to tell herself the tears that pressed at the thought were because she was afraid of being stuck indefinitely, but in reality they were partly for Fax, too. He might be the selfish bastard he saw himself as, but that didn't make him any less a hero to the people he was trying to save. And that included her.

He came off as cold and uncaring, but he'd cared enough to protect her, over and over again. And his note had gone even further. What he'd said about her being strong had mattered; it had made her consider exactly where and when she'd started thinking of herself as a wimp.

Trying to be as self-analytical as she knew how to be, she'd thought back and tracked it to her teenage years. It wasn't that her mother had called her a wimp—never that. It was more that anytime Chelsea had asked about her parents' divorce, her mother had gone on and on about how she'd tried her best to keep the marriage together and failed. She'd made Chelsea promise not to really, truly commit to a man unless she was sure he would work as hard as her to make it last.

Over the years, that had evolved into a sharp maternal pressure against failure, not just in relationships, but in everything. And so, Chelsea had realized as the shadows lengthened and the day turned to dusk, she'd started picking goals she knew she could meet, and she'd started giving up on things that seemed to come with a high probability of failure.

Like the FBI. And her love affairs.

She wasn't a wimp, she realized. She was terrified of failing.

Was that it? she wondered. Was it really so simple? What if—

The sound of tires crunching on gravel derailed that train of thought in an instant.

She whipped her head around, craning to see through the small crack between the drawn blinds and the window frame. The truck—assuming it was Fax—was out of view, leaving her to tense as she heard a car door slam.

Then another, and a third.

Panic flared, hard and hot, and she yanked at her bonds, realizing that while Fax had been trying to keep her safe by holding her in place, he'd also made her an easy target.

What if Muhammad had caught him but not killed him right away? What if he'd tortured him for her whereabouts first?

Her stomach roiled and her heart hammered up into her throat as three sets of footsteps approached the motel door. Seconds later, there was a loud slam and the door flew inward under the force of a man's kick.

Chelsea screamed, unable to stay quiet and still, unable to do anything but shriek in horror as three figures lunged through the door and bolted toward her, moving fast, their hands outstretched.

"Chelsea!" Those hands grabbed at her, tugging at her bonds. "Oh, my God, Chelsea, are you okay?"

The words penetrated, as did the identities of her attackers…or rather, her rescuers.

"Sara?" Chelsea's voice broke on surprise, and a jolt of fledgling hope. She looked from her boss to the two men who had accompanied her. Familiar, trustworthy men. "Seth? Tucker? What—" She broke off then, because it was too huge to say aloud, her surprise too great.

To her embarrassment, she started sobbing, stuttering questions and explanations that made no sense, her words tumbling over one another as her brain tried to deal with the realization that her friends had found her, that Fax had somehow let them know where to go. Which meant he wasn't coming back for her.

The thought shouldn't have hurt as much as it did.

"We've got you," Sara was saying, holding her and stroking her, and saying her name over and over while Tucker crouched down and went to work on the cuffs, quickly releasing her from her bedside imprisonment.

Seth had been the one to kick in the door, but now he stood back, watching her.

He knew something, Chelsea realized. Or else he thought he knew something and he was looking for confirmation. But what was it? Had he found out something about Fax's undercover work, or was he trying to figure out whose side she was on?

"Come on." Tucker held out a hand. "Let's get you out of here." He pulled her to her feet and Sara draped a coat over her shoulders—this one was burgundy wool and too large all over, reminding Chelsea that she'd been wearing another of Sara's coats when she and Fax first met. The memory brought a fresh burst of tears.

Get a grip on yourself, she thought fiercely, reining in the weepies through sheer force of will. *You're tougher than this.*

And, she realized with a small start of surprise, she was.

Only days earlier, she'd thought of herself as a small person capable of doing only small things, but somehow in the midst of the fear and sneaking around Fax had put her through, she'd gained a new degree of mettle.

Or so she hoped, because she was about to do something the old Chelsea never would've contemplated.

She stopped as they passed Seth. Looking the FBI agent in the eye, she said, "Where is he?"

"We have him in custody."

Nerves shimmered through her, alongside a kick of relief that at least he was alive. For the time being, anyway. "'We' as in the Bear Claw PD or the FBI?" she asked, though she wasn't sure which answer would be preferable.

"What do you know, Chelsea?" Seth asked softly, his eyes intent on hers. "And I don't mean what have you guessed or what has he told you, but what do you really know for certain?"

She hesitated, because she didn't know the FBI agent as well as some of the others, and what she did know suggested that while he was a strong personality and went his own way when necessary, he typically worked within the confines of his position. He was a company man, and she was about to ask him to work way outside the limits.

What she needed could potentially get Seth—and the rest of them—fired if it didn't work out as planned. Worse, they'd probably all go to jail.

She took a deep breath, then stepped off the deep end, into a half-baked plan that not only had the potential to fail, it probably would. But the thing was, she didn't care anymore. Fax was worth the risk. "I'll tell you everything, I promise," she said. "But first I'm going to need your help."

IT WASN'T UNTIL FAX found himself back behind bars that he realized two things: one, it was far more difficult to plan a valid-seeming escape without gadgets and outside help; and two, the only thing that'd kept him sane during his incarceration was the knowledge that someone out in the real world knew he wasn't actually a criminal.

Before, he'd been in jail because he'd chosen to be for the greater good. He'd had an excuse to feel noble and martyred.

Now, as the holding-cell door clanged shut and the guard locked him in alone, he just felt like a failure. He'd helped three deadly terrorists escape back into the world at large and hadn't been able to complete his mission.

He'd blown his cover by trusting the wrong person. He had six civilian lives on his conscience—three guards—not counting al-Jihad's accomplice—one morgue attendant and the two cops who'd been guarding Chelsea had all died as part of his botched mission. And what did he have to show for it?

Not nearly enough. He'd only identified one potential terrorist contact within federal law enforcement, and only then because the guy had come after him at the ski lodge. The agent's ID tagged him as Michael Grayson, a midlevel operative out of the Denver office, but that was all Fax knew.

Besides, he thought on an uncharacteristic beat of depression, what was the point? He didn't have anyone to report to anymore. He had to assume that Muhammad had been telling the truth and Jane was dead, her network obliterated.

Perhaps records of his undercover work still existed somewhere, but it'd be twenty to life before he'd be free to search for them, and it wasn't like he had friends on the inside ready to go to bat for him.

In the aftermath of Abby's death, he'd let those connections fall away. Some he'd even intentionally severed as part of making himself into the agent Jane had needed—one with no ties, no regrets.

No heart. The thought came out of nowhere, but it resonated more than he liked. Since when did he think things like that? Since he met Chelsea, that was when. She'd awakened something within him that had been long dormant, since Abby's death, or maybe even before that, when he'd realized the woman he'd been in love with wasn't the one he'd thought he'd married.

He'd married a fantasy. One that had looked an awful lot like Chelsea did in reality.

Sure, they were different types physically, but Chelsea had the core values he'd grown up with, the ones that lent themselves to a house in the suburbs, with a white picket fence and a couple of kids. He'd wanted that once, had thought he'd found it, only to have it disappear.

In response he'd disappeared, becoming something even his own family had turned away from. A man who thought in terms of acceptable risk and tied his lover to a bed in a boarded-up motel, and left her alone.

He was worse than a bastard. He was heartless. He was—

"There you are," a familiar male voice said, interrupting Fax's self-recrimination.

He stiffened and turned to face the man who stood alone on the other side of the holding-cell bars, wearing the uniform of a Bear Claw cop and pointing a gun in his direction.

"Muhammad," Fax said evenly. "I'm surprised you bothered to have me turn around. You're not the type to shy away from shooting a man in the back."

Al-Jihad's second in command sneered, but didn't disagree. "You're going to tell me where the woman is before you die."

"Not happening."

"You're not the only one with access to designer drugs." The terrorist tapped a code into the keypad and swung open the door to the holding cell, mute evidence that al-Jihad's reach was growing longer by the day. Now, it appeared, he had friends within the Bear Claw PD itself. Keeping his weapon trained on Fax's midsection, where a bullet might be fatal but death would be slow and agonizing, Muhammad tossed a pair of handcuffs onto the floor at Fax's feet. "Put these on. We're leaving."

Fax bent and grabbed the cuffs. Then he lunged forward, straightening as he attacked, so his head slammed into the terrorist's midsection.

It was a suicide attack, but he'd rather die now than risk giving up Chelsea's location under the influence of powerful truth-telling drugs.

Muhammad shouted and reeled backward, but stayed on his feet and brought the pistol down, slamming it into the back of Fax's head.

Fax rolled, absorbing some of the blow and deflecting the rest, but bells still chimed in his skull as he threw himself at the other man, landing a punch to the bastard's gut and then going for his throat, intending to choke the life out of him. He wanted Muhammad dead, wanted revenge on behalf of the guard's wife who'd lost both husband and son, for the morgue attendant who had been Chelsea's friend, and for the cops who'd given their lives to save hers.

Fax got a grip on Muhammad's throat and bore down, but the other man brought the gun to bear and fired.

The bullet whistled past Fax's shoulder and the report deafened him, stunning him just long enough for Muhammad to break free.

Fax reoriented, though his sense of hearing was limited to a high-pitched whine. Muhammad was on his feet, standing in the holding-cell doorway, pointing his weapon directly at Fax.

Instead of firing, he jolted, then turned and looked toward the door connecting the holding area to the main PD. Seeing something he didn't like, he spun and ran for the side exit, leaving the holding-cell door wide open.

Fax didn't waste any time. He broke for the doorway, but he was already too late. Just as he cleared the opening, a big man wearing street clothes burst through the door that led to the PD. He carried himself like a cop, and locked on Fax the moment he was through. There was another man behind him, and they looked like they meant business.

Fax didn't know if they were al-Jihad's contacts or upstanding members of the Bear Claw PD, but they were his enemies either way.

Roaring, Fax swung.

The cop dodged and shouted something, but Fax couldn't hear over the whine of temporary nerve deafness. He could only see the other man's lips moving, his eyes sparking with annoyance. Then the big guy grabbed him and his buddy got the other side and they were hustling him, not back into the cell or the PD, but toward the rear exit.

Which meant they were on the terrorists' payroll, Fax realized with a sick lurch. They were dragging him to wherever al-Jihad was holed up, and when they got him there, they'd pump him full of drugs and ask him where Chelsea was hidden.

"No!" he shouted, struggling to break free. He almost made it, only to have the guy on his right side grab a choke hold and bear down.

Gagging, Fax staggered. The first guy keyed in the code needed to get them out the back door, and waved them through, looking worried.

Fax's hearing was starting to come back online, enough for him to hear an engine revving in front of them, and men shouting behind.

Then they were through the door, and Fax froze—not at the sight of the nondescript but powerful sedan the men were dragging him toward, but at the sight of the woman sitting in the driver's seat.

Chelsea. He wasn't sure if he said her name aloud or only thought it, but it was a magic word, unlocking his limbs and brain so he could lunge forward and dive into the vehicle. The two cops piled in after him, and she hit the gas before they were all the way in, peeling away from the PD and accelerating across the city, headed for the highway.

Behind them, he imagined the other cops were too stunned to immediately pursue. They'd been betrayed by their own, by Chelsea and two strangers who had zero reason to help him.

Fax dragged himself up and onto a seat and the others did the same. He caught Chelsea glancing at him in the rearview mirror, and he said, "How did you do it?"

Her eyes went cool in the reflection. "It's called having friends, Jonah. You should try it some time."

Chapter Ten

Chelsea drove them back to the deserted motel in the silence that'd fallen after Fax's few attempts to start conversation.

"Save it until the team's all assembled," she'd snapped, trying to make it clear that he wasn't in charge anymore. At least not of her or her friends.

After Sara, Seth and Tucker had rescued her from her motel prison, she'd told them everything about her association with Fax and his claims to be an undercover fed. She'd left out the part about the sex, but could tell that Sara had guessed.

Seth, who'd heard part of it before, had interjected that he'd investigated the claim and found nothing in any of the databases that supported Fax's story, or Jane Doe's existence. However, he was willing to admit that he was no computer expert, that it was possible the files existed and he didn't know where to look, or didn't have the proper clearance.

Besides, Chelsea had argued, the very nature of Jane Doe's team meant that the records were buried deep, if they existed at all.

That was when Tucker and Seth had asked her if she

really truly believed that Fax was who he said he was, and her plan was the only real way to protect Bear Claw—and the U.S.—from al-Jihad's terror network.

"I believe him," she'd said simply, and her friends had nodded and moved on from there, agreeing to help her break Fax out of the Bear Claw PD and launch their own, completely illegal, completely unsanctioned op during the following day's festival, with the intent of taking out al-Jihad and his men and flushing out the conspirators within the Bear Claw PD and the local FBI field office.

Granted, the decision had been significantly hastened by the fact that Seth hadn't much liked some of the answers he'd gotten when he'd started looking deeper at Fax's background, and noticed that his dishonorable discharge didn't mesh with his numerous commendations.

The FBI agent had been even less pleased to learn that his questions had tipped off someone who'd gotten word to al-Jihad that Fax was an undercover agent, Chelsea his contact. In fact, he'd been furious—but in Seth's case, fury apparently translated into cold efficiency.

He and Tucker had planned the jailbreak, but most of their plan hadn't been necessary because they'd gotten there on Muhammad's heels—a lucky break that Chelsea was trying not to think too hard about. What mattered was that Fax was out of the holding cell, and they were on their way to rendezvous with the rest of the group, which would include Fax and Chelsea, Seth and Tucker, along with Sara, who'd stayed behind to get a couple more of the hotel rooms ready, and Seth and Tucker's wives, Cassie and Alyssa.

Chelsea hadn't wanted to involve the other women, but Sara had been adamant about being included, and the guys had refused to shut out their wives, who were decorated cops in their own right.

That had been borderline annoying, but Chelsea had squelched the negative thoughts, knowing they came straight from jealousy. She wanted to be part of a relationship like that, formed of both partnership and love. It wasn't that she didn't want her friends to have that sort of love, either. It was just that she wanted it, too…yet had the self-destructive tendency to be attracted only to men who were completely unable to give her what she wanted.

Or maybe not, she thought on a burst of the new self-awareness she'd gained during the long, quiet day. Maybe it wasn't so much that she had bad taste in men—maybe it was that she gave up at the first sign of trouble. Maybe the long string of near misses were cases of her running away rather than putting all her effort into saving something, taking the risk that she might fail.

Well, not this time, she told herself. *I'm not giving up this time. Not on Fax or his operation.*

She glanced at him in the rearview mirror, only to find him watching her. Their eyes locked in the reflected image, and a flare of warmth kindled in her midsection.

Deliberately, she looked away and forced her eyes back on the road just as the turnoff leading to the motel came into view. They'd deal with business first. Then they'd deal with what might be the start of something important, if she was willing to fight for it, and he was willing to change for it.

Which, she acknowledged, was a big "if."

She pulled up the long, winding drive that led to the deserted motel. They'd decided to stick with the same place, on the theory that the electricity and water hadn't yet been turned off, and it offered all the concealment that had prompted Fax to choose it originally.

The closed-down motel was practically a campground, tucked into the tree line at the edge of the state park. It wasn't visible from the street and there weren't any houses for a couple of miles on either side, which meant they didn't have to worry about the lights attracting unwanted attention from locals who knew the place had gone out of business. It was a good hideout, just as it'd been a good prison.

Chelsea parked Seth's car and climbed out.

"Come on." She led the way to the room where Fax had imprisoned her, figuring there was a certain sort of irony to using the room for a strategy session.

Upon entering, she saw that Sara had gotten rid of the cuffs and chain, and the bucket. The room was back to looking like a cheap, tired motel room, with a sagging king-size bed and bare patches on the walls. The rickety desk held a pile of pizza boxes and a couple of cases of soda and sparkling water, and the cooler was now full of ice.

"All the convenience of home," Sara said wryly as Chelsea entered, but her eyes were locked on the doorway behind her.

Chelsea knew without looking that Fax had come in behind her—she could feel his presence itch along her nerve endings like fire, and she could see the anger in Sara's eyes.

Her friends might have agreed to help Fax, but they'd done it for her sake, not his. They had, each in his or her own way, let Chelsea know they hated how he'd involved her, endangered her. Sara was even more worried, having figured out they were personally involved.

Chelsea had done her best to defend Fax's decisions, but knew her friends were seriously reserving their judgment.

Stepping aside, she waved him into the room. "Fax, this is Sara."

Fax nodded. "The head ME."

"Chelsea's friend," Sara corrected with a distinct snap in her voice, and the two of them spent a few seconds measuring each other.

Outside the motel room, the rise and fall of male and female voices heralded the arrival of Alyssa and Cassie, who had stayed behind—keeping a very low profile—to see how the PD members and FBI field agents handled the incident, figuring that might give them some insight into the conspirators' identities.

Within moments, all four of them came through the door. Rock-solid Tucker and blond, tomboyish Alyssa were followed by dark-featured Seth in full-on brooding mode, with imp-faced, steely-eyed Cassie at his shoulder.

That meant that Chelsea suddenly found herself in a dingy motel room crowded with six other people and one pretty serious standoff, with her friends glaring at the man who had been, for one short night at least, her lover.

Sara shifted her glare to Chelsea, and she could practically see it in her friend's eyes: *Your taste in men stinks.*

"No kidding," Chelsea muttered under her breath, but moved to Fax's side. "Back off," she said. "He had a job to do, and made the choices he needed to make in order to get it done."

"But it's not done, is it?" Sara said softly. "Not even close."

"Which is where we come in," Chelsea said, although they'd already had this fight and she'd won it. "Something really bad is going to happen tomorrow if we don't stop it, and you five are the only ones I trust to help us." She turned to Fax. "I hope I won't regret this."

She half expected him to say she already should. Instead, he tilted his head in Seth's direction. "Agent Varitek?"

"Yeah," Seth allowed.

"Who did you talk to on the inside?"

Seth hesitated for a long moment, then said, "I'm not naming names right now. Suffice it to say the channels shut down way before they should have."

"Which tells me nothing."

Seth shrugged. "Sorry. That's the way it's going to be."

Fax gritted his teeth. "Then why bother to bust me out? Why not just leave me to Muhammad and his nine-millimeter?"

It was Sara who answered, "You can thank Chelsea for that."

All eyes fixed on Chelsea, including Fax's. She felt her cheeks heat and made a point of not looking at him. But he said, in a voice intended mostly for her, "Thank you."

It was a small thing that shouldn't have mattered. Because it mattered too much, she snapped, "I didn't do it for you. I did it for all the people who are going to be at that concert tomorrow."

"I'm surprised you didn't blow the whistle and have them cancel the whole thing," he said, still speaking softly, as though they weren't the center of attention.

"I was going to," she answered honestly, looking at him fully for the first time since they'd entered the motel room. "Except you were right. It's not just about the festival, and it's not even just about al-Jihad and the other escapees. We need to root out the evil, not just clip a few branches."

And oddly, the word *we* didn't seem so strange. She was involved up to her neck and she wasn't backing down this time, wasn't retreating even though the odds of success seemed very slim.

Chelsea stepped away from Fax, distancing herself from him and aligning with her friends. "You've got backup now, Jonah. Tell us what to do."

And with that, she handed him leadership of the small group, trusting him with her friends.

For a few seconds he looked as if he was going to refuse. Then his shoulders relaxed and his jaw unlocked, and something flickered across his face that might've looked like exhausted relief in another man, but on him simply looked like a moment of calm. "Thank you." This time he said it right out loud, and meant it.

"You're welcome," Seth said. "I think."

The subtext was clear—he might accept Fax as group leader for now, but they were all going to be watching him very, very closely.

"Well, I'm glad that's more or less settled," said Chelsea, deliberately breaking the tension by moving across the room and reaching for one of the pizzas. "Who's hungry?"

Fax was turning to answer her just as a set of headlights cut through the darkness. Reacting instantly, he turned the motion into a lunge, catching Chelsea around the waist and bearing her to the ground beneath him.

"Down!" Alyssa shouted, going for her weapon as the others scrambled to kill the lights and take positions.

"Stay!" Fax hissed, shoving Chelsea into the corner beneath the desk. "Don't you *dare* move." Then he was gone. Seconds later, he returned and shoved Sara in beside her, hissing the same warning.

Chelsea grabbed Sara's hands and they clung to each other while the professionals took up position around the room. She couldn't see anything—the headlights had cut out—but she could feel the incredible tension in the air, and hear a few low-voiced exchanges from the others.

Had Muhammad followed them from the PD? That was the only thing she could think had happened, unless—

A whistle sounded outside, interrupting her train of thought: several short bursts and one long, in a pattern of some sort.

The tension in the room changed, and Fax cursed—a succinct and physically impossible two-word oath.

Then he whistled back a different combination.

A third was returned.

Moments later he opened the door a crack, then all the way, and reached to flip on the exterior lights. A woman stood in the doorway opposite him, tall, gorgeous and statuesque, despite the fact that her once high-end clothes were wrinkled and stained, as though she'd been wearing them for several days under uncertain circumstances.

Chelsea scooted out from underneath the table and stood, tugging Sara with her.

It took her a moment to place the look in the woman's eyes. When she did, a chill ran the entire length of her spine and then centered in her stomach on a moment of queasiness. Her eyes looked like Fax's had when he and Chelsea had first met.

"Chelsea," Tucker said from his firing position beside the bed. "Do you know her?"

"No," Fax answered for her. "But I do." His voice had regained its cool, detached flavor, but Chelsea knew him well enough to hear the tremor of emotion beneath the words when he said, "This is Jane Doe."

"It can't be," Chelsea said stupidly as strange dread flooded her veins. "Jane Doe is dead."

"I'm harder to kill than al-Jihad and his men thought," the woman said. She looked from one to the other of the people inside the motel room, skipping over Chelsea and Sara and lingering on Seth, apparently either recognizing him from the Bureau, or instinctively knowing that he ranked within the group.

She spoke only to Fax, though, when she said, "I never saw it coming. One minute I was at my desk, the next I was waking up in a storage facility outside the city two days later. I don't know who hit me, or with what, or why they didn't just kill me outright." Her eyes hardened. "You can be sure, though, that when I figure out who it was, they'll pay."

Chelsea had to suppress a shiver at the venom in those last two words.

"How did you find us?" Seth asked. He hadn't reholstered his weapon. None of them had.

Jane jerked her chin back in the direction of her vehicle. "I had some equipment stashed for a rainy day, enough to monitor the local chatter. When I heard that Fax had turned up at the Bear Claw PD, I headed into town to see what I could do, but you'd gotten there ahead of me. When Muhammad tore off in one direction and you guys headed up here, I went with my gut and followed you." Her eyes went cool and slid in Chelsea's direction. "I hope I won't regret my choice."

Irritation prickled through Chelsea, but she didn't say anything. This was Fax's world, not hers. It was his call.

"What about the others?" Fax asked quietly.

Jane shook her head. "We were running an op a few weeks ago and it went very bad. At first it seemed unrelated, but now I have to assume that the bastard who's behind this set them up, too." She paused. "It's just the two of us now."

Chelsea didn't like the sound of that one bit, but Fax avoided meeting her eyes as he digested the new information.

After a moment he nodded. "We were just getting ready to pull together a plan." Without asking the others, he sketched out what they knew, acting as though there was no question whatsoever that she could be included.

Logically, it made sense, Chelsea knew. But that didn't stop the situation from putting her on edge. She didn't like the intrusion, didn't like the woman, especially when Jane said in a superior tone, "Of course, you realize he's targeting the stadium."

Fax nodded. "We know."

But that was another thing Chelsea had spent a good amount of time thinking about during her imprisonment. "Maybe not."

That got their attention. Fax frowned at her. "What are you talking about?"

"Remember those schematics you told me about? The ones you saw in the cabin? You said yourself they didn't look anything like the stadium or the other buildings at the ski resort. Well, I was thinking about it today, and I'm pretty sure what you described could correspond to the structures the old mining company used to cap off the played-out mines. The ski resort has reinforced them over the years and has been using them to store stuff they need out on the slopes." She paused for effect. "As of two weeks ago, the huts were stocked with equipment the engineers said the resort might need if we have another bad rainstorm and there are more landslides. That includes explosives."

She'd already discussed the theory with her friends; Cassie had actually been the one to mention the explosives. They had all agreed that Fax's description of the schematics fit with the huts. Given that the engineers were in the process of figuring out how to stabilize the slopes, which had become badly eroded in places, it seemed reasonable to suspect that al-Jihad might not be targeting the stadium itself, but rather the mountainside directly above it.

But Jane barely gave the theory a three-count before she shook her head. "No. He's targeting the stadium directly."

She turned away from Chelsea, dismissing her.

"Fax?" Chelsea said, looking right at him, willing him to back her up.

Their eyes locked. Then he looked at Jane. "The schematics I saw could be the huts she's talking about."

It wasn't exactly a ringing endorsement.

"We go with the evidence, not a 'could be,'" Jane said curtly.

"We haven't seen your evidence," Seth said levelly, coming up so he was standing shoulder to shoulder with Chelsea. The others murmured agreement and followed suit, so it was six against two.

The numbers didn't seem to bother Jane, though. She simply sniffed. "We're going after al-Jihad and his cell members at the stadium, end of discussion. Join us or don't join us, your call. But I'm warning all of you right now that if you even breathe a word of warning to anyone regarding an attack on the stadium, I'll personally see to it that you're held under the USA PATRIOT Act for as long as possible, without an arraignment or trial."

The threat hung in the air, a nasty, unfriendly thing. Chelsea felt the heat of a flush climb her neck and touch her cheeks. She was furious with Fax for his stillness, his lack of support, his instant switch of allegiance the moment his old flame was back in the picture.

Damn him.

He looked at her now, not to make amends, but to say, "So, what's it going to be?"

She jerked her chin in the air. "We'll discuss it and get back to you."

Then, before she embarrassed the hell out of herself by crying—or screaming—in front of Fax's gorgeous, totally in-control boss, she stalked out of the room with her friends at her back.

FAX WATCHED THEM GO and tried to tell himself he was making the right call. Somehow, though, right and wrong had gotten mixed up inside his head, blurring together until things that might've seemed very clear-cut to him before were all jammed together in an indecipherable mess.

He was seriously reeling. Within the space of three hours he'd gone from being a prisoner, to almost getting killed, escaping again, and now to being—what?

Jane's reappearance couldn't have been timed better, but maybe that was what rang faintly false.

Why and how had she shown up now? he wondered, and felt seriously disloyal for even thinking the question. Jane had saved him. She'd taught him. She was the one person he knew he could trust.

But at the same time, he didn't like the look her arrival had put in Chelsea's eyes—a mix of accusation and hurt that made him want to go to her and explain.

But explain what? He owed Jane his allegiance. Surely she could understand that.

Caught in his own head, Fax waited while Jane grabbed a slice of pepperoni and started wolfing it, as though she hadn't eaten in the more than seventy-two hours she'd been out of the loop.

Fax said, "You mentioned having some equipment with you?"

"I've got a couple of portable surveillance units in the car," she answered. "Some weapons, a couple of laptops and a decryptor that's only working about half the time." She paused, shrugging. "It's not nearly what we're used to working with, but we can make do."

She dug in to a second piece of pizza, apparently too hungry to worry about the grease on her chin when she was normally fastidious about her appearance. That was consistent with her explanation for the past few days, as was her bedraggled appearance.

And why was he even questioning it? He'd been hoping against hope that Jane would reappear and give him the bona fides he was lacking without her, the leadership she was known for. Hell, he'd wanted to see her for her own sake, and because she was one of the few constants over the past few years of his life. He should be relieved and excited, not wary.

Maybe Chelsea was right. He'd been undercover so long he'd forgotten what it meant to have friends.

"It's good to see you, Jane," he said, and meant it.

"Same goes." They shared a look and he felt something loosen in his chest, a feeling of homecoming for a man with no home.

She understood him, knew how he thought because she thought the same way. He wasn't alone anymore.

But he hadn't been alone before, had he? He'd had Chelsea at his back.

Without her, the room felt empty.

"The stadium is the logical target, but al-Jihad has to know we'll figure that out," Fax said carefully. "What if he's doing what Chelsea suggested? Bringing the mountain down on the stadium could have even more of an effect than bombing it."

But Jane didn't even hesitate before she shook her head. "No, he's going to hit the stadium directly and personally. He wants to prove he can do it despite the added security the PD has put in place since his escape."

"Personally?" Fax said, surprised. "As in, he's going to be on scene?" Men like al-Jihad rarely got their hands dirty on the day-to-day workings of terror. Typically, they preferred to stay above it all and orchestrate.

"This time, yes. He's making a point." She paused, looking at him as though trying to figure out how much to tell him. Finally she said, "I think he's trying to set up a larger group, incorporating half a dozen or so of the biggest names in the anti-American theater. This is his calling card, his show of strength."

Fax cursed bitterly. "It's part of a recruiting campaign."

She nodded. "That's what we got from the chatter we were picking up right before I was taken out." She spread her hands. "Since then I've been monitoring when I can, but I don't have anything new to add."

He took a deep breath, sorting through the possibilities. "Is there someone on the inside you can trust? Someone you can get word to who'll give us more manpower and a sanction?"

She shook her head, eyes going sad. "Three days ago I would've said yes. But I'm pretty sure the one man in the organization that I would've gone to was responsible for my abduction, and for taking out the rest of the team after the fact. It had to have been him—he was the only one who knew exactly where the team was and the sign-countersigns they were using."

"I'm sorry," Fax said, knowing that she might not show it, but the betrayal had to cut deep.

She shook her head. "It's the business." And the thing was, she looked mad, but not hurt. As he would've been under the same circumstances a few months earlier.

"Do you know what form the attack is going to take?" he asked, forcing himself on task.

"Not precisely, but I've got a strategy mapped out." She sketched out how they could get in close to the stadium, and use one of the portable surveillance units to scan the airways and digital satellite data streams, searching for key words and flagged voices. That way, they'd be able to identify phone or radio traffic between the on-site terrorists, including al-Jihad, and his big conspirators.

Fax frowned. "Are you sure they'll be in contact with one another? Seems like needless exposure to me."

"It's all part of this big conglomerate al-Jihad is trying to set up. Trust me, the intel is solid."

And, really, that was all he needed to know. If Jane said this was the best plan, then it was the best plan, hands down.

They spent maybe another fifteen minutes discussing the details, and then wound down. By that point, Fax was sitting in the single chair with his feet up on the desk, while Jane was propped up against the headboard of the king-size bed, working on her second bottle of water.

When their discussion had trailed off to silence, she

took a long pull of water, then exhaled. "I'm sorry, but I've got to ask. Is the woman going to be a problem?"

He didn't ask how or what she knew. He also didn't automatically say, *No, of course not.* Instead, he lifted a shoulder, and said, "I'm trying very hard not to let her be a distraction."

Jane arched an eyebrow. "Trying? As in, not succeeding?"

"It's complicated."

"Interesting." She looked at him long and hard, and maybe her smile went a little sad around the edges. "That's not a word you ever used to describe us, I'm betting."

"There wasn't really an 'us,' though, was there?"

"No. Not really. Which doesn't answer my original question."

"I know." He stood, draining his soda and hitting a three-pointer in the bathroom wastebasket. "You sleeping here?"

She looked around and wrinkled her nose, then stood and joined him near the door. "I'll smell like pizza if I do. I'll take something farther down."

They parted out in front of the motel; she headed for her car and retrieved a laptop, then walked to a room at the far end of the row.

Fax stood where he was, hesitating. He wanted to talk to Chelsea, but also wanted to talk to Varitek and the others, to apologize, maybe, or see if they could find a compromise between the two groups.

He appreciated Jane's confidence, but knew her plan would benefit from additional bodies.

Jane stopped and turned near the end of the row, her body cloaked in shadows. Her voice was quiet when she said, "Problem?"

What she really meant, he knew, was *Make your choice.* He couldn't straddle the line between the two groups and be an effective agent. He needed to be clear on his priorities, and on the chain of command.

He shook his head. "No problem."

She held his eyes for a long moment before nodding. "Good to hear." Then she turned and went into her room, not looking back.

A year ago—heck, even a couple of weeks ago—he might have followed.

Now he turned the other way and headed for the woods, needing to walk off the frustration that rode him, digging greedy claws beneath his skin and warning him that what he wanted wasn't in Jane's room.

He didn't know where he was going, didn't know what drew him onward along a narrow hiking trail leading away from the motel. Using the moon to light his way, he followed the trail.

Within a short distance, the track opened up to a picnic area, a wide stone shelf that dropped away to nothing on the far side, creating a vista that was no doubt perfect for pictures and barbecues during the day. At night, though, in the moonlit darkness, it was perfect for privacy.

And romance.

Chelsea sat on one of the picnic tables with her feet on the bench and her chin in her palms, staring out into the night. She turned when she heard his approach, but said nothing, just looked at him.

She was what had drawn him out here, Fax knew. Somehow, with some sort of internal surveillance that was tuned only to her, he'd known she'd be out here. Had known there were things he needed to say to her.

Because of it, because she deserved better than what he'd given her so far, he stepped off the trail and crossed to her, stopping when he was just a few paces away.

He took a deep breath. "We should talk."

Chapter Eleven

The old Chelsea probably would've agreed in a rush, *Yes, we do need to talk. I'm glad we're on the same page.*

The woman she'd become since first meeting Fax—tougher and more aware of her own worth and ability—simply looked at him and said, "I think pretty much everything's been said, don't you?" She lifted a shoulder. "You're back in the fold. You don't need anything from me."

"That's not true." He said it so quickly that she might've thought it was a knee-jerk response, except he wasn't the sort to do or say anything without thinking it through first.

"Isn't it?" She turned away and looked back out across the vista, where moonlight hit on a canopy of pine, with occasional glints of silver tracing the path of one of the tributaries that fed into Bear Claw Creek.

She'd told herself she'd come out to the picnic area for some privacy, but now she acknowledged the lie.

She'd known he would come after her. Now that he was there, though, she didn't know what came next.

After a moment, he hitched himself up and sat beside her. "You're wrong. I do need you."

The words sounded like they came hard to him, but she had little sympathy. "You cuffed me to a bed and left me alone because I threatened to go to the cops. Let's face it, that's not the sort of thing a guy does if he's looking for a long-term relationship."

A muscle pulsed at the corner of his jaw. "I did what I had to do."

"You did what came easy to you."

"It wasn't easy." His words were low and intense, and he surprised her by taking her hand in his, and threading their fingers together. "I won't apologize, because I'm not sorry. But I will say that it bothered me more than I'd expected it to."

"Because you'd spent so much time in solitary confinement," she said, trying not to feel the way their palms matched up just right, or the fine shimmer of warmth that trailed up her arm from the simple contact.

"Because I was leaving you behind."

The simple statement sliced through her, leveling her carefully built defenses. She floundered for a few seconds before saying, "I don't know how I'm supposed to feel about that."

"Me either." He moved a little closer to her on the picnic table and laid their joined hands on his muscular thigh. They were touching at hip and shoulder now, and she had to force herself not to lean into him as he continued, "I wasn't looking for anyone, you know. I don't have room in my life for a friend, never mind a lover."

"You slept with Jane." She hadn't meant to go there, but how could she not? She might've suspected the relationship before, but the moment she'd seen them together she'd known for certain. It was in the way they'd looked at each other, the way they'd leaned close to talk, well within each other's space.

"We had mutually agreeable sex. That doesn't make her my lover."

She winced. "That's cold."

"This isn't." He lifted their joined hands and pressed his lips to her knuckles, sending a frisson of heat radiating through her. "This is different, whether I want it to be or not." He paused, then admitted, "I hated leaving you here, but I didn't know what else to do. It wasn't about you calling the cops, either. Not really."

She didn't want to ask, didn't want to let him weaken her. But the feel of his body against hers and the good pressure of their fingers intertwined had her saying, "What was it about?"

"I was afraid." He said the word like it was a curse. "When I saw your police detail go down and I knew Muhammad and the others were out there, gunning for you, I couldn't handle it. I was scared and furious, and I couldn't get to you fast enough."

His voice was so raw, the emotion etched so clearly on his face in the moonlight, that her heart turned over in her chest. She squeezed her fingers on his. "You did get to me. You got me out of there, kept me safe. I'm fine."

"You might not be the next time. These guys are killers, Chelsea. If they want you dead, you might as well already be in the meat wagon."

Her blood heated, not just at his words, but at the emotion beneath them, which was more than she'd expected, more even than she'd hoped for on the few brief occasions she'd allowed herself to hope.

Which didn't change the way his face had lit when he'd seen Jane in the doorway, or the way the two of them had leaned close together, shutting the others out, including her.

"Why are you here, Jonah?" she said quietly, wishing he would go away, because if he didn't she was likely to do something she'd regret.

He didn't pretend to misunderstand. "Damned if I know."

"You should be with Jane."

"What if I'd rather be with you?"

"Can you honestly say that?"

His silence was answer enough, and Chelsea felt something wither and die within her. She pulled her hand away from his and stood. "I didn't think so." She turned to face him, her throat tightening a little at the moonlit sight of the man who had become too important to her in too short a time. "Let's not make this any harder than it already is, okay?"

She didn't really expect an answer, didn't get one. A moment of silence drew out as they stared at each other, knowing there really wasn't any answer to the gulf separating them—one of experience and priority, of lifestyle and goals.

Then she turned away, her eyes filling with angry tears as she returned to her room alone, leaving him in the darkness.

SHE WAS RIGHT, damn it. Fax knew it, knew he should leave things well enough alone. They'd had their moment and it'd been a good one, but neither of them had thought going in that it was going to be more than a flash in the pan, a night or two in the midst of chaos. He wasn't the sort of guy for more than that.

So why did he feel like kicking the crap out of the

picnic table and howling at the moon? Why did he want to follow her and pick a fight, argue the impossible?

"You were in prison, idiot," he muttered as he dragged himself off the picnic table and headed back toward the scattered lights coming from the motel. "You were bound to get hooked on the first woman you saw."

Which sounded logical enough. Too bad he couldn't convince himself it was the truth. He'd gone longer between lovers before. Hell, after Abby died, it'd been more than two years before he'd taken Jane up on her no-strings offer, and they'd only been together maybe a dozen times total, and then only when it made sense.

He and Chelsea made no sense whatsoever. Yet damned if he didn't hesitate when he reached the front of the motel, knowing he should get some sleep in his own drab room, but wanting to knock on Chelsea's door instead.

Let's not make this any harder than it already is, she'd said, and he knew she was right. Thing was, he wasn't sure he wanted to take the easy way out this time.

"Looking for company?"

He turned at the question, feeling a complicated mix of emotions at the sight of the woman backlit in her motel-room doorway.

The wrong woman.

He summoned a smile for Jane, one that felt like respect and trust, and nothing more. "Hey."

"I'll take that as a 'no.'" She didn't look like it bothered her one way or the other, but her expression hardened as she approached him.

She was wearing a T-shirt and yoga pants, no doubt borrowed—or more likely commandeered—from one of the other women. Even in the casual clothes, she looked like a leader, like a warrior in the battle against terrorism.

Tilting her head, she looked at him long and hard, then said simply, "You'll want some time off after this, to make your decision."

"I made my call a long time ago." Or rather, circumstances had made it for him. Maybe back then he could've gone in a different direction, made a different choice, but he'd seen and done too much in the intervening years.

He couldn't go back to real life now. He could only protect it for others.

"Are you sure? If your head's not in the game…" She let the sentence trail off, but he had no trouble filling in the blank. If he wasn't for her he was against her, and she'd leave him behind rather than let him interfere because of conflicted loyalties.

He knew, because it was what he would've done in her shoes. At least it would've been a few weeks earlier. Now, he couldn't be entirely sure what he would've done in her place. He only knew that he damn well needed to be in on al-Jihad's takedown—not just because he'd spent the past two years working toward it, but because the bastard was after Chelsea and her friends, and the residents of Bear Claw.

He couldn't give Chelsea the commitment and the caring that she needed, but he could damn well protect her, and the people she cared about.

"I'm so far into the game it's not even funny," he grated, letting Jane see the determination in his eyes, and an edge of threat. He was in this one whether he went with her or through her. It was her choice.

Her lips curved ever so slightly and she nodded. "That's what I wanted to hear." She turned and headed back to her room, but paused at the threshold and looked back. "You've always been my best. After this, we'll rebuild, and you'll be in it every step of the way. Two teams—one mine, one yours. You have my word."

His own team. It was an honor, a promotion. And it would consume his every waking moment from there on out.

Fax nodded. "I'm flattered."

"And?"

"I'm in."

"Good." She didn't say another word, just headed into her room and shut the door at her back.

Fax just stood there for a moment. Then he said, "You heard that, I take it?"

Three rooms down, Chelsea's door opened from the cracked position it'd been occupying. She stood framed in the doorway as he crossed to her, trying to read her expression and failing.

Wearing bike shorts and a plain T-shirt, she should've looked soft and vulnerable. Instead, she looked supremely self-contained as she tilted her head and said, "I heard."

"And?"

"What exactly is it that you want me to say?" Her eyes glittered, but with temper, not tears. "Congratulations?"

"Say you understand," he said, the words coming from nowhere, from somewhere deep inside him, emerging before he knew he was going to ask.

She smiled with zero humor. "I understand that leading a team will be far easier—and way more comfortable—for you than trying to make a change."

Anger flared, more familiar than the nerves that shimmered too near the surface. "That's low."

She lifted a shoulder. "Truth hurts. You didn't—still don't—want to trust me or my friends, because that might've proved that the way you live your life isn't the way it has to be, that you've got other options if you'd only be brave enough to reach out and grab for them."

"I'm not the one who thinks of myself as a wimp."

"Neither do I. Not anymore. No," she said softly, her focus turning inward, "I've given up too many times because I was afraid to try something I might not succeed at. But not anymore. I'm done wimping out."

"Is that what this is about?" he snapped. "Leading your friends up the mountain on the basis of zero evidence isn't exactly going to prove that you're brave. Seems to me you're heading away from the fight."

"You're getting nasty. That means you know I'm right."

He stepped closer, until he was in her space, crowding her, breathing the same air she was. "It means I'm getting annoyed with this conversation. What exactly do you want from me right now, Chelsea? Another apology?"

"No. I want you to come inside." She stepped back, into the motel room where he'd left her cuffed that morning, thinking it might be the last time he saw her.

She'd been unconscious, her eyelashes lying on her pale cheeks, her lips curved faintly on some dream he could only guess at, and envy.

His brain locked on the memory and on the invitation.

"You want…" He trailed off, sure he'd misheard.

But she crooked a finger. "I want you. Inside. Now."

His feet moved before he knew he'd made the decision, propelling him into her motel room. His hands worked of their own volition, closing and locking the door, and putting the pitiful chain in place. But before he could touch her, he forced himself to stop, forced himself to be sure this was what she wanted.

He lifted a hand and brushed a strand of hair away from her mouth, in a gesture of tenderness that felt both foreign and right. "I can't be what you need."

She raised an eyebrow. "You think I haven't figured that out? Please." But she caught his hand in hers, and pressed his palm to her cheek. "This is it, Jonah. It's been a hell of a week, but as of tomorrow, it's over. Back to real life for me, back to the shadows for you. This is our last night. I'd rather not waste it being mad at each other for things we can't or won't change."

He knew he should do something, say something; knew he should either move in or away from her, but he couldn't do a damn thing. He didn't trust himself to get it right, didn't trust himself not to hurt her in taking what he wanted more than he wanted his next breath.

He'd nearly talked himself into being the gentleman when she leaned up on her toes and touched her lips to his.

And he was lost.

CHELSEA KNEW she was making a big mistake, but she had to believe it'd be a bigger mistake to let him walk away without taking what she could get of the magic they made together. If it was just sex, then that was all it would be. And if, deep down inside, she knew it was far more than that on her part, she'd deal with that heartache tomorrow.

Tonight she wanted the man, *her* man, for this one final night they had together. So she kissed him, and was prepared to hang on tight if he tried to pull away.

She wasn't prepared for him to kiss her back. Which was exactly what he did, grabbing on to her and leaning in hard, taking her kiss from an invitation to a demand in the space of a second.

Heat speared through her. Want. Longing. And raw, no-holds-barred lust.

Whereas the night before had at least been cloaked with the illusion of romance, now there was none. He bent her over his arm, ravaging her lips and throat, his grip on her so tight she could do little more than sag back and moan with the feel of him, and the heat that spiraled up within her.

He bore her to the bed where he'd chained her that morning. Chelsea had a brief flash of wishing Sara hadn't disposed of the cuffs, followed by a hard blush brought on by the thought.

Fax's rusty chuckle let her know he'd read her expression, or else his mind had paralleled hers. She opened her eyes to find his face very near hers, his eyes gone flinty with passion.

He was breathing hard, with quick rasps—they both were. They were twined together on the yielding surface of the mattress, although she wasn't sure when they'd gotten there or how. Her T-shirt was up around her throat, and his hands were on her breasts, chafing them, working them until her entire body was a coil of sensation.

She arched back and cried out, dragging at his clothes, at his hard body atop hers, needing more, demanding more.

They parted only long enough to shed clothes and pull aside the cheap bedspread he'd stolen from the airport hotel, and for him to don the second and last of the condoms she kept in her purse. Then they were back on the bed straining together, chasing each other through the flames that licked around her, inside her.

He thrust into her without preamble, a tremendous surge that had her biting back a cry. He buried his own shout in her mouth, both of them aware that they weren't alone at the motel, yet at the same time unaware of anything but the slide and slap of flesh and the raw need that drove them together and apart, together and apart.

She came fast and hard, clamping around him, vising her calves behind his hips and driving him deeper and deeper still. He plunged into her again and again, spurring her onward, prolonging the pleasure until it passed beyond her comfort zone to something that wrenched her gut and warned that she would never be the same, she would never have another lover who could measure up to what she had experienced with Fax.

Then he cut loose, going rigid against her and muffling a long, hollow cry against her throat. She felt him pulsing within her, felt the long, drawn-out shudders that wracked his big, strong body, and she wrapped herself around him, giving herself to the moment, to the man, as she came again.

Tears tracked from the corners of her eyes and mingled with the sweat that prickled her body and then cooled, binding them together as surely as their flesh was united.

She'd been lying from the start. It hadn't just been sex for her. Not by a long shot.

Fax shuddered one last time and went limp against her. He looped his arms around her waist and hung on like he never meant to let go, and she allowed it because she was helpless to do otherwise, helpless to stop another tear from building and breaking free.

"Crushing you," he muttered thickly, and rolled to his side, taking her with him, rearranging them so they were spooned together, her back to his front. Then he pulled the coverlet over them both. He murmured something else, low and sweet, and too slurred for her to understand.

Within minutes, he was asleep.

Chelsea, on the other hand, was wide awake. She knew what she had to do and hated it. She wanted to stay in his arms, wanted to draw out every last precious second they had left together. But, really, their time had already run out. She was already using borrowed hours, time stolen from the people who trusted her, who needed her.

Slipping out from underneath Fax's sleep-heavy arm, she rose from the bed. Forcing herself not to look back, not to regret, she got dressed in her jeans and heavy shirt, and carried her shoes to the door.

There, she did look back. And immediately wished she hadn't.

Fax looked fierce even in his sleep. He'd pulled her pillow to his chest, cradling it as though he was still trying to protect her, trying to keep her close. Only, he'd protected her well enough, but he'd never let her close, never let her inside.

And after what she was about to do, he never would.

"Now it's my turn to say I'm sorry," she said, hanging on to the door frame to keep herself from going back to the bed and touching him, kissing him the way she wanted to—the way that would be guaranteed to wake him, guaranteed to give him a chance to stop her. Which wasn't an option. So instead she touched her fingers to her sex-swollen lips and blew him a kiss. "Goodbye, Jonah."

She closed the door quietly behind her, and tiptoed away from Jane's room. The other woman couldn't know what they planned.

At her quiet knock, Seth opened the door to the room

he and Cassie were sharing. He was dressed for action, and the others were gathered at his back. "Thought you weren't going to make it," he said, his eyes narrowing on hers.

"I'm here now," she said, refusing to explain, or make excuses. "Let's go."

A KNOCK ON THE DOOR roused Fax an hour past dawn. He was alone.

More than that, the sheets beside him were cool to the touch, and something inside him said that Chelsea had been gone for a while.

She went for breakfast, he told himself, knowing it was a lie and hating the dismay that shot through him, the worry.

After yanking on his pants and shirt, he opened the door. He was unsurprised to see Jane on the other side, and equally unsurprised to see that she was alone. "They're gone," he said. It wasn't a question.

Jane nodded. "Around 2:00 a.m."

Fax stiffened. "You heard and didn't stop them? Didn't come get me?"

"What would you have done?" Faint scorn laced her voice. "Get your head out of your pants and into the game, Jonah. If they're not fully on board with the plan then we're better off without them."

"What if they go to the cops?"

"They won't. They bought into that much of it." She jerked her chin in the direction of the mountain. "They're on their way up there, which is just as well for us. It'll get them out of our way while we do the real dirty work."

She held his gaze, awaiting a response.

But what could he say? She was his boss. She'd saved

his life and been what he'd needed, when he'd needed it. Chelsea and the others were… Damn it, he didn't know what they were anymore.

Chelsea had gotten to him in a way no other woman had since Abby. Hell, his feelings for her made the feelings he'd had for Abby look like a cheap imitation of lust and caring and—no, he wouldn't call it love, couldn't use a word like that, when he knew damn well it'd be a lie.

"Your call, Jonah," Jane said. But they both knew he'd made his choice long ago and had reaffirmed it just the night before. He was her man in all the ways that really counted.

He jerked his head toward her vehicle. "Let's go. Two of us will be enough."

It would have to be or Bear Claw was in serious trouble.

He'd deal with Chelsea's defection later. Or maybe not. Maybe he'd just leave town. It might be easier for both of them that way.

Chapter Twelve

By 9:00 a.m. Sunday, Chelsea and the others were in place.

They split up: Sara went with Tucker and Alyssa, while Chelsea stayed with Cassie and Seth. They hid off to the side of the main fault line, one group for each of the two mine-top huts they believed would be al-Jihad's target.

The huts were low steel structures built into the side of the mountain. More importantly, they flanked a hundred-foot-wide swath of unstable mountainside, which had been weakened by mining efforts and seriously destabilized by the recent rains.

Although the engineers swore it would stay put until they got their terracing and trenches in place, allowing them to trigger a so-called controllable avalanche, it looked precarious to Chelsea, and the cluster of buildings making up the ski lodge, which she could see at the base of the mountain, looked very small in comparison.

The idea of someone bringing the mountainside down on the stadium was enough to have her stomach in knots, but she breathed through it, knowing they were there to prevent exactly that.

Since cell transmissions could be detected, they'd agreed on a simple system of whistles and birdcalls to communicate.

The stealth proved unnecessary, though, as nine o'clock turned to ten, then eleven with no sign of company. The six friends were alone on the mountainside, and the parade had to be past the halfway point by now. There should be some activity if this was truly the terrorists' target.

Either they'd guessed wrong or there'd been a change in plans.

As she waited, Chelsea tried to keep herself from imagining how Fax must've felt when he woke up and found her gone, found all of them gone. She told herself it served him right for chaining her to the bed—fair was fair. But no matter how hard she tried to be, she wasn't the vindictive sort. If there'd been another way to do what she felt she needed to do, without going behind his back, she would've.

Unfortunately, he'd made his loyalties all too clear, and Jane had come out on top of that particular battle.

Sorrow and anger mixed inside her, reminding her of what she'd walked away from. Or rather, what he'd chased her away from. Because he'd made it crystal clear: he didn't want her enough to change.

Well, guess what? She'd already changed and she didn't intend to backpedal and return to the woman she'd been before. If he couldn't handle the person she was becoming, he didn't deserve her.

But even though he'd told her himself that he didn't deserve someone like her, she couldn't help thinking their main issue wasn't what she did or didn't deserve; it was whether he wanted what they'd had together enough to make the change...and the answer was a resounding "no."

Damn him, she thought, checking the time and wincing when she saw it was quarter to twelve.

"This is no good," Cassie said quietly. "Maybe we should consider heading down the mountain and hooking up with Fax and his—" She broke off with a glance at Chelsea and finished with, "boss."

Which so wasn't what she'd been thinking.

"They won't have us at this point," Chelsea said quietly. "She's probably already leaked a hint that we might show up there. The second we make an appearance, we'll be guests in our own jail."

Or rather, what had been their jail before they'd gone renegade. Chelsea didn't regret making the call for herself, but she was seriously wondering if she'd torpedoed her friends' careers based on nothing but her own insistence that Fax wasn't like the others.

Only he was, wasn't he?

"Hey." Cassie touched Chelsea's arm, giving it a squeeze. That meant more than it might've otherwise, because Cassie wasn't the touchy-feely type. "This isn't your fault. If it were easy to anticipate what this bastard was going to do, he wouldn't have gotten away with half the stuff he's accused of, and he would've been in a cage long before this."

"And he would've stayed there," Seth agreed.

"We should've listened to Jane." Chelsea's shoulders slumped. "I was trying to prove a point and it backfired." She'd wanted to make Fax take her side. Instead, she'd split their forces.

If she didn't fix the mistake fast, there was a good chance that innocent people were going to die. And she did *not* believe in acceptable levels of collateral damage.

In her world, one unnatural death was one too many.

"I'm going to take a look around," she announced, rising to a crouch that kept her below tree level in the undergrowth beside the low Quonset hut. "If the coast is clear, I think we should go down the mountain."

"Keep your head low," Seth said, but he didn't tell her not to go, which she took as proof that he also thought they were in the wrong place.

"Count on it." She worked her way out of the thicket, walking along the faint brush marks they'd left in obscuring their trail. They'd tested each step carefully to make sure they didn't wander onto unsafe ground, so she knew if she followed the marks she ought to be okay.

She kept careful watch, but saw only mud, stones and uprooted trees thrown around by the last big slide. There was no sign of anybody else on the mountain, no sign that al-Jihad and his men had ever considered attacking the site.

"Damn," she muttered, though she wasn't sure why she'd thought there might be something, some indication that—

The blur came at her from the side, a whistle of motion and a thump of impact that spun her and drove her staggering back.

Panic came hard and hot, and she screamed at the sight of Muhammad's face, the murderous satisfaction in his eyes.

Then there was another thump, and the world went dark.

FAX HAD A BAD FEELING about the setup at the stadium. It smelled wrong to him, felt wrong. If he'd been alone, he would've banged a U-turn halfway there and headed up into the mountains. Or maybe he would've kept going, figuring the others could handle whatever his gut told him was up there, while he needed to deal with the situation at the stadium.

The danger was up the mountain and in the stadium, and inside his own skull, buzzing and tugging at him, and making him crazy.

Or was that the woman making him nuts? Was it Chelsea and the way she'd seduced him, exhausted him to the point that he hadn't noticed the six of them leave the motel?

Part of him was furious at her deception. Another part of him was a little impressed. Not that he'd ever tell her that. Not that he'd ever get the chance to tell her.

Jane drove fast, weaving in and amongst the traffic as the parade ended and the crowds geared up for the concert. Her jaw was set, her eyes locked on the road with the single-minded determination that'd made her the best of the best and that had drawn the two of them to one another.

They'd been good together because they'd been the same. Still were.

When that rang faintly false and bumped up against the churn in his stomach that said they were headed the wrong way, he tamped down both sensations and checked his weapon for the fifth time since he'd gotten into the car.

"You're fidgeting," Jane said without looking at him.

"I'm fine."

"If you say so."

They didn't speak again until she'd pulled into a spot at the stadium. They each got out of the car, and Fax took a good, long look at the horseshoe-shaped rows of stadium benches, which rose high into the mountain air. He muttered a curse and then said, "What are we thinking? We couldn't cover this place on our own if we had two dozen highly trained operatives. And where is the surveillance equipment?" He turned toward Jane, saying, "I thought—"

"Fax," Jane interrupted, her voice tight.

He turned and froze in place at the sight of the man standing beside her, sharp-featured and weasely. Lee Mawadi.

Fax's blood iced in his veins. The bastard had Jane by the arm, and was holding a gun to her side, its muzzle pressed into her waist. He had the stones to smirk. "Not as smart as you think you are, huh, Fairfax?" He dug the weapon in harder, wringing a cry from Jane as he grated, "Toss your weapons back in the car. And don't try anything or the bitch here gets a few new holes."

Fax did as he was told as killing rage speared through him. He two-fingered the gun, then tossed it in the passenger's-side footwell.

"Now who's the lemming?" Lee jeered.

Fax didn't reply, didn't get a chance to, because suddenly the bastard was letting go of Jane and turning the weapon on Fax, and Jane wasn't doing a damned thing except standing there. Watching.

In a second of ice-cold reality, Fax understood what his gut had been trying to tell him since the night before, the instinct he'd ignored because he'd thought it was a mixture of lust and guilt.

Jane's reappearance had seemed too convenient because it *was* too convenient. She'd been working for al-Jihad all along.

Which meant Fax had, too. Maybe not all along, but for a while, at least.

Hell, he'd probably gone to jail for the bastard.

How could you? he wanted to ask her, but he could tell from her stone-set expression that she wouldn't answer, didn't care what he thought of her, didn't give a single damn about him.

She'd never claimed to care about anything but taking down al-Jihad and even that had been a lie.

"Steady, Jonah," she said, waving for Lee to lower his weapon. "Think it through. Think of the advantages."

"I'm way ahead of you." He smiled mirthlessly, cooling his expression even though his blood was quickly heating once again with anger, with panic.

Jane had known the others were headed up into the mountain.

For all he knew, they were already dead.

Jane's face softened with a hint of approval. "You already knew about my change in allegiance."

"I guessed," he said. "Good to know the time in prison hasn't dulled my instincts too much."

"He's lying," Lee hissed, bringing his weapon up once again. "He never would've sent the bitch to Muhammad. He's too much of a goddamn prince for that."

"And you're too much of a rodent to understand the concept of developing an asset for future use, then disposing of it when it ceases to be useful." Fax forced a smile, although his stomach roiled as he said, "Trust me, she came in *very* useful for a while."

That startled a chuckle out of Lee, who let the gun drop a notch.

It was all the opportunity Fax needed.

Moving fast, he lunged for the weapon, grabbing Lee at the same time that he swung a kick in Jane's direction, forcing her to stumble back, out of range. He fought with Lee, kicking and punching as the smaller man squirmed to get free and struggled to bring the gun to bear.

"You don't want to do this, Jonah," Jane said, her voice edged with irritation or maybe fear. "Don't be stupid."

"No." Grunting with the effort, he yanked the gun away from Lee and subdued the bastard with a choke hold. When Jane came at him, he dodged and grabbed her, and whipped her arm up behind her back as well. "I've been stupid for way too long already."

Using the gun to keep them pinned down, he yanked off Lee's belt and used it to bind their hands together at the smalls of their backs.

Then he turned toward the stadium, pointed the nine-millimeter in the air, and fired off four rounds in quick succession.

Screams and shouts erupted, and the people who'd been streaming into the arena only seconds earlier started scrambling to get out. Already set on a hair trigger after the prison break, the citizens of Bear Claw didn't wait to see where the shots were coming from or where they were aimed.

They bolted en masse, creating instant chaos.

Satisfied, Fax returned his attention to his two prisoners. He was just in time to duck the full-power kick Jane had aimed at his privates. Her foot struck him a glancing blow in the groin that sent a slash of pain through him and had him staggering.

They'd gotten free somehow, and Lee was already running. Jane paused and grabbed Fax's gun from the passenger's seat of her car.

She came up firing and she wasn't aiming into the air.

Fax hit the deck and rolled partway under the car, then scrambled up again. There were more screams, more chaos, and cars started peeling out of the parking lot. By the time Fax was up and oriented, Jane and Lee were both gone. Not good.

On the upside, though, the stadium was more than half empty, and—

An explosion roared from the main entrance, slamming him to the ground.

He heard more screams, dulled now by the ringing in his ears, then the thump of more explosions, the squeal of tires and the crashing impacts as cars collided, starting a chain reaction of accidents, with cars accordioning into each other in the drivers' mad rush to get the hell away from the bombs.

Which meant nobody was going anywhere, Fax realized as he levered himself up and took in the scene.

The stadium was wreathed in ugly gouts of black smoke that rose from each of the collapsed entrances. There were thousands of people still trapped inside and probably the same number stranded outside in the parking lot and road beyond, which had become impassable due to wrecked vehicles.

In the distance, he could hear sirens and emergency vehicles approaching, but it'd take too long for them to fight through the jammed roads. In the meantime, thousands of people would remain trapped in the bowl-shaped depression where the stadium had been built at the base of the mountain…right below the threatening shelf of a potential landslide.

Chelsea and the others were up there, Fax thought, his heart hammering painfully against his ribs. For all he knew, they were already dead, killed by al-Jihad and his ruthless terrorists as they cleared the way for the next stage of the plan.

It wasn't a case of the landslide or the stadium: the bastard had targeted both.

"I should've seen it," Fax said, cursing himself as he fought through the mob, headed for the road below, which was rapidly jamming with cars. "I should've known."

But he didn't, he hadn't. And because he hadn't been thinking clearly, innocent people that he cared about—yes, *cared,* damn it—might already be dead.

He hurled himself down the steep incline to the road, his feet barely moving fast enough to keep up with his momentum. He staggered when he reached the level strip of grass beside the road, but righted himself and kept running until he found what he was looking for.

The red SUV was empty, parked in the farthest lane with the driver's-side door open and the motor running. No doubt the driver was one of the many people who'd gathered at the edge of the road, shading their eyes and staring up toward the smoking stadium, talking in high, excited voices.

Fax climbed in the driver's seat and slammed the door, then hit the button to lock the vehicle tight. He was most of the way out of the nose-to-tail line of cars when a man ran at him, waving his hands and shouting.

Fax cracked the window and shouted, "Police business. You'll get it back."

Then he hit the gas and sent the SUV hurtling across a strip of grass and into the wide ditch separating the eastbound and westbound lanes of traffic. The SUV dug in and bounced hard and its tires spun. For a second, Fax was afraid the thing was going to dig itself into place and he'd be stuck. Then it tore free with a roar and a lurch, and started climbing up the other side.

He didn't wait for a break in the rubbernecking traffic

in the other lane. He just hit the gas and aimed for a gap that wasn't quite big enough for the SUV. Paint scraped and the vehicle shuddered and bounced as he fought it into a straight line following the road.

Nearby drivers swerved, honked and swore at him, but he didn't care. He leaned on the horn and flashed the high beams like a crazy man, and weaved in and out of the near-gridlocked traffic.

The other drivers must've thought he was with the emergency rescue personnel or something, because they started getting out of his way, just a few at first but then more and more of them, opening up a pathway until he was free, on the open road headed for the turnoff that would lead him up the mountain.

Once he was speeding along and not focused solely on the driving anymore, his brain kicked back online, and all he could picture was Chelsea's face as she'd slept, all he could imagine was that same face, still and gray, with her stretched out on a table in her own morgue, dead because he hadn't listened to her, hadn't trusted her, or his own instincts.

"No," he said aloud, denying the image, denying all of it. He would be in time to get to her, would be in time to save her.

Failure was *not* an option.

Chapter Thirteen

When Chelsea regained consciousness, it took a few moments for her eyes to clear and her brain to process what she was seeing. Memory returned with a brutal slap when she saw dirt, ledge stone and uprooted trees all piled in a disarray, tilted at a seemingly impossible angle.

She was still up on the mountain. But where was her attacker? Where were Seth, Cassie and the others? Moving her eyes first, then her head, she craned to see. When her neck twinged, suggesting that she'd pulled muscles in the struggle, she winced and moved her body instead.

Or rather, she tried to move her body. It didn't budge, because she was tied fast.

Panic slapped through the mist of unreality, warning her that the situation was very, very real. Her heartbeat accelerated and her blood fired in her veins, telling her to run far and fast.

Or stand and fight.

Slow down, she told herself when her mind started to race in terror. *Think it through.* For some reason, she heard the last three words in Fax's voice. Instead of making her mad or sad, as it probably should have, the sound steadied her. It made her think of his warm, solid body and the mask he could drop over his eyes, making it seem like he was running cold when she knew from experience that the blood running in his veins was very, very hot.

She closed her eyes and pictured him, imagining the worry lines that cut beside his mouth from having taken on too much weight for far too long, and the unexpected dimple that winked on one cheek on the rare occasion when he smiled for real.

Holding that image in her mind, she consciously slowed her breathing and counted her heartbeats.

The panic receded somewhat. It was still there, no doubt about it. But it was manageable, more or less. She could think. She could plan.

Okay, she thought, opening her eyes. *What's the deal?*

Unfortunately, calming down hadn't improved her immediate situation much. She wasn't in danger of hyperventilating anymore, but she was still bound to a big tree at the edge of the landslide.

Worse, she could see a heavy work boot sticking out from behind the precarious tilt of the earthen overhang.

She recognized it as one of Tucker's boots. As she watched, it moved, swinging from side to side as though he was fighting the same sort of bonds she was.

Her heart seized on the sight and she gave a low cry of horror.

A masculine chuckle—low and nasty—greeted her response, and Muhammad stepped around in front of her, moving gingerly on the shifting soil at the edge of the slide.

He looked at her for a long moment, his eyes blatantly lingering on her breasts then flashing back to her face as though daring her to say something, challenging her to a fight she couldn't possibly win.

When she said nothing, merely glared at him with all

the hatred that pounded in her veins, he sneered and turned his attention to the overhang. "You should've died that afternoon at your house, bitch. Then your friends wouldn't have gotten dragged into this." He fiddled with a small, flat handheld unit that might've been a PDA, might've been a phone, and said with a fake-sounding note of revelation, "Granted, then they probably would've been down at the stadium helping with crowd control and listening to that horrible excuse for a band. Which means they would've died anyway, once I did this."

Without warning, he lifted the handheld and pressed a couple of touch-pad keys.

"No!" Chelsea cried, realizing the unit was a detonator of some sort. "Don't!"

But it was already too late. There was a series of sharp explosions nearby, six of them, one after the other, *rat-tat-tat,* like machine-gun fire.

By themselves, they were little more than firecrackers. Combined with the instability of the ground, though, they were devastating.

A low rumble started, humming in her bones and rising up through the audible wavelengths, shaking the tree she was bound to, making it sway and dip.

Looking surprised that the earth shift was fanning that far out, Muhammad shoved the unit in his pocket and started backing up, moving quickly but carefully. When he reached stabler ground, he sketched a wave in Chelsea's direction. "Bye, bitch. I hope it hurts."

The hatred vibrated in the air between them, less because of what she'd done to complicate al-Jihad's plans and more because of what she was—an American and a woman.

Her stomach twisted in knots at the thought that Muhammad, and men like him, were going to win this time.

The tree shuddered, dipping alarmingly, and she cried out. Her words were lost beneath the growing roar, and suddenly the world was moving around her, underneath her. The overhang gave way and crashed like a breaking wave, sending tons of earth and rock onto the place where she'd seen Tucker's foot.

Chelsea screamed as her closest friends died. Tears blinded her and she choked on her sobs, on her terror. Then the earth was moving, faster and faster, gaining mass and momentum as it went, crashing its way toward the stadium. And Fax.

"Jonah!" she screamed, knowing there was nobody up on the mountain with her anymore who cared about her cries, except to feel pleasure in her pain.

Then the tree she was bound to pulled free of its root system, or the earth gave way beneath it, she wasn't sure which, she only knew that she was moving, tilting, and starting to slide, then stopping again as the entire mountainside paused, teetering on a pinpoint of balance that she knew could give way at any second.

Tears poured down her face. "*Jonah!*" she screamed again, even though she knew there was no hope of an answer.

Yet incredibly, she got one.

"Chelsea!" He was suddenly there, appearing out of nowhere, his face streaked with mud and sweat and set with horrible tension as he skidded along beside the tree she was tied to, yanking at her bonds. "Hang on!"

"What—" she gasped. "How?"

"Long story." He met her eyes briefly, and she saw a

light in them that hadn't been there before, a mix of anger and something else, something that was simultaneously softer and hotter than his usual expression. "Short version is that you were right and I was wrong, but I'm not apologizing. I'm telling you I love you instead."

He gave a huge yank and the ropes came free.

Heart pounding from surprise and fear, and more adrenaline than she'd ever weathered in her life, she threw herself against him. *"Jonah!"*

He grabbed on to her, held her hard and started dragging her up and across the mountain face, moving fast, not seeming to care that the earth sponged and fell free beneath them, that their mad dash for safety was triggering small landslides that merged into bigger ones.

"Hurry," he urged, dragging her along. "We've got to get out of here before—"

A huge freight-train roar cut him off, and the side of the mountain collapsed onto itself, and hurtled down the slope toward Bear Claw.

"Up here!" Jonah dragged her up onto a huge rock ledge, one that shuddered but held as the earth and smaller rocks pounded past it. He pulled her up, wrapped his arms around her, and held on so tightly she couldn't breathe.

She hugged him back just as tight, crying. "Jonah, the others…" she managed between sobs. "They were under the ledge when it gave."

He said something that she didn't catch, sure it was the roar of the avalanche. "What?"

Putting his lips close to her ear, he said, "They weren't under the ledge. I got them free while you distracted Muhammad. I sent them down the hill and told them to—" He broke off as a new sound echoed above the freight-train rumble, a heavy thump of detonations, one after the other, not the *rat-tat-tat* that had started the landslide, but the deep throated *whump-whump-whump* of heavy-duty explosives.

A cloud of earth shot up into the sky at the leading edge of the slide, and the avalanche changed course, flattening and dropping off, fanning out and eventually stopping.

The terrible roar diminished to a hiss, then a scattering of pebbles.

Chelsea stared, mouth agape. Then she turned to Fax, hardly able to believe what had just happened.

"You sent them to blast a channel between the slide and the stadium," she said in wonder.

He followed her gaze. "Looks like it worked."

"You let them go," she said and started to shake. "You took care of them first before you came for me."

Fax stiffened against her. "That doesn't mean—"

"No, no." She shushed him with her lips on his, letting him feel the smile in her kiss. "You trusted them to get the job done, and you trusted me to stay alive long enough for you to come for me. You did it right, Jonah. You saved us all."

A shudder went through his big body. "I almost didn't."

She heard him clearly, heard the pain and fear in his voice, because the landslide had trailed all the way to silence, piling into the trench her friends had blasted using explosives from the lower Quonset hut.

"But you did. Thank you." She pressed her lips to his, and he hesitated only a moment before he leaned into the kiss, opening to her and—

The click of a semiautomatic weapon being racked for firing echoed on the suddenly still air, freezing them both. Only for a second though, because before Chelsea could react, before she could even process the fact that they were in danger, Fax had twisted, bearing her to the ground and covering her as a bullet whistled over them both.

Then Fax lunged up with a roar, and charged Muhammad, who must've come back to make certain she was dead. As Fax came, he scooped up a handful of clay. Chelsea saw him grab Muhammad's gun with the hand that held the soil. Then Fax let go and danced away.

Al-Jihad's second in command roared something in a language Chelsea didn't know, spun toward Fax and fired point-blank.

The bullet impacted the pebbles and clay Fax had jammed down the barrel, and the weapon roared and jammed, blowing back in the terrorist's hands. He screamed and grabbed for his wrist as it spurted blood, and Fax took him down with a roundhouse to the jaw.

Muhammad went sprawling, bleeding and howling and clutching at his injured hand.

Fax kicked the gun away and then stood, breathing hard, staring down at his fallen enemy.

Chelsea gave the deep lacerations a quick look, and glanced at Fax. "He won't bleed out as long as he keeps pressure on."

"Then we'll tie him so he can." With more expediency than gentleness, Fax bound the sobbing man hand and foot, and searched him, dumping the contents of Muhammad's pockets into his own.

Seeing the transfer, Chelsea arched an eyebrow. "You planning on sharing that with the cops?"

Fax stilled, then turned slowly, that cool blankness dropping down to shield his expression, although she sensed that his blood was running hot and hard beneath. "Jane betrayed me—she was working for al-Jihad all along. Which means there may not be any way for me to prove my story, and even if I can, the authorities could still decide I'm a liability and a criminal." He drew a deep breath. "What if I said my next stop was Mexico?"

If it was a test, it was the easiest one Chelsea had ever taken. "Then I'd ask if I could swing by my place for a bathing suit."

He straightened, crossing to her and taking her hands in his, fitting their fingers together. "And if I said I wanted to turn myself in and offer up evidence against Jane in exchange for WitSec protection?"

She swallowed, knowing this was it, this was the rest of her life, staring at her with cool blue eyes that hid nothing of his feelings, once she knew where to look. "Then I'd ask if I could say goodbye to my friends before we left." Her voice shook a little on the words as she continued, "How about you? What's your opinion of taking on a most likely unemployed, blackballed medical examiner who's wishing she'd gone on that FBI interview way back when? For that matter, given that WitSec would make me change jobs anyway, what's your opinion of being with someone who suddenly doesn't know what she wants to be when she grows up?"

He inhaled a long, shuddering breath, then blew it out slowly so that he was almost whispering when he said, "I can't think of anything I'd like more. Employed, unemployed, spy, doctor, pathologist…I don't care what you wind up doing next, as long as I'm part of it." He dropped his forehead to hers. "I love you, Chelsea. We'll figure out the rest of it together, okay?"

Hope bloomed inside her, hard and hot, expanding to fill every inch of her body as she nodded, feeling her smile stretch so wide it pulled at the skin of her face as she rubbed her cheek against his, against the place where that elusive dimple flickered to life. "I love you back, Jonah. And, yeah, the rest will wait. This won't." She turned her lips to his, inviting a kiss, demanding it.

He'd just groaned and opened to her when a Bear Claw PD chopper buzzed up from below and hovered right above them, tilting to give its occupants a clear view.

Hoots and hollers filtered down, and Chelsea felt a laugh bubble up as she raised her hand and waved at her friends. "Guess they made it okay," she said, counting five heads pressed together in the windows. "And I'm guessing at least someone in the PD is grateful for our help. They sent the chopper after all."

Fax straightened away from her, although he kept an arm looped protectively around her waist as he surveyed the helicopter. She saw him look at the tree line as though considering making a break for it, and she elbowed him in the ribs. "Don't even think of it. These are my friends."

He looked at her for a long moment unspeaking, then nodded. "Mine, too, if they'll have me." He raised a hand to the chopper, gesturing for them to throw down a line, as there was nowhere to land.

And as he hooked them in and they were lifted up into the sky, Chelsea, who'd never been a big fan of heights, clung to his solid bulk and watched the ground fall away, knowing that as long as she was with him, she could do anything. Even fly.

The exultation was short-lived, though, because her friends weren't the only ones in the chopper—there was also a grim-faced man who immediately grabbed Fax and engaged him in low-voiced conversation, somehow isolating the two of them even in the crowded quarters of the helicopter.

The moment they touched down near the stadium, that same man whisked Fax away into a dark sedan with tinted windows and government plates.

Fax didn't look back as the vehicle pulled away. And in the days that followed, he didn't call. There was no word of him, not even a rumor.

It was as if he'd disappeared.

Chapter Fourteen

It was three long, agonizing weeks before Fax's boots hit Colorado soil once again.

The last time he'd arrived in the Bear Claw area, he'd been cuffed and flanked by blank-faced U.S. Marshals, who he suspected would've shot to kill and enjoyed it, believing that he'd tortured and murdered two FBI agents.

This time he was alone and dressed in casual civilian clothes. The jeans and button-down shirt still felt a little strange after living so long in prison clothes.

He was carrying a duffel bag filled with new clothes, because when he'd gone back to the storage unit he'd rented right after Abby's death, the things inside the musty garage-size box had looked tired and irrelevant. So he'd picked out a few boxes of stuff he thought he might want some day and donated the rest to a local shelter.

Then he'd cleaned out his offshore bank account, which had grown fat with the undercover pay Jane had funneled there through a shell company, and used the money to buy some essentials during the few breaks he'd been allowed between debriefings.

Those breaks had been few and far between. The

grim-faced agents in charge hadn't outright refused to let him leave the bunkerlike maze of rooms located beneath an innocuous-looking building in downtown D.C. They'd made it clear, though, that the more he stayed put and answered the same questions over and over again, the higher his likelihood of making it out of there with some hope of a continued career within federal law enforcement.

He'd stayed and he'd given up everything he knew or even suspected about the op that he'd thought had been designed to draw out al-Jihad's conspirators, but had really been intended solely to help the murderer escape from the ARX Supermax prison. He told them everything, not because he wanted his career back, but because his main motivation for having entered the world in the first place remained unchanged. He wanted to help bring down al-Jihad and others like him, who attacked U.S. politics by killing noncombatants: women and children. Families.

Out of necessity, the info flow hadn't just been one way. The agents questioning Fax had revealed that al-Jihad and Lee Mawadi remained at large, as did Jane Doe. Worse, she had managed to use her equipment to feed misinformation to the cops on duty along the parade route.

That, combined with the chaos at the stadium and the lack of manpower on the mountain, meant that not only had all of al-Jihad's men escaped—with the exception of Muhammad, who was staying grimly tight-lipped so far—the conspirators remained undetected.

For a time, the investigation had focused on FBI agent Michael Grayson, the man who had arrested Fax in the stadium the day before the attack. Even more damning than his seemingly not-so-coincidental presence at the stadium, was that he'd also been the point of failure for a carefully worded warning sent by Seth Varitek early on the morning of the parade.

Grayson had received the information, determined it was a prank, and unilaterally decided not to add the manpower Varitek had suggested. In doing so, he had very nearly helped doom thousands of Bear Claw residents.

Despite that sign of complicity, a thorough investigation turned up no evidence that Grayson was linked to al-Jihad or any other terrorist. Instead, it turned out that the agent was suffering through the tail end of a very nasty divorce and had been living on caffeine pills rather than sleep or food.

Not surprisingly, he'd been pulled out of the field and would undergo major reviews and potentially lose his fieldwork status. But while it was a good thing to deal with an agent on the edge, with Grayson cleared of suspicion, they were left with few theories and even fewer clues regarding the structure of al-Jihad's terror cells or the whereabouts of the terrorist leader, Jane Doe or Lee Mawadi.

One of their few leads was Lee Mawadi's ex-wife who lived in a remote area roughly between Bear Claw and the ARX Supermax prison. She had divorced him shortly after his arrest for the Santa Bombings, claiming not to have had any idea of his criminal involvement. She'd quit her job as a magazine photographer and changed her name and had all but gone into seclusion in an isolated cabin high in the mountains. All of which was consistent with her claim that she hated her ex…except for the fact that her cabin was less than thirty miles from the prison.

If she had wanted to completely separate herself from her ex-husband…why had she chosen to live a short drive away from where he'd been incarcerated?

When asked, she'd told agents it was atonement, a reminder of the terrible mistake she'd made. Living near the peak of a low mountain, within sight of both the prison and Bear Claw City, she was constantly reminded of the people who'd died in the Santa Bombings.

Maybe she was telling the truth, maybe not. Regardless, the feds were keeping her under very tight surveillance.

The task force dedicated to bringing al-Jihad down was being headed up by a no-nonsense career agent named M. K. O'Reilly. There were still major questions of who could and couldn't be trusted, but Fax's gut said O'Reilly was clean. Then again, he'd missed the signs that Jane had turned. In retrospect it was far too easy to pick up on the little hints, the small inconsistencies, and the way she'd progressively cut him off from all his other contacts, until he'd been dealing with her and her alone.

He was furious with himself for being oblivious to the clues. Oddly, though, Jane's betrayal—not just of him but of the country he'd dedicated his life to protecting—didn't kick him back into the black hole of distrust he'd occupied in the months after Abby's death, the pit Jane herself had rescued him from.

Instead, he was able to hate Jane for the betrayal without hating himself, without withdrawing from the people around him.

That was Chelsea's doing, he knew. Any time the blackness encroached on his soul, he thought of her smile, her gentle sanity, and the way their hands had fit together, the way *they* had fit, even though on paper they never should've worked.

At least he'd told himself over and over that they

worked, holding it as a lifeline, a mantra when things had looked their worst, when the grim-faced agents had hinted that he should plan for an extended stay, another incarceration, this time without the luxury of knowing deep down inside that he was one of the good guys, that he didn't belong there.

Then one day the threats had disappeared. In their place had been a job offer and an open door.

He was a free man now. He could dress how he wanted, could go where he wanted.

Which was what had brought him to Bear Claw.

When he got there, though, he pulled his rental over to the side of the road beside the *Welcome to Bear Claw City!* sign at the outskirts of the metro area.

And he sat there, wondering whether he'd blown it by not calling Chelsea in the intervening weeks, not letting her know where everything stood. The thing was, he hadn't wanted to call until he knew he was going to be able to come back to her.

"Well, you're back," he said to himself, staring up at the welcome sign. "Time to do your worst and hope for the best."

Still, it was a long time before he started driving again, and when he did his pulse was kicking, because for the first time in a long, long time, he was going to lay his heart—rather than his life—on the line.

For the first time in a long, long time, he cared.

More than that, he loved. He'd told her before, in the heat of the moment. Now it was time to see if she'd really meant it…because he sure as hell had.

SITTING IN HER small office in the ME's complex, Chelsea took another long look at the e-mail that had dropped into her computer's in-box. The return address was a government system, and there was an official seal at the upper left of the letter itself. The words *congratulations* and *please report* swam before her eyes, which misted at the realization that she was being offered a second chance at her dreams.

One of them, anyway. The other one appeared to be long gone, damn him.

Anger and heartache scratched at the back of her throat and she would've cursed herself for thinking of Fax. But if she started doing that, her days were likely to turn into a never-ending string of four-letter words, because she couldn't get him out of her head or her heart.

He'd swept into her life, turned her safe little universe upside down, told her he loved her and made her love him, and then disappeared without a word.

Jerk, she thought for the thousandth time and tried to find the anger that had sustained her for the first couple of weeks. It'd faded, though, leaving sadness behind—for herself, because she wanted the life they could've made together and for him because he'd been unable to break free of the patterns and beliefs that had bound him for too long. He was stuck in the past.

Well, not me, she thought, reading through the e-mail for the third time, finally beginning to believe she'd actually been accepted into the FBI's initial round of candidate screening.

She wasn't a shoo-in by any means, but she'd taken the first step.

"I have good news and bad news," she said when she heard someone come through the door, assuming it was Sara because she'd just called over and left a voice mail telling her boss that they needed to talk.

"Me, too," said a voice that was definitely *not* Sara's.

Chelsea froze. Then she looked up from her monitor, moving slowly, half convinced that he'd disappear, proving to be the same figment she'd imagined too many times to count.

But he didn't disappear. He stayed put, with one shoulder propped against the door frame, his arms crossed over his chest, his forearms bare where he'd rolled up the sleeves of a crisp blue button-down shirt.

The shirt was jarring in its very normalcy, as were his new-looking jeans and belt, which seemed to be trying to make him look like a regular guy. They failed, though, because there was nothing average about his solid build and angular face or the powerful emotion in his eyes when he looked at her.

Chelsea's breath went thin in her lungs as she stood and moved around the desk to approach him.

Stopping just outside his reach, she lifted her chin. "What's your news?"

"You first," he said, challenging her. Teasing her.

And at that moment she knew it was going to be okay. She didn't know where he'd been, but in that instant she knew he'd come back for her, and this time he was there to stay. She knew because she could finally see the warmth in his eyes, the love.

Her heart beat double time beneath her skin with a powerful combination of nerves and excitement. "I re-applied to the FBI and they've invited me to D.C."

"Of course they did. They're not stupid." The way he said it made her wonder whether he'd had something to do with the quick response. "What's the bad news?"

Her elation dimmed slightly. "It means leaving Sara in the lurch. With Jerry and Ricky both gone, she's shorthanded as it is. Worse, Mayor Proudfoot wants to replace her with someone more susceptible to pressure. He's leaning hard on IAD to investigate the office." She took a deep breath, then let it out. "But Sara's tough. She can take care of herself."

When she said it that way, it seemed obvious. Why had it taken her so long to figure out that she had to let go sometimes?

She tilted her head, taking a long look at the man who'd helped teach her that, by showing her the extreme of what could happen to a person who tried to take the world's problems on his shoulders and forgot to have his own life in the process.

"What about you?" she said, feeling her whole body shimmer with the warmth of his nearness, with the certainty that he'd come back for her. "What's your good news?"

"I'm here," he said simply, "and I'm staying. Not in Bear Claw, necessarily, but wherever you are. That's where I want to be."

He took her hand in his, and their fingers fit perfectly.

She stepped into him, leaned into him. "What's the bad news?"

"Same thing. Whether it's good news or bad depends on your perspective." He took her other hand, folded his fingers around hers and raised her knuckles to his lips. "That's assuming that you're willing to forgive me for taking a few weeks to get things squared away and make sure I didn't have to write you from the ARX Supermax, and you're happy to see me and you still want us to be together. In that case, then it's good news."

His eyes said he already knew what her answer

would be, as did the touch of his lips against hers, bringing heat and want.

"And if I'm not willing to forgive?" she said against his mouth, letting go of his hands to wrap her arms around his waist, anchoring herself to his strength.

"Then it's bad news, because I have no intention of giving up what we could have together. I don't care how long it takes, I'm going to stick it out and make it work." His eyes were intent on hers. "So, which is it? Good news or bad?"

She smiled as the warmth that'd gathered in her heart moved outward, radiating through her body like need. Like love. "Oh, it's good news. Very, very good news."

And as they kissed, twining together in her office doorway, she knew that no matter where she chose to go from here, what she chose to do, she wouldn't be doing it alone. She had a partner now. A lover.

A friend.

* * * * *

[illegible]

[illegible]

[illegible]

[illegible]

[illegible]

[illegible]

TYCOON PROTECTOR

BY
ELLE JAMES

2004 Golden Heart Winner for Best Paranormal Romance, **Elle James** started writing when her sister issued a Y2K challenge to write a romance novel. She managed a full-time job, raised three wonderful children and she and her husband even tried their hands at ranching exotic birds (ostriches, emus and rheas) in the Texas Hill Country. Ask her and she'll tell you what it's like to go toe-to-toe with an angry 350-pound bird! You can contact her at ellejames@earthlink.net or visit her website at www.ellejames.com.

I'd like to thank the wonderful authors who contributed to bringing this continuity together, making it come alive with action, adventure and romance. None of this could have happened if not for our terrific editors for their support and belief in us as authors. A great big, special thanks for making my dreams come true.

Chapter One

Jackson Champion stood on the Bayport Container Yard loading dock, sleeves rolled up, his cowboy hat tipped back on his head. Overhead illumination eclipsed the moon, making the busy container yard brighter than day with light reflecting off the low ceiling of clouds.

Despite the solid concrete beneath his feet, Jackson's body still swayed to the rhythm of the ocean. It usually took more than twenty-four hours for him to get his land legs back after several weeks at sea. His two-month reprieve, delay of the inevitable, call it what it was—okay, escape was the right word—had come to an end.

The time had come to face the consequences of a night spent in Ysabel Sanchez's arms. Yet here he was delaying the face-to-face he owed her by sticking around to direct the off-loading of cargo from his ship. A task the stevedores and deckhands normally managed quite well without his presence.

Cranes lifted containers from the ship, stacking them in the container yard with artful precision. He didn't have to be there, but he told himself he wanted to supervise the unloading of the special cargo he'd shipped for his remaining friends and founding members of the Aggie Four Foundation, Flint and Akeem. Just one more delay tactic. A twinge of regret passed over Jackson. One of their four had died recently; the pain still ached like an open wound.

The crate full of expertly designed Rasnovian saddles would bring a good price at Akeem's auction. But the money wouldn't buy a replacement for Jackson's pending loss. An inevitable defeat from any angle he chose to view it.

The woman was sure to leave him. No doubt about it. She had every right. Hell, she had the right to sue him for sexual harassment if she wanted to get legal on him. Not that Izzy would do that. She was one classy lady, grown from the same stock as he was. The stock of hard knocks. A grin threatened to spill across his face. She hated being called Izzy.

No, Ysabel wouldn't sue; she'd walk out on him. The two months enforced reprieve could be viewed as running away from his problem—although the problems he'd encountered while away had needed his on-site decision power. Jackson chose to call it delaying the inevitable. He'd missed her and he'd miss her even more when she was gone entirely out of his life.

He rolled the kinks out his shoulders and located the stevedore superintendent, the one man on the dock with a clue as to where the container holding the saddles was located and when it would be unloaded.

Being the owner didn't make him any more anxious to interrupt the complicated task of unloading a cargo ship. Weight distribution meant everything to the successful completion of the task.

His skin twitched in the side of his jaw, impatience settling in like a case of poison ivy, making him want to scratch all over. Now that he was back in Houston, he was anxious to get to the office and see what had happened in his two-month absence from the corporation he'd built from the ground up, Champion Shipping, Inc. Everyone would have gone home for the evening, except perhaps Ysabel. If he could catch her alone, maybe he could apologize and promise not to let it happen again.

His groin tightened at just the thought of that one night of the most incredible sex he'd ever experienced. Rebound sex, he'd called it. And it could cost him his most valuable employee. Ysabel Sanchez—executive assistant, master planner and right-hand man…er, woman. Ysabel was the one person he could count on to ground him in reality, tell it like it was and pick the right tie for every occasion. Even in his absence, she managed the day-to-day operations without a snag. She'd kept his schedule straight, reminded him of his social obligations and arranged his itinerary long-distance. The woman was phenomenal in more ways than he could enumerate.

Then why was he so hesitant to head back to the office?

Because he knew as soon as they were face-to-face, she'd hand him her resignation and walk out. Ysabel wasn't a one-night-stand kind of woman. She'd want the happily-ever-after, something Jackson hadn't believed in since his mother left him and his father twenty-seven years ago.

And after the fiasco with his ex-fiancée, Jackson was even less inclined to commit to that particular lifestyle than before. Not that Ysabel was anything like Jenna Nilsson.

The stevedore superintendent, Percy Pearson, glanced his way, Jackson's cue he could ask his question without interrupting the man's concentration.

Jackson closed the distance and held out his hand to the man. "Percy, good to see you. Have you seen the container with the special cargo yet?"

The man checked his handheld cargo tracking device. "Unloaded fifteen minutes ago. Should be in the second row of containers in that section." He pointed to a row of containers on the dock.

"Thanks." Jackson strode to the end of the row and found the container marked "Special." When he circled behind the container, he noted the container door had been opened and part of the shipment had been removed. "What the hell?"

A forklift carrying a pallet with a crate on it headed away from the ship and the open container, moving faster than was authorized in the chaotic structure of the container yard.

"Mr. Champion? I'm Tom Walker, the super said I could find you here." A young man probably in his early twenties hurried up to Jackson. He wore a crisp new business suit and shiny black wing-tipped shoes, fresh off the shelves. "Miss Sanchez sent me over. I'm the new management trainee on the executive rotation."

Was this Ysabel's idea of a joke? Not that he had time to worry about it when someone had pilfered his goods. "Did you see that?" Jackson pointed to the forklift. "I think that forklift driver took off with my property."

"Was he supposed to?" Tom asked.

"No." Jackson's gut tightened, anger rocketing through his bloodstream the farther away the forklift moved.

"You want me to chase him?" Tom stared down at his wing tips and shrugged. "I could probably catch him if I was wearing my running shoes."

"No, I'll take care of it." Jackson ran for an idle forklift he'd spotted standing between the containers. He hopped aboard and in seconds had the machine running. With the skill of one who'd done his share of stevedoring in his younger days, he backed out of the containers and turned toward the disappearing forklift. With a flip of a lever, Jackson shifted into forward and pushed the accelerator all the way forward.

Before the forklift moved two yards, Tom jumped on the back and held on to the cage surrounding the seat.

"What are you doing?" Jackson asked.

"Miss Sanchez told me I should stick to you like glue, no matter what."

"She did, did she?" Jackson pushed the vehicle faster, swinging around the corner the other forklift had taken.

"Yes, sir. Wow! I didn't know this rotation would be this exciting!" he shouted over the whine of the engine pushing the forklift to its limits.

Jackson didn't know his return would be as eventful as his two-month trip. He could use a little calm and boredom about now.

The thief had a lead of at least a football field's length, maneuvering past containers and personnel, narrowly missing several longshoremen unhooking a pallet from a crane's cable.

The forklift made a sharp left turn, sliding between rows of neatly stacked containers in weathered shades of orange, red and silver.

Rage spurred on Jackson. When he reached the spot where the other forklift had spun to the left, he didn't slow down. His forklift skidded to the right, skinning the side of a metal container, the clash of metal on metal sending sparks flying.

"You all right back there?" Jackson called out, a quick glance back at the young man made him smile.

The guy's suit was dirty, his face smudged with grease from the forklift and his teeth shone white in a face-splitting grin. "I'm still here, aren't I?"

Jackson could admire a tough kid. "You passed your first test."

"Oh, yeah? What test is that?"

"Keeping up with the boss!" He poured on the juice and sent the forklift shooting forward, but he could no longer see the other machine. "Where the hell did he go?" Slowing his own vehicle, he was about to give up and get the police involved when a shout behind him made him jump.

"There!" From his perch on the back of the forklift, Tom could see farther. He waved his arm back behind him, jabbing his finger to the right. "He went down that aisle."

Jackson slammed the forklift in Reverse and spun around, heading back the way Tom pointed. Like the young man said, the runaway forklift was making tracks across the container yard and would have gotten away if not for Tom's sharp eyes and quick response.

As he closed in on the other forklift, Jackson prepared for a fight, but he didn't get the chance.

The forklift jerked to the left, crossing Jackson's path.

Jackson stomped the brake and swerved to the right.

The forklift skidded back to the right and then left. Clearly the driver had lost control and was headed straight for a container.

"Look out!" Jackson called out, but the forklift driver drove full speed into the twenty-foot container. A small explosion blasted wood crating and metal in all directions.

"Get down!" Jackson threw himself off the forklift and dragged Tom off the back. Before they could hit the ground, another explosion shook the earth as the propane tank on the wrecked forklift erupted in a fiery ball of flame.

"WELL?" Delia's voice carried through the wood paneling of the bathroom door.

Ysabel stared down at the wand, blood rushing from her head, making her dizzy. As she'd suspected, but prayed otherwise, a blue line.

"Izzy? Are you all right?" Delia's voice was soft but insistent, bringing tears to Ysabel's eyes. She'd need her sister more than ever now.

Given all the other signs, Ysabel shouldn't have been surprised at the results of the test, but she'd hoped that maybe she was wrong. Maybe she'd missed her period because of stress and maybe that same stress had caused her stomach to be upset every morning for the past month. Yeah, and maybe pigs could fly.

So she was pregnant. She'd handled bigger problems for Champion Shipping; she could handle the matter of a baby, no problem. Ysabel opened the door and holding the wand up for her sister to see, stepped out of the bathroom.

Delia squealed and hugged her sister so hard she couldn't breathe. "I'm so excited. I get to be an auntie!"

Ysabel pried her sister loose and stepped back. "I'm glad someone is excited. You know it changes everything."

Delia's smile stayed in place. "So? Is that such a bad thing?"

"Only when the baby happens to be Jackson Champion's." Ysabel turned and paced the short length of Delia's living room floor in her Houston apartment. "Jackson's back in town." She stopped and sucked in a long shaky breath. "Holy Mary Mother of God, I'm about to be jobless."

"And pregnant. Why resign now? It's just not like you to quit anything, *mi hermana.* You sure you want to give up the best job you'll ever have?"

"I can get another." Ysabel ran a hand through her sleek light-brown hair that had worked its way out of the normal tight ponytail at the nape of her neck.

"Paying as well as the rich *gringo* pays you?" Delia huffed. "Not likely."

"Don't call him *gringo,*" Ysabel automatically defended, dropping her hands to her sides, her fists tightening almost as much as the knot in her gut. "I'll find another job."

"So when are you going to tell him?" Her sister's brows winged upward. "The man has the right to know."

"I know, I know. I just can't risk letting him find out until I get far enough away from him."

"You really think he'll sue for custody? A playboy like Jackson Champion?"

Ysabel snorted. "The man keeps what's his. How do you think he got so rich?" He kept everything but the women in his life. For some reason he seemed to go through women like an addict goes through drugs. As far as Ysabel knew, she'd been around longer than any of the females close to him because she hadn't slept with him. Up until she made the *Big Mistake.*

"Ysabel, a child is different. It'll only slow him down."

"Not if he hires a nanny to raise it."

"Madre de Dios!" Delia crossed her arms over her chest. "No niece of mine will be raised by a perfect stranger. She has more than enough family in the area to raise her properly."

A sad smile lifted the corners of Ysabel's lips. "If all goes as I intend, I won't be in this area much longer."

Delia's eyes glistened. "But where will you go? Mama will be devastated if she doesn't get to spoil her first grandchild."

"It can't be helped. I won't lose my baby to anyone and I refuse to let him live a disrupted life of joint custody. He deserves a chance to be normal."

"Without a father?"

A pang of regret hit Ysabel square in the chest. "You and I both know Jackson rides life in the fast lane. He doesn't slow down long enough to notice anything but the business."

"He took enough time to get engaged."

"Only because it was on his scheduled time line of 'things to do before I die.' *I* penciled that in on his goals sheet when he wasn't looking one day. The man wouldn't have bothered if I hadn't." He'd totally missed the point, too. Ysabel could still feel the pain of watching him court woman after woman to find one who could provide the right corporate-wife image. He'd thought he'd found it in Jenna Nilsson. The witch. He'd even had Ysabel order an engagement ring for the woman. Wow. She shook her head. The memory still made her chest ache.

"Still, he did get engaged," Delia offered, wincing when Ysabel glared at her.

"For what it was worth!" Ysabel threw her arms in the air. "She was cheating on him from day one with an old boyfriend."

"You knew?"

Heat filled her cheeks. "Yeah, but I didn't have the heart to tell him. The man is clueless when it comes to women. He deserved her."

"Wow, and here I thought you were in love with the guy."

"Emphasis on past tense." Ysabel tossed her long, straight hair behind her shoulder. "I'm so over him."

"Right, that's why we've been talking about him for the past…" Delia glanced at her wristwatch, "thirty minutes."

Anger surged in Ysabel's chest. "Of all people, I thought you'd understand." She grabbed her purse and keys. "I'm going back to my place."

"You mean you're going back to the office, don't you?" Delia stood and followed Ysabel toward the door. "I don't know why you bother to keep an apartment, you practically live at the office. What are you going to do when you aren't working there anymore?"

"I *don't* live at the office and I *am* going to my apartment," Ysabel lied. She'd thought of a few things she'd wanted to straighten in Jackson's office before he showed up bright and early tomorrow.

Delia rolled her eyes. "Whatever."

As she reached for the door, her BlackBerry phone sang out the tune to *Mission Impossible,* the one she'd assigned to Jackson Champion's phone number. Her heart leaped into her throat, threatening to choke off her air. Ysabel dug in her purse for the device. "Where is that damned thing?"

"Calm down. He'll just keep ringing until you answer."

"I am calm!" Her fingers curled around the smooth black rectangle and she jerked it from her purse. For a moment she stared down at the name displayed across the miniature screen. Jackson Champion. Her breath caught in her throat and her fingers froze.

"Tell him, Ysabel. Tell him he's going to be a father."

"No, I can't. I have to quit first."

"You owe him that much."

Ysabel's hands shook. "I can't."

"At least answer the phone." Delia reached over her sister's shoulder and punched the Talk button. Then she leaned back against the wall, her brows rising up her smooth forehead in challenge.

"Ysabel? Ysabel! Are you there?" Jackson's voice barked out from the phone, jerking Ysabel out of her stupor.

Her hands shook as she pressed the phone to her ear. "Yes, I'm here."

"I need you down on the Bayport Terminal ASAP."

"Tell him," Delia whispered.

With Delia staring at her like her gaze could bore a hole into her conscience and Jackson's voice sending goose bumps across her skin, Ysabel shook her head. "I can't."

"What do you mean you can't?" Jackson asked. "I need you here now! And set up a meeting with the Aggie Four—Flint McKade and Akeem Abdul—for first thing in the morning. We've got big problems."

Ysabel resisted the urge to pull out a pen and jot down his instructions on the handy notepad she kept in her purse. She took a deep breath and straightened. It was now or never. "I quit."

"You what?" Jackson shouted.

Ysabel held the phone away from her ear until Jackson stopped yelling. "You heard me. I quit."

"That's what I thought you said. I don't know what's going on, but quitting at this point in time is not an option. Get down to the terminal now!"

It was just like the man to ignore her when *she* wanted something. Ysabel's stubborn streak set in with a vengeance. "Maybe you didn't understand what I just said."

"I understood just fine. I also have an employment contract that requires you give me two weeks notice."

Jackson paused, breathing heavily in the phone. “Look, I’ve had a lousy voyage with a man gone overboard. You sent me a trainee when I just got back in town, a crate full of what I thought were Rasnovian saddles just exploded in front of me, I have a dead man lying at my feet and the police are trying to arrest me for murder. Either you get down here now or I’ll sue you for breach of contract!”

Chapter Two

"I tell you, as far as I knew, the box contained hand-crafted Rasnovian saddles, not explosives." Jackson held his temper in check. Now was not the time for letting loose. Not with a rabid, foaming-at-the-mouth detective ready to accuse him of God knew what.

Detective Brody Green nodded toward the area surrounded in yellow crime scene ribbon, a snarling sneer lifting his upper lip. "Obviously, the box wasn't full of saddles. Our crime scene experts are leaning toward explosive detonators. Would you care to explain that?"

Jackson's back teeth ground together. "Champion Shipping doesn't transport explosives or detonators. Nowhere on my manifests was this indicated or I would have put a stop to it before it left the port of embarkation."

Brody's lips twisted into a mirthless smile. "Right. Still, I'll need to question you and all your employees involved in the loading and unloading of this particular ship. And I'll bet the Department of Homeland Security will want to talk with you as well."

"Fine. I have nothing to hide." Jackson ran a hand through his hair and looked around for the hundredth time. Where was Ysabel?

As if reading his mind, Tom, the executive rotation trainee, stared down at his watch. “She said she’d be here in twenty minutes. That was…twenty minutes ago.” He looked across the container yard and grinned. “Just like clockwork. How does she do it?”

The skin on the back of Jackson’s neck tingled. He didn’t need Tom’s words to tell him Ysabel was behind him. The day of reckoning had arrived and Jackson was no more prepared for it than he’d been two months ago. *Face the music, Champion.* Face it and lose her.

Sucking in a deep breath, he slowly turned.

Ysabel Sanchez strode across the heated concrete, her heels clicking, her long straight hair swaying around her shoulders in a curtain of light. Her full hips mesmerized him in the glare of the overhead lights.

Jackson’s mouth went dry and his groin tightened. Two months should have erased all physical yearnings he might have had for his executive assistant. It worked for all the other women he’d dated since he’d escaped puberty.

Ysabel wasn’t like the other women. She carried herself as if she were a Spanish queen, poker-straight, a haughty tilt to her chin, all business and no nonsense. Yes, that was the Ysabel he wanted to remember, but he had the other Ysabel branded in his mind and every nerve ending in his body since that night he’d spent in her arms.

Jackson had witnessed the softness and tenderness beneath the hard-core front she put on for Champion Shipping. Her Spanish heritage showed in the full curve of her breasts, the light olive tone of her skin and the rounded swell of her hips. Soft, moss-green eyes saw through his soul to the man he’d hidden beneath the rough exterior since his first day in the foster care system. The woman had a knack for reading minds. If Jackson believed in magic, Ysabel Sanchez was most definitely a witch.

His hands ached for the straight, light brown hair that

sifted through his fingers like strands of the finest silk. Beneath that cool, professional exterior lurked a fiery passion he hadn't seen before. The urge to pull her into his arms and pick up where they'd left off that night in his bed nearly blew away his icy reserve. Damn the woman to hell!

Jackson suppressed a moan and struggled to keep his hands in his pockets and maintain a professional face in front of the detective and the kid. Neither of them had a need to know of his transgression or his secret lust for his executive assistant. That was his cross to bear.

Without a "Hello" or a "Good to see you" after two months out of the office, Jackson skipped the niceties and went straight for dealing with the more immediate problem. "Detective Brody, Ysabel Sanchez."

Ysabel extended a graceful hand. "Detective."

The detective's eyes narrowed, his lips tightening. "Miss Sanchez." He didn't take her hand, just raised his notepad a degree and made a show of jotting down notes with the government black pen. "For the record, what is your relationship to Mr. Champion?" His glance skewered her.

Sensing the detective's rising ire, Jackson jumped in and answered for Ysabel. "Miss Sanchez is my executive assistant."

"Right." Detective Brody's gaze swept her from head to toe. "We should all have our very own *assistant* like Miss Sanchez, shouldn't we?" A nasty smile slid across his face as he glanced at Jackson and Tom.

Tom's brows rose and Jackson's anger spiked to dangerous.

"Don't overstep your boundaries, Detective," he warned, his fists clenching at his sides. If the man wasn't sporting a badge and a gun, Jackson would have taken a swing and to hell with the consequences.

But with a man being loaded onto a gurney for transportation to the morgue and an unexplained shipment of explosives, Jackson couldn't afford to lose his cool. No matter how warranted.

Ysabel's lips spread in a tight smile, her hand dropping to her side. "Could someone fill me in on what's going on?" She glanced up at Jackson, her gaze quickly shifting to Tom.

A twinge of annoyance made Jackson's chest tighten. So things weren't right with her either after the two-month absence. So much for time and distance diminishing memories. Damn, he had a lot of backpedaling to do to convince Ysabel not to leave Champion Shipping. And he had to. She'd become his lifeline to sanity in a business that seemed to have mushroomed overnight.

Detective Brody stepped between Jackson and Ysabel, completely ignoring her and addressing only Jackson. "Could you direct me to whoever is in charge of offloading the cargo from your ship?"

Longing for a minute or two with Ysabel to set the record straight—although a minute wouldn't be nearly enough—Jackson grit his teeth. "Sure." He turned to Tom. "Could you enlighten Miss Sanchez? I'll be back." He hoped.

"Yes, sir." Tom practically snapped to attention at the request.

A small smile quirked the corners of Ysabel's mouth.

Warmth filled Jackson's chest. That was the easy smile he remembered from his assistant before he'd slept with her. The warmth chilled almost as quickly as it came on. What he wouldn't give to put things back to the way they were.

He walked away, leading the detective toward Percy Pearson, the superintendent responsible for offloading the cargo.

All the while, he could feel her gaze boring into his back. Yeah, he'd screwed up. If only he could get her alone and try to undo the mistake and make things right again.

Fat chance.

YSABEL clutched her purse to keep her hands from shaking. Her first face-to-face contact with the man who had tied her in knots for the past two months hadn't gone nearly as she'd planned. She'd wanted to get him alone, hand over her resignation letter and walk out. A clean break. The less said the better. After he'd walked—no, make that ran—from his apartment following the most incredible night of sex she'd ever experienced, she had a firm understanding of what he expected from her.

Nothing. And she should expect nothing from him.

She might have been able to hide her true feelings and gone on, business-as-usual just like she had for the past two months—which hadn't been hard considering the man had disappeared off the face of the earth physically, if not so much by e-mail and voicemail. Unfortunately, the result of their mental lapse in their otherwise professional relationship was the baby growing in Ysabel's womb.

Her hand rose involuntarily to her still-flat midsection. She'd harbored more than a professional yearning for her boss pretty much since she'd gone to work for him five years ago. Determined to keep her job, she'd squelched her natural desires and pretended that his constant parade of different women didn't hurt. After a while she'd begun to see a pattern in his dating. Date twice and dump. The women he dated were primarily money-hungry gold-diggers, mostly interested in his wealth and social standing. They hadn't been given a chance to know the man beneath the charming, if somewhat distant, exterior.

Being his assistant, Ysabel saw what made Jackson Champion tick. When he didn't think she was looking or he didn't notice she was in the room, she saw what made him hurt and knew more than he'd ever tell her about himself by simply observing. In order to better understand her boss, she'd done a little digging of her own and knew he didn't have family. Tossed into the foster care system at the sensitive age of seven, he'd been passed from one family to the next, never feeling the love of parents.

When he'd been more than a bear to work for, Ysabel reminded herself that the man had to be hurting inside still, never having resolved issues of loneliness and neglect from his childhood.

The only family he claimed was the Aggie Four, the close-knit group of friends he'd made while attending college at Texas A&M. An unlikely group of young men brought together by hard times, their own isolation and a need for friendship. He'd die for any one of them and they'd do the same.

A wave of sadness washed over Ysabel. The Aggie Four was now down to three. Even after three months, Viktor Romanov and his family's deaths still burned in her chest. She could imagine how Jackson felt. As his assistant, Ysabel had been involved in many meetings of the Aggie Four and come to know the men Jackson valued as friends on a more personal basis.

The young prince of Rasnovia had struggled to bring his country into the future. With the help and financial support of the Aggie Four Foundation, they'd combined forces to rebuild the small nation after its split from Russia. Democracy and capitalism had been introduced and flourished until a group of rebels overran the Romanovs, killing them and plunging the country into civil war.

A lot had happened in the past few months to all of the Aggie Four. She suspected it was more than coincidence. She sucked in a deep breath and turned to Tom, a smile spreading across her face. "So, how was your first day with the great Jackson Champion?"

Tom grinned. "Wow, the man's a dynamo! I'd no sooner gotten here then he was leaping onto a forklift and chasing after another." He filled her in on what had happened with the runaway forklift driver and the ensuing explosion.

"Any idea what caused the explosion?"

Tom's smile faded. "The firefighters found evidence of detonators in the debris. The detonators might have set off the propane tank on the forklift. The man driving…" Tom shook his head. "Not pretty."

The wind shifted, pushing the damp smell of charred wood and flesh toward Ysabel. Her stomach lurched. She'd had only two bouts of nausea in the past two weeks. That plus the missed period had clued her into the fact she might be pregnant. She pressed a hand to her mouth and willed her stomach to behave.

Jackson stalked back toward Ysabel and Tom, his face set in tight lines. "Detective Brody is breathing fire and trying to come up with reasons to throw me in jail."

Ysabel swallowed hard, hoping her stomach would stay down. "Why?"

"He wants to pin the shipment of detonators on me and Champion Shipping, not to mention slapping a murder charge on me for the thief's death." Jackson ran his hand through his hair, making the dark locks stand on end. "I'll need that emergency meeting of the Aggie Four to happen first thing tomorrow morning."

She nodded, afraid to open her mouth. Another waft of pungent air hit her and her stomach burbled.

"We'll meet at McKade's ranch house. I could use the fresh air." He glanced around the container yard, shaking his head. "If the Department of Homeland Security sinks its teeth into this, it could shut down Champion Shipping indefinitely."

Ysabel knew they could and she understood the impact to their customers and cash flow. They could lose millions.

"The detective said I could go but to expect more questions." Jackson turned to Tom. "Did you drive your own car?"

"Yes, sir."

"No need for you to ruin your night. I'll see you tomorrow in the office."

Tom nodded, shooting a look from Jackson to Ysabel for confirmation.

Ysabel nodded. "See ya tomorrow."

"Okay, then." Tom gave them one last look as though he was afraid he'd miss something important or exciting by leaving, then he turned and strode toward the parking lot.

Alone at last, Ysabel quelled an urge to run after Tom. She didn't want to be alone with Jackson. So much remained unsaid and even though she'd wanted to clear the air, now that she had the opportunity, she couldn't find the backbone to make it happen.

Jackson fixed that for her. He took one more look around then headed off toward the parking lot, his pace eating the distance. "Come on, I want to swing by the office. I'll need a list of all employees working the shipment here and in Rasnovia where we picked up the saddles. Then we'll need to compile a list of anyone who might have it in for me, although I suspect that could be a long one. You don't make as much money as I do without accumulating enemies."

"I know this isn't a good time for you, but what part of 'I quit' didn't you understand?"

Jackson stopped dead still. He didn't turn, didn't look at her, but his shoulders stiffened. "And what part of 'lawsuit' didn't you understand? I need you now to help me figure out this mess. After that, we'll discuss your severance options." He didn't wait for her response, but continued toward the parking lot.

Ysabel hurried to keep up. She was used to racing after Jackson even on a good day. He didn't waste time and he didn't suffer slowpokes. If only her stomach would cooperate. Several steps brought her closer to the source of the smell and she saw the emergency personnel zipping the remains of the forklift driver into a body bag.

The charred skin and the stench of burned flesh sent Ysabel over the edge. Her stomach heaved. She dropped back and held her hand over her mouth. *No, please, not now.* Tears welled in her eyes.

Jackson, aware he'd lost her, stopped and turned, a frown creasing his brow. "Is everything all right, Miss Sanchez?"

She wanted to throw something at him and hug him at the same time. Damn the man! Of course everything wasn't *all right.* And she couldn't tell him why. She could only hope that she didn't disgrace herself in front of him. Now would *not* be the time to display weakness. "I'm fine. Just winded," she lied and quickly clamped her hand back over her mouth.

Unconvinced, he retraced his steps and stood in front of her. "Are you feeling well?"

His concerned tone pushed the tears over the edge of her eyelids. They made a trail down her cheeks. She couldn't move, couldn't straighten fully without losing the contents of her stomach. Damn, why had she eaten that pizza with her sister? If she never saw another pizza again, it would be too soon.

Jackson's fingers clamped around her wrist and he tugged her hand down. "What's wrong Ysabel? Why the tears?" He scanned her face and looked down at her bare lips. "Your face and lips are pale. Perhaps you should sit down. Do I need to have the emergency personnel check you out?"

"No!" Her eyes widened. Fear he'd find out her secret made her reply more sharply than she'd intended. "No, I'm fine. Really. I must have eaten something that didn't agree with my stomach." Beads of perspiration sprang up on her brow. If only he'd back off and leave her to handle her *problem* on her own.

Jackson pushed a strand of hair behind her ear. "I think you should see the EMT." He glanced behind her.

Afraid he'd wave down one of the emergency responders, Ysabel straightened, pulling her hands out of his and swallowing the bile rising in her throat. "No, really." She smoothed her hands down her skirt and forced a smile. "See? I'm better already."

His frown deepened as though he didn't believe her for a minute. Then he shrugged. "Okay, then let's get out of here."

Holy Mary, Mother of God, that smell! A gentle gust of coastal wind pushed the horrible smell across Ysabel's nostrils and she was a goner.

Her stomach upended, regurgitated pizza and apple juice launching from her insides. Poor, unsuspecting Jackson, who still stood directly in front of her, didn't have a chance.

She emptied the contents of her miserable gut on his trouser legs and shoes.

Jackson yelped and jumped back, but not soon enough to avoid her unplanned aim.

Unable to stop, Ysabel retched and retched, tears squeezing from between her tightly shut eyelids.

Then she felt hands pulling her hair back behind her head and warm fingers holding her shoulders. The same hands that had stroked every inch of her body with such smooth sensuality, now held her gently, providing support and comfort.

Jackson's tenderness did nothing to stem the flow of tears coursing down her face. If anything it only made them worse.

When her stomach let up, she was able to ease to an upright position. Embarrassed and certain she was an undignified disaster, Ysabel turned her back to Jackson. "Leave me alone," she moaned.

"I can't." He turned her toward him and patted her face with a clean cotton handkerchief, drying her tears and mopping up what he could of her gastronomic pyrotechnics.

"I'm sorry. I guess the smell got to me."

He smiled and smoothed her hair back from her face. "It happens to the best of us."

"But not to me." Ysabel grabbed his wrist and relieved him of the scrap of cloth, her lips pressing into a tight line. She couldn't take much more of his concern. Not when she had to get away from him and Champion Shipping forever. Not when her heart was shattering into a billion pieces.

What a dope. How could she be so stupid to fall so completely in love with her boss?

Chapter Three

Jackson insisted on driving Ysabel's compact red car with its sparkling set of rosary beads dangling from the rearview mirror, folding his six-foot-two-inch frame behind the driver's wheel. After tossing her cookies at the container yard, Ysabel was too shaky and weak to maneuver Houston traffic—or so Jackson reasoned after wrestling the keys from her stubborn, unwilling hands.

Truth was, his own hands were shaking and he wasn't feeling so steady. Not that he'd ever admit it. The great Jackson Champion had narrowly missed being blown up and faced the possibility of going to jail all upon return from a two-month sabbatical from his home in Houston. But what had him confused and shaking inside was Ysabel being so violently ill.

Ysabel, the one constant in his life. The person he'd come to depend on for just about everything. The woman he'd betrayed by taking her to his bed in a fit of rebound sex.

His hands gripped the wheel so tightly that his knuckles whitened. Late at night the traffic in Houston was almost tolerable. He didn't have to sit in jammed lines of vehicles and pray his car didn't overheat in the unrelenting Texas sun.

"I thought we were going back to the office." Ysabel sat beside him, her normal color almost returned to her face, back in professional mode and ready to take on any challenge. She was amazing.

And that was the problem. She didn't know when to take time out for herself. She'd let him drive her into the dirt before she cried uncle. His lips pressed together. Wasn't it time to take others into consideration for once? Had he been that incredibly selfish? "I'm taking you back to my place."

"No!"

Her sharp reply made him risk a glance her way. In the light from the dash, her eyes rounded and she gripped her purse like the rail on the edge of a sheer drop-off. Was she scared of him?

The muscles in his chest pulled tight, especially the big one conducting blood through his system. He'd done that. Made her afraid of him, but that didn't change the fact she'd thrown up in the container yard and that he didn't think she should be left alone. "You're not well."

"Now that my stomach is empty, I feel just fine. Let's get to the office and pull up that information you wanted. I can't—don't want to go to your place…." Her voice trailed off and she chewed on her lip.

Jackson's teeth ground together. She didn't trust him to keep his hands to himself. He couldn't blame her. After all, he'd taken advantage of her giving nature two months ago and taken her to his bed. He shouldn't expect her to warm to the idea of being alone with him in the place he'd slept with her.

It had all unraveled because of his stupid, selfish attitude. So his ego had taken a hit after being jilted by his fiancée. He'd had no right to demand Ysabel meet him at his place after office hours. He'd been so obsessed with finding out why he'd been summarily dismissed by Jenna without so much as an explanation. It completely set him aback. Why would any woman walk away from marriage to a billionaire?

Ysabel tried to make him see that he hadn't been marrying for the right reasons. Love had never entered the equation with Jenna. He'd decided he needed a wife and Jenna had seemed to fit the bill.

Ysabel had argued that good breeding stock, with connections in the corporate world wasn't enough to base a marriage on.

He'd countered that he didn't want children nor the messiness and entanglement of love. No one ever won when love was involved. All he wanted was a wife to grace his dinner table when he entertained his important guests.

Ysabel had been equally passionate that love and family meant everything and that he should be glad Jenna called it off before Jackson had made the biggest mistake of his life.

Ysabel's green eyes had flashed with her zeal. Having called her to his condo late at night, she'd come immediately, dressed in a jean skirt and a skimpy camisole.

For the first time in their five-year relationship as employee and boss, Jackson saw past the professional facade she donned every day, and he was shocked. Shocked and completely and irrevocably turned on. Ysabel wasn't the sensible, icy exec he'd thought she was. She was fiery and sassy, strong and determined.

That's when he'd kissed her. The kiss led to more until he woke up the next morning with her lying next to him in his bed.

He'd come awake staring down at her, thinking how right she looked with her light brown hair splayed across his pillow, and how he could get used to having her wake up next to him every day of his life.

Then reality hit him like a rockslide. He'd steered clear of relationships for a reason. They never worked. Divorce happened and kids were abandoned and grew up in broken homes or foster homes. Like him.

He couldn't do that to any kid of his, couldn't bring a child into the world knowing he might not be in his life to give him the love and support he'd need. Knowing that most marriages were doomed to failure.

"Okay, then, I'm taking you home. You don't need to be working when you're sick."

"Really, I'm fine." She reached out and laid her hand on his arm.

An electric shock ran from where she touched all the way through him, making his heartbeat increase, pumping blood like an overworked piston through his bloodstream. His gaze dropped to where her slender fingers curled around his sleeve.

As quickly as she'd placed it there, she withdrew her hand and clasped it in her lap, pleating the fabric of her linen skirt, clearly nervous in his company.

What a mess he'd made of his relationship with the only woman he'd ever trusted. He'd destroyed her trust.

"I don't want to go home," she insisted. "We need to work quickly to get this matter resolved."

A heavy lump settled in his gut and his jaw tightened. "So you can resign?" He took a turn a little faster than he'd intended, tires skidding on the still-hot pavement.

"*Madre de Dios,* Jackson! Could you slow it down? I'm not partial to getting car sick and I don't relish being involved in a wreck."

"Sorry." He slowed, taking the turns at a reasonable speed, recognizing the physical effort it took him to keep his foot from ramming the accelerator through the floorboard. Once he'd eased onto Interstate 45 heading into downtown Houston, he willed his fingers to loosen their grip.

"In answer to your previous question…" She sighed. "Yes. Partly. I want to have this situation resolved before I leave the corporation. More than that I want to stop whoever is using Champion Shipping to smuggle deadly and illegal substances." Her hands balled into fists. "We need to nail the bastard."

A smile pushed Jackson's lips up on the edges. That was his Ysabel. She had been the most loyal employee on his payroll, doing everything in her power to ensure the success of Champion Shipping.

"Thanks." He shot a glance her way. "I guess that's all I can expect."

Her shoulders rose and fell on a deep breath. "Jackson, we need to talk."

The lead weight in his gut flipped. "We need to talk" always meant she needed to say something and he wasn't going to like it. He risked another glance her way, trying to read the expression in her profile and failing miserably. Out of the far corner of his eye, he caught a flash of headlights glaring off his side mirror. Before he could turn and look, a dark sedan raced up beside the compact car and slammed into the driver's side.

Having relaxed his grip on the wheel, Jackson wasn't prepared for the impact. The car jolted and skidded to the side, bounced against the concrete guard rail and swerved across three lanes of traffic. The dark sedan slammed into the back panel, setting the car into a spin.

"Holy Jesus!" Ysabel cried out, bracing her hands against the dash.

Jackson fought to regain control of the car, bringing it to a hair-raising stop on the far shoulder against a concrete barricade, facing oncoming traffic.

The smell of burned rubber and exhaust fumes filled the interior of the small car.

Ysabel scrambled for the door handle, frantically trying to unlock it.

"Stay in the car, Izzy." He grabbed her hand, stopping her crazed attempt to get out. "We don't know if that guy will come back and hit us again."

"I don't care. I have to get out." She flung the door open and it crashed into the concrete. Then she dived out onto the ground.

Jackson jumped out and rounded the car.

Ysabel crouched on her hands and knees heaving, her entire body shaking with the effort. But nothing came up. The sound of her tortured gasps tore at Jackson's heart.

He dropped to the ground and gathered her against him. "Izzy, sweetheart, breathe." He sat back on the pavement, settling her in his lap. "Breathe, baby."

Her pale face glowed in the moonlight, her cheeks shining with tears. "I'm sorry."

"What have you got to be sorry about? I should have been paying attention."

"I'm not usually sick."

"I know, and that has me worried. I'm taking you to the hospital."

She stiffened. "No."

"I won't take no for an answer." He climbed to his feet, carrying Ysabel with him. "We're going to the hospital. This isn't right."

"No. I'll refuse treatment. Just take me home."

"Okay, so no hospital. But you're going home and I'm calling in my physician. End of subject."

She stared at him, her face close enough to kiss, her eyes rounded, with dark smudges beneath them.

The need to take her lips was more than an urge, it was an obsession. If he didn't think she'd slap his face, he'd have followed his desire. But Ysabel had had more than enough excitement for one day. He set her in the car and strapped on her seat belt, adjusting her seat back so that she lay fully reclined. "Don't worry about a thing. I'll take care of you."

AN hour later, Jackson had reported the hit and run to the police and managed to get the corporate physician to pay a house call at Ysabel's apartment. With Jackson pacing the floor of her compact living room, Ysabel lay on her bed behind her closed bedroom door, a cold stethoscope pressed to her chest, willing the doctor to declare her fit and get the hell out.

Dr. Adams folded his stethoscope and shoved it into his bag. "How long have you known?"

"Known what?" Ysabel asked, her gaze darting to the closed door of her bedroom. Could Jackson hear their words through the wooden panels? She couldn't afford for him to find out now. She had to think, make plans and get the hell out of Houston.

"It doesn't take a brain surgeon to figure this out." Jackson's corporate physician smiled as if making a joke. "You've missed a period and you're throwing up, otherwise you're perfectly healthy."

She buttoned her shirt and climbed off the bed, putting distance between them. "I don't know what you're talking about."

"I've done the math. Question is, have you?" He waited, unmoving.

She teetered on the edge of lying again, but she'd had enough lying. "How accurate are home pregnancy tests?" Ysabel asked, her voice a soft whisper.

"They've been pretty accurate as long as you've gone past a period. I take it you've tested positive for pregnancy?"

Ysabel spun, a finger to her lips. "Shhh! I don't want anyone to know."

"You mean you don't want Jackson to know?"

"That's not what I said," she argued, her words guarded, her brows drawing together. The doctor had guessed about her pregnancy, would he also guess the father of the child to be Jackson Champion?

Dr. Adams laid a hand on her shoulder. "You don't have to worry. I respect doctor–patient confidentiality. Your secret is safe with me."

"Thanks." Ysabel swallowed the vile taste of guilt and nodded. "What are you going to tell Mr. Champion?"

"I'll tell him it *might* have been a mild case of food poisoning and that you'll be fine. Not the truth but not exactly a lie." He squeezed her shoulders in a reassuring grip. "Ysabel, I hope you have the good sense to let the father in on your secret. A man has a right to know he's got a child on the way."

She stared up into the man's eyes, tears forming in her own. After a long pause, she dipped her head. "I will." As soon as she knew how she could retain custody when the father of her child could buy half of Houston with the amount of money he had.

"Fair enough." Dr. Adams opened the door and stepped out into Ysabel's small living area decorated in bold shades of red, yellow and orange. "She's fine, Jackson. Nothing a good night's sleep won't cure."

"But why was she throwing up?"

"Hard to say without blood tests, probably food poisoning, but it appears as if the worst has passed."

"Don't you think we should take her to the hospital and run those blood tests?" Jackson stared over Dr. Adams's shoulder to where Ysabel stood in the doorway.

Butterflies turned somersaults in Ysabel's stomach. "I told you it was nothing. We don't need to waste any more of the doctor's time or burden the hospital with nothing but a little bit of food poisoning. Go home, Mr. Champion. Like the doctor said, I could use a little rest."

Jackson's forehead furrowed. "I'm staying."

"If you stay, I'm sure to get no rest at all." As soon as the words came out of her mouth, Ysabel realized how they could be misinterpreted and her face heated. "Just leave. I'll be at work bright and early in the morning."

"Take the day off. I can survive without you for a day." He plunked his cowboy hat on his head. "I don't like leaving you."

"*Madre de Dios!* You don't live here and I haven't invited

you to stay. So get out." She softened her words with a twisted smile.

The doctor nodded. "Leave the girl alone and go home, Jackson. She'll be fine."

His steps dragging, Jackson allowed the doctor to escort him out of Ysabel's apartment. Not until the door was closed behind them and their footsteps faded down the hallway, did Ysabel let out the breath she'd been holding.

If she'd known that was what it would be like to see Jackson again, she'd have asked him to stay away longer. Too tired to think, she stripped, took a quick shower and fell into her bed.

As her eyes closed, she thought of all that had happened in the past three hours.

She'd learned she was pregnant, tendered her resignation, Jackson had nearly been killed and they'd almost been run off the road by a homicidal maniac.

Yup, that pretty much summed up the day. She yawned, wondering what was in store for the next morning. Reaching down, she pulled the sheet up over her head as though that would keep the chaos away.

"FLINT? It's Jackson. We need to meet."

Dr. Adams had given him a ride back to the building he owned in downtown Houston where he had the penthouse condo on the twenty-fifth floor. He preferred the wide-open spaces of his ranch west of Houston, but his business necessitated a residence in the city.

Standing at the floor-to-ceiling window in nothing but his boxer shorts, he pressed the cell phone to his ear.

"Do you know what time it is?" Flint McKade grumbled into his ear.

"Two in the morning. I know it's late and I'm sorry to wake you, but I've got some serious problems. I'm going to need the help of the Aggie Four." His hand tightened as it hit him in a fresh wave of anger and sorrow that the Aggie Four was down to three now. Viktor's loss hit him harder when he needed the full support of the friends he'd grown to love and respect. He missed Viktor.

As much as he missed his dead friend, he needed the support of the ones still living. If he didn't find out who planted the detonators in that container, he'd not only be up on charges of murder for the death of the forklift driver, but he'd also be the prime suspect in the possible plot to commit an act of terrorism against the United States.

"What's the problem? Want me to come now?" Flint's voice perked up, all sleepiness vanishing.

"No, that's not necessary. Contact Akeem and let him know we're having an emergency meeting tomorrow at your ranch at noon."

"Will do." Flint paused. "You know we're with you, buddy, whatever the problem. Hang in there. There's nothing we can't overcome." That had been their mantra throughout school at Texas A&M. The mantra had followed them through the years of building their empires.

Jackson's throat tightened. He hoped they could overcome this mess, which right now seemed insurmountable.

FROM the rented apartment on the twenty-third floor, a man stood in darkness, staring through his binoculars at the building two blocks away. Things were going according to plan. The Department of Homeland Security would be heating up and all indications should point to the three remaining members of the Aggie Four.

Jackson Champion stood silhouetted against the window of his condo, unashamed of his nakedness and unaware he was being watched at that very moment. He appeared to be talking on his cell phone. Probably talking to one of his cronies about the accident at the terminal.

The hit and run on the interstate wasn't part of the plan, but he chalked it up to an added bonus. Jackson ought to be feeling the squeeze by now. If not, he would be soon.

Chapter Four

"Tom, I need you to scan the employee files of the ship that delivered that cargo yesterday. I want a list of all the employees, their backgrounds and the date they started work for Champion Shipping."

"Yes, ma'am." Tom sat behind his desk outside Ysabel's office and logged on to the computer. "I heard about the accident on the freeway last night. I'm glad no one was injured."

"Yeah." So was Ysabel. They had been too close to death for her liking. Now that she was carrying a baby, she had to be more careful—think of someone beside herself in the equation.

She paced the floor of her office, having arrived later than intended. For the first time in the five years she'd worked for Champion Shipping, she just couldn't drag herself out of bed at her usual five o'clock in the morning. Partly because of the late night at the terminal and mostly because of the exhaustion of the first trimester of pregnancy.

She'd Googled pregnancy online and read about it while nibbling on crackers, hoping to keep her stomach down when every little smell set her off. All she needed was to throw up in front of Jackson again and he'd have an ambulance there so fast she wouldn't know what hit her. No, she had to keep her morning sickness from him at all costs. The best way would be to avoid him altogether.

"Miss Sanchez!" Jackson bellowed from the corner office next to hers.

So much for avoiding the man. As she left her office, she paused, staring at Tom, trying to think of a way to keep from being alone in the same room with Jackson. At the rate she was going, he'd have her secret figured out. A man who'd accumulated as much wealth as Jackson had wasn't a complete moron. She smiled at the younger man. "Tom, will you go see what Mr. Champion wants and tell him I had to run an errand?"

Tom cast a glance toward the billionaire's office, a frown furrowing his unlined forehead. "Are you sure? He called for you."

Guilt smacked her in the gut. She reasoned that the consequences of Jackson learning about her secret outweighed the guilt in her conscience.

"Miss Sanchez!"

Ysabel jumped and rolled her eyes. "*Fine*. I'll see what the man wants." She trudged her way toward his office, her feet dragging with every step. With her hand on the doorknob, she squared her shoulders and pushed the door wide. "Mr. Champion, is there something I could get you?"

"I thought I told you to take the day off." He stood with his arms crossed over his chest, his feet wide, his back to the glass windows that were openly displaying a gloriously bright morning in downtown Houston.

Ysabel blinked, trying to read Jackson's expression. The glare of light from the windows effectively cast his face in the shadows and more likely exposed every line, crease and smudge of her own face in minute detail. From the glance in her bathroom mirror that morning, she wasn't looking her best. Far from it. "If it makes you feel better, I slept in. I just got here."

His eyes narrowed and she squirmed under his inspection. "How are you feeling this morning?"

She pushed her lips into a cheerful smile she didn't nearly

feel. "Completely fine." *As long as I don't look at food before noon.*

He stared at her hard for another ten seconds before his arms fell to his sides. Jackson dropped into the plush leather seat behind the massive desk crafted by an artist in south Texas from the finest mesquite available in the state. "Good, then I'll need you to come with me when I meet with the Aggie Four at noon.

Her breath caught in her throat and she swallowed to clear it. "Here in Houston?" She crossed her fingers behind her back, praying the group would meet nearby, otherwise she'd be stuck in Jackson's truck, alone with the man for the forty-five minutes to an hour it took to reach the ranch west of Houston.

"We're meeting at the Diamondback. Be ready to go in forty-five minutes." His focus shifted to the papers requiring immediate attention on his desk, his attitude one of dismissal.

Grateful for the respite, Ysabel turned toward the door. Before she could exit, two men stepped into the doorframe, blocking her path.

"Mr. Jackson?" The first one crossed the threshold.

Ysabel recognized him as Detective Brody Green from the container yard the previous evening. Her chest tightened. Why would they come to Champion Shipping instead of having Jackson come to them to give his statement?

Instead of slipping out of the office to leave Jackson alone, she stepped back and allowed the lawmen to enter.

Jackson stood. "Detective Green, I hope you have some good news for me."

The man's mouth tightened. "Sorry, Mr. Champion. Can't say that I have." He jerked his head toward the man beside him. "Fielding?"

The man stepped forward, his hand extended to Jackson.

"Mr. Champion, I'm Special Agent Bob Fielding, with the Federal Bureau of Investigations. I'm working this case in conjunction with the Department of Homeland Security."

Ysabel's heart dropped to her stomach. Was the other shoe about to fall? Would they shut down Champion Shipping?

"Mr. Fielding. What can I do for you?" Jackson asked, his voice polite, his expression that of an expert poker player.

The agent withdrew a pad and pen from his jacket pocket. "I have a few questions for you regarding the explosion yesterday. That and I regret to inform you that we'll have to shut down the offloading of the remaining cargo on your ship until it has been thoroughly examined." Fielding tapped his pen to his note pad. "This incident, the radiation-poisoning incident at the Diamondback Ranch, plus the explosion and deaths of three men on one of your airplanes raises a boatload of other questions for the Aggie Four Foundation. Oh, and I also heard that you had a man go overboard on the sail across the ocean."

Jackson's face remained unflinching, his gaze shifting from Agent Fielding to Detective Green. The only indication of his ire was the muscle twitching in his jaw.

Familiar with his ability to hide all emotion, Ysabel picked up on the dangerous level of anger brewing beneath the surface. She stepped forward in hopes of diffusing the situation. "Do you have any idea how long the investigation will take? You do understand that time is money. By shutting down the offloading of the ship, you tie up the berth for longer than originally contracted."

"I'm sorry, Miss—" Fielding glanced from Jackson to Ysabel.

Ysabel redirected his attention to her by shoving a hand in his direction. "I'm Ysabel Sanchez, Mr. Champion's executive assistant. Do we need to call in our legal staff?"

Fielding's brows rose with his shoulders. "That might be

a possibility. We have four agents assigned to the ship along with two sniffing dogs. We should be able to complete our scan in a day. Two tops."

"If you see that it will go longer, please let us know at the earliest possible moment. Other ships use the Port of Houston and the port maintains a tight schedule." She moved toward the door. "If that's all..." She waved toward the door. "I'll see you out."

Detective Green practically snarled at Ysabel. "Oh no you don't. That's far from *all.* And you'll definitely want to bring in your legal staff for what I have to say."

"And what is that?" Jackson stepped between Detective Green and Ysabel, his voice dangerously low.

"That forklift driver who died last night, Stephan Kenig, was dead before he crashed. Someone shot him in the head."

Ysabel gasped.

Jackson remained stoic. "And this has *what* to do with me?"

Green pinned Jackson with a narrow-eyed stare. "We found a gun close by. My bet is that the ballistics will match with the bullet we found in the victim."

Ysabel frowned. The man who died was the criminal, not so much a victim, and Detective Green was now treating Jackson like he was the criminal. "Again, what does this have to do with Mr. Champion?"

"Please, get to the point," Jackson said, his voice sharp, his fingers tightening into a fist.

"The point is," Detective Brody's mouth turned up in a smirk, "we ran a scan on the serial number. The SIG SAUER registration is in the name of Jackson Champion. Mr. Champion, we need you to come with us to the sheriff's office. We'll need fingerprints to match with those we found on the gun."

"I don't know what's going on here, but I didn't shoot

that man. I was chasing him because I thought he was stealing my saddles."

Green snorted. "Nevertheless, your gun appears to be the one that killed him."

"Detective." Tom Walker stood in the open doorway. "I was with Mr. Jackson during the chase. I can vouch for him. He didn't have a gun and he didn't shoot the other forklift driver."

Green didn't look happy to hear Tom's admission. "Are you willing to sign a statement to that effect?"

Tom's shoulders straightened until he looked as though he was a soldier standing at attention. "Absolutely."

"You'll have to come to headquarters, as well. I'll need a sworn statement from both you and Champion."

Jackson nodded toward Ysabel. "Call my attorney and meet me there."

Ysabel nodded as Detective Green slammed cuffs onto Jackson's wrists.

Jackson's jaw tightened, but he didn't wince.

Anger surged inside Ysabel at the rough treatment. "Is that necessary? Mr. Walker just told you Mr. Champion didn't do it. I'm sure he won't try to run from the law for something he isn't guilty of."

The detective snapped the cuffs shut. "Procedure."

Agent Fielding shook his head. "I don't think that's necessary."

"This is a local issue. If you have a problem with the way I handle it, take it up with my supervisor." Green shoved Jackson through the door.

Ysabel could have sworn Detective Green smiled as he led Jackson through the bay of offices, past Champion Shipping employees, treating Jackson like a common criminal.

Ysabel ran to her office, snatching up her BlackBerry and purse. "Come on, Tom, let's get there."

The elevator Jackson and the lawmen got into closed before she could get on. She jammed her finger on the down button, her toe tapping against the granite tiles while she waited for another car and someone to answer her call to the corporate law firm.

"Halston, Young and Franklin Law Firm, how may I help you?" a perky secretary said into her ear as the elevator door dinged open.

"This is Ysabel Sanchez with Champion Shipping. Mr. Jackson requests the immediate presence of Mr. Young at the sheriff's office. Let me stress, Mr. Young needs to be there ASAP."

"I CAN'T believe Detective Green dragged you into the station." Flint McKade paced the floor of his spacious office, his cowboy boots tapping against the wood flooring.

Jackson rubbed the back of his neck, tension pulling at the muscles there. "Yeah, he seemed to get a big kick out of parading me through the office in cuffs. My employees will get a good laugh at that." He shrugged, unfazed by the memory of his startled employees. Ysabel would give them the straight scoop. "Thank goodness I had a witness riding on the back of my forklift or I'd have been at the sheriff's office a lot longer than the two hours it took my lawyer to straighten out the mess." Jackson turned toward the door to the office. Where had Ysabel disappeared to? "What I'm pissed about is that someone broke into my home and stole my gun."

"I thought you had a brand-new security system installed last year?" Akeem Abdul leaned against the wood-paneled walls, his boots crossed at the ankle, looking laid back except for the intensity in his dark eyes. If not for the jeans, boots and denim shirt, he'd appear the most ferocious sheik in any desert—fierce and loyal to his friends.

"I did. I used the firm Deke recommended. They installed a state-of-the-art system. No one should have been able to enter without detection." His friend from college days at Texas A&M, Deke Norton, had promised him no one could penetrate the system without his explicit permission. Jackson smacked his hat against his leg. "I've got a call into Deke's security specialist to review the entire system."

Flint stopped in mid-pace. "What is Homeland Security saying?"

"The FBI agent in charge made noises that the detonators, the plane explosion, the man going overboard on my ship and the radioactive traces you found here at the ranch are making it look bad for the Aggie Four Foundation. They'll be poking around all of us with questions soon."

Flint nodded. "That explains the call I had from your man Fielding this morning. He wants to meet with me this afternoon. He'll be working the angle of the radiation-contaminated parts they found in the horse blankets smuggled with that last shipment of Arabians out of the Middle East. It's been three months and they still haven't pinned who brought in those parts. They suspect it's the rebel faction that staged the coup in Rasnovia, but they have no firm proof."

"Gentlemen, the evidence is looking bad for us." Jackson slapped his hat against his jeans again, frustration making him wish he could punch something or someone. "For me in particular, since my shipping business is the one bringing in the bad goods."

"You're not in this alone." Akeem pushed away from the wall, strode across the floor and held out a hand to Jackson.

Jackson clasped it with both hands. "Thanks."

"That's right," Flint said, closing the distance and covering their joined hands with his own. "The Aggie Four is a team and we'll see this thing through."

"This is reassuring." Ysabel walked in carrying a tray of

iced tea Flint's cook, Lucinda, had prepared. "Have you figured out how to keep our man Jackson out of jail?"

Akeem reached for the tea, "Nah, we thought we'd let him rot there, while we spend his fortune."

"Yeah," Flint grinned. "The man has more than enough to share."

Ysabel rolled her eyes. "Like you two don't? Give me a break. No, really, what are you planning?"

Flint abandoned his smile, deep furrows etched across his forehead. "We plan a thorough search into our employee databases for answers to who's behind the smuggling."

"You two have had dealings with Detective Green before, haven't you?" Ysabel asked.

Akeem nodded. "Sure, he was on the case when Flint's sister Taylor's son, Christopher, was kidnapped."

"Yeah and he was there to investigate the explosion and shootings on the airplane that took the lives of three of my men," Flint added.

Jackson twisted the brim of his cowboy hat. "I don't trust the man."

"Any reason in particular?" Akeem asked.

"He seemed more than happy to jump on any excuse to bust me."

"I noticed that." Ysabel set her tea glass on a coaster. "It was as though he enjoyed seeing you booked and fingerprinted. He was outright angry when Tom's sworn statement kept you from occupying a jail cell."

"Do you still have connections inside the sheriff's office?" Akeem asked.

Jackson nodded to Ysabel. "That would be Ysabel's connection. One of your cousins, right?"

"Mitch Stanford. He's married to my cousin Rosa." Ysabel retrieved her BlackBerry from her purse and scanned the contact names until she found Mitch. "I'll give him a call and ask him to keep an eye open for anything that might surface concerning the case."

"Thanks." Jackson stared down at his Stetson, lost in thought. "Why are these things happening to us?"

"It's as if someone has it in for the Aggie Four Foundation, maybe us in particular," Akeem said, as he gazed out the window at the acres of lush green pastures.

"You think they had anything to do with Viktor's death?" Flint paused to stare at a picture hanging on the wall of the four of them when they were in college, arms linked over their shoulders, all wearing swim trunks on South Padre beach. The senior trip they'd scrimped and saved their hard-earned money for.

Jackson had a copy on his desk in his office. The Aggie Four had been there for him since they'd all vowed to become billionaires back in their college days. And damned if they didn't all make it.

"Viktor's death was half a world away in Rasnovia," Ysabel observed, her hand poised over the BlackBerry.

Her voice jerked Jackson out of his thoughts, his head snapped up and he stared across at her. A raw, festering ache reverberated through his body at the sight of her. Ysabel had tendered her resignation.

Yet she sat on the leather, wingback chair, her slim knees crossed, long gorgeous legs tipped in sexy black heels. She could wear a brown paper bag and still make a man's blood boil.

He pulled his gaze from those legs and forced his mind away from how they'd wrapped around his waist and how she'd cried out his name in lust-filled passion. No, now wasn't the time to get a rise or worry about how he could keep his prized executive assistant.

"That's true. Viktor and his family were murdered in Rasnovia." Jackson's chest tightened, but he forced himself to move on. "The smuggling also *began* half a world away. The shipment with the saddles and detonators originated in Rasnovia."

Akeem perched on the edge of Flint's desk. "I'm amazed you were able to ship anything out of Rasnovia with a civil war ravaging the country since the royal family's death."

"Given what the police found in that box, I'm beginning to think it's not so amazing." Jackson captured Ysabel's gaze. "Have you heard anything on that database scan of employees?"

"Not yet. I have Tom working it."

"You sure he's the man for the job? He's so new to the company."

"If you'd read his résumé, you'd have noticed he won numerous awards for breaking into supposedly air-tight computer security systems. He knows his way around a computer."

Jackson shook his head and stared at her as if she'd lost her mind. "You hired a hacker?"

"He's only a hacker in a good way. Pinkerton confirmed his background check. Besides, I liked him."

A surge of something akin to anger pushed through Jackson, making him want to lash out at the young guy Ysabel had hired. "You trust him inside Champion Shipping's computer systems?"

"Absolutely." She crossed her arms over her chest, the stubborn tilt to her chin one he'd seen before when she'd fought for a point in which she believed.

Flint grinned at the exchange. "You know Ysabel's instincts have paid off for you in more instances than you can count. You better keep her on the payroll."

Akeem chuckled. "Yeah, I'd hate to see her go to work for the competition."

Their seemingly innocuous comments hit Jackson square in the gut. What they didn't know was that Ysabel had more or less given her two-week notice. Although the noncompete clause in her contract would keep her from going to work for his competitors, she wouldn't be working for him anymore. And that's what he didn't want to think about or acknowledge.

"What about the road-rage incident last night?" Ysabel reminded him. "If someone has it in for you all, wouldn't they try to run the rest of you off the road, as well?"

Akeem nodded. "Sadly, when you've clawed your way to the top like we have, you accumulate enemies along the way. Some even out to cause us trouble for the cash."

"Christopher's kidnapping." Ysabel's hand rose to cover her stomach, making Jackson think she might be having a relapse of yesterday's sickness. Instinctively, he moved forward several steps before he stopped himself. She'd be ticked if he hovered over her like he had yesterday. But that couldn't stop him from keeping a close eye on her.

"What got me about that whole kidnapping scare was that the police seemed to know what was going to happen almost before it did," Flint said.

"Like how did they know where the kidnappers were taking the boy almost before Taylor and I got there?" Akeem asked.

"An insider leaking it out," Flint stated. It was his nephew who'd been in danger, his sister who'd gone after him with only Akeem to protect her. Akeem had been there for her. Both Flint and Jackson would trust the Texas sheik with their own lives and had on more than one occasion.

Jackson shook his head. "More like an insider giving the orders." He shot a look toward Ysabel.

"I'm on it boss. I'll let my cousin know to keep a look out for a dirty cop while I'm asking him to keep us posted on the investigation."

"*Señor* McKade?" Lucinda appeared at the door.

Flint nodded toward the housekeeper/cook. "Yes, what is it?"

"*Señor* Norton is here to see you."

"Deke?" Flint's brows tugged inward. "I don't remember scheduling a meeting with Deke." He shrugged. "Send him in. Maybe he can shed some light on this mess."

Jackson raised a hand. "I'd rather not mention it yet. I want to find out more before we share inside information outside this room. If word gets out to the press that Champion Shipping and the Aggie Four Foundation are involved in international terrorism, we could be ruined."

"And you don't want our financial adviser to know this." Flint nodded. "Gotcha." He tipped his head to Lucinda. "Show him in."

"*Sí, señor.*" She backed out of the doorway and hurried away.

"Not that I don't trust Deke, but he is a financial adviser after all. I don't want to put him in the position of knowing something about the market before it happens." Jackson stared around the room at each of the individuals there. "Because of his friendship with all of us it could be considered insider trading."

A moment later, Deke Norton opened the door and strode in. "Did you see the news?" He walked across to the flat-screen, plasma television set hanging on the wall over the fireplace and pressed the power button.

"Why?" Jackson hadn't had time to watch the news between running his corporation, spending two hours at the Harris County Sheriff's Office and then heading out to the Diamondback Ranch to meet with the Aggie Four. Who had time to watch the news when your world was crumbling around you?

"You'll want to see this." Deke nodded toward the screen.

A local Houston news anchor blinked into focus. "Late breaking news." He glanced down at a sheet of paper in his hand. "Houston shipping mogul and former most eligible Texas bachelor, Jackson Champion, was taken into custody today as a possible suspect in the murder of a forklift driver last night at the Port of Houston."

"Damn." Jackson slapped his Stetson against his knee.

"Shh!" Deke turned up the volume. "It gets worse."

"Preliminary investigations indicate that he may have shot the man to silence him after the forklift driver discovered a smuggled shipment of detonators coming off a Champion Shipping cargo ship. Houston police detectives, the sheriff's office and Homeland Security are scrambling to find out just how bad the threat is." The reporter stared into the camera. "The shipping giant who already owns half of Houston, is under FBI, Houston P.D. and Homeland Security scrutiny."

Akeem shook his fist at the screen. "Where did they get that crap?"

"Here we go again," Flint punched the Power button, switching the television off. "The press making a mockery out of our judicial system. Since when were they elected judge, jury and executioner? Makes you sound guilty without all the evidence."

"How did they get that information?" Akeem asked. "It's not public knowledge, is it?"

"Only an insider in the investigation would have that information to peddle." Once again Jackson's gaze shot to Ysabel.

She opened her mouth to tell him she'd ask her cousin José, who worked at that particular television station, to get with her cousin at the sheriff's department to find out who the anchor's source was. A glance at Deke made her close her lips and rethink her words. "I'll get on it."

"Let me guess..." Akeem shook his head, smiling. "Another cousin?"

Flint asked, "How many cousins do you have, Ysabel?"

She stood, digging her cell phone out of her purse. "Too many to count." Most of her family and extended family lived in the Houston area. She'd hate to leave them to start over by herself.

Once outside Flint's office, Ysabel breathed a sigh of relief. Torn between wanting to know what was going on and wanting to be as far away from Jackson as possible, she felt as though her insides were tied in knots. She worked her way back to the kitchen where Lucinda was preparing a light snack for the men.

Lucinda handed her dry saltines. "Take these. They will help settle your stomach."

"Why do you think I need them?"

"It happens to most women during the early months. The nausea, the upset tummy."

Ysabel stared down at her belly. "How did you—"

"Know you are with child?" Lucinda laughed and lifted the tray. "I could see it in your face, in the way you hold your hand over *la niña* and the way you stare at *Señor* Jackson." She patted Ysabel's belly. "She will be beautiful like her mama and papa."

Ysabel dropped into a chair, the crackers clutched in her hand. If Lucinda could tell just by looking at her, what was to keep Jackson from knowing?

She dragged in a deep breath and fought back the tears so ready to fall at just about anything. Shoving a cracker in her mouth, she focused on keeping it down while she thumbed through her BlackBerry for her cousins' numbers. This smuggling stuff had to resolve quickly so that she could get on with her life and away from Jackson.

Chapter Five

"Mr. Champion, I think I've found something." Tom Walker jumped up from his desk and followed Jackson into his office. The staff had left for the day, except for the young manager trainee.

Ysabel had insisted on stopping at her apartment on their way back from the Diamondback Ranch, something about a date with her sister.

How could she consider a date with her sister more important than what was happening to Champion Shipping? And although she'd insisted they needed to talk the night before, she'd done anything but talk on the way back from the ranch.

She'd spoken less than ten words the entire hour and a half it took them to get back to Houston in rush-hour traffic. Jackson didn't like it. He'd rather she ranted and raved like any self-respecting woman angry at not getting her way. At least then he might get a clue as to what was going on in her convoluted head.

But she'd sat in the passenger seat of his pickup, her hands folded in her lap, her focus on the windshield, not him. He'd tried several times to start a conversation. He'd asked about the cousins she'd called, she'd answered in monosyllables. Gone was her willingness to exchange ideas with him, to argue about politics and condemn his lack of a personal life.

By the time they'd reached Houston, he was so frustrated he'd wanted to grab her by the shoulders and shake her out of the silent treatment.

But she'd flung the truck door open and jumped out before he could stop her. Damned woman!

"Sir? Did you want to hear what I found?" Tom repeated.

"Yes, yes, of course." Jackson turned toward the eager young man, much like himself at the tender age of twenty-two. "What did you find?"

"I did a scan on all employees hired in the past six months, both here in Houston and also in several of your Middle Eastern locations, as well as those in Rasnovia."

Jackson's spirits improved slightly, his attention firmly rooted on the trainee. "And?"

"I pulled up the employee photographs of twenty people and sent them to Miss Sanchez's cousin at the Harris County Sheriff's Office and he ran it through a database of persons of interest." Tom smiled. "We got a hit on four of the men. One of them was the forklift driver, Stephan Kenig. They match up with a group the CIA have been tracking who've been spotted in a Syrian terrorist training camp in the past year." The young man handed him a computer printout with employee personal data and the pictures of the men.

Jackson glanced at the names and shook his head, amazed at the amount of information the guy had accumulated in such a short time. "Her cousin told you all that?"

Tom shrugged. "I've been on the computer and phone most of the day passing information. But it was Miss Sanchez who called and told me what her cousin found out. She wanted me to tell you that she was on her way back to the office and should be here in about…" Tom glanced down at his watch and looked outside Jackson's door. "Now." He grinned and stepped out of the doorway.

Ysabel walked into the office. Gone was her professionally tailored skirt suit. In its place was a pair of faded blue jeans and an oversize sweatshirt, the neckline torn out and hanging over one shoulder like an eighties dance queen. She looked young and vulnerable, more like a teen from the barrio than a high-powered executive assistant. She dumped her purse in a chair and pushed her sleeves up past her elbows. "Did you look up the address on the man here in Houston?"

"Got it." Tom handed her a sheet of paper. "Greg Voleski, aka Gregor Volsky."

"Have you passed the addresses on to my cousin at the sheriff's office yet?" she asked.

The young man handed her a copy of the papers he'd given to Jackson. "I was just about to hit send on the e-mail when Mr. Champion showed up."

Ysabel pressed her lips together. "Send it and then go home for the evening. You've done more than enough for the day."

"But if there's anything else I can do…" Tom stared from Jackson to Ysabel, his gaze stopping with Ysabel as though she was the boss, not Jackson.

Jackson fought the smile threatening to break through. Ysabel ran the corporation as well as he did. Sometimes better. And his employees respected her abilities and intelligence.

Ysabel smiled at the trainee. "Get some rest. I need you sharp for whatever comes up tomorrow. Now get that info to my cousin, pronto!"

Tom darted through the door.

Jackson crossed the floor, closed and locked the door behind Tom. "He's going to make a hell of a good employee."

"I know." Ysabel moved a step away from Jackson and stared down at the paper in her hand. "I know where this apartment building is. It's near to where I grew up in my old neighborhood."

Jackson leaned over her shoulder to look at the address. "If he even thought there was a chance the law was onto him, he'd be long gone."

Ysabel's eyes narrowed. "Then let's get there before he has the chance."

"No way. The man's a trained terrorist." Jackson tried to take the paper from her.

She jerked her hand back, but not before his fingers closed on the sheet. She held tight. "Like you said, he's probably long gone. What would it hurt to go check out his place and see if there's anything that would help us in our investigation?"

"Ysabel." Jackson didn't like where she was leading. "Let the police handle it."

She refused to release the paper, staging a mini tug-of-war with him. "The Aggie Four agreed to the idea that there is someone crooked on the police force or in the sheriff's office. Are you going to trust them to do it right?"

She had a point. And she wasn't giving up the paper. If he didn't agree to go with her to this man's apartment, he wouldn't put it past her to go on her own. Fear pinched his chest, an image of the dead forklift driver's charred remains firmly rooted in his memory. "Okay. You've convinced me. Give me the paper and *I'll* go." He tugged on the paper, determined to get it from her. Instead, he ended up ripping it in half.

She retained the half with the address on it, holding it up behind her, out of his reach. "I'm going with you."

"If you weren't already quitting, I'd fire you on the spot for insubordination." He reached over her shoulder, grabbing the scrap of paper. Their fingers connected, a charge of electricity exploding through his nerve endings like gasoline in a combustion engine.

She held on, refusing to let him have the address. The result was to bring him closer to her than they'd been since *The Night.* The exotic scent of her hair wafted up to assault his senses, the warmth of her skin teasing him with its nearness.

"Go ahead," she said, her voice but a whisper as if she couldn't quite catch her breath. "If you remember, I wanted to resign, but you had to throw an employment contract at me like a prenup agreement in a divorce case." Her gaze dropped from his eyes to his mouth, her breathing becoming more shallow and erratic. She wasn't immune to him like she'd led him to believe with her silent treatment and aloof behavior.

"I need you Ysabel." *More than I ever thought possible.* But he had to keep it on the professional level. "And you owe me a two-week notice."

Ysabel's eyelids drooped to half mast and she swayed toward Jackson. "Does everything have to be on your terms and your terms only?" Her words had dropped to a murmur, as if she couldn't get enough air into or out of her lungs.

"Damn right." She had him tied in a knot so tight he couldn't remember how to breathe either. He let her have the paper, his hand curling around the back of her neck feathering through the silky smooth hair falling down to her waist.

"Someone needs to teach you a lesson on compromise." Her own arms twined around his neck and she brought his mouth exquisitely closer to hers.

He stopped a breath away from her lips. "And I know just the one who can do it." Then his lips closed over hers, his other hand circling her waist, drawing her soft body against his harder one.

Two months hadn't been nearly long enough to erase Ysabel from his mind, hadn't been long enough to make him forget how she felt against him, the taste of her lips, the warmth of her hands on his skin.

His body remembered, his mind rejoiced and he fell into

her like a dehydrated man fell into an oasis pool, lapping up the very essence of her.

Her mouth opened on a moan and his tongue delved in, twisting and toying with hers. She tasted of mint and chocolate, the sweetness wrapping around him, drawing him deeper into her.

When her head dropped back, he stole the opportunity to lavish kisses along the smooth line of her throat, nipping at the vein pumping madly beneath the skin.

She tugged at his shirt, pulling it from the waistband of his jeans so that she could slide her hands beneath it. Long, tapered fingers climbed up his taut abs, skimming over his ribs to rest against the muscles of his chest.

His fingers slipped beneath the sweatshirt hanging loosely from her shoulders, finding the gentle curve of her waist, the silky skin feverish to his touch. His hands climbed ever upward until his palms cupped the swell of her breasts.

She had beautiful breasts, full and lush, tipped with the prettiest rosy-brown nipples a man could ever want.

His mouth watered with the need to taste them. He grabbed the hem of the sweatshirt and ripped it up over her head, tossing it to the floor.

She flicked the buttons of his shirt, loosening them one at a time, until he thought he might come undone if she didn't finish in the next two seconds. Before she could release the bottom two buttons, he saved her the effort, ripping them apart.

Then he pulled her to him, her lace-covered breasts tangling in the hairs on his chest, teasing his senses with the wispy scrap of material. He reached behind her and flicked the hooks. Then he slid the straps over her shoulders…slowly…his gaze drinking in the way she spilled into his palms.

The hard ridge beneath his trousers tightened painfully.

When her hand reached between them and stroked him,

he gasped. He'd dreamed of this every night for the past two months, his sleep disturbed with images of Ysabel standing before him naked.

Now she was here, naked from the waist up. As if driven by the demons of his nightmares, he reached out and unbuttoned her jeans, tugging the zipper down until he could see the lacy black panties beneath. The slight swell of her belly complimented her full hips and made him want more. She wasn't model-thin like many of his previous women. Not Ysabel. Her Hispanic heritage gave her curves in all the best places.

He dropped to one knee and kissed her belly button.

She raised a hand and brushed it across his cheek, a sad kind of shadow crossing her eyes.

"Do you want me to stop?" he asked, unsure whether he could at this point.

She shook her head and pulled his head to her belly, where he pressed his lips, tonguing her belly button.

Clutching the edges of her waistband, Jackson tugged the jeans downward, trailing kisses across her belly button and down to the thin elastic of her panties. He hooked his thumbs beneath the elastic surrounding her thighs and stroked the fine, curly hairs beneath, rubbing over the sweet spot that made her crazy.

She cried out, her hips pressing closer.

With his body straining to hold back, Jackson jerked the jeans and panties the rest of the way down. The past two months fell away and Jackson was back in the heaven of Ysabel's arms.

She slipped out of her shoes and clothes, standing before him in nothing but skin. Tingling, sensitized skin that yearned to feel his skin against it.

"You're so beautiful." His hands slid up the backs of her calves and he pressed a kiss to her kneecaps. "Stubborn, sexy, beautiful Ysabel."

His words made her melt inside. She wanted to believe she meant something more to him than any of the other women he'd paraded past her over the years. If he even gave her a hint that this would go beyond another one-night stand, she'd blurt out that she'd fallen in love with him the day she'd interviewed for the job as his executive assistant.

That was the problem. She knew his track record. Knew the name of each woman he'd taken to bed since she'd come to work for him. Knew what happened afterward, how he stopped calling, stopped dating and eventually forgot about them.

Knowing all that, why didn't she stop him?

Because she wanted him so intensely, she'd risk a broken heart for one last time with him.

His thumbs massaged her inner thighs. It felt so good, her knees fell open as if they knew what to do even if Ysabel couldn't make sense of her chaotic thoughts.

Jackson's fingers parted her folds and he took her in his mouth, tonguing her until she thought she would explode into a zillion little pieces if he didn't quit.

She pulled away, her breathing ragged, coming in short, rapid gasps. The need for oxygen came secondary to the other kind of need pulsing through her, making her wild with desire.

Jackson rose in front of her. Hooking his elbows beneath her knees, he lifted her into his arms.

Ysabel wrapped her legs around him, settling over the bulge in his trousers, wishing he were as naked as she was, feeling very much the seductress, naked and wanton in the CEO's office. Instead of shocking her and making her cringe with guilt and shame, it empowered her. She'd brought him to this point. He desired her, even if he could never love her.

He carried her across the carpeted office and settled her bottom on the cool, slick surface of his desk.

Before he could change his mind, she reached for him, making quick work of his belt, button and fly. She wanted him inside her, filling that place that had been empty since the day he'd left her alone in his apartment.

His jeans slipped to his ankles, caught on his boots, his boxer shorts quickly followed.

She took him in her hands, loving the sexy feel of silk on steel. Gently, slowly, greedily, she guided him to her, pressing him against her opening.

Jackson paused, sucked in a shaky breath and let it out slowly. "We weren't careful before, we shouldn't risk it a second time. I have protection in my wallet."

"Don't worry," she said, clasping his buttocks in her palms she guided him home, his shaft filling and stretching her deliciously moist channel. He was so hard, warm and sexy, she couldn't wait.

Fully encased inside her, his muscles straining against her fingers, Jackson froze. "Are you sure? I could pull out at the last second?"

Rocking against him, in the age-old rhythm of mating, Ysabel couldn't take his reticence much longer. She wanted it all and she wanted it now. "No. Really. It's already taken care of. I can't get pregnant." At the back of her lust-filled mind, she almost laughed hysterically. Nice of him to worry now, when it was way past too late. She couldn't get pregnant because she already was.

He grasped her face between his hands and kissed her with such tenderness, she thought she would die. "We still need to talk," he said, smoothing a stray tear from her cheek.

"Later." She leaned back, bracing her hands in the middle of his desk, her breasts thrusting toward the ceiling, her hair feathering across her back.

His hands on her hips, Jackson's thrusts built a delicious friction inside her, heating her core to the point of meltdown.

As the thrusts increased in tempo, tension built inside her until she felt as taut as a cocked bow. Then she shot over the edge, hurtling into the most intense sensations she'd only experienced one other time in her life. The first and only other night she and Jackson made love. The night they'd made the baby growing in her belly.

Jackson clutched her tightly against him, filling her to full and held her steady as he emptied his seed into her.

Ysabel's legs dropped down and she wrapped her arms around him, hiding her face against his chest, tears wetting her cheeks. All too soon, she'd leave. Jackson would forget about her and she'd only have memories of this night together. Memories and a baby to love.

"What's this?" He tipped her head back and brushed a thumb beneath her eye.

"Nothing."

"Did I hurt you?"

"No." *But you will.* She pushed him away and dropped to her feet, her cheeks burning, guilt raging through her. He had the right to know about his baby. But she couldn't tell him now. The urge to run hit her like a panic attack. "I just have to go."

"But we need to talk."

"No, we don't." She grabbed for her jeans, her legs shaking so hard, it took her several attempts to get them in the pant legs and pull up. Tossing the sweatshirt over her head, she yanked it down over her naked breasts and ran for the door.

Jackson's hand caught her before she turned the handle. "Stop. We can't leave things like this." His brows dipped downward, his blue eyes strangely sad and pensive.

Now wasn't the time to feel bad about leaving Jackson. If she didn't do it now, she'd only feel worse when he dumped her later. "We shouldn't have done this. It only complicates the situation."

"Damn it, Ysabel!" he exploded. "Having you in my life complicates everything."

She stared up at him for a moment, then her gaze dropped to her bare feet. "Yeah. But not much longer. You have to put up with me for only thirteen more days, then I'll be out of your life for good." She jerked loose of his hold and dived for the door. If she didn't get out, she'd dissolve into a weeping mess at his feet.

"Ysabel!" he yelled after her.

She glanced back to see him scrambling for his clothing.

With a head start, she'd make it to the elevator before him. In a mad dash she raced for the elevator bay.

Relief washed over her when she spied the open elevator. She dashed in and punched the lobby level. The door closed, ever so slowly.

"Ysabel, wait!"

Jackson ran toward the elevator, pushing his arm through a sleeve as he raced across the granite tile, skidding to a stop just as the door closed completely. As the elevator jerked and silently descended toward the ground, fists pounded on the metal door above. "Ysabel! Damn it! This is crazy. I know where you live!"

Ysabel stared up at the ceiling of the elevator car, fully expecting Jackson to break through it and shake the truth out of her. When he didn't, she leaned against the mirrored wall and slid to the floor, her tears drying.

She'd only managed to delay the inevitable and piss off Jackson at the same time. She had to come to work the next day or risk being sued for every cent she owned, and right now, she needed all the money she could find to help her through the next few months of job hunting and settling in a new town. No, she couldn't avoid him, but she needed breathing space, if only for the remainder of the night.

Going back to her apartment right away wasn't an option.

He'd be sure to show up there and demand an explanation she wasn't prepared to give.

She'd left the address of the other suspect in his office, forgotten in her desperate attempt to recapture something she'd never had in the first place. Ysabel closed her eyes and visualized the paper Tom had given her. Her photographic memory kicked in and numbers and letters appeared in her mind. She remembered.

Too distraught to go home, she might as well check out the apartment where Greg Voleski lived. She didn't know what she'd do once she got there, but she had to do something, rather than wait around for Jackson to show up and expose her secret. The fireworks in that situation were sure to be devastating. What could be worse at Greg's apartment?

Chapter Six

When Jackson reached the parking garage, Ysabel's taillights blinked at him, rounding the corner to the exit, mocking his attempt to catch up with her. He made a mental note to talk with the elevator maintenance man. No elevator should be that incredibly slow.

He ran for his truck, throwing himself inside. She'd be out of the garage before he could catch her and even at night there would be enough traffic in downtown Houston he'd have a hell of a time following her.

So he had to outthink her. Where would Ysabel go?

If she were smart, she'd go straight home and wait for Jackson to catch up to her and shake some sense into her head. But then Ysabel was a woman and she didn't think like him—a mere man.

Jackson pulled out onto the street and looked both ways. No sign of Ysabel's bright red compact car, only lights from other people hurrying home after a late day at the office. Why couldn't they have gone home earlier like normal people?

Jackson chuckled. Because they were like *him.* Driven by some force, whether it was the almighty dollar, an unreasonable deadline or an evil boss bent on ruining their social lives, the people leaving downtown late were much like he'd been two months ago. Compelled to work his life away, all his efforts concentrated on increasing his already-massive fortune. When had becoming a billionaire become an obsession? When was enough enough?

Jackson's truck idled as he pondered which direction to take—his current predicament a metaphor of his life.

At an early age, he'd vowed never to be poor again. He and his college buddies, the Aggie Four, made a pact to become billionaires and they had. Now what?

Now he found himself defending his corporation and his friends from a vicious attack, one that could ruin them, and all he could think about was Ysabel and the screwed up way he'd handled their relationship. Never mind he could go to jail and lose everything he'd worked so hard to attain. Never mind someone was out, possibly to kill him. He couldn't leave things the way they were between himself and his executive assistant. Hell, he'd already violated one of his self-imposed cardinal rules: Don't get involved with your employees. Maybe she was right by resigning.

His gut tightened. To hell with her being right. She couldn't quit. He needed her.

Jackson slammed his palm against the steering wheel. "Where the hell did you go, Ysabel Sanchez?" he shouted to his windshield.

Think, Jackson. Think like a female. Think like Ysabel.

She'd expect him to show up at her apartment. Hadn't he shouted he knew where she lived? Yeah, she'd think he'd go there first. Therefore, she'd avoid going there until later.

Her sister's apartment? Jackson glanced at the clock on his dash. Already past ten o'clock at night, she wouldn't bother her sister this late. Would she? Jackson had been there on one occasion when he'd dropped off Ysabel after a trip to New York City. He could probably figure out where it was again. But was that where she'd be?

Then he remembered what they'd been fighting over when he'd lost his mind and kissed her. She'd insisted on coming with him to Greg Voleski's apartment.

When he'd been gathering his clothes off the floor of his office, Jackson had shoved the scrap of paper into his pocket and grabbed the papers Tom had given him with the other two men's names. He reached for the torn paper now and studied the address. Would Ysabel remember it? With her superb memory, probably. Would she be stupid enough to go there at night in a neighborhood of questionable safety?

Hell, yes! Rather than go home and risk running into him, she'd place herself in a dangerous situation. She didn't have the address with her and would assume Jackson would think she'd forget. And she was just stubborn enough to go alone to a place that hadn't been safe even when she'd been growing up there.

Jackson switched on the GPS unit in the dash of his truck and keyed in the address. Once on the road to the apartment building in southwest Houston, he tapped the speed dial number for Akeem on the hands-free cell phone device also built into the dash of his customized pickup.

Akeem answered on the first ring, his voice coming over the speaker phone loud and clear. "Hey, Jackson. What do you know?"

"I need you to use your connections in Rasnovia to find two men who were on Champion Shipping's payroll." He filled in Akeem on what Tom and Ysabel's cousin at the sheriff's office had learned and the names of the two men.

"I'll get right on it. Hey, Jackson, I've been thinking about it, you might consider beefing up your personal security. I know you don't like the idea of a bodyguard, but with one attempt on your life already, it might be time to break down and get one."

Jackson had rejected what must have been hundreds of

sales calls from personal protection agencies. Since his name came out in the Houston newspaper as one of the most eligible bachelors in the state of Texas, listing a rough accounting of his assets, he'd been getting nonstop phone calls. It was enough to bring out not only every gold digger this side of the Mississippi, but others from around the world.

The article had brought out the weirdos, solicitors and every charity wanting a piece of Champion Shipping assets. Ysabel had managed to run interference, deflecting even the most insistent. Jackson didn't have the patience. However, he'd turned to his friend Deke Norton for advice on installing new security systems in all of his residences and offices. He still wanted to handle his personal security on his own, primarily by keeping a low profile when out and dressing like any other Texan, in discount store jeans and cowboy boots. Besides, they were more comfortable.

"Thanks, Akeem. I'll think about it." He clicked the Off button as he turned off the main road into a Southside neighborhood where streetlights illuminated the peeling paint and general state of disrepair common among low-rent properties managed by slum lords or subsidized by the government.

Young men, wearing the ultra-baggy shorts whose crotches hung down below their knees, loitered in groups against the sides of buildings, the tips of their cigarettes glowing bright red in the shadows. Chains hung from their belt loops to their pockets, the shiny silver glinting in the light from the corner streetlight.

Jackson reached beneath his seat for the handgun he kept close by, his own personal bodyguard, in his opinion.

As he waited at a stoplight for the red to change to green, he took in the ominous air of the neighborhood. He'd thought he had it bad growing up in foster homes. However, this neighborhood had him beat. He couldn't imagine a kid of his walking alone or in a group down one of these streets.

He tried to convince himself that it couldn't be as bad as he was making it. Lots of people lived here, young and old. But the reports of drive-by shootings always came out of these poorer, more desperate living conditions.

A cold wave of dread washed over him. Ysabel was out here somewhere if she really did come to investigate Voleski's apartment. Jackson hoped like hell she'd gone to her sister's instead.

The GPS unit led him deeper into the community until he rounded a corner and the three-story apartment building appeared filling the block to his right.

He pulled into the parking area, his shiny new truck a glaring contrast to the dilapidated vehicles lined up on the broken pavement. At the end of the parking lot, he spied a bright red compact car with rosary beads hanging from the rearview mirror and his stomach dropped. Ysabel.

Ysabel knew exactly where the apartment complex was. She remembered hurrying by it when she was a young girl on her way to the neighborhood elementary school. One of the teenagers who babysat her on occasion had told her a woman had been found strangled to death in one of the apartments. From that time on, Ysabel got a severe case of the creeps passing by the building. She'd even walk two blocks out of her way to avoid the area altogether.

Her bright red car stood out as a new car, but the bangs and dents from the collision the night before made it fit in somewhat with the other dented vehicles in the parking lot. Still, to avoid drawing attention, she'd parked at the very end next to the Dumpster, hoping the smell of rotting garbage was enough of a deterrent to keep anyone from stealing the car or its various parts while she snooped around Gregor Volsky's apartment.

When she got out of her car, she'd begun to think maybe she'd made a huge mistake. A pregnant woman had no right to risk her own life, much less her baby's, by sneaking around a potential terrorist's apartment. Standing beside her car, she'd hesitated.

Hell, she was here already, what would it hurt to see if anyone was home? She didn't have to barge in or make her presence known.

Ysabel climbed the steps to the second floor and followed the concrete catwalk to apartment 212. Thankfully, the streetlight didn't shed much light from either end of the street, casting this particular apartment into the shadows.

The blinds were drawn and as far as Ysabel could tell, no lights were on inside.

"If you're looking for *Señor* Voleski, he moved out this morning."

Ysabel jumped, her heart slamming against her ribcage.

A small, leathery-skinned woman with thin, graying blond hair leaned against the open door of apartment number 213, her arms folded over her chest, a cigarette dangling from her lips.

Ysabel forced a smile, her stomach rebelling at the scent of burning tobacco. "I'm sorry, what did you say?"

The older woman's eyes narrowed. "You aren't one of his relatives, are you?"

"No, I'm not, why?"

"He gave me most of his stuff, said he wasn't coming back." Her eyes widened as though a thought had come to her. "You're not here to repossess his stuff or something, are you? Because if you are, he didn't give me nothin'." She stepped back into her apartment and hurried to close the door.

Ysabel stopped her by pressing a foot into the space, regretting her movement when the door crunched her toes into the doorframe. She winced, but didn't cry out. "Wait. I'm not here to collect anything. I just want to know where I can find Mr. Voleski."

"I don't know, he mumbled something about gettin' on some ship tonight and that he wouldn't be back to this rat hole ever again, or any other rat hole for that matter." She shrugged. "His words. Why are you looking for him? Is he in some kind of trouble?" She stared down at the foot preventing her from closing the door and then her glance rose to Ysabel. "Because if he is, I don't know *nada*." She removed the cigarette from her lips and blew smoke into Ysabel's face.

How she kept from launching the contents of her belly onto the blonde, Ysabel didn't know, but she did long enough to ask, "Can you tell me anything about him?" She waved a hand in front of her face to clear the smoke.

"No. I didn't talk to him much, he didn't talk to me at all. That's the way it is. Most people mind their own business."

"Did you overhear any odd noises coming from his apartment, ever see what he kept in there?"

"No. I mind my own business. I took a few things, but nothing worth much. I don't think he told the apartment manager he was leaving. Again, not my problem if he skips out on the rent. The door's not locked. He left like he wasn't ever coming back. Me and 215 helped ourselves. Not much left, but you're welcome to it."

Ysabel moved her foot. The woman had helped with more information than she would have thought to ask. Too bad she'd been through the man's belongings before Ysabel had a chance to look. "He didn't by chance have a computer or any electronics, did he?"

The door closed a little more. "Nothing you'd want. Just some busted clocks and radios." She shut the door before Ysabel could ask any more questions.

Ysabel returned to apartment number 212 and reached for the doorknob.

Something thwacked against the doorframe next to her head and splintered wood caught in her hair.

What the hell?

Ysabel ducked low, the wrought iron railing providing little barrier to whoever was throwing things at her. She peered up at the hole left in the wood. A small hole the size of a bullet showed up black against the dirty white of the faded paint. Crap! Someone wasn't throwing things; he was shooting at her!

She dropped to her belly hugging the concrete.

"Ysabel?" The voice coming from the stairwell made her heart leap.

"Jackson?" she whispered. "Jackson?" her voice growing in strength. As quickly as her relief flared to life, it plummeted. "Get down! Someone's shooting at me."

Instead of heeding her words, his footsteps pounded the rest of the way up the metal and concrete stairs. "Ysabel, get down!"

"I *am* down. *You* get down," she yelled back at him, afraid he'd burst into full view, giving the shooter a broad target to aim for.

Another bullet winged over the top of her head, close enough she felt the air whiff her hair. "Damn!" She couldn't believe it. She'd only stopped by to check things out. It wasn't as if she was going to try to make a citizen's arrest or anything. She was a woman, not some macho cop. A pregnant woman who had no business putting herself or her baby at risk.

Great. She was wasting time second-guessing and bemoaning her poor judgment instead of getting the heck out of there.

"Ysabel? Talk to me, sweetheart," Jackson whispered loud enough for her to hear him. "Are you all right?"

He'd called her sweetheart. Ysabel's eyes pooled and she reached up to brush aside the ready tears. Her hormones had made her entirely too weepy for an independent, self-assured single woman. "I'm fine, but if you get yourself shot, I'll kill you."

A soft chuckle warmed her insides and made her think that perhaps everything would be okay if she just kept her cool. Jackson would help her out of this mess. Although how he'd do that without getting shot himself, she couldn't fathom.

He couldn't get to her without making himself a target and she wasn't getting anywhere by playing dead. She squirmed an inch, mimicking the low crawling soldiers from the black-and-white war movies she'd watched with her father back when she was a little girl. Keeping her head and belly as close to the concrete as possible, she inched her way across the landing, thankful that she wasn't any farther along in her pregnancy. Low-crawling would be out in a month or two. Not that she planned to ever low-crawl again, if she could help it.

Another bullet pinged against the wrought iron railing.

"Damn, Ysabel!" Jackson swore. "I'm coming for you."

"*Madre de Dios!* Don't!"

"Then for heaven's sake, stay still. I'll be back."

"What do you mean, you'll be back?" When he didn't answer, she almost raised her head to look for him, before she remembered the shooter had nailed the wall just above her head in a previous shot fired. "Jackson?"

Had he backed down the stairwell to go find their shooter? Didn't he know he could get himself killed? "Damn him!" she grumbled, her heart lodging in her throat. "He doesn't have the sense God gave a gnat. He'll get himself killed and then he'll never know he was going to be a daddy."

Suddenly, her insistence to keep her pregnancy a secret seemed like an incredibly selfish act. Jackson had every right to know he was going to be a father. Maybe then he wouldn't be so stupid crazy and think he had to go tackle some insane shooter.

Those darned tears welled in her eyes, blinding her. She had to make it to that stairwell and stop him, but how could she see when she was crying like a blubbering baby? She squinched up her muscles and wiggled across the concrete another few inches, the coarseness grazing her palms and elbows. "Jackson Champion, you better not get yourself killed," she whispered, the tears falling in earnest now.

She'd almost made it to the stairwell when she realized the bullets had stopped slamming into the building around her. Except for the noise from cars passing on the streets around the building, she couldn't hear anything.

Then from the far corner of the building, an engine revved and tires squealed.

"Damn!" Jackson's voice shouted from somewhere in the parking lot below.

The vehicle sped away until all was quiet again. Too quiet.

"Jackson?" she called out, her voice shaking. For several long seconds, he didn't respond.

Then his voice sounded from the corner of the building where the vehicle had taken off from. "He's gone, Ysabel. You can come down."

"Jackson?" She rose to her knees and peered through the wrought iron railing. "Are you okay?"

"I'm fine, just pissed. He got away and I didn't even get the license plate."

"But you're okay?" She grasped the railing and strained to see him, her entire body shaking.

"Yes."

Ysabel stood on trembling legs and brushed the dirt off her hands. "Good, because I'm going to kill you."

"You'll have to come down here to do it then." His dark silhouette appeared below her and he smiled up at her, the lights from a first-floor apartment glinting off his teeth.

"I will, after I've checked out Gregor's apartment."

The teeth disappeared. "No way, Ysabel. You get down here, right now."

"Apparently, you can't tell me what to do anymore than I can tell you to stay away from a deranged shooter." She turned her back on him and strode for apartment number 212, anger fueling her pace.

Footsteps pounded on the concrete and steel steps. "Ysabel! Don't you dare—"

She grabbed the knob and flung the door open. "I dared."

He caught her around the waist before she could step across the threshold into the apartment and flung her out of the doorway and behind him. "Are you insane?"

"No, I'm informed. Now move aside." Although she spoke to him with that tone she reserved for employees overstepping the line, she was thrilled at the way he'd rushed to protect her. Not that it meant anything. He'd protect any one of his employees. That's just the way Jackson Champion worked. Rough around the edges, but his bark was definitely much worse than his bite and he really cared about the people working for him.

Ysabel knew that behind his corporate shark exterior was a man who needed love just like anyone else. Like her.

"What a mess." Jackson hovered in the doorway, looking in without moving forward.

"His neighbor said he'd moved out, but didn't take anything."

"Looks like he took a lot."

"That would be 213 and 215. He told them they could have what they wanted." She leaned up on her tiptoes and gazed over Jackson's shoulder. "Looks like that was just about everything but the trash." Dirty clothing, old pizza boxes and broken furniture were just a few of the items littering the filthy carpet. The musty smell of misuse, stale food and lack of simple hygiene wafted out to Ysabel, making her gag. She swallowed hard, determined to look for anything that would tell her what the man was planning.

Jackson looked inside and scanned the parking lot behind him. "Okay, we'll both go in, but only because I can't leave you standing out here for our friend to come back and use as target practice."

"So magnanimous of you." Ysabel sucked in a deep breath of semi-fresh air before she slid past him into the apartment. With a finger pressed beneath her nose to stave off the overwhelming stench, she looked around the apartment. "What exactly are we looking for?"

"You tell me." He touched a hand to the middle of her back as he stepped in behind her. "I just followed you here."

"You were supposed to go home and leave me alone." Warmth spread from where his hand rested on her. Despite her words, to the contrary, she was glad he'd followed her.

"*You* were supposed to go home and leave Gregor's apartment alone."

"Seems to me, we both have a problem taking orders." She liked their open banter, which had been a part of the boss–employee relationship from the first time they met in her interview. She was certain Jackson hired her because she gave as good as she got on sarcasm. It was almost like old times, before they'd committed the ultimate folly and slept together. If not for the baby growing in her belly, she might have been able to push aside her feelings for the man and get on with the business of being his executive assistant again, and nothing else.

The baby changed everything.

Ysabel stepped away from his touch. "I guess I expected to find bomb parts or something."

"I'm not seeing anything that even resembles bomb-making materials." Jackson nudged a lump of dirty clothes aside to look beneath. "Not that I'm sure what those are. But there aren't any pipes or gunpowder, fertilizer or electronics that might indicate a bomb factory." He ducked into the miniscule bedroom and adjoining bathroom and called out, "Maybe he took them with him?"

In the kitchen, Ysabel froze. "What did you say?"

Jackson emerged from the bedroom and stared across the room at Ysabel, his brows dipping low. "Which part, about the material or about his taking them with him?"

"Madre de Dios," Ysabel whispered, making the sign of the cross over her chest.

Jackson closed the distance between them and clutched her arms. "What?"

She stared up at him, her body going cold. "He told the neighbor he was leaving on a ship and not coming back."

As her words sank in, Jackson's face tightened. "One of my ships. Jesus." He grabbed her hand and dragged her toward the door. "Come on, we have to find out which one."

Chapter Seven

Ysabel climbed in the truck beside Jackson and held on to the armrest as though her life depended on it. She didn't even squawk about leaving her car in the parking lot. Another reason Jackson admired his executive assistant. She knew. A car could be replaced, lives couldn't.

She buckled her seat belt and stared straight ahead, up for the challenge no matter what it was. "Where to?"

"Port of Houston." He had backed out and was racing down the street toward the interstate before he remembered to buckle his own seat belt.

"We don't know that's where he went," she stated.

"He's only got a badge to work with Champion Shipping vessels and equipment. If he's getting on a ship like his neighbor said, it has to be one of ours."

"Maybe he's just getting on a ship to catch a ride home, wherever that is." Ysabel had always played his devil's advocate, brainstorming with him on ideas that made his corporation grow and prosper.

She could be right in this case. The man might just be catching a ride home, but Jackson wouldn't bet on it. Gregor was a suspected terrorist. One of his compatriots had already died, obviously before completing his mission to blow up something besides himself. Jackson ground his teeth together but didn't reply. No use worrying Ysabel any more than she already was.

He didn't have to say anything, the woman was smart. "Same old Jackson Champion," she said, shooting him a tight smile. "You're not willing to risk the lives of your other employees if there's even a fraction of a chance he'll try something stupid."

"Right."

Ysabel pulled her BlackBerry from her purse. "Well, then, I'd better get busy. Because we don't have time to swing by the downtown Champion building to check our databases, I'll call the harbormaster at the Port of Houston and find out if any of Champion Shipping's freighters or petroleum ships have left the port today."

"I don't know what I'd do without you." He kept his words light, but his hands tightened on the wheel. With the threat of her resignation lingering between them, he'd have to learn how to do without her soon enough.

Ysabel didn't return his glance or respond to his comment about what he'd do without her, instead concentrating on her cell phone.

Her lack of response was more disturbing than if she'd responded to his statement. He'd thought they were almost back to normal after the scare at Gregor's apartment, trading sarcasm and insults, like two close friends. Had this latest scare set them back?

His hopes of keeping her on staff were dwindling drastically and he didn't know what to do to convince her to stay. Why did women have to be so damned difficult to understand?

Time to think about how to keep Ysabel later, the more immediate issue being Gregor. If the terrorist got on a petroleum ship, there was no telling what he'd do. Many of the petroleum ships left the port empty on the way to distant locations halfway around the world.

When he reached the freeway, he pressed his foot to the accelerator, giving the truck everything it had, pushing to the speed limits and over.

Ysabel ducked her head, pressing her ear to her phone with one hand and holding on with the other, asking for the harbor-master or anyone who could tell them which Champion ships had left the port that day. She dug in her bag for a pen and notebook, scribbling madly. When she was done writing, she spoke slowly and clearly, "Listen carefully. Contact the captains of those ships and find out if one Greg Voleski is on board." She paused, then continued. "It could be a matter of life and death. Call me as soon as you know." She gave him her cell number, clicked the BlackBerry off and sat staring straight ahead, her finger hovering over the Talk button on her phone.

The Port of Houston loomed ahead, the lights from the Barbour's Cut and Bayport terminals illuminating the sky like daytime. The port never slept, containers had to be moved day and night. New ships traversed the Houston Shipping Channel heavily loaded with cargo or fuel.

When Ysabel's phone buzzed, Jackson pulled to the side of the road, shifted into Park and rolled the window down to breathe in the smell of the water and listen to Ysabel's end of the conversation.

"Champion Shipping, Miss Sanchez speaking." She listened for a moment, pressing her phone to one ear and her hand over the other ear to block out all street noise. Then she looked across to Jackson, her face pale in the lights from the dash and the container yard. "Gregor's on the *Grand Aggie Four* petroleum tanker." Her focus shifted to the phone again and she repeated what she was hearing. "It's passing through the Houston Shipping Channel between Pelican Island and Port Bolivar right now."

Galveston. Jackson knew the area, it was a narrow strait through which ships entered and left Galveston Bay. A potential choke point for shipping traffic.

He reached for the BlackBerry, but before Ysabel could hand it to him, a distant boom filled the night air, cutting through traffic noise from the street beside them.

Ysabel yelped and dropped the phone. "What was that?"

His stomach lurched, cold dread washing over him. "Give me your phone." Jackson lunged across the seat desperately searching for the device she'd dropped.

She found it in the side pocket of the door and handed it to him, her hands shaking.

"Was that an explosion?" he yelled into the phone. All he could hear on the other end were people shouting.

"What's happening?" Ysabel leaned close, pressing her ear against his hand holding the BlackBerry.

"All hell's broken loose," he said, straining to understand the muffled shouts. Someone was shouting, "Call the Coast Guard!"

The harbormaster came on the line. "I have to clear this line for emergency response."

"This is Jackson Champion of Champion Shipping. What happened?"

"Your petroleum tanker, *Grand Aggie Four,* just exploded in the Houston Shipping Channel. Now please, I must clear the line so we can get to work." The line went dead.

Ysabel sat back in her seat, her face blanched. "He blew up the ship."

"That son of a bitch blew up my ship." Jackson tossed the phone in her lap and set the truck in drive, pulling a sharp U-turn in the middle of the road. He knew the captain of that ship personally, had discussed the nature of the shipping industry and the impact of terrorism at length over a bottle of the finest whiskey. They'd always known terrorism was a possibility, but when it hit one of your own…

Ysabel hung on to the door and her BlackBerry. "What now?"

"Call Tony Ingram."

"The helicopter pilot?"

"Yeah, we're going up to have a look."

She thumbed through her contact list stored in her phone until she found the pilot and punched in his number. "Mr. Champion requests your presence at corporate headquarters. Prepare the helicopter for flight, pronto."

Jackson kept one of his helicopters on the roof of Champion Shipping's headquarters building. He aimed his truck for that one now. The trip back to the heart of Houston took less time than the drive to the port terminals.

Ysabel thanked God the police force wasn't out in droves like they were during rush-hour traffic. When they arrived at Champion Shipping headquarters building, Jackson parked on the street in a no-parking zone and ran in, so focused on getting to the helicopter that he barely noticed Ysabel breathing hard, struggling to keep up with his longer stride.

He tossed the truck keys to the night security guard on the front desk. "Get someone to move my truck." And then he ran to the elevator.

The elevator dinged open immediately and he held the door, waiting for Ysabel to catch up.

When she tumbled through, gasping for air, he felt a twinge of guilt. "I'm sorry."

She held up a hand, sucked in a breath and said, "I know, you want to see what's happening." Another breath rattled into her lungs. "Me, too. I'm just out of shape."

With a quick glance at her slim figure with curves in all the places a woman ought to have them, he shook his head.

"Yeah, right, out of shape." He passed his access card through the elevator's lock mechanism and pressed the button for the roof. With nothing to do but wait for the elevator to climb to the twenty-first floor, Jackson had a chance to study Ysabel.

Her cheeks were pale and her shoulders drooped as though she were exhausted.

"You look all done in." He frowned. "Maybe you should go home."

"What?" She straightened, pushing her hair back behind her ears. Although some color returned to her cheeks, it didn't hide the dark smudges beneath her eyes. The woman was beat and Jackson felt responsible.

"You haven't been feeling well lately and what with the attack tonight—" He frowned. "I insist you catch a taxi home. Get some sleep. I can have one of the security guards escort you there."

"Madre de Dios!" Ysabel planted her hands on her hips, her green eyes sparkling in the muted elevator lights. "You may be my boss—temporarily, I remind you—but you're *not* my keeper. I know my body better than you do, so stop trying to tell me what I do and don't need."

Jackson's back stiffened. "You're as stubborn as a mule, did you know that?"

"Takes one to know one."

"Yeah, well, if I wasn't in a hurry, I'd make sure you went home." And tuck her in bed to make sure she actually went to bed. The thought of Ysabel in a bed made Jackson's heart pound a little faster.

"If I wasn't a lady, I'd tell you what you could do with your bossiness."

He snorted. "Nothing's stopped you before." Jackson's blood was pumping through his veins, his anger and desire rising with each word they batted at each other. Why did she have that effect on him? She made him mad enough to either shake her or kiss her. Both options held too much appeal to ignore.

Thankfully the elevator door opened before he could do either.

Ysabel was the first one out, pushing through the heavy metal exterior door to the roof, wind from the helicopter blades whipping hair into her face.

Jackson clamped a hand over his cowboy hat to keep it from blowing over the side of the building.

Sitting inside the helicopter, checking over the instruments, Tony Ingram waved them forward.

Jackson climbed into the front seat next to Tony. Ysabel slipped into the backseat and buckled her seat belt, praying her morning sickness didn't extend past eleven at night or morph into motion sickness. Maybe Jackson had the right idea and she should have gone home. The smell of aviation fuel was doing nothing for the stability of her stomach.

Then the thought of the people aboard the *Grand Aggie Four* being injured or killed brought her out of her own troubles and made her focus on the Houston skyline.

The helicopter lifted off and made a sweeping turn southeast toward Galveston, leaving Ysabel's stomach behind, or that was what it felt like. Lights from the Houston skyline twinkled in the blackness of the sky like a million Christmas lights lit up all at once. She barely noticed the city's beauty, instead concentrating on retaining the contents of her tummy, thankful she hadn't had more than a handful of crackers before leaving her apartment earlier that evening. So much had happened in between, she'd forgotten to eat.

Ysabel couldn't hear the words Jackson was saying to Tony, so she slipped the flight headset over her head, the reassuring crackle making her feel more connected in the noise of the aircraft.

"I don't see flames or anything yet," Tony was saying.

"Hopefully, you won't," Jackson replied, his voice mechanical and filled with static. "The ship was empty, on a scheduled run to Saudi Arabia."

Tony switched his mike to another frequency and then switched back. "Coast Guard's helo is up and they say they have boats in the water. Should be able to see something soon. I can't get too close with the Coast Guard down there working. I'll swing wide so you can get a view of all sides without interfering with other air traffic."

Jackson pulled out a pair of binoculars and peered out the window.

As Ysabel looked out at the lights stretching the length of Galveston, she zeroed in on the gap between Pelican Island and Port Bolivar. She'd been across that strait many times as a young girl on the ferry that connected the two strips of land.

The *Grand Aggie Four* sat still in the water surrounded by fire boats, pumping water onto the side and deck of the ship. Without binoculars, Ysabel couldn't estimate the amount of damage, but a dark smudge of soot stained the column of the bridge.

"Jackson, I have to cut this trip short," Tony said into the headset.

"Why? What's wrong?"

The tightness of Jackson's voice made Ysabel lean forward in her safety harness, craning her neck to see the instrument panels as if she knew anything about what they should look like.

"I'm losing oil pressure." Tony had a white-knuckled grip on the control stick.

Ysabel's heart thundered against her chest. "Is losing oil pressure a bad thing?" she asked, her voice crackling in her ears.

"Could be." Tony's gaze ran over the instruments and he leaned toward the window, peering out. "Damn. We must have blown a hose. You better brace yourself and look for a place to land."

Land? Ysabel looked out at the moonlight reflecting off the water of Galveston Bay. As far as she knew, helicopters didn't land on water.

Tony tilted the control stick toward the closest land. "I won't have much control, so get ready for a rough landing."

Ysabel clutched a hand over her belly. "Holy Mary, Mother of God," she whispered. How could this be happening?

The helicopter spun in circles, losing altitude at an alarming rate. Lights from Port Bolivar seemed to rush up at them in rotating swirls.

There were houses down there. What if they landed on one?

"Can you aim this thing for Fort Travis and the beach?" Jackson called out over the mike.

"I'm trying," Tony grunted, both hands on the stick, struggling to stabilize the spinning aircraft and direct it to a relatively clear landing area.

With her heart stuttering and her breathing coming in ragged gasps, Ysabel closed her eyes, praying to God to keep Jackson, Tony and her unborn child safe. The spinning motion continued, but she kept her eyes closed tightly.

"Brace yourself for impact!" Tony yelled.

Calm settled over Ysabel as she let her imagination carry her toward the earth. The bumpy swirling of the chopper was nothing more than the wind gently rocking her and the baby. When she opened her eyes, they would be on the ground.

One…two…three…

Ysabel opened her eyes as the helicopter hit with a bone-jarring thud. Metal crunched, the skids buckling beneath them. The body of the chopper leaned, setting the thundering blades at an angle. One hit the ground, snapped off and flew toward the sea, followed by another.

Ysabel tried to duck, but the restraints held her tight in her seat. With parts flying in all directions, all she could do was watch and hope none hit the people inside the helicopter.

The engine stopped, the broken blades rotated to a stop and stillness settled over the smooth grassy landscape of Ft. Travis historic park.

Then Ysabel took her first breath in what felt like hours. With the breath came panic. “Jackson?” When he didn’t answer, she knew she had to get the heck out of the chopper. Her fingers clawed at the straps, searching for the buckle. At last she found it and released the catch. As soon as she was free of the restraints, she toppled forward, hitting the back of the seat in front of her. The door beside her jerked open and Jackson stood there, his eyes wild, his hat missing and his hair standing on end. He was the most beautiful sight to Ysabel.

He dragged her out of the chopper onto her feet and crushed her against his chest. “Oh, Jesus, I thought this was it.” His hands roved over her body as if reassuring himself she was alive. Then he was kissing her, his mouth slanting over hers, his tongue delving in to taste hers. When he stopped long enough to breathe, his breath brushed against her cheek. “I thought I’d lost you.” He kissed her again, this time taking it slow, as though he cherished every caress.

“You two all righ—” Tony rushed around the tail of the helicopter and skidded to a halt. “Uh…right?”

Jackson broke away from the kiss and stared down at Ysabel. “Are you?”

Her face flaming at being caught kissing the boss, Ysabel pushed against Jackson’s chest. “I’m fine.” When he didn’t let go, she pushed harder. “Really, you can let me go.” The more she pushed, the more panicked she felt as if his arms were chains around her. Her puny efforts were weak at best and to her horror, her eyes filled with tears. Dizziness made her head spin, mimicking the motion of the spiraling helicopter before it landed. If he didn't let go, she was afraid she'd throw up yet again. "Please," she begged, her voice choking on a sob.

His eyes narrowed and he eased his hold.

As soon as his arms loosened around her, she regretted her haste to be free. The spiraling sensation intensified and Ysabel's vision blurred. Without warning, her knees turned to noodles. *"Madre de Dios…"* she said as she crumpled to the ground.

Chapter Eight

"She's coming around," someone whispered.

"Delia?" Ysabel's eyes fluttered open to the soft lights of her own bedroom. "Delia? Is that you?"

"Shh, *mi hermana.* I'm here." Delia lifted Ysabel's hand and squeezed gently.

Images of the helicopter spinning to the ground blasted through Ysabel's memory and she sat up straight. "Jackson?"

"He's fine, the pilot's fine, you're fine. Lay back and sleep." Delia fluffed an extra pillow behind her and gently pushed her back against them. "You're not taking care of yourself. Mama will be angry that you are not taking very good care of her first grandchild. You won't hear the end of it when she gets back from Monterrey."

"Did I pass out?" Ysabel laid back, the soft pillows feeling wonderful after the crazy day. "What time is it? Or should I ask what day it is?"

"Relax. You've slept for only eight hours. You could use another ten, if you ask me."

Ysabel sat up again. "Eight hours!" She glanced at the clock on the nightstand. "I'm supposed to be at work." She shoved the sheet aside and swung her feet off the bed.

"You're not going anywhere." Delia stood in Ysabel's way

so she couldn't get out of the bed without running into her sister. "Doctor's orders. You're not to get out of bed until noon."

"Doctor?"

"Yeah, Jackson had his physician make a house call."

The blood drained from Ysabel's face and she lay back against the pillows. "Did he…"

"Tell Jackson you were having his baby?" Delia frowned. "No, but he should have."

"No." Ysabel pushed a hand through the tangled mass of hair. "I have to find the right time."

"You need to tell him soon. The poor man was beside himself, convinced you should be admitted to the hospital. But you kept telling him no."

"I did?" Ysabel smiled weakly at her sister. "I must not have been too out of it."

"You were out of it enough that Jackson stayed beside your bed until I arrived. If I hadn't pushed him out the door, he'd have stayed through the night. The man's a wreck."

Ysabel's heart jumped in her chest and then settled back into a slower rhythm. She knew better than to get her hopes up where Jackson Champion was concerned. Exhaustion was making her loopy. "He'd do that for any employee."

Delia shook her head. "I don't know. The man was worried enough to stick by you when he had a blown-up ship in the Houston Shipping Channel."

"He should have been out there."

"The doctor told him you'd be fine after a little rest, that you didn't need someone to babysit you. But did Jackson go out to check on his ship? No, ma'am. Not until I'd arrived and told him he had to leave or face the wrath of Delia."

Since when had Ysabel Sanchez become a liability to her boss? She didn't like it one little bit. She was an independent self-starter who didn't need anyone else. Yet at the back of her mind, she liked it a little too much. A girl could get used to having a man worry about her for a change. Any man but Jackson Champion.

"So?" Delia planted her hands on her hips. "What are you going to do about him?"

What was she going to do? She obviously had to tell him or he'd have her committed to a hospital and learn about the baby from someone besides her. She tapped a finger to her chin. Question was, when? "I'll tell him, but the timing has to be right."

Delia rolled her eyes. "As far as I'm concerned you've already passed the right time and gone straight to no-matter-when-you-tell-him-you're-screwed."

"How bad is it?" Akeem settled in one of the leather chairs in Jackson's office.

"No one died, except the man who set off the explosion, and the ship's not sinking." Two things he was relieved to learn early that morning when he'd finally gotten the first response personnel to fill him in. "It appears as if the damage is to the side of the ship. That's about all I know at this point. The Coast Guard won't let anyone on board until the accident has been thoroughly investigated. The crew has been evacuated and treated at local hospitals."

"In the meantime, you have to wonder if there are any more terrorists working at Champion Shipping." Flint McKade pushed his cowboy hat to the back of his head and rubbed his temples. "I don't like it."

Jackson turned to Akeem. "Have your people in Rasnovia found the two men identified as terrorists? I'm afraid what happened last night here in Houston could happen anywhere Champion Shipping assets are."

Akeem shook his head. "They've disappeared. However, my contacts in Rasnovia were able to get into their apartments. They left behind a computer that didn't work."

Jackson sat forward. "Where is it?"

"It's at the airport in Rasnovia, awaiting your orders. You'll have to smuggle it out. There's still so much unrest since Viktor's family was overthrown."

"I'll have a Rasnovia plane there within an hour to collect it." Jackson leaned forward and punched his intercom button to Ysabel, before he remembered she wasn't in.

"Yes, sir?" Ysabel's voice came over the line, clear and calm.

It took him a full five seconds to realize he shouldn't be hearing her voice, not until the next day. "What the hell are you doing back in the office?"

"Working," she said, her tone firm, her words terse and no-nonsense. "What can I do for you?"

Jackson's blood pressure rose and he would have told her off, but the curious faces of his friends made him reconsider. Instead he forced himself to rise slowly from his chair. "I'll be right back."

As he passed by his two friends, he could swear that out of the corner of his eye he saw Akeem shooting a grin at Flint. When Jackson turned and glared at the man, Akeem looked all innocence. The chuckles behind him did nothing to improve his mood as he pulled the door closed behind him.

Ysabel sat with her head bent in conversation on her cell phone.

Jackson waited, not very patiently, taking the opportunity to study her, while she concentrated on the caller's message.

Dark circles smudged the skin beneath her eyes and her arms looked almost painfully thin. Had she lost weight or had she always been that skinny?

An image of her naked in his bed flashed through Jackson's mind. No. She'd lost weight in the two months he'd been gone. Damn it! Why didn't she get off the phone and go home?

When she showed no sign of hanging up, Jackson grabbed her phone from her hands.

"What the—" She glared up at him. "Give it back."

"Miss Sanchez will call you back," he said into the phone and then he clicked the Off button.

She leaped from her seat and lunged for the phone, but it was too late. "Hey! That was Fielding from the FBI."

"I don't care if it was the man on the moon." He poked a finger at her. "You're supposed to be home in bed. Doctor's orders."

"I don't take orders from anyone."

"I'm the boss."

"We can fix that right now." She grabbed her purse from one drawer in her desk and a sealed envelope from another. "My resignation." She shoved the envelope at him.

Jackson refused to take it. "I have a contract."

Color flared in her cheeks like twin red flags. "Screw your contract." She slipped the strap of her handbag over her shoulder. "I can't take any more of your bossiness."

"You can and you will or I'll see you in court."

All the angry color drained from her face and Ysabel backed away a step, chewing her bottom lip, her eyes rounding like a deer in a face-off with a rabid hunter.

Where had the fighting tigress gone? From raging temper to scared to death in seconds, this woman was not the unflappable executive assistant he knew so well. "What the hell happened to you while I've been gone?"

Tears welled in her eyes and she appeared to be thinking about what she'd say. When a sob escaped her throat, she clapped a hand over her mouth. "You idiot." Then she turned and ran for the ladies restroom outside the door to the executive office suite.

"What the hell's going on?"

Tom Walker popped up from his desk on the other side of the spacious office. "Was that a rhetorical question or did you want me to follow her and find out?"

Jackson stared at the young man as though he'd lost his mind. "No, hell, no. I'll see to it." He followed Ysabel through the glass doors and into the hallway. The door to the ladies' room swung gently to a stop.

Determined to get to the bottom of Ysabel's problem, he stormed through the door.

One of his employees from accounting stood in front of the mirror applying lipstick. When she glanced in his direction, she gasped. "Mr. Jackson!" The lipstick she held clattered into the sink basin, leaving a long red streak of color against the porcelain. "What are you doing in here?"

"Oh, tell me he didn't come in here." Ysabel cried out from behind a stall door.

"Damn right I did." He glared at the woman retrieving her lipstick. "Get out."

"Yes, sir." She left the mess, lipstick and all, in the sink and scampered through the door.

With only one pair of legs showing beneath the stall door, Jackson rest assured he and Ysabel were alone. "Now will you tell me what the hell is wrong with you?"

"I don't know what you're talking about."

"Damn it, Ysabel! Get out here and explain yourself."

"I make it a point not to explain myself." A loud flush emphasized her words and she stepped through the door, her head held high, her eyes tear-bright. "Do you think it dignified for a man in your position to be standing in the ladies' bathroom?"

"Dignity be damned. I own the company and—" he caught himself before he said the first thing that came to his mind.

"And you own me? Is that what you were going to say?" Her gaze sharpened into slits. "I promise you, no one owns Ysabel Sanchez. Not you, not this company. No one." She stormed to the sink and twisted the knob hard, blasting a spray of water onto her hands.

"I didn't say that. I know no one owns you. I do, however, own a contract that binds you to this company for an additional two weeks."

"One week, five-and-a-half days."

"Whatever! While you work for me, I can tell you when you can be in or out of the office. I want you to go home now."

"If I leave this office, you have no control over my movements. I could go back to Gregor's apartment for all you know."

The sucker punch hit him square in the gut and he sucked in a breath at the thought of Ysabel back at that apartment where she'd been shot at. "You wouldn't be stupid enough to go back there, not after last night."

"You don't know anything about me, Jackson Champion."

"That place is now a crime scene. I know that you're smart and you wouldn't do anything to place yourself or any other Champion assets in danger."

"Oh, so not only do you own me, but you consider me a Champion asset? Well, you know what you can do with your assets." She stormed by him letting the door swing shut in his face.

Before he could push through to follow Ysabel, another woman from accounting entered the ladies' room, jerked to a stop and clapped a hand over her mouth. "I'm sorry. Am I in the wrong bathroom?"

"You could say that." Jackson ducked around her and shoved through the door. "Ysabel!"

He had to run to catch up to her at the elevator. She'd just punched the Down button and stood tapping her sexy foot against the granite tiles.

The elevator door opened, but Jackson stepped in front of Ysabel. "Where are you going?"

"You wanted me to take the day off, remember? I'm taking the day off."

The thought of her leaving the building without him

gripped his chest like a giant fist and squeezed. "No. I don't want you to take the day off."

"Make up your mind, Mr. Champion. I'm not a yo-yo on a string you can sling around."

"I don't trust you to go home to bed."

"That's your problem." She reached around him to keep the elevator door from closing. "Now, if you don't mind, I'm leaving."

"No, I need you to work."

She let go of the elevator door and crossed her arms beneath her breasts, the action pushing them upward, emphasizing their fullness.

Tired as he was, his body reacted to her stance by sending a jolt of energy to his groin. How could she have lost weight everywhere else and gained more cleavage at the same time? He didn't remember her breasts being so plump and heavy.

Jackson scrubbed a hand over his face, reminding himself she was an employee and he had no business staring at her in that way. He had no business making love to her two months ago or last night, for that matter. Hell, the lack of sleep, worrying over his ship, freaking out over crash-landing a helicopter with Ysabel in the back and then Ysabel passing out in his arms was making him crazy.

"Just come back to the office. You can ease back into work. In fact, I have something that needs immediate attention."

"Let Tom do it. He's quite capable."

"He doesn't know as much as you do. I need a plane to fly to Rasnovia within the next hour to make a pick up."

Ysabel's eyes brightened. The woman loved a challenge. "That won't be easy with all the unrest since the uprising."

"That's why I need you to handle it." He tipped his head to the side. "But if you think Tom can handle it, I'll let him. Of course, it could be a life-and-death mission for the pilot and that kind of responsibility is a lot to ask of someone with limited experience.

She nodded, her gaze shooting to a corner as if she was already thinking through what she'd have to do to make it happen. Then her eyes narrowed. "Don't think I'm going to change my mind about leaving Champion Shipping at the end of my two-week notice. I'm not."

"Understood." Jackson fought off a smile. The woman was stubborn but good and she couldn't resist a challenge.

When she turned toward her office, the bell on the elevator dinged, the door slid open and Jenna Nilsson stepped out.

Jackson smothered a groan. The last person on earth he wanted to see was his ex-fiancée. If it hadn't been for her dumping him two months ago, he'd never have slept with Ysabel, placing the huge strain on their relationship and threatening her future employment with Champion Shipping.

Ysabel turned toward the door, her eyes narrowing slightly. If Jackson hadn't been watching for her reaction, he might have missed it.

Jackson stared at Jenna, trying to remember what he saw in the woman. Granted she was beautiful and would make a beautiful decoration at dinners, but what else? She had been mediocre in bed compared to Ysabel's fiery passion. He'd never been in love with her. All he'd wanted out of the relationship was to check off a box on his list of things to do to prove his success. Marriage had been a taboo, certain to fail in his books, just like the majority of marriages today. He'd only taken the risk with Jenna because there was no love lost between them.

Since the day she'd walked out on him, he'd never been more grateful to anyone in his life. Dumping him had shown him what an arrogant bastard he'd become, thinking marriage was just another task to be accomplished.

His one night with Ysabel had shown him how wrong

he'd been. She'd told him how important marriage was, how he deserved love and his potential wife deserved it, as well. He hadn't been that upset about Jenna leaving because he'd never loved her, never could. He needed a woman who was his equal in intelligence, drive and determination. Someone who could stand up to him in an argument and give as good as she got. He didn't want a doormat to let him walk all over. Ysabel said he needed someone who would love him with passion and be his equal in all things.

It was that night that Jackson realized he needed to marry someone like Ysabel. Strong, confident, smart and beautiful. She'd always stood up to him when he was wrong, including when he announced he was going to marry Jenna. She'd been the one to point out that he was a fool to marry for anything other than love. If all he wanted was a pretty woman to grace his dinner table when he entertained, he could hire an escort service.

Ysabel had been with him for five years, refining his rough edges and guiding him through the social intricacies of doing business with people of foreign cultures.

With Jenna and Ysabel standing in front of him, Jackson knew beyond a doubt he could never marry a woman like Jenna and why he'd ever thought he could baffled him now.

When Jenna stepped out of the elevator, Ysabel fought the sudden urge to leap forward and shove her back in before the door closed behind her. Better yet, wait until the elevator dropped to the bottom floor and push her into the open shaft.

"Mr. Champion is very busy, Ms. Nilsson. Perhaps you could come back another time?"

Completely ignoring Ysabel, Jenna advanced on Jackson and slipped her arms around his neck, a determined glint in her eyes. "Hi, Jackie, aren't you going to say hello to your fiancée?"

Ysabel's back teeth ground together. Why this woman insisted on calling Jackson Jackie was beyond her.

"Ex-fiancée, Jenna." He unwrapped her arms from around his neck. "Remember? You dumped me for another man."

Her pretty pink lips pursed in a sexy pout, making Ysabel want to scratch her baby-blue eyes out. "You're not still mad about that, are you?" Her beautiful brows rose into her pale blond hair. "Jackie, honey, if you'd returned my calls, we could have straightened out this whole mess months ago."

"Maybe I didn't want to straighten out this mess as you call it."

Ysabel wanted to cheer at his words, but she kept her mouth shut. If she jumped on Jenna and scratched her eyes out, Jackson might get the hint that she had more than an employee's interest in the big boss of Champion Shipping. She didn't want that to come out, especially in front of the ex. No matter what, she couldn't appear jealous, catty or in love with Jackson in any way. Her break from his employment would be hard enough for her as it was. If he thought he could play on her emotions for him to try and talk her into staying, she'd be hard-pressed to fend him off. All he had to do was crook his finger and she'd probably fall right back into his bed. She was a sucker for the Champion charm. As evidenced by her present condition.

"Can we go somewhere to talk?" Jenna shot a pointed glare at Ysabel. "Alone?"

"I'm sorry, Jenna. We have nothing to talk about. Ysabel—Miss Sanchez is right. I'm too busy right now."

The blonde's pouty lips slimmed into a narrow line. She sucked in a deep breath and forced another smile. "Why don't I stop by later this evening at your condo? We really need to talk."

"Seriously, Jenna." Jackson hooked her arm and steered her toward the elevator. "I don't have time and I meant it. It's over."

Her voice rose, her eyes widening. "You can't mean that."

"I assure you, I do."

Ysabel fought to keep a smirk from lifting the corner of her mouth. The woman deserved to be tossed out on her butt. After dumping a man as beautiful as Jackson Champion, she should be committed for evaluation in a mental institution.

Rumor had it she was involved with another man while she'd been dating Jackson and that she hadn't given up the other man even after Jackson asked her to marry him. She didn't deserve Jackson Champion.

And you do?

Ysabel's shoulders sagged.

He stood in front of her talking softly to Jenna as he firmly placed her in the elevator.

Jenna's face pinched into a frown. "Jackie, honey, really, we should work things out. We make a beautiful couple. Think of how beautiful our children will be. Please, Jackie, at least have dinner with me."

Ysabel's breath caught in her throat at the image of Jenna and Jackson having little blond-haired children with blue eyes. He couldn't go back to Jenna. He had a child on the way with her, Ysabel. Didn't he realize what a mistake having children with Jenna would be?

To Jackson's credit and Ysabel's relief, the man shook his head. "It'll never work." Then he punched the Down button. As the doors closed he turned to face her.

Ysabel's face flooded with heat. She'd been staring at him and his ex the entire time. And thinking he couldn't have children with anyone else was just wrong, when she planned on leaving him and taking his child with her. She spun and would have dashed back to her office, but Jackson stuck out a hand and snagged her elbow.

"Whoa, wait a minute."

"I'm on my way to place that call. Is there anything else you want?"

He held her elbow and stared down into her face. In a low, deep voice, he answered, "I want so much more."

Mesmerized by his tone, Ysabel had to remind herself to breathe. If he insisted on being this close to her for the remaining time of her two-week notice, she'd be back in his bed before nightfall and she could do nothing to stop herself. "I'll work for you until my two weeks are up, but don't touch me ever again." She jerked her elbow free and fled before she threw herself into his arms and begged him to be her one and only.

He didn't reach for her, didn't try to stop her as she ran from him. Part of her wanted him to, the other part knew what a mistake it would be.

Fool! She was a complete fool! For the past five years, she'd fought her growing attraction for the man she called boss. All that pretense had been a complete waste of time. She was a goner and the sooner she got the hell out of his office and life the better. She was just an executive assistant. He was a billionaire! *Get a grip and get on with your life, girl.*

Ysabel sat behind her desk and pretended not to notice Jackson as he passed her and entered his office.

She'd make her call and leave, unable to trust herself in his presence, not with her hormones intensifying every emotion. Pregnancy was making her crazy.

After she'd arranged for an airplane from a nation other than the good old U.S. of A., and in particular, Champion Shipping, she hung up the phone, grabbed her purse and headed for the door. Her cell phone rang before she made it out of her office.

"Ysabel, it's Mitch."

Ysabel dropped back into her seat. "What have you found?"

"Not much, unfortunately. Detective Green is keeping a tight rein on all the information about your man Voleski even to the point he isn't sharing it with the FBI agent."

"That's odd."

"No kidding. I can't dig too much without alerting Green to my activities. You might have to do some digging on your own. You have information about him through your company. Start there."

"Thanks, Mitch. I will." She clicked the Off button and sat tapping her pen against a notepad.

"Anything I can help you with?"

Ysabel spun her seat to face Tom and an idea came to her. "Tom, check Greg Voleski's employment data and find out what bank he does business with. He should have a routing number listed on his direct deposit. Chase it down and see if it leads anywhere else. You know, transfers to other accounts, deposits to his account other than from Champion Shipping payroll." Ysabel's lips twisted. "Can you do that?"

Tom grinned. "I shouldn't tell you this, but I once hacked my way into an account in the Cayman Islands. It was easy." He held up his hands, his eyes rounding. "Don't worry. I know right from wrong. I didn't steal anything. I just happen to love a challenge."

Her lips curled into a smile as she gathered her purse. "Consider this a challenge. Anything you can find on Greg Voleski or Gregor Volsky will help."

Ysabel left the office. She had no intention of going home to bed when she had some checking to do of her own. If the detective wasn't sharing information, she had to get it for herself. She'd be damned if she let Champion Shipping take the fall for the terrorist attacks. Not that she had any obligation to help Champion Shipping when she planned to quit in one week and five days. But still, Jackson didn't deserve the fingers pointing at him and the Aggie Four Foundation.

When she stepped out of the elevator into the parking garage below the building, she passed a sheriff's deputy SUV sitting in the handicap parking zone. Detective Green sat in the driver's seat talking to someone in the passenger seat. Ysabel couldn't see the face of the person on the other side, but she could see long blond hair. Detective Green shot a glance her way, his eyes narrowing.

Ysabel shivered. To say his look was cold would be an understatement. Glacial fit the description. She hurried to her car and slid behind the wheel, pulling out of her designated parking place. Once outside the parking garage, she drove up the street, made a U-turn and waited on the opposite street corner to see who came out. If the detective exited, she might catch a glimpse of the person he was talking with. Why she cared, she didn't know, but somehow it seemed important. So she waited.

The wait didn't last long. A silver BMW slid out of the parking garage and onto the street.

From her vantage point, Ysabel could clearly identify the driver—Jenna Nilsson, combing a hand through her long blond hair. Hadn't she left the building more than twenty minutes before Ysabel? Was she the blonde Detective Green had been talking to in the front seat of his SUV? If so, why? What did she have to do with the case?

Ysabel made a mental note to ask Jackson when she saw him the next day. In the meantime, she headed for Greg Voleski's apartment in the shadier part of Houston. With it being daylight, she should have no troubles. It was times like last night that got sticky.

Before she made it to the street where Gregor had lived, her BlackBerry chirped and Tom's number displayed on the screen. Nervous tension washed over her and she passed the street she should have turned on. Tom's call could mean good news. Maybe he had something for her that would save her from going to the apartment where she'd been shot at the night before?

Then again, Tom's news could be more of the same—bad news for Champion Shipping.

Chapter Nine

Jackson sat in his chair behind his desk glaring at the desk calendar. When had Ysabel become so aggravating? If she'd just do as he told her, everything would be fine.

"Anything we can help you with, buddy?" Flint asked, a gleam twinkling in his eye.

Jackson glanced up almost surprised at the presence of his two friends. He'd been so deep in thought, he'd completely forgotten that he'd called a meeting of the Aggie Four. "We need to get this whole situation under control before the Aggie Four Foundation is blamed for everything." If he could solve his corporation's issues, he could spend time figuring out how to get his life back in order. And Ysabel. Huh! Like he could manage that woman.

"We agree. While you were out *counseling* your employee, Flint and I turned on the news."

Jackson glanced toward the screen mounted on the wall opposite his desk. The screen was black. "What, are they ripping Champion Shipping to shreds over this latest fiasco?"

Flint nodded. "Pretty much."

"And if that wasn't enough, they're putting two and two together and coming up with five. They've included the Aggie Four Foundation in the accusations, not to mention tying everything back to political unrest in Rasnovia. The

Rasnovian rebels are claiming responsibility for the explosion on the *Grand Aggie Four.* The news reporters aren't going to let you off so easily."

If the paparazzi thought they could milk a story, they would milk this one for all it was worth. "Great." Jackson pushed away from his desk and stood, running a hand through his hair. "What next?"

A light tap on the door and Tom poked his head inside. "Mr. Champion, a Detective Green is here to see you."

Akeem's lips twisted into a grimace. "You had to ask."

Jackson didn't want to have anything to do with Detective Green. The man had been nothing but antagonistic toward him since the explosion on the dock. He'd rather work with Special Agent Fielding of the FBI than Detective Green. He sighed. "Show him in."

Tom backed out of the way.

Detective Green barged in like he had every right to be there. "Jackson Champion, I need you to come down to the station for questioning."

"I've already given my statement to Agent Fielding of the FBI."

"Are you refusing to come with me?" Detective Green thumbed the handcuffs tucked into his thick utility belt.

"I'm not refusing anything. Unless you have a warrant for my arrest, I'll come down to the station in my own vehicle, on my own time. You're not parading me through the offices like a criminal again. I put up with it once. Next time I'll have your badge."

Red stained Detective Green's neck, climbing up into his cheeks. "You think you can walk all over regular people like they mean absolutely nothin'? It always has to be your way, doesn't it? You just intimidate or buy your way out of anything. You rich guys think you can get away with making promises you don't intend to keep, regardless of the consequences. Well, I call bull. Someday really soon, you'll get what's coming to you."

Jackson raised his hands, surrender style. "I have no idea what you're talking about. Have I done something to offend you in any way?"

"I'm tired of you wealthy SOBs getting away with murder."

"Whoa, slow down there, cowboy. Are you accusing me of murder now?" Jackson stepped toward the man, his fists clenched. "Because if you are, I'll sue you for slander faster than you can say 'Your honor, I royally screwed up.'"

"I'm not accusing you of nothing. But if you don't get down to the station in the next hour, I'll have that signed warrant to arrest your ass." Detective Green glared at the others in the room and then stalked out, slamming the door behind him.

"What the heck just happened here?" Akeem asked, his jaw hanging open.

"Looks to me like Detective Green's got a bug biting his butt about something." Jackson relaxed his fists.

Flint stared at the closed door, his brows high on his forehead. "No kidding."

Jackson planted his hands on his hips. "I get the feeling it's more than just investigation of this case."

"You're not going down to the station are you?" Flint asked. "He's liable to throw you in jail for just looking at him."

"I'll get my attorney to pave the way. I'll see if Agent Fielding is around, as well."

"Sounds good. Want us to come with you?"

"No, that's not necessary."

"Then I'll be at the ranch, ready at a moment's notice," Flint slapped Jackson's shoulder and grinned. "Stay out of jail, will ya?"

Akeem stuck out his hand to shake Jackson's. "I'll be at the auction house. Let me know what you find out about that computer. And if you need me for anything…"

"I know, all I have to do is send up a flare and you two will be here." Jackson smiled. He could count on his friends.

Flint and Akeem left, promising to think back through all that had occurred in the past few months leading up to the explosion on the *Grand Aggie Four.*

Jackson followed Akeem and Flint. Outside his office, he rounded the corner to Ysabel's desk, intending to take her home before he stopped in at the sheriff's office. Her chair was empty. "Damn!"

His hand on the door exiting the executive suite, Akeem stopped in his tracks and turned. "What's wrong?"

"Ysabel's gone." Jackson slipped his cell phone from the case clipped to his belt and punched the speed dial for Ysabel. After several rings, the call rolled over to her voice mail. "Damn." He glanced around the office. "Tom!"

Tom's head bobbed up over the top of his five-foot-tall cubicle walls. "Yes, sir."

"When did Ysabel leave?"

The younger man disappeared and reappeared outside of his cubicle. "About an hour ago."

"Did she say where she was going?"

"No, sir. But I might have an idea." He paused long enough to make Jackson grind his teeth.

"Well?"

"Before she left, she told me to dig into Greg Voleski's employment file for the bank he had his check direct deposited to." Tom shot a look at Flint and Akeem.

Jackson nodded. "You can say anything in front of them. I trust them implicitly."

"She told me to find out anything I could about bank deposits, transfers or anything under Greg Voleski's accounts." Tom shuffled his feet. "I don't know if I should be telling you this."

Jackson stopped himself from reaching out and shaking

the younger man. "Ysabel told me you're an excellent hacker and this is an emergency. What did you find?"

"He transferred all his money from the account where his check was deposited into another account under the name of Anna Chernov. And that's not all. A sum of two hundred fifty thousand was also deposited to Ms. Chernov's account the day before yesterday."

"Where did the two hundred fifty thousand come from?"

"I'm working on it. Face value, the money looks to be from a charitable foundation from some foreign country. But the more I dig, the shadier it gets. Corporations owned by other corporations, owners that can't be traced and hidden or numbered bank accounts in the Caymans and Switzerland. It's a veritable jigsaw puzzle."

Tom handed Jackson a sticky note. "That's the address of the woman here in Houston whose account Greg Voleski dropped his money into."

Jackson closed his eyes and inhaled deeply. "Bottom line is that you gave Ysabel this same address, am I right?" He opened his eyes and pinned Tom with a stare.

Tom sighed. "Yes, sir. She might have gone there."

"Thanks." Jackson spun on his heels and raced for the elevator, Akeem and Flint jogging to keep up.

Once in the elevator, Jackson's toe tapped against the tiled floor, a million scenarios spinning through his head, none of the outcomes good for Ysabel.

"Need help on this one, Jackson?"

"Maybe. Did you two ride together?"

"Yes," Akeem answered.

"If you could swing by Ysabel's apartment to see if she made it home, that would be great. Call me when you get there and let me know." As he handed them the address, the elevator doors slid open into the parking garage. Jackson climbed into his pickup; Akeem and Flint spun out in Flint's

Diamondback Ranch truck. Out on the street, they turned in opposite directions.

Jackson punched the address into his GPS and followed the directions, navigating through the streets to southwest Houston, the neighborhood with one of the highest crime rates in the city. The sun crept toward the horizon too fast for Jackson's comfort. He hoped he got to Ysabel before she did something stupid, like get out of her car.

YSABEL stared out at the cracker-box house with faded, peeling pink paint. Somewhat safe inside her air-conditioned car she'd retrieved earlier that day from Gregor's apartment building, she was glad she'd gotten it back relatively unscathed from its night in a less-than-safe part of town.

The late-afternoon sun slanted over a huge oak tree in the front yard, casting long shadows over the rotted eaves and patched roof. Bushes crowded around the sides and front, growing as tall as some of the windows, shrouding them in mystery. In the front yard, a rusted-out car tilted into the dirt on three dry-rotted flat tires and one missing wheel. The hood stood open, the engine as rusted as the paint job.

The place reeked of the desperately poor. Having grown up on the edge of just such a place, Ysabel's heart leaned toward pity for the woman she'd come here to see. Anna Chernov. The woman Gregor Volsky had left his last dime to—granted, two hundred and fifty thousand dollars couldn't be considered pocket change.

A group of young men, probably teens, dressed in droopy pants and oversize T-shirts with a picture of a snake twisted across the front, loitered at the corner bus stop across the street. If she wasn't mistaken, they were watching Ysabel watching the pink house. Should she get out or should she call the police and let them handle this?

Her gut told her the police should handle this.

A curtain flickered in the front window and a woman's face peered through the dirty glass, an infant clutched to her chest. The fear in her eyes couldn't be mistaken. The curtain jerked closed and the house grew still.

Would she try to run out the backdoor? If this woman disappeared, they might never know anything about who deposited the large sum of money into Gregor's account the day before the ship exploded. Blood money for blowing up the *Grand Aggie Four.* The woman hiding behind the curtain might know something that could lead the police in the right direction—away from Champion Shipping and the Aggie Four Foundation.

Before she could change her mind, Ysabel flung open her door and ran for the house. At the front door, she pushed the doorbell and listened. Nothing. The bell didn't work, not that it surprised her. As far as she could tell, the house didn't even have central air. An old window unit tilted out of a small window on the side of the house, its quiet stillness evidence it didn't work. As hot as it was, the woman and her baby had to be steaming all closed up in the house.

Ysabel knocked on the door. "Anna, please open the door."

A baby cried out in the back of the house and a door slammed.

Her heart kicked up a notch, sending her blood pounding through her veins. Ysabel raised her hand to knock again, changed her mind and ran through the overgrown grass to the back of the house.

Ysabel stepped up on the broken concrete of the back stoop and glanced through the glass window on the backdoor.

A small woman with dark hair and pale skin juggled a baby in one arm and a large suitcase in the other, pushing it through the kitchen toward her. When she saw Ysabel, she screamed and dropped the suitcase. The baby wailed in her arms as she ran for the front of the house.

"No, don't run!" Ysabel cried out. She jiggled the doorknob and the door swung open. "Anna, wait!" Ysabel raced after the woman, afraid Anna would hurt herself or the baby she carried in her hurry to get away from the stranger at her backdoor. "Please, Anna, I won't hurt you."

As the frightened woman reached the front of the house, the living room window shattered, a bottle topped with a flaming rag crashed into the wall above a sagging plaid sofa. The smell of gasoline filled the air and the entire living room burst into flames.

Anna stood transfixed, staring into the fire, tears streaming down over the bundle of baby in her arms. She wailed in a language Ysabel didn't understand but guessed to be Russian.

With the fire rapidly spreading around her, Ysabel had to do something fast. She grabbed the woman around the waist and hauled her through the small house to the backdoor.

Afraid whoever had attacked the front would now be at the backdoor, Ysabel shoved Anna and her baby to the side and she flung the door open, ducking back into the kitchen. Smoke billowed into the kitchen gagging her. It was die in the flames or face whatever was waiting for them outside.

Ysabel chose to take her chances. She clutched Anna's arm and dragged her through the door and out into a back alley. The wind chose that moment to swoosh down among the trees and they were enveloped in a veil of smoke, giving them a chance to get away from the house without being seen. Once they reached the corner of the house two doors down, Ysabel pulled Anna into a crouch, hiding behind a large rollaway trash bin.

The wind shifted and died down, the smoke swirling upward. Fire engulfed the small-framed house, eating away at the chipped paint and bone-dry wood. The flames leaped into the darkening sky, catching in the towering oak, lighting it like a giant torch.

Anna curled up beside Ysabel, coughing, her eyes filled with tears. The baby cried softly until Ysabel took it in her arms and spoke soothing words to it until it quieted.

Too afraid to move and disclose their location, Ysabel waited in silence until fire-engine sirens wailed in the distance.

Whoever had thrown the Molotov cocktail into the house would leave or at least not attempt to cause them more harm with the police and firefighters arriving on the scene.

Ysabel pulled out her cell phone and called a taxi. She'd get Anna someplace safe and then figure out what to do next.

As she waited for the taxi to arrive one street over from the fire she turned to the woman who'd almost died in that house.

"Anna, what do you know about Gregor?" Ysabel held the baby, rocking it back and forth to keep it from crying.

A sob escaped the woman and she buried her face in her hands. "He's dead. Gregor is dead."

Ysabel laid a hand on Anna's arm. "I'm sorry. You must have cared for him a great deal."

Anna looked across at the baby in Ysabel's arms. "My baby's father is dead."

Although Ysabel should have guessed it, Anna's words struck her hard. The baby in her arms would grow up without a father.

Anna clutched at Ysabel's hand. "Gregor wasn't bad man. He was afraid. So afraid…" The woman doubled over, sobs wracking her body.

"What was he so afraid of?"

"A man…" Anna struggled for a word, "How you say make him afraid for life?"

"Someone threatened Gregor?" Ysabel's arms tightened around the baby.

"Yes! He tell Gregor he kill him and his family if he not do what man want."

"What did he want Gregor to do?"

Anna looked around the ground as if trying to form the right words. Then she made sounds of an explosion, her hands rising into the air. "Make big boom. Fire, lots of fire."

"Is that why he blew up the ship?"

Anna shook her head, more tears falling from her eyes. "No, he refused to make explosion. He blew up the ship and himself to make police see."

"To get their attention?" Ysabel asked.

Anna nodded, tears glistening in her eyes. "And to keep bad man from hurting me and Katiya." She bent over, her tears choking off her words.

Ysabel's head spun, her stomach tightening into a knot as she absorbed what Anna was telling her. "He blew up a ship to keep from having to blow up something bigger?" Ysabel's voice was barely above a whisper, cold trickling across her heated skin.

"Yes."

Chapter Ten

Four blocks from the address he'd entered into his GPS, Jackson came to a halt in traffic. Tapping his thumb on the steering wheel, he wondered what the heck had caused cars to come to a complete stop in a residential neighborhood.

The longer he sat, the more panic seized him. He checked his GPS for the remainder of the directions, pulled his truck to the side of the road and jumped out. People sitting in cars with their windows rolled down, shouted and honked at the traffic stopped dead in the road.

Jackson jogged past the line of vehicles, his pace quickening with every step. He turned left at the next street and looked ahead at a towering column of smoke rising from the tops of the houses. "Ysabel!" When he reached the street where Anna Chernov lived, several fire engines filled the narrow lane. Smoke billowed from the burned-out remains of a house, now nothing more than a blackened skeleton of a frame. Hoses trained a steady stream of water into the smoldering ashes. In front of the house stood a soot-covered compact car that may once have been red, a string of rosary beads hanging from the rearview mirror.

"Ysabel." Jackson pushed through the gawkers staring at the house until he reached a police officer. "Sir, were there any people inside?"

"Keep back, sir, and let the firemen do their job."

"I have to know, was there anyone inside that house?" Jackson grabbed the man by the collar to get his attention. "For God's sake! Someone I care about might have been in that house."

The cop's lips formed into a straight line. "Let go of the collar, mister."

Jackson dropped the man and stepped back, running a hand over his face, staring into the glowing embers being soaked with water. "I have to know."

The cop straightened his collar and sighed. "I'll see what I can find out. Wait here."

Jackson stood right where the cop told him and waited for the longest two minutes of his life, while the cop spoke with the fireman in charge.

The fireman spoke words Jackson couldn't hear and shook his head.

Jackson's chest tightened until he couldn't breathe.

The cop picked his way back through the crowd of rescue workers, stepping over the swollen water hoses. When he found Jackson, he shook his head. "As far as the firemen can tell there was no one in or around the house when it burned. We won't be certain until they can sift through the debris and that won't be until it cools. Probably tomorrow morning."

Jackson chose to cling to the hope that the preliminary investigation was correct and that no one died in the fire. If that was the case, where was Ysabel and why was her car still here?

With the scent of ashes clogging his senses, Jackson circled the neighborhood, searching for Ysabel. After thirty minutes, he gave up and headed back to his truck. The stranded cars had found alternate routes and dispersed, leaving the street clear for Jackson to turn around.

Pressing his foot to the accelerator, he sped back into the heart of Houston. He had to find Ysabel.

CLOSE to midnight, Ysabel climbed out of the taxi in front of her apartment building, smelling of smoke and exhausted beyond reason. If someone wanted to kill her at this point, she might welcome it gladly.

Her hand rose to her belly, a faint tightening in her uterus reminding her she really had to think more about her baby. From here on out, she would stick close to home and not go chasing after suspects or witnesses or anyone else even remotely dangerous.

She'd spent the last hour and a half settling Anna into a women's shelter her cousin Rita volunteered at. No one spoke Russian there and, for some misguided reason, Anna clung to Ysabel, refusing to let her go, as if she were a lifeline in a raging sea. Ysabel promised to stay with her until she fell asleep.

Anna had lain on a full-size bed, with baby Katiya next to her. Katiya cooed and waved a chubby fist, but the clean diaper and a belly full of warm milk worked its magic and eventually the baby had drifted to sleep, with her mother not far behind. Ysabel stared down at the two, wondering if she'd end up like Anna, in a women's shelter because she didn't have a job and couldn't find a job to support her baby.

Leaving Champion Shipping depressed Ysabel more than she'd let on to her sister, because leaving Champion Shipping meant leaving the only man she'd ever loved.

Tired but too jumpy from being attacked yet again, Ysabel sat in the backseat of the taxi, wondering what she was going to do for a car, a home, and a life after she quit her job in one week and four days. Options swirled in her mind, but none stuck. She'd worry about it tomorrow. Tonight she needed sleep.

With a weary smile at the security guard on the front desk, she dragged herself into the elevator and punched the button for her floor.

The upward motion almost made her long to sink to the

floor. The only thing holding her up was the handrail and the thought of picking herself up from the ground when the elevator stopped. She'd be better off collapsing in her own bed than on the elevator floor. What would the neighbors think?

The bell dinged at her floor and the doors slid open. Dog-tired, Ysabel stepped off the elevator and gasped.

Leaning against her door was a tall Texan, arms crossed over his chest, his cowboy hat pulled down over his forehead, making his eyes unreadable. Jackson Champion.

Ysabel stopped dead still. Blood raced through her veins, jump-starting her tired body. God, he looked like heaven. If only he were there because he loved her. If only he wasn't just coming to check on his *assets*.

She squared her shoulders and marched right up to him. "Excuse me, you're blocking my door." She reached out with her key, intent on unlocking the door and diving in before he opened his mouth to tell her what he thought of her little disappearing act.

Her hand didn't make it to the door. He caught it in his and held it.

She tried to pull her hand free, but he held firm. "Let go of me."

"Tell me that wasn't your car in front of what's left of Anna Chernov's house." He yanked her to his chest, his arm wrapping around her waist like an iron band, his eyes achingly intense. "Tell me you weren't there and I'll let you go."

As Jackson's gaze burned into her, Ysabel's knees melted and she almost fell. The strain of the day and those darned hormones kicked in, pushing tears to the corners of her eyes. Why couldn't she control her emotions any better than she was? Falling apart in front of *him* was *not* an option. She wouldn't.

Darn it! She was going to fall apart. "Jackson Champion,

why don't you just go away and leave me alone?" Her voice broke on a sob and she leaned her head against his chest.

"I can't." The arm around her middle tightened. The other slipped up her back, his hand tangling in her hair, tugging her head backward until she was forced to look at him. He leaned forward and kissed the tip of her nose. "You have a black smudge on your nose. Soot, right?" His grip in her hair tightened. "Why, Ysabel? Why can't you stay away from trouble?"

She laughed, the sound ending on a sob. "It seems to be following me." Her hand slid up his shirt, bunching in the material. A girl could get used to leaning on all that muscle, letting him take on the world for her. As tired as she was, Ysabel was more than tempted. With a sigh, she laid her cheek against him. His heart thumped against her ear, mirroring her own, the steady beats fusing into a matched rhythm.

"What happened at Anna Chernov's?" he asked, tucking a strand of hair behind her ear.

"I'm so tired, can I tell you later?" If she didn't lie down soon, surely she'd fall.

"Give me your key."

Without a fight, she handed over the key, refusing to give up the support of his arm and body. He turned her, fitting the key in the lock. When the door swung open, he scooped her up into his arms and carried her across the threshold.

"Better be careful, someone might think we were newlyweds," she muttered in a low voice. Ha! Like that would ever happen. More tears sprang to her eyes. Jackson Champion marry his executive assistant? Those kinds of happily-ever-afters only happened to spineless princesses in fairy tales, not to independent tough girls from the barrio.

Jackson's arms tightened around her. "So what? Would that be so bad?"

A lump choked Ysabel's throat and she swallowed hard, daring to look up into his eyes so close to her own. "You heard that?"

A smile spread across his face. "You're right here, what did you expect?"

"For you to be gentleman enough to ignore my hysterical ramblings." She struggled against his arms. "Put me down. I can walk on my own." Even though she forced her voice to be firm, she wasn't all that certain she could walk on her own at this point. Being carried never felt so good and pride aside, she'd be better off letting him.

Jackson kicked the door shut behind him and headed directly for her bedroom.

The closer he got, the harder her heart pounded in her chest. Exhaustion flew out the window, replaced by hot, pounding blood, pumping adrenaline throughout her body. Another scenario wrapped around her senses, the one where he'd carried her to his bed in his condo two months ago. The scenario that ended in his making love to her throughout the night. That particular story had ended in Jackson's disappearing act and her own discovery that she was pregnant with his child. Hers was no fairy tale with its requisite happy ending. Hers was the one that led to heartache and loneliness.

When he passed the bed and entered her bathroom, Ysabel put her foot down. "I can take it from here."

"Are you sure? Your track record over the past couple days hasn't been stellar, you know." He let her feet drop to the floor, but he retained his hold around her middle.

Leaning on Jackson Champion was wonderful, his strength seeping into her, taking over when her own knees refused to support her. But she couldn't rely on him to always be there for her. She had to depend on herself.

"Really. I can manage on my own." *And I will manage on my own with a baby when you are long gone.* "Now get out of here so I can get a shower."

"Okay, but I don't like leaving you. What if you pass out again?"

"I'm not going to pass out." *Unless you continue standing in front of me.*

If he stayed this close, she might hyperventilate. Or worse, she might hold her breath to keep from telling him she loved him and was carrying his child. That would be a huge mistake. The last thing she wanted was Jackson Champion feeling obligated to marry her or suing for custody of their unborn child. "You know where the door is, just lock it on your way out." She shoved him through the bathroom door and closed it between them. Then she leaned against the door, pressing her heated cheek to the cool wood paneling.

"I don't hear the water going," Jackson said, as if he were standing right in front of the door. "Can't shower without water."

"I don't need you telling me how to take a shower." An image of him running a wet soapy cloth over her breasts shot through her mind. He'd bathed her in his shower a lifetime ago, touching and caressing every part of her. Ysabel stifled a moan. Why did she have to dredge up all those old memories now? Something tightened in her lower belly and it wasn't her uterus. She wanted Jackson to throw open the door and do again what he'd done before. It took every ounce of internal strength to keep from opening the door and dragging him inside. "Go away, Jackson," she called through the door, her tone half-hearted at best.

"I'm going."

For several long seconds, she didn't hear a thing. For the first time since she'd had it installed, Ysabel was hating the wall-to-wall carpeting throughout her apartment that muffled every step Jackson took. When a door opened and clicked shut, she let out the breath she'd been holding. The man who'd completely complicated her life was gone. Or was he?

Ysabel peeked out the door of the bathroom. Her view of the apartment was limited to what she could see through her bedroom door. She didn't hear anything or see anything move. Good. A nudge of disappointment ached in her empty belly. After a quick shower, she'd fix something to eat. She had to stay healthy for her baby.

Leaving the door to the bathroom ajar, she stripped and climbed into the shower, closing the sliding glass door. Jackson's presence, along with his intriguing blend of aftershave lingered in the bathroom.

As she soaped herself, her imagination replaced her own hands with his, sliding down over her naked breasts. A moan rose from her throat. How she wished she hadn't been so hasty in throwing him out. With raging hormones completely unbalanced by the baby growing inside her uterus, she felt hotter, sexier and more turned on than she'd ever felt in her life. And what did that get her? Alone and naked in a shower, wishing for something she couldn't have. Tears spilled down her cheeks, mingling with the spray from the shower. Sobs wracked her chest and she leaned against the shower wall, unable to cope with the world weighing down on her shoulders.

Wrapped so completely in her misery, she didn't hear the shower door slide open. Not until Jackson stepped into the shower behind her did she realize he was there.

Strong arms pulled her against his blue chambray shirt. A big calloused hand pushed the hair out of her face and kissed the tears from her eyes.

"I thought you left." She laid her face against his damp shirt and inhaled the scent of Jackson.

His hand circled her waist and drew her naked hips against the rough denim of his jeans. "I'm glad I didn't."

She should be angry he hadn't gone, but she wasn't. Too tired to care about tomorrow, Ysabel sighed. "Me, too."

His mouth descended to claim hers, his lips sliding across, wet and warm. When he pushed past her teeth, he dived in, plundering her hungrily.

Warm water sprayed Ysabel's back, a heat more intense built inside. Clumsy fingers fumbled at the buttons on his shirt, eager to feel his skin against hers.

He pushed aside her hands and jerked the buttons loose.

Ysabel peeled the shirt over his shoulders, the heavily soaked fabric dropping with a plop to the tub floor. The jeans were next. She flicked the metal button loose and slid the zipper down, her gaze scraping along the opening. She almost came undone when she realized he'd gone commando, wearing no underwear at all.

His erection jutted forward through the opening, strong, straight and pulsing with his need. Jackson stripped the jeans off and gathered Ysabel in his arms, pulling her against the full, naked length of him.

Her soft skin reveled in the warm hardness of his muscles, the coarseness of the hairs on his chest and legs.

Jackson reached for the shampoo and squirted some into his hands, gently massaging suds into her long, smoky hair.

Ysabel closed her eyes and leaned back into the spray, the bubbles sliding down over her breasts. Heavier than bubbles, Jackson's lips followed their path, taking one turgid peak into his mouth, sucking gently.

Something deep inside tugged at her with each pull of his mouth on her nipple. Tension spread throughout her body.

With a hand full of soapy lather, he smoothed her body with large, sensual circles, trailing ever downward to that juncture of her thighs, aching for his touch.

She opened her legs to him and his hand glided between, cupping her sex. His finger stroked her folds, sliding across the ultra-sensitized nub of her desire.

When he fingered her there, Ysabel gasped, her hands climbing his shoulders to wrap around his neck. She pressed her hips closer, wanting more of his exquisite torture.

He flicked his finger over and over until she was practically climbing up his body to be closer still.

Ysabel intertwined her fingers around his neck and pulled his head down to kiss her, her hands sliding across broad shoulders. Her movements were spasmodic, erratic like the spasms of her nerve endings down there. Every part of her burned with her need to have Jackson inside her, filling her, loving her until she forgot all about tomorrow. Forgot about leaving him and starting over somewhere far away. Right at that moment, she wanted him and wouldn't stop until she had him.

His hands cupped the back of her knees and he lifted her, pressing her back against the cool tiles of the shower walls.

She wrapped her legs around his waist, anticipating the pressure of him inside her.

Poised at her entrance, he paused, dragging in a shaky breath. "I have protection in the back pocket of my jeans."

"No need," Ysabel gasped. "I can't get pregnant. Please, Jackson." She eased down over him, his full length sliding into her, the delicious friction making her breath catch in her throat. "Ah."

He paused. "Am I hurting you?"

"Yes, by stopping you're killing me." Pushing down on his shoulders and flexing her legs, she rose up and then eased back down. "Please, Jackson, make love to me." Normally, she hated begging, but now wasn't the time to be normal. Now was the time to throw caution and all her inhibitions to the wind and just *feel.*

Jackson braced her against the wall and holding her hips

in his big, capable hands, pumped into her, his movements strong and decisive. His lips pressed into a line of deep concentration, his head thrown back, his eyes half-closed.

His unrelenting strokes pushed her toward the edge and over, her body bursting with sensation.

Jackson drove into her one last time, buried deep inside her and held her there for a long, breathless moment. They stayed that way until Ysabel's legs slid down his sides. The brief spurt of lusty energy waned and she leaned into Jackson's neck.

He lifted her into his arms and pushing aside the sliding glass shower door, set her on the floor. With a large fluffy towel, he dried her from head to toe, squeezing the moisture from her long hair.

Too tired to think, Ysabel let him. His gentle caresses lulled her into a state of sleepiness she could no longer fight. When his hand smoothed over her belly, she could imagine him pressing his ear there to listen for the beat of their baby's heart. Jackson would make a good father. He deserved to know about his child. And she needed to tell him about what Anna had told her about Gregor.

When she opened her mouth to spill her guts, he surprised her by swinging her up into his arms and carrying her into her bedroom. He laid her among the sheets, pulling the comforter up around her. She couldn't remember when it had felt so good to be in bed. The warmth and comfort caressed her naked skin, reminding her of how tired she was.

Then he slid in behind her, spooning her body against his, her butt pressing against him, his hardness still apparent. If only she had the energy.

Her eyes drooped. She was going to tell him something. A yawn pushed the thought out of her head. What was it?

His arm curled around her, a hand cupping her breast. His breath stirred the drying hair behind her ear.

Tomorrow she'd remember what she wanted to tell him. Tomorrow was soon enough. Ysabel snuggled deeper into his arms and drifted off to sleep, the sound of a baby's cry drawing her into her dreams of a maid marrying a prince, where happily-ever-afters really did happen to girls like her.

Chapter Eleven

Jackson lay awake for a long time after Ysabel drifted off to sleep. The longer he lay there, the more his chest hurt. The events of the past two days crowded his thoughts, the uppermost being the near-misses on Ysabel's life. He had to do something to keep her safe until this mess was sorted out. The Aggie Four was under attack. Ysabel was a target, as well. Someone wanted her dead.

His arms tightened around her and she burrowed closer. He inhaled the scent of her herbal shampoo and the soap he'd used to clean her body. The woman was an enigma. For the first five years he'd known her, she'd been the model executive assistant, following the rules of boss–employee relations to the letter, with a little attitude to make it interesting. More than interesting. When Jackson had slipped up and gone to her, following Jenna's rejection, he hadn't expected to act on his desires where his competent assistant was concerned. He'd been as surprised as she was when he'd taken her into his arms and kissed her. Her passion enveloped him in a fire he couldn't douse and…well…that had been the end of his platonic relationship with Ysabel. Now that he knew what heat lay beneath her cool, no-nonsense facade, he couldn't forget.

His hand skimmed over her breast, the nipple tightening

into a hard bead. He didn't want to forget. He wanted more from her than polite conversation over a desk. What he wanted was to make love to her on the desk. Hard, fast, explosive passion. His blood quickened, racing through his veins.

Ysabel stirred against him, reminding him that she needed sleep, not to be woken to slake his selfish desires.

He closed his eyes, willing his lust to abate. An impossibility with her soft skin pressed against his thickening member.

Surely if he concentrated on what was more important than making love to Ysabel, he'd cool the heat.

Why would someone want Ysabel dead? She wasn't the billionaire. She wasn't involved in orchestrating the rebirth of Rasnovia with the Aggie Four Foundation. That had been the members of the Aggie Four. If a terrorist was out to bring down his band of friends for helping a struggling nation, why involve Ysabel?

After two hours, Jackson slipped from the bed and gathered his saturated clothing. He stuck them in Ysabel's washer on spin cycle and then tossed them into the dryer. While he waited for his clothes to dry, he paced her living-room floor, working the problem in his mind.

Two terrorists on U.S. soil. Both dead after trying to destroy Champion Shipping property. Two more in Rasnovia, loading bomb-making materials aboard Champion Shipping cargo ships. Had any more bomb materials slipped by the authorities? Did the terrorists have sufficient supplies to wreak havoc on U.S. soil? An icy shiver shot up his spine, making the hairs on the back of his neck rise to attention.

Another problem that guaranteed he wouldn't sleep was the knowledge that the gunfire at Gregor's apartment wasn't Gregor shooting at them to keep them from discovering anything among his personal belongings. At the time of the shooting, Gregor had to have been aboard the Grand Aggie

Four to orchestrate the explosion. Which meant another terrorist in Houston. Who could it be? None of his other employees had surfaced in their search. If he wasn't on Champion Shipping payroll, he'd be harder to find than the others. With over two million people in the city, the police and FBI would have a hell of a time tracking down one person.

Jackson performed an about-face and strode the length of Ysabel's living room floor. He'd get with Special Agent Fielding tomorrow and run through everything he knew and see if the FBI had any more information than he did on the mysterious shooter. Was the shooter the same one who'd tried to run them off the road the night before? Was he also the one who'd burned Anna Chernov's house to the ground tonight? Was it one man or a group of men?

With more questions than answers swirling through his mind, Jackson came to the conclusion that he needed help. Help finding the shooter. Help finding out who had paid Gregor to sabotage Champion Shipping. But most of all, he needed help protecting Ysabel.

Trouble was that he didn't trust anyone but himself to watch over her. He'd have to make sure she stayed with him every hour of every day until they caught those responsible for the attacks.

Jackson paused in the doorway to Ysabel's bedroom.

She lay curled on her side, naked to the waist, her hand resting across her stomach. Her straight brown hair splayed across her pillow, dark lashes emphasizing the shadows beneath her eyes. Full breasts, tipped with rosy-brown nipples pressed together, tempting him beyond redemption.

If he took on the responsibility of protecting Ysabel, how could he maintain the distance required of a boss to his employee? He hadn't managed in the past two days, so could he even hope to now that he knew her body, her passion?

Even as he pondered the dilemma, his groin tightened. A smile pulled at the corners of his mouth. Even Ysabel struggled to keep her distance, in a tug-of-war between pushing him away and holding him close.

A strange sense of satisfaction washed over him. She had feelings for him. As quickly as the satisfaction flowed through him, it ebbed away. Ysabel's conscience must be playing havoc with her work ethic. That had to be the reason she'd given her notice. Her honesty and integrity had been the reasons he'd hired her in the first place.

How could he keep her at Champion Shipping, knowing an affair with the boss went against everything she believed in? How could he let her go when he wanted to hold on to her forever?

Like now. The urge to hold her in his arms overwhelmed him, pushing him forward when he knew he shouldn't. Jackson climbed into the bed behind her, pulling her against him.

She turned toward him and pressed her face into the curve of his neck, nuzzling at the pulse beating there like a snare drum in a marching band. When her breasts pressed against his chest, he groaned.

He shouldn't have crawled back in bed with her, because now that he was there, he couldn't make himself leave.

YSABEL woke to the smell of food cooking in her kitchen. Her stomach rumbled in protest at being totally empty, the acids churning dangerously.

She stretched across the bed, rolling onto the opposite pillow that still smelled of Jackson.

Ysabel sat up straight, noticing for the first time that she had no clothes on. Heat burned in her cheeks and she grabbed for the sheet.

Jackson appeared at the door, a tray in his hands. "As

soon as you've had breakfast and get dressed, do you think you can manage a day at the office?"

Ysabel clutched at the sheet, her mouth going dry at the sight of him in nothing but jeans, his chest and feet bare. "Yes," she squeaked, cleared her throat and tried again. "Yes, of course." She cringed at her proper tone. What they'd done last night was anything but proper.

"Good." He strode across the room and set the tray in her lap.

She had to drop one hand to balance the tray. The sheet slipped low over one nipple.

Jackson leaned over her and tucked the sheet under her arm. Then he surprised her with a kiss on the tip of her nose. "Hurry up then. I made scrambled eggs and toast. Hope that's the way you like it."

Normally Ysabel ate eggs any way they came. Lately, even the sight of an egg made her stomach flip. She fought to control her gag reflex. At least until Jackson left the room, which he didn't seem to be in a hurry to do. She held the tray with one hand, her sheet with the other and stared up at him, her brows raised.

For a moment Jackson stood there. "You don't like scrambled eggs? I'm sorry. I should know that by now."

"It's not that."

"Is the toast overdone?"

Ysabel smiled, secretly thrilled that he wanted to please her.

"No, the toast is perfect." She pulled the sheet closer. "I've never eaten breakfast in bed."

"Never?"

"Not that I can remember. Certainly not naked." There, she'd said it, and the heat bloomed in her cheeks.

"You've been through a lot, you deserve to pamper yourself. But I get it. You want me to vamoose." He turned for the door. As he left the room, he glanced over his shoulder and gave her a wicked smile. "By the way, your sheet slipped on the left side."

Ysabel glanced down to where one of her breasts was fully exposed. "Why, you!" She dropped the sheet, grabbed a pillow and flung it at him.

He ducked out, his chuckle echoing into the living room.

Ysabel set the tray aside and climbed from the bed, glancing nervously toward the open doorway. She grabbed panties, a shirt and trousers from her closet and ran for the bathroom. Why she should be self-conscious about being naked in front of Jackson, she didn't know. He'd seen every part of her body now, more than once.

Her skin tingled in memory. A girl could hatch a few expectations out of his repeated attentions and Ysabel couldn't let that happen. Once she had her clothes on and downed a bite of dry toast, she'd have it out with Jackson and tell him that under no uncertain terms could they do again what they'd done last night.

Dressed, combed and having downed half a cup of decaf coffee and a slice of toast, she headed for the living room and the confrontation she fully intended to have.

Jackson stood at the window overlooking downtown Houston, with his back to her, his cell phone pressed to his ear. "That's right. I want a full security system installed by tonight. Can you do it? If not, I'll call around and see who can." He paused. "No, I trust that your people will give me a good deal. You've always come through for me before. Yeah, what are friends for? Thanks, Deke." Jackson hit the Off button, turned and ran his gaze the length of her. "Good, you're ready."

"Who was that?" Ysabel asked.

"A friend."

"What security system?"

"It's not important."

Too concerned about their fray into forbidden territory the previous night, Ysabel let the subject drop and thought about what she'd say to put an end to their indiscretions.

Before she could summon the courage to tell him she didn't want him to make love to her again, he hurried toward the door. "Grab your purse and let's get out of here."

"But we need to talk."

"Can we talk on the way to the office?" Jackson opened the door and held it for her. "Special Agent Fielding is meeting me there in twenty minutes."

"I'll take a taxi to pick up my car—"

Before she could finish her sentence, Jackson gave a grim shake of his head. "I believe your car was totaled last night. The fire at Anna's spread to your car."

With the door wide open, Ysabel stood transfixed. She didn't have a car. Last night she'd been too exhausted to gauge the ramifications and worry then. In the light of day, reality struck her. Without a car, she didn't have the independence she cherished so much. She needed to call the insurance company and get that ball rolling. If the damage was as bad as Jackson indicated, the adjuster would total her car, the one thing she'd hoped would last a lot longer. It had been the perfect car for her. It was paid off.

Quitting her job and not knowing how long it would take to find one even comparable made her stomach knot. She'd have to secure a loan within the next week and four days. The chances of getting a loan after she quit her job would shrivel up and blow away entirely. Not to mention, she hadn't banked on making a payment. That would cut into her finances considerably.

Jackson settled her in the passenger seat of his pickup and rounded the front of the truck to climb in. After he cleared the maze of the parking garage and emerged onto the street, he leaned back and glanced her way. "What was it you wanted to talk about?"

Ysabel sucked in a breath and let it out. Where to start? "About last night…"

"I'm sorry. I shouldn't have taken advantage of you while

you were so emotionally distraught. It wasn't fair of me and certainly not fair to you. Do you forgive me?"

Ysabel wished he wasn't being so nice. How much easier would it be if they were arguing and flinging accusations back and forth? Then she could blurt out the whole truth and not feel like such an incredible fool.

"It wasn't your fault. I'm equally to blame." She turned toward the window, avoiding his gaze. Now how would she say the rest?

"There, then that's settled."

"No, not really. You know it can't happen again, don't you? Promise me we won't do that again…." She twisted her fingers together in her lap.

"If that's what you want, I'll respect your decision."

"Good." She shot a glance at his profile, the toast in her stomach churning, ready tears springing to her eyes. She'd be damned if she let them fall.

Was leaving her alone that easy for him? Keeping her hands off Jackson was near to impossible for her. Thus the need to put distance between them, quickly. "I'll need to find a new car today."

His lips firmed into a straight line. "That'll have to wait. I need you at the office. Work is piling up and I can't afford for you to be out right now."

"But I can't function without transportation."

"Don't worry. I'll get you where you need to go after work." His tone brooked no argument. Traffic around them thickened, requiring all of Jackson's attention.

Ysabel sat back in her seat. Jackson playing chauffeur was not a solution to her problem. How could she maintain her distance if he insisted on driving her back and forth to work? As soon as she got to the office, she'd do some car shopping online. And when she'd put in her required eight hours at the office, she'd take a taxi to the dealership. Problem solved.

A trickle of relief spread through her, tempered by the knowledge that she still had to get through a day working for Jackson.

ONCE in the Champion Shipping corporate offices, Ysabel headed for the ladies' room, giving Jackson the perfect opportunity to set his plan in motion.

As he walked by the manager trainee's desk, he barked, "Tom, in my office."

The younger man shot out of his desk as though his butt had been loaded with a spring. "Yes, sir."

Once inside, Jackson closed the door and crossed to his desk before speaking. "I have a special project for you."

Tom's tense shoulders relaxed. "Great! What is it?"

"You're to stick to Miss Sanchez like fly paper."

"Yes, sir. Is there something in particular you want me to learn from her?"

"No. I just want you to keep her from leaving the building without my knowledge."

A frown pulled Tom's eyebrows together. "May I ask why?"

Jackson inhaled deeply and let it out. "Last night someone tried to kill her."

"Holy crap!" Tom's eyes widened.

"I don't think she quite realizes how much danger she's in, and it's up to the two of us to keep her from putting herself in harm's way."

Tom popped to attention and came very close to saluting Jackson. "Yes, sir! I'll stick to her like you said…like fly paper. Uh, sir?"

"Drop the sir, Tom. Call me Jackson. What is it?"

"What exactly is fly paper?"

"Never mind, just don't let her out of your sight."

"Got it." Tom performed a perfect about-face and left the office, his gaze panning the area for his new assignment.

Jackson smiled. He liked the kid. Maybe he'd make a good replacement for Ysabel, if she followed through with her threat to quit Champion Shipping.

Not that anyone, least of all Tom, could replace Ysabel.

Jackson sat behind his desk and stared at the mounds of paperwork that had accumulated in his inbox over the past two months. Ysabel kept him informed and in the loop on any major decisions via phone and fax. Today, he didn't have the focus to tackle any of it. Life-and-death threats tended to push finding the cause of those threats to the top of his priority list.

A light tap on the open door brought him out of his musings. Ysabel stood in the doorway, her cheeks unnaturally pink. "Mr. Champion, Special Agent Fielding is on his way up to see you."

"Good, when he gets here, show him in. And you'll need to stay, as well."

Her brows rose. "You need me?"

"You'll need to fill him in on what happened last night. You know, the fire, Anna Chernov?" His voice softened. "In case you don't remember, you were too tired to tell me everything. Actually, you were too tired to tell me anything."

Ysabel blushed and ducked out to meet the agent at the elevator.

A smile teased the corners of his lips. She'd been shy this morning about his seeing her naked. Now she was blushing over his comment about last night. He liked that.

His smile faded when Special Agent Fielding walked through the door. Jackson stood and rounded the desk to shake the man's hand. "Anything new on your end?"

Fielding's eyes narrowed. "Yes, but I'm not sure if it means anything."

"Then just spit it out."

"As you might have noticed, I'm getting little to no help from the sheriff's department. More particularly, Detective Brody Green."

"I'm not surprised. He's been nothing but antagonistic toward me from day one."

"Exactly. And it's been like pulling teeth to get information from him concerning the case." The agent inhaled and let it out. "I ran a check on him."

"And?"

"He's run up a debt to the tune of three hundred thousand dollars."

Jackson whistled. "That's a lot of cash on a detective's salary. You think he's feeling the strain?"

"That's my bet."

"You think he might be a little resentful of your fortune?" Ysabel entered the room, closing the door behind her.

"Could be."

She tapped a finger to her chin and stared out the window. "The question that begs to be answered is what does it have to do with this case?"

Fielding shrugged. "Maybe nothing." He turned his focus to Ysabel. "Jackson told me over the phone that you had a little excitement last night."

Ysabel nodded. "A little."

Agent Fielding pulled a pad and pen out of his pocket. "Start from the top and tell me everything you saw, heard and even smelled. I'd ask why you haven't spoken to the sheriff on this yet, but given Detective Green's demeanor, I can't say I blame you."

Ysabel nodded and glanced at Jackson before she began. She told him about receiving a tip that Gregor had a friend named Anna Chernov. She didn't enlighten him as to where she'd gotten the tip, just that she went to Anna Chernov's house on the southwest side of Houston. She filled him in on what Anna had told her about how she'd been afraid, what she'd said about Gregor sacrificing himself to save her and the baby.

"Where is Ms. Chernov now?"

Ysabel looked from Jackson to Fielding and back. "I'm sorry. She made me promise not to tell a soul where she is. She's afraid whoever started the fire at her house last night will find her and finish the job."

Agent Fielding nodded. "Is there a way you could set me up with a meeting with her, away from where she's staying?"

Ysabel nodded. "I'm sure I can."

"Good. Let's make that happen, let's say," Fielding glanced down at his watch, "four hours from now?"

Ysabel looked to Jackson. "I'll need transportation."

"You'll get it," he replied.

"Then four hours it is." She exchanged cell-phone numbers with the agent and arranged to call with the meeting location later.

"Back to the fire." Agent Fielding leaned closer. "Did you see anyone hanging around the house before you entered or after you left?"

Ysabel closed her eyes.

Jackson noticed the dark circles had barely abated after her night's sleep. He vowed to make sure she got to bed earlier tonight and to leave her alone so that she could actually sleep. Assuming she let him inside her apartment, otherwise he'd be sleeping in the hallway. He wouldn't leave her alone again.

"When I was still in my car outside Anna's house, I noticed a group of young men, maybe teens hanging around the corner across the street."

"Can you describe them?"

"They were wearing those baggy jeans with the crotch hanging down to their knees."

"Anything else? What about shirts, hair, piercings? Anything."

"All of them wore big T-shirts with a snake on the front."

Fielding sat back in his seat and jotted a note on his pad. "The *Culebras.*"

Jackson's chest squeezed tight. "Aren't they one of the most violent gangs in Houston?" He shot a glance at Ysabel.

Ysabel's hand rose to her stomach, her face pale. "I've heard about them."

Jackson felt sick to his stomach, too. Ysabel had been within spitting distance of one of the most notorious gangs in the city, known for drive-by shootings, stabbings and gang rapes. His gut tightened at what had almost happened to her and what could have if the gang had gone into that house before they set it afire. His grip tightened on the pen he held until his knuckles turned white.

Fielding nodded at Jackson without voicing the many dangers of being in gang territory, his eyes saying it all. "I'll get my people on it immediately. Someone is bound to have seen them, maybe even know some of them we can bring in for questioning. In the meantime, Miss Sanchez," his gaze shifted to Ysabel, "I wouldn't go anywhere near the area, especially alone."

She held up a hand. "Don't worry. I've sworn off all investigation on my part. Last night convinced me to leave it to the pros."

Jackson wished he could believe her. But knowing Ysabel as well as he did, he knew her independent nature might get her into trouble yet again. Between himself and Tom, they should be able to keep up with her. He hoped. What more could he do? Physically tie her down?

Akeem's words came back to him. What about a bodyguard? He pulled a pad of paper close and jotted down a note to call Deke. The man had contacts in the security business. Maybe he could recommend a reliable source. He'd steered him in the right direction to having a security system installed in Ysabel's apartment. She'd be mad he went behind her back to have it installed, but maybe not so mad when he told her it was at the company's expense, not hers.

"Is that all you have at the moment?" Fielding stood and tucked his pad and pen into his jacket pocket.

"No, that's not all." Jackson nodded to Ysabel. "Could you call Tom inside?"

She left the room, closing the door behind her.

"I'm worried about Miss Sanchez," Jackson said as soon as the door closed. "Three attempts on her life in the past two days is three attempts too many. Can you look into that angle, as well?"

"Sure will. Did you make a list of those people who might have it in for you? Or events that could have made someone mad?"

Jackson sifted through his drawer and surfaced a sheet of paper he'd been making notes on. "I've been in business for over fifteen years and nothing besides the uprising in Rasnovia came to mind."

"I read in the paper that you and your fiancée split two months ago. Do you think she might begrudge your relationship with Miss Sanchez?"

Jackson stared at Agent Fielding as if he'd grown horns. "What relationship? Until Miss Nilsson called off our wedding, I didn't have a relationship with Miss Sanchez, not that any of this is your business."

"If it means finding the person responsible for the attempts on Miss Sanchez's life, it's my business. In most cases, victims are killed by people they know. Was Miss Sanchez familiar with Miss Nilsson?"

"She knew her and met with her on occasion. It was bound to happen because Miss Sanchez is my executive assistant." Jackson shook his head. "But I can't see Jenna Nilsson as a murderer."

Fielding shrugged. "I'll check into it. I'm sure you're

right, but it won't hurt to do a little digging into her background."

Ysabel knocked and opened the door, leading Tom into the room.

"Yes, Mr. Champion?" The young man walked in, darting nervous glances at Special Agent Fielding.

"Relax, Tom. I want you to tell Special Agent Fielding what you've learned so far."

Tom gulped. "You want me to tell him?"

"Not how, but what." Jackson turned to the FBI agent. "Tom has it on good authority that Gregor Volsky received a sizable deposit into his account recently. Isn't that right?"

Tom let out the breath he'd been holding. "That's right. Over two hundred thousand dollars two days ago."

Fielding looked from Tom to Jackson. "I take it I'm not supposed to ask how you know this."

Tom looked to Jackson.

"Right. But if I were in the FBI, I'd have all of Greg Voleski and Gregor Volsky's accounts frozen and start tracing those deposits."

Agent Fielding pinned Tom with his stare. "You mean your *authority* hasn't informed you of the source of the deposit yet?"

"No, not really." Tom stood straight, clasping his hands together in the front, clearly uncomfortable with the questioning. "Only that it was from a numbered bank account in the Cayman Islands. I can get you that number if you'd like."

"Yes, I'd like." Agent Fielding pulled his pen and pad from his pocket and jotted down some notes. "Tell your source thanks and if he ever wants a job with the FBI to give me a call."

A grin stretched across Tom's face. "Yes, sir!"

Jackson frowned. He didn't want to lose Tom now that he'd proven to be so useful. Then again, he'd never hold the guy back from the glamorous job of being an agent for the FBI. "Tom can get you that number for the bank account on your way out. Let me know what you find out about the fire last night."

Agent Fielding nodded. "I will."

Jackson stood. "And if it's all the same to you, Agent Fielding, we'd rather you didn't let Detective Green know where you learned about the money transfers."

The FBI agent touched a finger to his temple. "You got it."

Tom and Ysabel turned to follow the agent.

"Miss Sanchez, a moment, please," Jackson said, feeling strange calling her Miss Sanchez when he'd seen her naked just that morning.

Ysabel grabbed Tom's arm. "Don't you need Tom, as well?"

"Not now. I need to speak to you alone."

Tom glanced down at her hand on his arm. "Are you okay, Miss Sanchez?"

Ysabel's hand jerked free of Tom's arm as if she just realized she'd been holding him back. "Yes, yes. I'm all right. Go ahead. I'll be fine, just a little shaky from the fire last night."

"Want me to get you a bottle of water or something from the cafeteria?" Tom asked.

Jackson's back teeth ground together. "I'll take care of it, Tom. You can go."

Tom gave Ysabel one last look and left.

Ysabel stayed where she was for a long moment facing the door, her back to Jackson. Then she turned, her shoulders stiff. "What did you need, Mr. Champion?"

"I need you to cut the bull. After last night, we should be on a first-name basis, *Ysabel.*" When she refused to correct what she'd called him, he shrugged. "Fine. That's not why I called you in here."

"What is it then?"

"I want you to take me to Anna Chernov."

She stared right at him, no expression on her face. "I can't."

"You can and you will."

"I'm sorry, Mr. Champion, I made a promise to her that I would tell no one where she is."

"You don't have transportation."

"I plan on remedying that as soon as I get off work."

"You need to take me to her now. I'm afraid whoever attacked her last night might find her before we get her to a safe location."

"She's safe where she is."

"Are you willing to bet her life on it? And the life of her baby?"

Ysabel chewed her lip, a frown knitting her brow.

"I thought not. Now take me to her so that I can get her to a safe location."

Chapter Twelve

"I don't make a habit of breaking my promises," Ysabel groused in the seat beside Jackson. "Turn left at the next corner."

"You're doing her a favor." Jackson negotiated the turn. "Besides, you don't have a car, you might as well let me get you there."

"Which reminds me." Ysabel's fingers tightened around her purse strap. "After we get Anna situated, could you drop me off at the nearest car dealership? I need to purchase a new car."

"You don't just walk into a car dealership without a clue as to what you want in a car and how much it's worth."

"That's easy for you to say. You've got a vehicle. Try being without one, even for a day." She tapped her fingernails on the armrest. "It'll make you crazy."

"If that's what's bothering you, I'll help you find a car tomorrow."

"No, I want to find my own car by myself."

Jackson didn't respond, but his grip tightened on the wheel, his knuckles turning white. Had her response hurt him or made him angry?

Not that she should care. The main reason she wanted to find her new car by herself was because she didn't want a car that reminded her of Jackson. Especially after she'd left

Champion Shipping and Jackson behind. The split would be hard enough without constant reminders. With a baby coming, she'd want to talk about the safest car with the easiest access to a child's car seat. All these things she needed to consider, now that she was expecting a baby. It was just as well her car burned up. A compact car wasn't necessarily the best choice for a new mom with a baby and a bulky car seat.

As they neared the road where the battered women's shelter was located, Ysabel wished she'd been more firm with Jackson. Anna might not trust her again. "Stop here."

Jackson glanced around at the small homes that didn't look big enough for a shelter. "Is this it?"

"No, it's two blocks from here, but I want to go in alone and talk with her first." She held up her cell phone. "I'll call you when I get to Anna's okay." Ysabel reached for the door handle.

His hand shot out and he grabbed her arm. "No. I won't let you go there by yourself."

"And I won't destroy that woman's trust in me. If she knows that I led someone here after promising her I wouldn't, she might run. How do you want this to go?"

"I don't want you to go by yourself."

"I'd prefer you stayed here until I return." She could tell by the stubborn set of his jaw he wouldn't consider that an option at all. Ysabel sighed, making a decision she hoped she wouldn't regret. "If you can't manage that, then follow me on foot, and *don't* let anyone see you. And when I get Anna to come out, head back to the truck so that she doesn't know you followed me to her."

"I don't like it." Jackson's grip on her arm tightened, almost to the point of being painful, but Ysabel kept her silence, letting him stew over his choices. "Okay, I'll follow at a distance."

Ysabel slipped out of the truck and leaned back in. "Give me a chance to get ahead of you before you follow."

Jackson nodded.

She turned to walk away, her thoughts on what she'd say to Anna to convince her it was all right to talk with the man her husband had tried to destroy.

Before she'd gone two steps, Jackson called out. "Ysabel."

Her steps faltered and she turned back toward the truck.

Jackson leaned against the hood of the vehicle, his feet crossed at the ankles looking sexy and relaxed. But the tightness of his jaw indicated the effort it took for him to stay put. "Be careful, will ya?"

She held up her hand with her cell phone. "I'll call if I get into trouble." When she turned away, she couldn't help the smile that lifted the corners of her lips. In his own way, Jackson Champion probably cared for her. Warmth spread inside her chest, hurrying her forward.

Not that relationships lasted with Jackson. He'd proven that time and again. Hadn't she seen the parade of women over the past five years, moving through his life like they were moving through a revolving door? None of them stayed. He didn't let them.

Except for Jenna. When he'd decided it was time to settle down, he'd made his decision to marry Jenna and she'd been the one to back out. He hadn't been emotionally scarred by her rejection, more matter-of-fact than anything. Not that Jenna was his type at all.

And who was his type? The little voice in the back of Ysabel's head taunted her. Another little voice answered, *Me! Me! Me!*

Keep your feet on the ground, girl. Jackson Champion is a player, and don't you forget that.

Fully aware of the man trailing her to the point the hairs on the back of her neck stood at attention, Ysabel tried to concentrate on what she'd say to Anna.

When she arrived at the shelter, she entered through the front door. Mrs. Rodriguez, the home's administrator called out from her office. "If you're looking for Anna, she left an hour ago."

Ysabel's stomach dropped. "Did she say where she was going?"

"She said something about a bank and money. Her accent was so thick, I barely understood her."

Nausea threatened Ysabel's finicky pregnant stomach. "Did she say when she'd be back?"

Mrs. Rodriguez checked her watch. "About now. She was only going to be gone for an hour. She left Katiya with me and I'm sure she'll wake up hungry before long." Mrs. Rodriguez waved to the playpen on the far side of her desk where a sleeping baby lay curled up in a blanket a fist pressed against her cheek. The baby jerked, as if sensing their attention, and then settled, her mouth making little sucking motions.

Ysabel's heart melted at the sight of the baby. Soon she'd have one of her own. Would she look like Jackson? In some ways, Ysabel hoped not. Forgetting Jackson would be hard enough without the constant reminder. But deep in her heart, she really hoped her baby would have his dark hair and blue eyes.

"There she is now." Mrs. Rodriguez's gaze focused on the window.

The front door opened and Anna stepped inside, her face and hair covered in a light scarf. When she saw Ysabel standing there, she rushed forward, wrapping her thin arms around Ysabel. "Oh, Miss Ysabel, I am happy to see you."

Ysabel hugged the woman and set her aside. "Can we go to your room and talk?"

Anna glanced at Mrs. Rodriguez.

"Go." The older woman waved her away. "Katiya is still sleeping. I'll bring her if she wakes."

Anna led the way to the back of the house where her small room was located.

Once inside, Ysabel closed the door and turned to Anna. "Are you all right? Are they treating you well?"

Anna smiled, nodding her head. "Yes, oh, yes. Mrs. Rodriguez has been very good to me and Katiya." Her smile faded and her brows pulled inward. "But I cannot repay her."

"She said you just went to the bank. Were you unable to access the money Gregor left you?"

"The bank tell me the account is frozen. I have no money and I can't get any more." She clasped her hands in her lap, tears springing to her eyes. "How can I pay for food for me and Katiya?"

Ysabel didn't like the idea that she'd been to a bank and liked it even less that the account had been frozen. If Tom was able to hack into Gregor's account, would someone else be watching it for signs of activity? A sense of urgency swarmed Ysabel's belly. If someone had been watching the bank, would they be able to follow Anna back to the shelter? Suddenly Jackson's suggestion that Anna might not be safe didn't seem so off-base.

Ysabel sat on the bed beside Anna and laid her hand over the other woman's hand. "The man I work for wants to talk to you about Gregor."

"Who is this man?"

Ysabel inhaled deeply and let it out. "Jackson Champion."

Anna shrank back, pulling her hand free of Ysabel. "The man Gregor worked for?"

"Yes."

"He will kill me for what Gregor did to his ship."

"No, Jackson will not kill you, he wants to help you."

"No, no, he will send me to jail, I will be deported. What will happen to me and Katiya?" She jumped up from the bed and paced the room.

"Anna, what if the men who burned your house down come back again?" She stopped short of saying "to finish the job."

Anna glanced around the room as if looking for her belongings. "I must leave. I go where they cannot find me."

"You don't have any money, Anna. You and your baby need food to live."

"I can't stay here. That man will come. I know it. He will find us."

Ysabel rose from her perch on the bed. "Did you see the man who paid Gregor, Anna?"

She shook her head, tears running down her face. "One time only and he was too far away to see his face. A big man." She raised her hand high above her head and a shiver shook her frame. "A big, bad man."

"He was tall?" Ysabel quelled her excitement. Anna wasn't much over five feet tall. Practically any man would tower over her. Although it wasn't much to go on, it was the most description anyone had reported so far. Anna might be the only person alive who could come close to identifying whoever was responsible for sabotaging Champion Shipping and possibly the Aggie Four Foundation. Which put her in danger. "Anna, if this man thinks you can identify him, he will definitely be looking for you. Mr. Champion can help you hide from him."

She shook her head. "No, no. I can't."

A light tap on the door made Ysabel jump and Anna cry out.

"Anna, a man is on the telephone, asking for an Anna Chernov," Mrs. Rodriguez's voice called out through the wood paneling. "I told him no one by that name lived here. I thought you should know."

Anna grasped Ysabel's hand. "He has found me. He has found me!"

Ysabel held her hands firmly between her own. When the administrator's footsteps faded down the hallway, Ysabel stared into Anna's eyes. "You have to come with me. If he found you here, he'll find you no matter where you run. You don't have the money to help you disappear. Mr. Champion does."

Anna's tears trickled to a stop. "You trust this Mr. Champion?"

Ysabel nodded. "I'd trust him with my life." *Just not my heart.*

Anna took a shaky breath and sighed. "Then I will come with you."

With a nod, Ysabel pulled her cell phone from her pocket. "I'm going to call Mr. Champion now and let him know where we are to pick us up in his truck. You're sure?"

The woman nodded.

A baby wailed in the hallway outside the room. Anna raced for the door and flung it open.

Mrs. Rodriguez carried Katiya toward them, smiling. "She's awake and hungry. That girl's got a set of lungs on her."

Ysabel dialed Jackson's number.

"Everything okay?" he answered, his voice taut.

"Yes." Ysabel glanced at Anna settling on the bed to feed the crying baby.

Anna pulled her shirt up and nestled the baby close to her breast. Like a baby bird eager for her mother's offering, Katiya turned her cheek into her mother's breast, mouth wide open and latched on.

Ysabel's own breasts tingled. Soon she'd be feeding her own baby. What would it feel like to have a baby suckling on her nipples? Her heart filled with longing. Seven months seemed a long time to wait. She wanted to hold her child now.

"I'm headed back for the truck. Don't go anywhere."

"We'll be here." Short of jerking the baby loose from her hold on Anna, they couldn't quite jump up and run down the street without Katiya screaming for her supper. The infant was an effective alarm system to anyone listening or looking for a woman carrying a baby.

Ysabel's toe tapped against the carpet. The sooner they left the shelter the better. If someone knew enough to call here asking for Anna, he might not be far behind. What was keeping Jackson?

Footsteps in the hallway hurried toward Anna's room.

With her breath caught in her throat, Ysabel ran for the door and nearly jumped out of her skin when someone knocked loudly.

"Ms. Chernov, there's a man out here claiming he's here to pick you up." When Ysabel yanked the door open, Mrs. Rodriguez practically fell in. "What should I do?"

"Is he wearing a cowboy hat and driving a pickup?" Ysabel asked.

"Yes, yes, he is. Do you know him?" The older woman's brows knitted into a concerned frown. "We don't like unannounced visitors here. What with this being a battered women's shelter and all."

"It's okay. He's with me and he's okay." Ysabel patted the woman's arm. "Anna, we need to leave."

Anna pressed a finger to her nipple, breaking the baby's suction.

Katiya sucked in a deep, sobbing breath and cried.

Ysabel took the baby into her arms while Anna straightened her clothing and grabbed the diaper bag they'd purchased the previous evening. Everything Anna owned was in that diaper bag. Which didn't amount to much—diapers, two outfits for Katiya and one change of clothing for Anna. That was it.

Ysabel held the whimpering baby against her chest and led the way out to Jackson.

The five or ten minutes Ysabel had been inside the house without him had been the longest of Jackson's life. When she walked toward him carrying an infant, he couldn't keep the smile from curling his lips. "What have you got there?" He leaned close and tickled the baby's chin, the scent of talcum and herbal shampoo mixing to form a not unpleasant combination. He brushed his hand across the baby's soft skin, wishing it was Ysabel's skin he stroked. "Hi, sweetheart. Want to go for a ride?"

Mrs. Rodriguez opened a closet door and tugged an infant's car seat out. "You can take this. I assume you won't be coming back to stay?"

Ysabel looked to Jackson.

He shook his head. They'd take Anna somewhere safe and he'd help her and her child to get a fresh start.

"We won't, Mrs. Rodriguez," Ysabel told the older woman. "But thank you for all your help. We'll return the car seat in a few days."

"Don't worry about it. You can return it anytime."

"Stay here," Jackson told Ysabel and Anna. He left the house first, and spent the next precious few minutes struggling to fit the car seat into the backseat of his pickup. Once he had the straps in place, his gaze panned the street and the nearby houses in both directions. After a long moment, he waved Ysabel and Anna to join him at the truck.

Carrying the baby, Ysabel hustled around the truck and climbed into the backseat. She had the baby strapped in and cinched in seconds. Anna climbed into the seat beside the baby and leaned over to plunk a pacifier in her mouth.

Ysabel dropped down out of the truck and rounded the tailgate, climbing up into the front passenger seat beside Jackson. "Where to?"

He started the engine and set the truck in gear. "The Diamondback Ranch. At least there, you can see your enemy coming from a distance."

Ysabel nodded and settled back in the cab for the hour-long ride in Houston traffic. "Anna said she saw Gregor speak to a big man. She thinks he's the one who ordered Gregor to smuggle the bomb materials and blow up the ship."

Jackson glanced in the rearview mirror at the woman in the backseat. Her pale face and shadowed eyes radiated her fear. "Would you recognize him if you saw him in a picture?"

Anna shrugged and looked down at her baby. "I am not certain. I was hiding and it was dark outside, he stood in the shadows." She yawned and leaned her head back against the seat. "His hair not like Anna's. White."

So the man had pale hair. A big blond man. Jackson wanted to ask more, but Anna's eyes closed.

The woman had to be exhausted, running from a killer and living in fear for her life.

Jackson concentrated on the road, leaving the woman alone. Soon Anna nodded off to sleep.

About that time, Ysabel reached a hand across and touched his leg.

Every nerve ending in that spot and others throughout his body leaped.

"I haven't asked her about talking with Fielding yet. It was all I could do to get her into the truck with you."

"I got that feeling. She's been through a lot."

Ysabel turned in her seat to look over her shoulder. "Do you think she'll be safe at the ranch?"

"Yes, Flint will make sure she's okay. And he'll arrange for her to get a new start someplace when this is all over."

"Good. I'd hate anything bad to happen to her and her baby."

The rest of the ride passed in silence. As they turned off the highway onto the long driveway to the ranch, Ysabel's cell phone rang.

She scrambled in her purse for the device and viewed the screen. "It's Tom," she said as she punched the Talk button. "This is Ysabel."

Jackson alternated checking his position on the road and studying Ysabel's expressions.

Her brows drew together. "You did? A corporation. Did

you find out who it belongs to?" A long pause. "A Houston address. Surely we can track down the owners. That's great, Tom. You're doing a fabulous job. We can look into it more tomorr—Tom?" She glanced across at Jackson. "Tom?"

Her face paled.

Jackson slowed the truck and pulled to the side of the road. "What's happening?"

"I don't know." She pressed the phone to one ear and a hand to the other. "I think he dropped the phone."

A loud banging sound erupted from the cell phone and Ysabel's hand jerked away from her head. "Oh, my God." Her eyes widened and she looked across the console to Jackson. "I think he crashed."

Chapter Thirteen

Her hands shaking, Ysabel called 9-1-1 and reported what she'd heard after Tom dropped his cell phone. Not that she could give them much more information because she didn't know exactly where Tom had been when he wrecked.

Jackson was on the phone and shifting into gear at the same time. Committed to delivering Anna to the ranch, they couldn't turn around until they'd safely delivered her into the care of Flint McKade.

When they reached the ranch, Flint was waiting on the porch with his wife, Lora Leigh.

Even before he'd switched off the engine, Flint was at his truck door, opening it. "I was able to contact the Houston dispatch. They found Tom's vehicle in a ditch off Interstate 45."

Ysabel climbed out of the pickup and rounded the hood to stand in front of Flint. "How is he?"

Lora Leigh joined Flint. "Still alive from what the dispatcher could tell us. They're having to cut him out of his car."

"Damn it!" Jackson slammed his palm against the steering wheel. "What the hell happened?"

"According to one of the police officers, someone ran him off the road on his way home from work," Flint said. "Witnesses say it was deliberate."

"Poor Tom." Ysabel's hand hovered over her belly, plucking at her shirt. "I can't believe someone would attack in broad daylight."

"Did anyone get a make on the car?" Jackson asked.

"A witness reported a dark-blue Saturn, a rental car. They were able to get a partial on the license. Special Agent Fielding is checking into it."

"Good." Jackson climbed down from the truck and opened the door for Anna, whose face had paled considerably at the news. "Could you take care of Ms. Chernov? I need to get back to town."

"You bet." Lora Leigh climbed inside and unsnapped the safety belts holding the baby and the car seat. "Come, Anna, I'll show you your room. And don't worry, Flint has a state-of-the-art security system inside the house. You'll be safe here."

"If there's anything more I can do, let me know." Flint held out a hand to Jackson and the men shook.

"There is one thing," Jackson said. "See if you can talk Anna into a meeting with Special Agent Fielding. Maybe he can arrange for a composite sketch of the man she saw with her husband."

Anna hesitated, her eyes wide. "No, I cannot risk it."

Jackson sighed. "Just hear what Flint has to say. We won't force you to do anything you don't want to do."

Anna's gaze met Jackson's. After a moment, she nodded. "I will listen."

Ysabel gave her a hug. "You'll be okay. Lora Leigh is a sweetheart. She'll help you with Katiya."

"Absolutely. We were able to borrow a crib from one of the ranch hands. Come see." Lora Leigh, carrying the car seat with the sleeping baby inside, led Anna into the house.

Ysabel climbed into the truck, her stomach churning, the awful acids burning for release.

Jackson slid into the driver's seat, his gaze on her as he started the engine. "Are you okay?"

"No. I'm not." Tears welled in her eyes, but she held on to them until Jackson turned the truck back toward Houston. "I shouldn't have involved Tom in this."

"Ysabel, you don't know if Tom's accident was due to the hacking he's been doing."

"Why else would someone deliberately run him off the road?" Anger surged through her. Deep down, she knew she wasn't angry at Jackson, but he was there and she had to lash out at someone or something. "What have we accomplished so far? Nothing!" She slammed her hand on the arm rest. "Nothing but a burned-down house, two dead terrorists and a kid on his way to the hospital. We're not exactly batting a thousand here. What are you going to do about it? How are you going to make it stop?"

Jackson's lips tightened into a thin line. "I don't know. But you're right. It's not fair that Tom, Anna and you got caught up in all this. I don't know what I can do to make the attacks stop, but I can do something about you and Tom. You're not to work on this anymore. In fact, as of today, your resignation is official. That way you're not involved with Champion Shipping at all."

Ysabel's anger shriveled up and died at his words, replaced by an ominous sense of dread. This was it. She'd finally gotten what she wanted. Then why didn't she feel better about it? When she should be relieved, she could think only about the emptiness of spending the rest of her life without ever seeing Jackson again. No more poking fun, arguing politics and comparing notes on how to improve Champion Shipping.

"Okay," she managed to say. Her hands clasped together in her lap, pressed over her belly. When she should be planning her next steps, her move and her job search, all she could do was sit and stare out the window, her mind a complete blank.

Jackson sat stone-cold silent in the seat beside her all the way back to the outskirts of Houston. As he maneuvered through the late-afternoon traffic, his cell phone rang. Flint called to give him the name of the hospital they'd taken Tom to.

"I can drop you at the office or take you with me to see Tom," Jackson offered.

"Tom," she said.

At the hospital, Ysabel questioned the volunteer at the information desk who located Tom's room in intensive care. At first, the nurses wouldn't let them in to see Tom because neither one of them was a family member. Ysabel tried to explain that Tom's family lived in Lubbock and they couldn't get there until late that night, but the nurses held firm.

Jackson took over. One call to the administrator and a reminder of how much money Champion Shipping contributed annually to the hospital and they were ushered into Tom's room.

Tom lay amidst an array of machines, wires and tubes. His young face bruised and lacerated, the dark smudges a sharp contrast against the crisp white sheets.

"We just gave him a sedative, so he won't be able to talk long, if at all," the nurse informed them, in a hushed voice.

"Hey, Tom." Ysabel lifted the young man's hand in hers, careful not to touch anything broken or bruised. A knot rose to her throat as she stared down into his battered face.

Tom's eyelids flickered open. "Did I die? Are you an angel?" His cracked lips turned up in a wry smile. He winced and the smile disappeared. "Guess I won't be smiling anytime soon," he croaked in a voice barely above a whisper.

Jackson rounded the bed to the other side and shook his

head. "And I thought I had the corner on the dare-devil driving. You sure know how to make an impression on the boss."

"Does this mean I get a raise?" Tom chuckled and coughed.

Jackson smiled down at the kid. "We'll talk about it."

Ysabel's heart swelled at the tenderness in Jackson's voice. He really was good to his employees. She'd never had a complaint. Hopefully, she'd find a new boss as considerate. A sob rose in her throat.

The younger man's eyes drifted closed. "Ysabel, could you tell the boss I'll be late for work tomorrow?"

Ysabel swallowed the lump in her throat and she gently squeezed his hand. "Don't worry. I'm sure the boss will let it slide this once."

"Not so sure. 'Specially because his girl is holding my hand." Tom's breathing evened out and his face went slack.

Ysabel's cheeks heated. Tom didn't realize how far from the truth his words were. The boss's girl. Ha! He'd just accepted her resignation, effectively cutting her out of his life forever.

The nurse appeared in the doorway. "You'll have to leave now. Mr. Walker needs rest."

In the elevator going down, Jackson spoke first. "I don't feel comfortable leaving Tom here without protection."

"I could stay with him."

Jackson shook his head. "No. You're exhausted, you need to get home. Not to mention, you've had your share of near misses." He flipped his phone open. "It's time to hire some help."

While Jackson called around for a bodyguard for hire, Ysabel did some calling of her own to her sister Delia.

Twenty minutes later, Jackson shut his phone and scrubbed a hand over his face. "I have a man on the way.

Once he gets here, we can go."

Delia chose that moment to hurry into the lobby of the hospital.

Ysabel faced Jackson. "I have my own transportation. If it's all right by you, I'll collect my things from the office tonight."

Jackson felt like he'd been sucker-punched in the gut. Oh yeah, he'd accepted her resignation. What the hell was he thinking? Had he really said she could leave? If Ysabel left, he'd have no way to protect her from whoever was trying to kill her. Panic seized him. "About that. I didn't mean it. I still want you to stay on for the full two weeks."

Ysabel smiled sadly. "You can't take it back, Jackson. You verbally accepted my resignation. That's as binding as a signed contract."

"But it's not in writing. It would be your word against mine. I could take you to court and keep you from leaving before the end of your two-week notice."

She shook her head. "Jackson Champion, you're a man of your word. You wouldn't lie in court to save your life. Just let me go. I'll be okay and so will you."

Jackson wasn't so sure. If he let Ysabel walk out of his life now, he'd never see her again. "If it's a matter of pay, I'll double your salary."

Her brows dipped. For a brilliant businessman, Jackson Champion could be clueless when it came to people. No, when it came to her. "It's never been about the pay, Jackson."

"Then why quit now?"

"I have to. That's all there is to it."

"Is it because of what's happened between us? I'll leave you alone, if that's what you want."

"No. Maybe someday I'll tell you. But for now, I can't." Her voice choked on the last words.

Her sister stepped up beside her and jabbed her elbow into Ysabel's arm. "Tell him."

Ysabel glared at her sister. "No. Not now."

"If you don't, I will."

Ysabel grabbed her sister's arm and jerked her toward the door. "Goodbye, Jackson. Come on, Delia. I don't need another conscience."

The two women hurried away, leaving Jackson standing alone in the lobby. She was leaving. Damn it! Ysabel was leaving and all the money he owned couldn't stop her.

Money hadn't changed her mind, not that he really expected it to. Ysabel wasn't driven to make millions like he was. For the first time since he'd known Ysabel he wondered just what did motivate her. She was always talking about her family. Obviously family meant a lot to her. She loved her family and hoped to have one of her own someday. Hadn't she told him that once upon a time?

Jackson's own family had abandoned him to the foster-care system, a system that hadn't been the ideal place for a child to learn what families were all about. He'd been shuffled from one home to another. What did he know about how a family worked?

Ysabel knew. Her large, extended family was spread out across Houston and south Texas, but they were close like a family was supposed to be.

Was that it? Did she want a chance for a family of her own? Did she want to leave him so she'd have time to date and find a man to love her like she deserved? Searing heat burned in his chest at the thought of another man holding Ysabel in his arms, making love to her sweet body, giving her children. Was he jealous? When Jenna had ditched him for an old boyfriend, he hadn't felt as though he couldn't breathe, or like he wanted to smash a man's face, or as if he couldn't live to the next day.

Jackson Champion had never been jealous before and he

wasn't sure he was now. But whatever he was feeling, he didn't like it.

If she was leaving to take the time to date and find a man to love her, could he convince her to stay if he told her that *he* loved her? Would that make a difference?

Ysabel had told him he was a man of his word. Could he tell her he loved her and mean it? Did he love her?

The question rammed him like a wrecker ball. Did he love Ysabel?

"Sir? Are you Jackson Champion?" A bulked-out man dressed in a tight black polo shirt and black trousers stopped in front of him, removing mirrored aviator glasses.

Jackson focused on the man, realizing for the first time since Ysabel had walked away that he was still standing in the lobby of the hospital.

"I'm Toby Layne. The agency sent me over. I'm your new bodyguard." He cracked his knuckles and flexed his muscles. "Whose body do you want me to guard?"

DELIA was waiting for her outside her apartment when Ysabel returned from the office, carrying a box with the personal items she'd unloaded from her desk. Although the box was heavy, the contents didn't amount to much—a few pictures, her framed college diplomas and her favorite stapler.

She and Delia had spent two hours on a hot dealership lot, choosing a car Ysabel couldn't have cared less about. She didn't have the heart to tell the salesman her only requirement was an affordable payment for a woman working for minimum wage. She'd cash in some of her 401K. That and her insurance payoff would equal a sizable down payment to keep her monthly outgo reasonable.

After promising her life away, Ysabel drove off the lot in a sedate four-door charcoal gray sedan any soccer mom would be proud of.

"Didn't I just see you an hour ago?" She balanced the box on her hip and fished in her purse with her spare hand. "What are you doing here? Don't you have a party to go to or whatever single girls do today?"

"Not until the weekend, *mi hermana.* I have a few minutes I can spend helping my pregnant sister leave the man she loves. Give me that." She reached for the box and held it while Ysabel unlocked the door.

Part of Ysabel wanted to be left alone to sort through the box and what was left of her life. The other part couldn't stand the thought of sitting by herself in her apartment, the four walls closing in around her. "Come in then. I could use some diversion."

Before she'd closed the door firmly, Delia started, "Why didn't you tell him?"

"If you're going to nag, just turn around and leave right now."

Delia set the box on the coffee table and raised her hands in surrender. "Okay, okay, I promise not to nag you about telling Jackson you're pregnant with *his* child."

"Good, because I really don't think I could take it right now." Ysabel choked back a sob, but she couldn't stop the rush of tears to her eyes. "I can't believe I'll never see him again."

"Oh, you'll see him all right." Delia wandered toward the kitchen and opened the refrigerator. "In court most likely. Girl, you don't have any food in your refrigerator. What are you feeding that baby?"

"I don't know." Ysabel flopped onto the brushed leather sofa and plopped her feet next to a box.

"Well, you can't starve yourself without starving your baby. I'm calling out for Chinese."

While Delia placed the order, Ysabel pressed her fingers

to her eyes, trying unsuccessfully to stem the flow of tears. "What is wrong with me? I never cry!"

Delia set the phone on the counter and hurried to sit beside Ysabel on the sofa. "You're pregnant. You're going to cry. Get used to it."

"Since when are you an expert on pregnant women?"

"Don't you remember? I stayed with our cousin Carmen during her last two months before José decided to appear. She taught me everything I need to know about babies." Delia raised her hand. "I do so solemnly swear I'll never have any of my own." Her face wrinkled in a horrified grimace. "How anyone could want to have children is beyond me. All that blood, screaming and pain."

"Thanks." Ysabel stared at her sister, without lifting her head from the back of the sofa. "I'll remember to bring you with me when I need a root canal. Nothing like telling it like it is to make a girl scared to death."

Her sister had the grace to blush. "Sorry. Now is not a good time to tell you all that."

"No, duh."

"The point was, you're pregnant, your hormones are whacky, you just said goodbye to the man you love. What's not to cry about?" Delia wrapped her in her arms and hugged her. "You go right ahead and cry. You deserve to."

Ysabel chuckled and hiccupped, pushing her sister away. "Thanks, but I need to get past this."

"You won't until you tell Jackson that he has a baby on the way."

Ysabel leaned her head back again, her head aching. "I know."

"Until you do, you won't be able to get on with your life. And it's not fair to run away before you do it. Jackson has the right to know where you and the baby are. He's the father."

"You promised not to nag." Ysabel laid her arm over her face.

"I know, I just feel so strongly about this and deep down, I know you do too. Your sense of fairness won't let you rest until you tell him."

"You're right." Ysabel sat up. "I can't think past that time. I should have told him as soon as I found out."

"Now you're talking."

Ysabel stood and straightened her pants suit. "Question is how?"

"How what?"

"How do I tell him?" Her head throbbed, her stomach knotting at the prospect of telling Jackson he was going to be a father. What man liked being broadsided by an admission like that? How would he take it? Would he be angry, disappointed, shocked?

"Why don't you try the straight and simple? 'Jackson, I'm having your baby.'"

Ysabel tapped a finger to her lips and stared out of her window at the lights of downtown Houston. Her apartment wasn't in the penthouse, but she had a good view of the rest of the city. She could see the light from Jackson's penthouse, albeit from a distance. Not that she could tell whether he was home. She'd left him at the hospital three hours ago. Would he be home?

Now that she wasn't working for him anymore, she might as well get it over with. He might be too distracted by what was happening with Champion Shipping to be concerned about her and a baby. "Okay, I'm going to tell him." Her decision made, she marched to the counter where she'd left her purse and slipped her cell phone from a side pocket.

Delia squealed. "You are *not* going to tell him over the phone, are you?"

Ysabel's finger hovered over the speed dial for Jackson's cell number. "Why not?"

"*Madre de Dios!* You can't tell a man he's going to be a father over the phone." She practically leaped at Ysabel, grabbing her phone. "You have to tell him in person."

Her heart hammered against her ribs. "No way. I can't." Even as she said the words, she knew that was exactly what she had to do.

"You have to." Delia slipped an arm around Ysabel's waist and pulled her against her side. "You know he deserves that much."

Ysabel huffed out a sigh. "I hate it when you're right." She stole the phone from her sister's hands and tossed it into her purse. "Then I'll go to his place right now and tell him. That way I can leave when I want to. If he comes here, I'd have a harder time getting him to leave."

"Good thinking." Delia smiled. Was there a little devilish gleam in her green eyes so much like Ysabel's? "Go on, *mi hermana.* I'll wait here in case you need someone to talk to when you get back."

"You'd do that for me?" Ysabel's eyes pooled again with her ready tears.

"Of course. I'm not leaving until that Chinese food gets here." She laughed, turning Ysabel toward the door. "Hurry up before it gets any later. It's already after nine."

"I'm going." Ysabel's feet dragged toward the door, every step bringing her closer to her last face-to-face with the only man she'd ever loved. Foolishly, yes, but loved nonetheless. "It takes only about fifteen minutes there, fifteen minutes back and a few minutes to break the news to him. I'll be back in less than an hour. Keep my food warm." Not that she'd want to touch it after telling Jackson the news. Right at that moment, she wanted to throw up and she didn't expect that feeling to go away even after she told him.

On the ride down the elevator and the walk out to her car, Ysabel told herself everything would be all right.

When she arrived at Jackson's building and entered the parking garage, her throat closed up and she fought to breathe normally. She hoped like hell telling Jackson wasn't going to be the biggest mistake of her life.

A frown pulled at her brow. Jackson's car wasn't in his assigned spot.

Why hadn't she thought to call him before she came over? She pulled her phone from her purse. Before she could place the call, a loud knock on her window made her scream and drop her phone.

Her pulse jumping, Ysabel starred out at Jenna Nilsson.

"Ysabel, help me, please," she cried. Her pretty face was bruised, her lip cracked and bleeding.

Ysabel shoved her car into park and jumped out. "Jenna, what happened?"

"It's my brother," she sobbed, her words garbled through the tears. "He's gone crazy."

"Your brother?" Ysabel hadn't known Jenna had a brother. She'd assumed she was an only child. Nothing in any of her conversations with the woman had indicated otherwise. She wrapped the girl in her arms and patted her back. "Take a deep breath and tell me about it."

"No, we can't stay here." She stared around the parking garage, her eyes wide, her hands shaking. "He'll find me and kill me."

"Then get in my car. I'll take you to the police station."

"No!" Jenna pulled free of her hold and stepped back, her head shaking back and forth. "No. You can't go to the police. He'll find me."

"But the police will help."

"No, you can't, because he's—" she dropped to her knees

and buried her face in her hands. “He’s—” More sobs muffled her words.

Ysabel squatted down beside Jenna. “Because he’s what?”

“Because he *is* a cop,” a deep, familiar voice said, before something hard and cold pressed against Ysabel’s back. “Don’t turn around, don’t move.”

Jenna shrank away from Ysabel’s captor. “Oh, God. No. Brody, you can’t do this. You can’t.”

“Shut up!” the man said.

Ysabel’s entire body shook at the realization that the man with a gun pointed at her back was a member of the sheriff’s department. The detective investigating the bombing case, Brody Green. “He’s your brother?” she asked Jenna.

“My stepbrother. You have to stop him. He’s planning to blow up—”

“I said shut up!” Brody stepped forward and slammed the barrel of the pistol against Jenna’s cheekbone. She crumpled to the ground without even a whimper.

Ysabel moved toward the unconscious woman. Before she could reach her, a hand grabbed her hair and yanked her back. “Leave her.”

“But she needs medical attention.”

“Let her die. She’s of no use to me now. She never could get it right.”

“What do you mean?”

“She was supposed to marry Jackson Champion. If she had, none of this would have gotten out of hand.” He jerked her toward his car. “Now get in.”

Chapter Fourteen

After checking over the bodyguard's credentials and briefing him on his duties, Jackson left the hospital, a full hour after Ysabel. Once in his truck, he drove around the city in a complete mental fog. For the first time in his life, he didn't know exactly what he needed to do. Ysabel had been the rock in his world, the one who kept him on track. Even during his two-month absence, he was comforted by the knowledge that she was back home, running the office, smoothing his path. There for him.

Too jittery to go home, he jumped when his cell phone rang, disappointment filling him when the number came up Unknown. To him that meant not Ysabel.

For a moment he let it ring. But the chance it might be news on who had attacked Tom made him reach for the hands-free button on the dash. "Jackson speaking."

"Mr. Champion, this is Special Agent Fielding. I realize it's late, but is there a possibility you could stop by our field office off Interstate 610?"

"What do you have?"

"We have the identity of who rented the vehicle that ran Tom off the road."

"I'll be there in ten minutes." Jackson turned onto Interstate 10 and floored the accelerator. Finally, a clue. Eight and a half minutes later, he skidded to a stop in the parking lot at the Houston field office of the Federal Bureau of Investigations on T. C. Jester Boulevard.

Fielding met him at the front door and led him through the maze of offices to a conference room set up with a computer and a large white board. On the board was the time line of the chain of events going back to when one of Champion Shipping's airplanes exploded on the tarmac carrying a shipment of Arabians for Flint and Akeem several months ago.

"Take a seat," the agent invited.

Jackson dropped into a padded chair, staring around at the room and its contents. "You guys have been busy."

"Yeah, but this might be the first real clue we've gotten in regards to the potential terrorist plot we think might be underfoot right here in Houston."

Jackson nodded, his gut clenching at the thought. Houston was anything but prepared for a terrorist attack. With over a million people in Houston proper, an attack would be devastating. "I know my ships might have been involved in transporting dirty bomb-making materials. I've tightened security and run another background check on all my employees working in and around the shipyards."

"Good. That will help. But we think the damage may already be done and dirty bomb materials are already here in the city. We just don't know where and when they'll strike."

"So what did you find?"

"The vehicle that ran Tom off the road earlier was a rental car, leased out to a J. Nilsson."

"Jenna?" Jackson sat back. "You think Jenna is capable of running a man off the road?"

"Anyone is capable of running another person off the road just by not paying attention. But no." Fielding shook his head. "Witnesses said the driver was a man. So we ran a check on your ex-fiancée. And you'll never believe what we found."

Jackson leaned forward.

"Jenna's half brother is none other than the sheriff department's Detective Brody Green."

Jackson scrubbed a hand over his face. "Why didn't I know that?"

"Did you run a background check on Miss Nilsson?"

"Yes." He'd had Ysabel schedule the background check after their first date.

"I'm betting Pinkerton didn't go any further than her mother and father. You see, her mother had a baby when she was a teenager. Brody. She gave him to his father to raise. It wasn't until Jenna's mother died in a car accident that she found out she had a brother."

Jackson crossed his arms over his chest. "So, her brother is a detective. You think he's the one who ran Tom off the road?"

"We dusted the car for prints and found nothing. He must have used gloves while driving. But he didn't use them when he filled the gas tank. We were able to lift a clean print and run it through our databases. We got a match on our detective."

"But why would he want to sabotage the investigation?"

"Could have something to do with that debt he's accumulated at the casinos in Biloxi, Mississippi." Fielding smiled grimly. "Remember, he's in over his head to the tune of three hundred thousand dollars."

To Jackson, three hundred thousand dollars wasn't that much these days. But on a detective's salary…

"Have you brought him in for questioning?"

"That's the problem, we can't find him. He didn't show up for work today and didn't call in."

"Great, the man's a potential menace and no one knows where he is?" The conversation he'd had with Detective Green played back in his mind. "Green doesn't like me."

"Yeah, I gathered as much. Do you think it had anything to do with your relationship with Jenna?"

"Now that I know he's her half-brother, I'd bet my fortune on it." Jackson tried to recall his exact wording. "He said something about SOBs like me making promises they never intended to keep and then backing out without care for the repercussions. He said, it would come back to haunt me someday."

"Do you think he's the one sabotaging Champion Shipping and the Aggie Four Foundation?" Fielding asked.

"I didn't get the impression he was smart enough to orchestrate anything that difficult. He's mad at me about something, but I'm not sure what." Jackson dug through his memory to think of what and all he had was his relationship to Jenna.

"Do you think he was counting on your marrying Jenna so that he could get his hands on some of your money to pay back his debts?"

Jackson chewed on that thought. "If he wanted me to marry Jenna so that he could get his hands on the money, why would he try to sabotage my corporation?"

"I don't know." Fielding tapped a pen to the table top. "You say Miss Sanchez has been targeted on several occasions?"

"Yes."

"Do you think he feels like she's a threat to you and Jenna patching things up?"

The recent image of Jenna in his office practically throwing herself at him sprang to mind. "Jenna tried to get me to take her back." He looked up at Fielding without seeing him. "If he thinks Jenna and I are getting back together, he doesn't know that it was Jenna who called off the wedding, not me. She's in love with another man."

"Maybe she's afraid of Green. Afraid he'll hurt her if she doesn't marry you. Maybe he thinks you dumped his sister for Miss Sanchez." Fielding grinned. "The chemistry between the two of you is pretty obvious even to a stranger like me."

Jackson stood up so fast, his chair shot out behind him, tipping over to crash against the tiled floor. "If Jenna hasn't told him the truth, he might keep trying until he succeeds in getting Ysabel permanently out of the picture. I have to go."

"Before you go, what did Tom find that could have Detective Green scared enough to run him off the road?"

Jackson paused in the doorframe. "He hacked into the Cayman bank account that transferred money into Gregor Volsky's account. He was able to trace the account back to a corporation here in Houston."

Fielding's brows rose. "Any idea which one?"

"None. We'll have to wait for Tom to come out of the sedative they've got him on. But you're welcome to the computer he used in my office."

"We're working on a warrant to search Green's home and office. Should have that soon."

"Great. Now if you'll excuse me, I need to check on Ysabel."

"Right. Do you want me to send an agent to her apartment?"

"No, I'll be there before any agent can be mobilized."

Fielding grinned. "She's a keeper, your Miss Sanchez."

Jackson nodded. "I know." He only wished he was keeping her. He'd practically kicked her out of his life by accepting her resignation. If he'd been in his right mind, he would have used the time he had left to convince her to stay.

The nights they'd spent in each others' arms had been pure ecstasy. Ysabel had been every bit as passionate as he had. But she'd never said anything about love.

Was love a factor in their relationship? He thought back over the years with Ysabel by his side at Champion Shipping. Her wit, humor and intelligence made him smile, kept him on his toes. He thought of all the women he'd paraded past her and her continued good attitude, if not a few sarcastic remarks about their IQ or lack thereof.

He couldn't think of life without her. If that was love…

Once outside the FBI building, he pulled out his cell phone and dialed Ysabel's number. After the fourth ring, her voice mail message played. "Ysabel, meet me at your place. It's important that we talk. Don't go out, don't open your door for anyone, including and especially Detective Green." He clicked the Off button and pressed harder on the accelerator. Why wasn't she answering? Was it because his number showed on the display? "Jesus, Ysabel, now's not the time to ignore me. Pick up the phone. Call me," Jackson said out loud.

He had to get to her before that lunatic Green did. Within minutes, he slammed his truck to a stop outside Ysabel's apartment building, threw it in Park and leaped down. The ride up the elevator, all fourteen floors, nearly killed him. Taking the stairs might have been faster. All the way up, he couldn't help the overwhelming sense of dread washing over him. What if she wasn't there? What if Green had gotten to her first?

The elevator door dinged and before the doors fully opened, Jackson squeezed through and raced down the hall to her apartment, banging on the door. "Ysabel!"

"Keep your shirt on," a voice called out from within.

Relief washed over Jackson. She was home. All that worrying for nothing.

When the door opened, it took him a moment to realize the person in front of him wasn't Ysabel. She looked like her, but she wasn't Ysabel. Delia.

Jackson pushed past her. "Where's Ysabel?" He strode through the apartment, his chest tightening with each step.

"Hello to you, too." Delia leaned in the doorway, a smile curling her lips. "My sister is on her way to your place. She had something important to say to you that couldn't wait."

"She shouldn't be running around the city at night. What's so important it couldn't have waited until morning?" Jackson returned to the door, wanting to shake someone for answers.

"I'm not at liberty to say. You'll have to ask her. She left fifteen minutes ago. She should be at your apartment about now." Delia stepped aside. "If you hurry, you might catch her."

"If she shows up before I find her, tell her to call me and stay put." Jackson hurried through the door and loped down the hallway to the elevator.

"Will do, big daddy." Delia called out behind him in a soft voice he almost didn't hear.

Once in his truck, he performed a U-turn and sped along the street toward his downtown apartment. He hoped he'd catch her before she left his building. Hell, he hoped he'd catch her before Green did.

YSABEL struggled to sit up in the backseat of Detective Green's unmarked sheriff's deputy sedan. The hard plastic zip strap cinching her wrists together behind her back wasn't helping her gain her balance. Jenna lay unconscious on the floorboard in front of her—at least Ysabel *hoped* she was only unconscious. She swallowed hard on the lump of fear threatening to choke off her air. Somehow she had to get out of this situation. Her baby deserved a chance to live. "Where are you taking me?" she asked the back of the man's head.

Green didn't answer, but the speed of the vehicle increased and the sound of the pavement smoothed as if he'd gained access to a freeway.

"Mr. Champion will be looking for me and the FBI is on to you. You know you're not going to get away with anything," Ysabel lied, hopefully.

"Shut up, you stupid woman. The FBI knows nothing.

They think a bunch of foreigners are responsible for what's been going on and as far as I'm concerned, they can keep on thinking that. They'll never suspect me."

"You're wrong," she argued, just to keep him talking. Maybe if she made him angry enough, he'd stop the car and get out. With her hands bound behind her back, she couldn't reach a door handle and she didn't know whether the doors had to be opened from the outside like most police cars.

"Detective Green, Jenna needs a doctor."

"Not where you two are going."

Dread filled Ysabel's empty stomach.

"Besides, it's her own fault. If she hadn't screwed up her wedding with that jerk, Champion, none of this would have happened."

"What did Jenna's wedding to Jackson have to do with kidnapping me?" Try as she might, she couldn't make the connection.

"Doesn't matter now—and it will matter even less when it's all said and done."

Ysabel took a deep breath and asked, "What do you mean when all's said and done?"

"I'm going to blow Houston off the map." Green laughed, sending a cold slither of fear washing over Ysabel's skin.

"You were the one importing all the bomb-making materials?" Ysabel asked.

"No, and that's the beauty of it. They'll never link me to that because I wasn't the one who had the stuff smuggled into America. The only people who know I'm involved are in this car and after today, you two won't be blabbing."

Because he planned on blowing them up with the rest of Houston. Ysabel didn't have to be a mind-reader to figure that one out, but she'd be damned if she let it happen. Her baby depended on her to use her brain and get herself and Jenna out of this alive.

"Why? You're a cop, sworn to protect the people of Houston. Why would you want to destroy the city?"

"Why do you think?"

"Someone made you mad?" she guessed, completely at a loss for a reason good enough to destroy so many lives.

"That's only part of it. Let's just say someone made me an offer I couldn't refuse."

Ysabel gasped. "You're doing this for money?"

"Hell, yeah. The Rasnovian dissidents would have done it for nothing, just to make a point and an example out of the Americans. I'm not that idealistic." He snorted. "Cold hard cash motivates me."

"That means one other person knows about your involvement besides Jenna and me. Aren't you afraid he'll get caught and take you down with you?"

"No way. He has more money than God. Enough to make sure he's never found out."

"Don't you know that bad guys never win?"

"Lady, when you've worked with the kind of criminals I've worked with for more years than I care to admit, you'd realize how wrong that statement is. The criminals are rarely caught. The bad guys are getting away with murder."

Ysabel wiggled her hands in the plastic strap. Unless she could find something to rub it against and break it, she wasn't getting loose from the thin, hard bond. She stared down at Jenna, wishing she could reach her to check for a pulse. The poor woman had a bruise the size of a baseball on her cheekbone and her eye was almost swelled shut. "Jenna," she whispered, scooting across the seat to lean over her.

Detective Green swerved, sending Ysabel rolling forward on top of Jenna.

She struggled to right herself, inch by inch, scooting her butt back up onto the backseat. When she looked down at Jenna, the woman's eyes blinked open.

Ysabel let out the breath she'd been holding. "Jenna, wake up, you have to help me."

Jenna's clouded eyes cleared and widened. She would have sat bolt upright if Ysabel didn't choose that time to roll back on top of her to keep her down.

"Shh, don't let him know you're conscious," Ysabel whispered directly into Jenna's ear, hoping the sound of the car engine and tires on the pavement kept Green from hearing her words. "Nod if you understand."

Jenna nodded, sucking in a labored breath. She couldn't breathe with Ysabel on top of her.

As quickly as she could, Ysabel scooted back up on the seat. "Why involve Jenna in your scheme? What has she done to deserve to die?"

"What do you care? She was in your way of marrying your rich boss."

"That isn't true." Ysabel stared down at Jenna, all the envy she'd felt for the other woman gone. She knew the reason Jenna had called off the wedding. She'd gone back to her ex-boyfriend. What she didn't understand was her desperate attempt to patch things up with Jackson after two months. "What did you mean if Jenna had married Jackson none of this would have happened?"

Detective Green snorted. "I would have gotten the money from her, instead of doing it the hard way."

"You think Jackson would have given you money through Jenna?" She snorted. "You obviously don't know Jackson Champion. So now you're being paid as a mercenary?"

"That's right."

"All for money?"

"When you don't have it and someone wants it from you, you'll do just about anything."

An icy shiver raked Ysabel's skin. "Including murder?"

"Babe, someone's gonna die and it ain't gonna be me."

Chapter Fifteen

Jackson's truck tires squealed as he rounded the corners into the parking garage beneath the downtown building where he lived. When he veered around the concrete column leading to his private parking space, he slammed on the brakes.

A brand new car stood blocking his space, the door wide open with no one inside. The car had to be Ysabel's.

Damn. Green had gotten to her.

Jackson whipped out his cell phone and punched the speed dial number for Special Agent Fielding.

After only one ring, the agent answered. "Fielding speaking."

"He's got her," Jackson said, his voice catching. He cleared his throat and tried again. "I think Detective Green has Ysabel." He explained what he'd found, ending with, "We have to find her before…"

"We'll find her, Jackson. Don't you worry."

"How? I have no idea where he would have taken her."

"We have a GPS tracking device planted on his work car and his home car. If he's out driving somewhere, we'll find him. Let me get my guys working on it. I'll get back with you as soon as I know anything. Don't do anything until you hear from me."

Jackson hit the Off button and sat staring at Ysabel's car. Don't do anything? Was the agent nuts? How could he just sit back and wait for something to happen? That something could be the death of the only woman he'd dared to love. He sat back against his plush leather seat, his stomach in knots, his head spinning with the realization he loved a woman. No. He loved Ysabel.

Now that he recognized how he felt, he wouldn't rest until he told her. If he got the chance.

Jackson slipped his shift into Reverse and turned his truck. He couldn't wait to go looking for her. He had to find her himself. As he drove out of the parking garage, he dialed Flint and Akeem on conference call.

"I need your help," he started without an introduction or anything.

"What's happening?"

Jackson filled them in on Ysabel's abduction and who he thought it might be.

"We're on our way," Flint said.

"I'm getting into my truck as we speak," Akeem added. "In the meantime, doesn't Ysabel have a cousin in the sheriff's department? Contact him and see what he can do."

"I will." Out of habit and with no real direction to turn, Jackson headed toward the Port of Houston. Once on the freeway, he dialed 9-1-1. When the dispatcher answered, he barked, "I have an emergency and need to speak with Mitch Stanford in the sheriff's department, immediately."

"Sir, is this a life-or-death emergency? Perhaps we can help you."

"This is Jackson Champion of Champion Shipping. This call is a matter of life and death. It's imperative I speak with Mitch Stanford and only Mr. Stanford. Now, please find him."

The woman put him on hold, piping Muzak into his ear. After two of the longest minutes of his life, the line clicked.

"Stanford speaking. What do you have, Mr. Champion?"

Jackson told Mitch everything he knew thus far.

"You think Green has Ysabel?" Stanford asked.

"I don't have anything but her empty car to go on, but my gut tells me yes."

"He didn't show up for work today and he hasn't called to report in. I'll get our people on it right away."

"Thanks." Jackson clicked the Off button and stared straight ahead. Where would the man take her?

His cell phone buzzed and he flipped it open. "Jackson."

"We've got a location on Green's work car."

"Where is it?"

"Headed east on Pasadena Freeway toward the Port of Houston." Agent Fielding paused. "Mr. Champion, you should let the FBI and the police handle this."

"He has Ysabel," Jackson said through clenched teeth, his fingers practically crushing the phone in his hand. Already headed that direction, he slammed his foot to the floor, closed his phone and dropped it into the cup holder.

DETECTIVE Green drove, oblivious to the life-or-death struggle in the backseat of his sedan.

Ysabel turned her back to Jenna and scooted up far enough that the other woman could reach the plastic zip tie holding her wrists together.

Jenna tugged at it while Ysabel kept Green engaged in conversation to cover any sounds they might make.

"Why do you hate Jackson Champion so much?" Ysabel asked.

"He's just like all the fat rich men who walk all over the little guys. They never seem to have enough money, just take, take, take. Well, I plan to give him a little more than he bargained for."

"What did he do to you personally?"

"He didn't marry my stupid little sister like he was supposed to. He was too good for her."

"Why do you care? You weren't marrying Jackson."

"No, but her marriage meant money to me."

"Just because she married Jackson didn't mean she'd have access to all of his money."

"She damned well better have. I told the stupid bitch not to sign any prenuptial agreements. We made a deal. I'd keep her ex-boyfriend out of jail on drug charges and she'd pay off a few debts for me."

"Debts?" Ysabel asked.

Jenna pulled Ysabel's hair until her head was close enough that she could whisper, "Three hundred thousand in gambling debt, my brother didn't know when to quit."

"None of your damned business! She owed me for saving her stupid boyfriend." He gunned the accelerator and the car fishtailed, sliding off the road into gravel. "It's showtime."

He stopped the car and got out.

"I'm sorry, Ysabel, I couldn't loosen it," Jenna called softly.

Fearing Green meant to shoot them here and now, Ysabel aimed her feet at the door as it opened. "Be ready, Jenna. When I say go, get out and run as fast as you can."

"But I can't leave you."

"Yes, you can and will. Just do it," she hissed.

The door jerked open and Brody Green leaned in. "Come on, we have alternate transportation."

Ysabel cocked her legs and kicked out as hard as she could, catching Brody in the jaw.

The surprise attack sent him staggering backward. He slipped in the gravel and fell.

"Go, Jenna, go!"

Jenna rolled out of the car and struggled to her feet.

Before she could get two yards from the car, Green was up and onto her, grabbing her around the middle. Although she kicked and screamed, he held tight.

As soon as Jenna left the car, Ysabel had scooted to the edge of the seat. Now she leaned forward and propelled herself out of the car and ran toward Green, head down like a charging bull.

She caught him in the middle of his back, aiming for his kidney.

He grunted, his grip loosening on Jenna. She dropped to the ground and rolled to the side, kicking at his ankles to get away. She crab-walked backward, scuffling in the gravel, but slipping too much to get her feet under her.

Green kicked her in the side. A sharp snap sounded clearly in the night sky and Jenna doubled over, clutching her ribcage. "Oh, God," she wheezed.

Ysabel's head hurt from hitting Brody so hard that she barely managed to remain upright. It took her too long to right herself. By the time she dug into the gravel to run, Brody had her by the waist, squeezing so hard that Ysabel was afraid for her baby. She ceased her struggles immediately, certain she wasn't going to get away this time without grave damage to her unborn child. She'd have to bide her time and watch for another opportunity. For now all she could do was study her surroundings. Darkness surrounded them, lit by the nearby glow of hundreds of lights reflecting off the clouds. They must be close to a refinery or the shipyards. But where?

Green twisted her around and slapped duct tape over her mouth. He did the same for Jenna, zip-tying her hands behind her, as well. Then he marched them farther down the gravel road, surrounded by bushes and tall grasses they couldn't see over. They rounded a curve in the dirt path and stopped behind a maintenance van.

Green slid the rolling door upward and shoved Jenna in first with such force that she slid across the metal floor and banged into the stack of boxes inside. She lay still, her eyes closed, her body limp.

Afraid he'd hurt her baby, Ysabel stepped toward the truck. "You don't have to push. I'll get in." As she stepped up into the van, a hand slammed between her shoulder blades, sending her sprawling forward. With her hands cinched behind her back, she had no way to break her fall. At the last minute, she twisted, landing on her side to avoid injury to her abdomen. Her hip hit the hard metal floor, shooting shards of pain throughout her body. Her vision blurred as she slid into Jenna's soft body. With every bit of effort she could muster, she fought the blackness. She could not afford to pass out. Not with a nutcase ready to blow up her and everybody in Houston. Despite her best attempt, darkness consumed her.

When she came to, the van rumbled to a stop.

Muffled voices barely penetrated the thick metal walls. Ysabel tried to scream, but the engine revved and the vehicle moved forward. She banged her heels against the floor, trying anything to make enough noise to attract attention.

At last, the van stopped and the door slid up and Brody Green's deep voice filled the interior. "Last stop, ladies."

JACKSON took a turn too fast, struggling to maintain control of the truck. Headed east on the Pasadena Freeway, almost to the Bayport Terminal, his phone rang again, displaying Agent Fielding's number in the window.

"Jackson, we sent an agent by Green's house. In his garage, we found traces of bomb-making materials and a diagram of the Champion Shipping oil storage facility near the Port of Houston. If he has what we think he has and he gets inside the oil tank yards, he could blow the Port of Houston off the map. If the explosion is big enough, he could cause some major damage to the City of Houston. We've mobilized all of the first responders and the bomb squad. Stay out of the facility, Jackson. You're no good to anyone dead."

"I hear you."

"But you're going to ignore me, aren't you?" Agent Fielding snorted. "I guess if one of my employees was kidnapped, I'd go in as well."

"She's not just an employee," Jackson admitted. "Ysabel is the woman I love." He said it out loud and couldn't take it back. Nor did he want to.

"I thought so. I'm right behind you by about ten minutes. If you could wait, I'll go in with you."

"No can do. But I'll carry my phone. Let me know when you arrive. I'll have it on vibrate."

"The Houston Port Authority is notifying the terminal operators to stop and hold all vehicles entering the oil storage facility."

"What if he's already in?" Jackson pulled onto the road leading to the Champion Shipping oil storage facility, his heart racing the closer he got. For years, he'd fooled himself into believing that amassing a fortune was the most important thing he could do with his life.

With the very real possibility of losing Ysabel, he'd finally come to realize friends and family just might be more important than any monetary gains. He'd trade all of his fortune to save Ysabel. Every last cent. As he pulled up to the guard house, he was met with a security guard, gun pulled, ready to shoot. The man stood firm, his short hair and solid bearing bespoke a prior service commitment. Jackson liked to hire prior military personnel to guard Champion Shipping facilities. They had the stamina and strength to stand up to anything.

"Step out of your vehicle," the guard demanded.

Jackson dropped down, his hands held high. "I'm Jackson Champion. If you'll let me get my badge out, I'll prove it."

"Slowly, I have my finger on the trigger and I'm not afraid to shoot."

"I believe it." Jackson eased his wallet from his back pocket and removed his badge, holding it out for the guard.

After inspecting the picture and Jackson's face carefully, the guard lowered his weapon but didn't put it away. "Mr. Champion, glad you're here. Maybe you can explain the terrorist alert we received."

"It's just that. We have a potential terrorist threat and we think he might be aiming for this facility. Have any vehicles passed through this gate in the past couple of hours?"

"I just came on duty. Let me check the log." He ran inside the guard booth.

Jackson followed.

The guard booted the computer screen and logged in. "Yes, twenty minutes ago, a maintenance van drove through." The guard shot a glance at Jackson. "You don't think…"

His heart squeezed tightly in his chest. "Yes, I do. Open the gate. I'm going in."

"Yes, sir!"

As Jackson jogged toward his truck, he called out over his shoulder, "The cavalry will be arriving any minute. Let the bomb squad through. I'm afraid we're going to need them."

"You sure you don't want me to go in with you, sir?"

"No, I need you to man the gate in case the van or anyone comes out before I do."

"Yes, sir!" The guard popped to attention and saluted before he remembered he wasn't in the military anymore. His face red, the man hit the gate release button.

Jackson blew through the opened gate, leaving the stunned guard pacing, his gun drawn.

He hadn't gone very deep into the maze of oil storage tanks when he found the van, the rear door open, the interior empty.

The hum of the harbor and the nearby container yards drowned out smaller sounds. Jackson shut down his engine. Much as he'd like to drive through the oil storage yard, he couldn't risk Ysabel's life on rash movements.

He set his shift into Neutral, pushed his truck out of sight of the van and climbed down, reaching beneath the seat for his older, trusty Glock, since his SIG Sauer had become a property of the state in the murder of Stephan Kenig. He knew how to use the gun, had spent a lot of time out at the ranch practicing with Flint and Akeem, each becoming expert with their choice of weapon. But he'd never had to shoot at a man.

His jaw tightened. If it came down to Ysabel or Green, he'd shoot the man in a heartbeat.

He returned to the van, popped the hood and yanked the wires to the electronics. Without serious work, the van would go nowhere.

Jackson eased around the first large storage tank, his eyes adjusting quickly to the darkness, the only light the glow coming from the container yard and the security lights on the corner fences. Long shadows around the base of the tanks could hide not one but a dozen men.

The clang of something hitting metal echoed through the tank farm, making it difficult for Jackson to pinpoint. He left the shadow of the first tank and ran across an opening to the next, careful not to scuff the gravel, thus giving away his position.

Another clang bounced off the towering holding tanks, this time sounding closer.

Checking the alleys at the corner of four tanks, Jackson took a breath and held it, listening for anything—a voice, a footstep, breathing. But the hum of machinery and generators in the distance, drowned out the softer, more subtle sounds. He let his breath out and ran kitty-corner to the tank diagonal from him, he hoped in the direction of the clanging noise.

As he slid around the shadowed side of the tank, he could see the next tank and the ladder snaking upward around the metal cylinder. At the base of the ladder, someone stood straight and unmoving.

For several long seconds, Jackson stood quietly studying

the dark figure. Then it moved a foot, banging it against the metal railing of the ladder. A small foot. A gentle breeze lifted a lock of hair, blowing it across the person's face.

Jackson sucked in a breath. "Ysabel." He was halfway across the open space between the storage tanks before he remembered that there was a killer on the loose in the tank farm. He could have set a trap for him, waiting for just such a moment to take out Jackson Champion. The thought only slowed him for a second. He didn't care whether he lived or died, but he'd be damned if he'd let Ysabel die on his watch.

Her eyes widened and she shook her head violently, her voice muffled by a thick length of silver duct tape over her mouth. Tears glistened in her eyes and on her cheeks.

Anger surged through Jackson. Brody Green was going to pay for this.

He reached for the ropes tying her to the staircase. Before he could lay a hand on them, she kicked his shin.

"Ow!" Jackson stared down at her and dropped his voice. "Why did you do that?"

"Mmm mmmttthh," she said through the tape.

"I'm sorry, Izzy, I can't understand you." He reached out and grabbed the end of the duct tape, easing it off her face, hating how much it must hurt.

When he got it off halfway, she said, "Rip it."

Startled by her demand, his hand jerked the tape the rest of the way off.

Ysabel gasped, more tears falling. "Don't touch me, Jackson."

"I have to get you out of here. Green's going to blow up the place." He reached again for the ropes crisscrossing her body.

"No, Jackson! He's going to blow up this place using me. Just leave."

"What do you mean?"

"If you move that rope, the explosives will go off. You can't save me, Jackson." Her voice broke and she gulped. "Save yourself."

"I won't leave you." Without touching her, he peered behind her. As she'd said, a metal box with wires was tied to the ropes holding her in place. What looked like a lump of clay was stuck to the side of the box. Plastic explosives. His blood chilled.

"Green's still here and he has Jenna. I think he took her to the next row of tanks. You have to help her if you can."

"I won't leave you," he repeated. Frustration overwhelmed him. Jackson was a man who liked to take charge, grab the bull by the horns and to hell with the consequences. But Ysabel's life was on the line and he could do nothing.

Ysabel's tears stopped flowing and she drew in a deep breath. "I'll be okay, Jackson. Find Jenna and see if you can get her out first."

"But—"

"Please. Just go."

Jackson cupped her face in his hand. "I'll be back. I promise."

"No." She shook her head. "You have to find Jenna and get out. Green's got enough explosives here to blow a new channel in the Port of Houston. Get out and warn the rest of the city."

"I'm going, but I *will* be back. You're not getting rid of me that easily, sweetheart." He leaned down and captured her mouth with his, the moment bittersweet. When he broke off the kiss, he pressed his lips to her temple, breathing in the scent of her shampoo. "I love you, Ysabel."

Then he turned and left.

Ysabel dropped the pretense and let the tears flow. "Please, Jackson, save yourself," she sobbed quietly. Her belly tightened, reminding her she'd never told him about his baby, and still couldn't. Jackson wouldn't leave knowing Ysabel was carrying his child and he had to leave to save himself and Jenna.

Afraid to move her arms or hands and set off the bomb earlier than the twenty minutes Detective Green had set on the timer, Ysabel stood straight and still, wishing she'd been smarter and fought harder to get free of Detective Green. Her baby deserved to live.

If she got out of this alive, her first task would be to tell Jackson about their baby. Getting out alive was the big IF.

Chapter Sixteen

After putting a tank between himself and Ysabel, Jackson crouched in the shadows and flipped open his cell phone, speed-dialing Agent Fielding.

"Did you find her?" Fielding answered.

"Yeah. How soon 'til the bomb squad gets here?"

"Fifteen minutes, tops."

"That might be too late. Tell them to hurry. Green has Ysabel wired to the bomb." His voice caught on the lump in his throat. Ysabel had been so vulnerable and brave. He refused to let her die.

"Jesus. I'm almost there. What about Green?"

"I haven't located him yet, but I disabled his escape vehicle. He won't get far."

"Good. See ya in a few." Fielding rang off.

Jackson wove between the tanks until he spied another figure tied to the stairs snaking around the side of a tank. Her long blond hair glinted in the pale light, hanging down over her face.

Even though he didn't love her, he couldn't leave Jenna to die. With time so precious, Jackson spared a moment to scan all directions, straining to see into the shadows. Then he ran across the open space to Jenna. She dangled in the ropes, unconscious, but her chest rose and fell steadily. Jackson checked the ropes binding her to the stairs. No bombs.

He pulled a knife from his pocket and sliced through the ropes. Jenna fell into his arms and moaned.

"It's okay, Jenna. I've got you now." He lifted her into his arms and carried her back toward Ysabel.

"My brother…" she muttered. "He's going to kill me and Ysabel."

Jackson's lips firmed into a straight line, his hands tightening on Jenna's legs. "Not if I can help it."

He ducked into the shadows and eased around the tank Ysabel was tied to until he could see her, standing so still and scared.

A shadow moved at the base of another tank.

Jackson set Jenna on the ground. "Shh. Stay down and close to the tank so that no one can see you. I think I've found your brother."

Jenna grabbed his arm, her face pale in the moonlight. "Be careful, Jackson. He's a monster."

Anyone who would tie bombs to a woman in the middle of an oil-tank farm was a certifiable psychotic. "I know. Stay."

Before he could get to Ysabel, the moving shadow broke free at the base of the oil storage tank and ran across the opening, straight toward Ysabel.

Brody Green grabbed a handful of Ysabel's hair and yanked back her head. "Tell him to give me his truck keys," he demanded, his voice coarse and gravelly.

"No."

"Tell him or I'll shoot you now." He pressed the pistol he was holding against Ysabel's forehead.

Fighting the urge to charge out and kill Green with his bare hands, Jackson leveled his pistol on the man and called out from the shadows, "Let her go." He couldn't fire until he got a clear shot, otherwise he'd risk hitting Ysabel or the oil tank behind her.

"Well, well, the great Jackson Champion finally shows his face." Green tugged on Ysabel's hair, but she didn't cry out. "I would have thought you'd send in your paid minions rather than risk your own rich self."

"Let Miss Sanchez go," Jackson said in a low, clear voice.

"Now then, you know I can't do that. Maybe if you hadn't sabotaged my van, I'd have left and you wouldn't be choosing between your truck and your girlfriend."

"She means nothing to you, Green. Let her go. Your bomb will make a big enough splash with the media without tying her to it."

"Ah, but she means a lot to you, doesn't our Miss Sanchez? She's the reason you wouldn't marry my sister, wasn't she?"

"No, she's not, but that doesn't matter now, does it? I know you're not smart enough to dream up an attack like this all by yourself, Green. Who paid you to blow up the tank yard? I'll double what he's paying you to let her go and I promise you safe passage to the border of Mexico."

"You think I'm fool enough to trust you to keep any promise? Give me the keys to your truck or I shoot her now and save her from being blown to bits in the blast."

"You can have the keys. Take the truck, just leave Miss Sanchez." Jackson took the keys out of his pocket and tossed them through the air to land at Green's feet. "Take them." Then he quickly stepped out of the position he'd been in so that Green couldn't get a bead on him based on the trajectory of the keys and the direction of his voice.

Green pointed his gun into the shadows. "No funny business, Jackson."

"I wouldn't dare."

"Good, because I don't have any qualms over shooting a woman."

Jackson's teeth clenched. "Or beating them up, right?"

"So you found Jenna, did you? That woman is too stupid to live. I should have shot her a long time ago."

Ysabel snorted. "Pleasant thoughts for a brother, don't you think?"

"Shut up." Green punched Ysabel in the face. Then pointing the gun at her head, he bent low to retrieve the keys Jackson had thrown.

While Green bent over, Ysabel kicked out, catching the man's gun hand with her foot. "It's not nice to hit women."

His weapon flew through the air and dropped several yards away.

"Freeze, Green. Or I swear I'll blow your butt from here to eternity."

"Bitch!" Brody stumbled and fell to his knees.

"This is for Jenna." Ysabel swung her foot again, landing another blow to Green's temple, sending him face-first into the dust.

"And don't call me bitch," she said, her voice strong, despite her potentially deadly position.

Jackson's chest swelled. She was beautiful, even facing death. But he didn't have time to dwell on her stunning performance.

Brody rolled to his side and snatched his gun up into his hand. Then he rolled again, popping up onto his haunches, aiming for Ysabel.

Jackson fired his Glock. The bullet hit Green in the chest, the impact knocking him backward to land with a hard thump in the dirt.

Easing forward, Jackson pointed his gun at Green's head and reached down to check for a pulse. "He's dead."

"Madre de Dios," Ysabel prayed softly. "Where is Jenna?"

"I'm here." The woman stepped out of the shadows and ran to Ysabel. "I'm so sorry for what he did." She stopped short of Ysabel and stared at the maze of ropes and charges. "If only he'd taken me instead of you."

"I'm okay, Jenna. You have to get out of here, now." Ysabel looked to Jackson. "Please, take her out of here. Please."

Jackson grabbed Jenna's elbow. "Come on, you need to get somewhere safe." He reached down and collected his keys from the dirt and ushered her back the way he'd come. When he made it to his truck, he opened it, shoved Jenna into the driver's seat and handed her the keys. "Drive and don't stop until you're out of Houston all together."

The woman shook her head. "No. I won't leave her."

"That's my line." Jackson smiled. "Please, just go."

"You love her, don't you?"

"More than life." He rolled down the window and shut the door. "Now go."

"Okay, but only because I know you'll save her. You're a good man, Jackson Champion. She loves you, too, you know?"

"I hope so, because when this is all over, I'm going to ask her to marry me. Now I have a date with a girl and a bomb."

"God bless you."

Jackson sent a few prayers of his own to the big guy as he jogged toward Ysabel. Before he got to her, his phone vibrated in his pocket. He jerked it out.

"Jackson, I'm at the gate with the bomb squad. We'll be there soon."

"Thanks." Jackson blinked back tears and looked up at the sky. "Thanks." But the day wasn't over until Ysabel was free and the bomb was defused.

YSABEL stood in silence feeling, rather than hearing the silent ticking of her life going away. In the near distance she heard the sound of a truck pulling away.

Tears flowed freely down her cheeks, blurring her vision. He'd gotten away. Thank God, he'd gotten away.

A hand on her arm made her jump. She blinked back her tears.

Jackson stood in front of her, gently brushing away the moisture from her cheeks. "Hey, it's not over yet."

"You're supposed to be gone. Jackson, oh, please, go!"

"I can't." He cupped her chin and smiled down into her eyes. "I want to be with you."

"But you have to go."

"I can't leave the woman I love."

"No, you can't love me. You have to live."

"But I do love you and I won't go until you come with me."

A lump of tears jammed her throat and she swallowed hard to clear the blockage. "I couldn't bear it if you die."

"I'm not going to die and neither are you."

"But the bomb—"

"It's not going to go off." He turned and waved toward a group of men converging on them dressed in heavy padding and shielded helmets. "You see, the cavalry has arrived."

More tears sprang to Ysabel's eyes. "In case they don't get me out of this, I just wanted you to know—"

Jackson frowned. "Save it. You can tell me all about whatever you want to say when we get you out of this."

"But—"

"I won't listen. You and I are going to have a long, *real* talk when this is over. And I don't mean at the pearly gates." He smiled. "Not that I'd be going that direction necessarily. But I don't plan on you or me leaving this world anytime in the near future."

A man dressed like a dark marshmallow stepped up to Jackson and laid a hand on his arm. "Sir, please leave the area while we do our job."

Jackson refused to budge. "I'm not going anywhere without Ysabel."

The man shook his helmeted head. "It's your life, buddy. Just give us room to work."

Stepping back, Jackson stayed close enough Ysabel could see him. "I'm here for you, babe."

"I wish you'd go. I need you to tell my parents, my sister and the rest of my family that I love them. If you don't go, who will tell them?"

"They're *your* family. They deserve to hear it from you. And I couldn't begin to find them all. What do you have, a hundred cousins in the Houston area alone?"

Jackson was cute when he was picking on her. Ysabel hadn't realized how much she'd missed their brand of teasing and she gave him a watery smile. "Something like that. I love a big family."

"I do, too. It took me years to realize it, but that's what I've always wanted." Jackson crossed his arms over his chest, his brows rising in challenge. "Maybe someday we can have one of our own."

Ysabel's chest tightened as hope filled her. "What do you mean?"

The man working on the wires behind her grunted. "Sounds like he's proposing. I hope this is the right wire."

Jackson reached for Ysabel's hand. "I love you, Ysabel Sanchez."

Ysabel smiled across at him. "I love you, too, Jackson Champion." If she died in that moment, she'd die a very happy woman.

A soft snick sounded behind her and she held her breath, waiting for the huge explosion.

Instead the man in the padded gear straightened and held up a wire. "The man was an amateur. This job was too easy." He took off his helmet and smiled at Ysabel. "Which is a good thing for you considering we only had another minute to work with." With a few quick snips, he removed the detonator and the plastic explosives. "You can untie her now. My work is done."

Ysabel sagged, dragging in a deep breath. "It's over?"

"Yes, ma'am. We have a dog searching through the rest of the tank yard to make sure he didn't leave any more presents. But I think Mr. Jackson surprised him before he could arm any more charges."

When the last rope dropped from Ysabel's arms and Jackson had cut the blasted zip tie from her wrists, she stood in front of him. For the second time since she'd known him, Ysabel felt shy and nervous. "Did I really tell you I love you?"

"I heard it." The guy from the bomb squad said. "But then people will say the darnedest things when they think they're going to die. I won't hold you to it."

"But I will." Jackson lifted her hand and pressed a kiss into her palm. "I meant every word I said. And to prove it…" He dropped to one knee.

The blood rushed to Ysabel's cheeks, her heart pounding so hard in her chest she couldn't breathe. She was very afraid she'd pass out and make a fool out of herself before he… Before he what? Dare she hope? *"Madre de Dios."*

Jackson looked up at her in the dim lighting, his own eyes shining and serious. "Ysabel Sanchez, will you marry me?"

"Why?" As soon as the word was out of her mouth, she clapped a hand over her lips.

With a smile, Jackson tugged her hand until she was forced to sit on his one knee. "Didn't you hear what I said not even five minutes ago?"

"The man said he loved you, lady. Isn't that reason

enough?" The bomb squad guy stripped the padding off his chest, shaking his head.

Jackson shot him a glare. "I can handle this, if you don't mind."

The guy raised his hands in surrender. "Right, sorry. Didn't mean to steal your thunder."

"Are you sure?" Ysabel's words came out breathy. She could hardly breathe and quite possibly might hyperventilate.

"More sure than I've ever been about anything in my life." He stood and pulled her into his arms. "Did you mean what you said?"

"About loving you?" Ysabel's chin dipped. "Yes, I've loved you for a very long time."

"And you've been there for me, but I couldn't see you." He tipped her chin up. "I'm sorry I've been so blind."

A tear slipped down her cheek. "You're forgiven."

He touched his lips to hers, but pulled back without kissing her. "Does this mean you'll marry me?"

"Yes." She said. Then throwing her head back, she shouted, "Yes!"

Then he crushed her to his chest and kissed her, his mouth slanting over hers, his tongue delving in to taste hers.

Ysabel's hands slipped up his arms and clasped behind his head, holding him close so that the kiss might last forever.

Inside her blood bubbled, her nerves bounced as though her entire body would light up like firecrackers.

Jackson Champion had asked her to marry him. Her! Ysabel Sanchez.

Then the bubbles burst and her heart fell to her stomach. What would he say when he found out she'd been keeping a secret? A secret she had no right to keep from him?

Ysabel, pushed back from him.

"What's wrong?" he asked, nuzzling her neck and nipping at her earlobe.

"I can't marry you, Jackson."

His head came up, a frown drawing his brows together. "What do you mean you can't marry me? You just said yes."

"I haven't exactly been truthful with you."

"What *exactly* do you mean?" He stared down into her eyes, a smile curling the corners of his lips. "Don't tell me you're already married and I didn't know about it."

"No, no. I'm single all right. With a boss like you, who has time for a social life?" She gave a half-hearted laugh and gulped back another round of tears. "I didn't tell you something I should have told you days ago." She stepped out of his reach and turned her back to him, afraid to see the anger in his eyes when she finally told him.

He reached for her hand and tugged. "You can tell me anything."

Ysabel looked at their joined hands and then up into his eyes. "I'm going to have your baby."

Jackson's frown deepened. "Of course you're going to have my baby. We're going to have half a dozen, if I have anything to say about it. Don't you want children?"

"Oh, yes!" She squeezed his hand. "I meant I'm going to have your baby in exactly seven months."

His eyes narrowed as if he was doing the math in his head, then the brows rose. "You're pregnant?"

Ysabel cringed and answered shakily. "Yes."

Jackson ran a hand through his hair, standing it on end. "You're really pregnant? From that time…"

"Yes and yes." Her nerves stretched to the limit, Ysabel held her breath. "I'm sorry I didn't tell you right away."

He pulled her hand, drawing her closer, his gaze fixed on her belly. "I'm going to be a daddy?" Instead of angry glares and harsh accusations, his words came out softly reverent. Then he looked at her, love shining from his eyes.

If she'd had any doubts, they were wiped away immediately. "Yes, you're going to be a daddy."

His eyes suspiciously bright, Jackson kissed her lips with a gentle brush. "Thank you."

Ysabel laughed, relief making her giddy. "Well, in that case," she pulled him closer, "can we make it a quick wedding?"

"The sooner the better."

"And can I invite my family?"

"Every last uncle, aunt and second or third cousin." He lifted her off her feet and spun her around. "I'll give you the biggest wedding Houston has seen, with more sparkle and bling than all of Tiffany's."

"I don't need a big expensive wedding. I just want you." She cupped his face and kissed him. "But you'll have to be careful, I'm not sure how much roughhousing the baby can take."

"Oh, yeah." Jackson grinned and let her slide slowly down his body. "You concentrate on taking care of Jackson, Jr. and let me take care of the details. I know what, I'll hire a wedding planner."

"That would be lovely."

"How's next week?"

"To meet the planner?" she asked.

"No, to get married."

"Next week?" Ysabel squeaked. "You've got to be kidding."

"Is that too soon?" Jackson's eyes rounded. "I thought you couldn't wait to marry me."

"I can't wait, but a week?" she squeaked again.

"Just leave it to me. All you have to do is show up."

She frowned. "I don't know about this. A man planning a wedding?"

"I went from nothing to worth well over a billion dollars."

He crossed his arms over his chest. “I can do anything I set my mind to.”

“I’m sure you can.” She ran her hand over his chest, loving that she was free to do it and could do it the rest of her life. “But a wedding? I fear the great Jackson Champion might be in over his head.”

He grabbed her around the waist and pulled her into his arms. “Trust me.”

Epilogue

"I don't know why I couldn't be out at the ranch to get ready for the wedding there." Ysabel fluffed the satin of her long white wedding dress and tugged at the strapless bust line. "I should have gone for sleeves."

"In this heat?" Delia sat on one side of her dressed in a sea-foam green bridesmaid dress.

On Ysabel's other side Lora Leigh McKade gave a dreamy smile. "I can't wait to see the expression on your face when you see what Jackson's done. It's perfect, just perfect. Oh, and Anna sends her love and congratulations."

"How are she and Katiya?" Ysabel asked.

"Doing fine. Flint, Akeem and Jackson used their clout to give her a new home, a new name and American citizenship. She's going to be fine."

Ysabel smiled. "I'm glad." The poor woman had been through a lot. Thinking about Anna only drew her mind away from her coming nuptials for a minute and the nervousness bubbled right back up in her belly. She drew in a deep breath and let it out. "This is making me crazy. Isn't the bride supposed to plan the wedding? Hand me another cracker will ya, Del? I think I'm getting nauseous."

Delia handed her the entire box. "You better slow down

or you'll be throwing up crackers in your wedding dress." Her sister reached for her hands. "Oh, sweetie, you're shaking."

"I can't seem to help it. Maybe if I'd been in on the planning, I wouldn't be such a wreck."

"Jackson wanted you to be relaxed, not to be troubled about anything." Lora Leigh patted her leg. "He's such a worrywart about you and the baby. It's kind of cute."

Ysabel's lips twitched. "I'm glad he's glad."

Delia snorted. "Glad? The man's ecstatic!"

He was, which filled Ysabel with more happiness than she felt she deserved. Not only was Jackson happy, but he'd also been pushing for her to move in with him even before the wedding.

Needing a little time to get used to the idea and to get her affairs in order, Ysabel insisted on staying in her apartment until after the wedding. She used the excuse that she didn't want to give the paparazzi any more fuel to add to the media circus than they already had.

As they turned onto the road leading to the Diamondback Ranch, Ysabel's palms sweated and butterflies erupted in her stomach. "I'm getting married," she said in a whisper.

Delia hugged her close, brushing a tear from her own eye. "*Sí. Mi hermana* is getting married."

As they neared the ranch house, the cars parked in neat rows on the grass numbered in the hundreds with uniformed security officers directing even more cars to designated positions.

"Madre de Dios!" Ysabel raised her hand to her mouth. "He must have invited all of Houston."

Lora Leigh sat back, a smug look on her face. "We had to hire a service to help get the invitations out in record time. Some were hand-delivered. Jackson doesn't do anything in a small way."

Ysabel frowned at the pretty blonde. "You knew and you couldn't have at least warned me? I'm not sure I can stand in front of all those people, much less walk down the aisle. It'll take forever!"

With a laugh, Delia patted her hand. "Don't worry, you can do this. You've been in tougher boardrooms."

The guards waved the limousine down the drive to the house. Once they came abreast of Flint and Lora Leigh's home, they could finally see the wedding party.

Ysabel touched a hand to her chest.

The huge expanse of green grass was filled with a big white tent festooned with garlands of ivy, mixed with red and white roses. Outside the tent stood row upon row of folding wooden chairs facing an ornate gazebo, also festooned with ivy and roses.

"It's beautiful." Tears sprang to Ysabel's eyes.

"I tried to help him with the details, but Jackson insisted on all of this and then some." Lora Leigh sighed. "I couldn't have done better if I'd tried. Wait until you see the ice sculptures and the dance floor in the party tent."

"Ice sculptures?" Ysabel couldn't begin to take in all the tasteful decorations, the people milling about in the shade. Her gaze panned the crowd, but she couldn't find Jackson. Panic seized her chest and she feared she'd hyperventilate. "How did he pull this off in one week?"

Lora Leigh laughed. "The man is driven."

"I'd say he's more than driven," Delia added, her eyes round in her face as she stared out at the setting fit for a princess. "He's a human dynamo."

The limousine stopped at the side entry to the large house and the chauffeur opened the door for the ladies.

Lora Leigh got out first.

When Ysabel stepped out, her knees refused to work. Lora Leigh grabbed her elbow and braced her until she steadied.

"Come on, we want to do our last-minute primping and Mama wants to give you something."

"Mama and Papa are here?" Joy welled in Ysabel's heart. "They told me they couldn't make it."

"Oops." Delia grimaced. "That was supposed to be a surprise. Jackson had them flown in from Monterrey on his private jet. You should have seen their faces."

"Come, ladies, let's get this show on the road. There are people waiting in the heat." Lora Leigh herded them into the house and into a large living area, set up as a dressing room for the bride.

A small, thin woman with straight brown hair and green eyes the exact shade of Ysabel's hurried forward, her eyes shining with tears. *"Mija!"* She opened her arms wide and engulfed Ysabel in a tight hug.

"Mama." Ysabel fought to keep the tears from flowing.

"I was so worried when I heard about the bomb. And I couldn't get a flight back because Homeland Security had shut down international flights into and out of Houston."

"You're here now, and that's all that matters. Where's Papa?"

"He's lecturing Jackson." Her mother set her back to look at her in the eyes. "Such a rush. You would think he *had* to marry you."

Ysabel's gaze darted to Delia. "You didn't tell her?"

"Are you kidding?" Delia shook her head. "If I'd told her you were pregnant, all of Houston would know before the sun went down."

"Ysabel!" Another round of exuberant hugging and Ysabel started feeling oxygen-deprived.

Thankfully Delia stepped in. "Mama, please. Jackson is trying to make an honest woman of her. Let her get down the aisle so that he can." She untangled her mother's arms from around Ysabel and ushered her sister to a seat. "Sit, before you fall."

For the next ten minutes, the bridesmaids and mother of

the bride fussed around Ysabel, until she couldn't stand it another minute. Finally, she cried out, "Please let me have two minutes to myself. I need to breathe."

IN another room on the other side of the house, Jackson paced, a cell phone to his ear. He'd considered having it surgically attached after all the calls and preparations he'd made over the last week. This wedding would be perfect if it killed him getting there.

"Exactly where are you?" he demanded into the phone. The jeweler hadn't arrived with the custom-fitted ring and diamond necklace Jackson had ordered to be delivered for the wedding.

"Oh, thank goodness, we're on the drive to the house now," the man answered and hung up.

Jackson glanced at his watch. The wedding began in ten minutes. He barely had time to get the necklace to Ysabel before she made her entrance.

Flint pounded his back between his shoulder blades. "Breathe, man, before you fall flat on your face."

"I am breathing, damn it." He stopped and dragged in a deep breath, realizing for the first time he had been holding his breath.

"If I didn't know any better, I'd say our friend Jackson Champion is having a panic attack," Akeem addressed Flint as though Jackson wasn't in the room.

"For a man who was almost blown halfway to Louisiana, you'd think he could handle one little ol' wedding."

"Little?" Akeem snorted. "Have you been outside? It's a circus out there."

Jackson frowned. "Do you think it was too much? I wanted her to have a fairy-tale wedding. Isn't that what all women want?"

"Not necessarily. Some of them like more subtle displays of love. A quiet ceremony on the courthouse steps is enough."

"Or a quick trip to Vegas for an authentic Elvis wedding." Akeem actually kept a straight face for all of two seconds. Then he was grinning.

"No, really, do you think she'll like it?" Jackson glanced out the window.

Flint nodded. "All kidding aside, you did a great job. Any woman would be happy."

Jackson let out a long slow breath. "She's not any woman. She's Ysabel. And after that scare in the tank yard, I didn't want her to have to do anything but show up."

"Yeah, right. Do you know how hard it is to find a wedding dress in a week? I have it on good authority that it's a nightmare." Akeem grinned. "Taylor came home exhausted every night after shopping with the bride-to-be."

"Same with Lora Leigh," Flint added.

The frown deepened on Jackson's brow. "Had I known, I'd have had a tailor flown in from France to design and sew the damn dress." He glared at the men. "Why didn't you tell me?"

Flint shrugged. "The women made us promise."

Jackson glanced out the front window again. "Did you find out anything about the mysterious man who paid Detective Green to blow up the tank yard?"

"Not yet."

"Green told Ysabel the man was richer than God. What kind of clue is that?" Jackson shoved a hand through his hair and faced his friends. "If we don't find the man behind these attacks, none of us or our businesses are safe." Including his soon-to-be wife and baby. The thought of someone trying to hurt him by hurting them made every ounce of rage burn inside him.

"I hired a man Deke recommended to pick up where your man Tom left off hacking. Unfortunately, what little Tom found has since been expertly brushed beneath the rug. By the way, Tom's here. He threatened all the nurses and doctors so they'd release him in time for the wedding."

Jackson stared out at the drive again. "I've hired a bodyguard for Ysabel. I'd appreciate it if you didn't tell her. She wouldn't be very happy about it."

Flint raised his hand, scout-style. "Wild horses couldn't drag it out of me."

Akeem mimicked Flint. "Same here."

"At least the heat is off the Aggie Four Foundation and Champion Shipping for the time being. Let's hope it stays that way." Jackson studied the black Lincoln Continental inching its way toward the house. When it stopped, he could make out the jeweler's store logo emblazoned in gold lettering on the side panel. "He's here."

"We'll take care of it." Akeem and Flint ran out of the room and returned less than a minute later with a small man in a black suit clutched between them. "Look what we found."

"About time." Jackson strode to the jeweler and held out his hand. "Well, where are they?"

The little man's hands shook as he dug into his suit jacket and pulled out a long flat case. He held it out to Jackson. "I hope these meet with your approval."

Jackson opened the flat box and pulled out a strand of diamonds, a wedding band and diamond engagement ring with a three-carat diamond set in white gold. "I'm not the one who has to approve." He glanced at Flint. "What room is she in?"

"The den on the other end of the house. But it's bad luck to see the bride before the wedding."

"Then you take it." He shoved the necklace into Flint's hands. "Tell her I wanted her to have it and would have given it to her sooner, but well…"

Flint frowned and held out his hand. "Just give me the damned necklace."

"Never mind. I'll deliver it myself." Jackson strode from the room and across the house to the den where Ysabel awaited her cue.

Without knocking he flung the door open. "Ysabel?"

She stood, her long hair swept up on top of her head, curled into loose ringlets. The dress fit her to perfection, her baby tummy not even showing this early in her pregnancy.

Jackson's mouth went dry and his chest swelled to the point he thought his buttons might pop off his shirt and tuxedo jacket.

"It's bad luck to see the bride before the wedding," she said, a smile shining in her eyes.

"You could never be bad luck to me." He stepped through the door and closed it behind him. "I told your mother I'd take care of the something new. I'm sorry I'm late." He stood staring at her, unable to get enough of her. "I've missed you over the last week. Arguing with my new executive assistant isn't as fun as with you."

Ysabel frowned. "What's she like?"

"Temporary. I want you back by my side as soon as possible."

Her frown switched directions. "Good. I don't want to be one of those arm-candy wives who stay home and redecorate because they're bored." She met him halfway and held out her hand. "Something new?"

"New?" He stared down into her moss green eyes, wanting nothing more than to hold her in his arms forever. "Oh, yes." He dug in his pocket. "Turn around."

"Okay." Slowly she turned, the long train on her gown twisting beautifully. She faced a full-length mirror, her gaze finding his in the reflection.

"Close your eyes."

After she'd done as he asked, he slid the diamond necklace around her throat and clasped it in the back. "Okay, you can look."

He stood behind her, staring at her reflection and the look on her face when she opened her eyes.

Ysabel blinked, then her eyes widened. "Are those real?"

Jackson nodded. "Do you like them?"

"Like them?" She touched a finger to the sparkling diamonds, her own green eyes sparkling as bright. "I love them." Then she spun and flung her arms around him.

He kissed her temple and traced a line of kisses to her earlobe. "My baby deserves a little bling, and there's a lot more where that came from." He slipped the engagement ring on her finger.

"*Madre de Dios!* It's huge!" She tipped her hand back and forth, light glinting off the marquis diamond. Then she cupped his face in her hands and stared into his eyes. "I love you, Jackson Champion, whether or not you give me diamonds. You know that, don't you?"

With a smile, he kissed the tip of her nose, then her lips. "I certainly do. That's why I love you so much. You're the real thing, Ysabel, and I want to spend the rest of my life with you."

She leaned up on her tiptoes and kissed him, drawing him into her mouth with all the love she felt. "Then what are we waiting for, cowboy? Are you ready?"

He smiled down at her and gave her his arm. "More than ready to begin the rest of our lives."

* * * * *

Mills & Boon® Intrigue
brings you a sneak preview of…

Debra Webb's
Secrets in Four Corners

Sheriff Patrick Martinez is the law in Kenner County and nobody is going to be threatened under his watch – least of all his long-time love, Bree Hunter, and her little son who he wished was his!

Don't miss this thrilling first story in the
KENNER COUNTY CRIME UNIT
mini-series, available next month from Mills & Boon® Intrigue.

Secrets in Four Corners

by

Debra Webb

[illegible]

[illegible]

[illegible]

Sheriff Patrick Martinez is [illegible] Kenner County [illegible] [illegible] [illegible] [illegible] [illegible] [illegible] [illegible] [illegible]

Don't miss the thrilling next installment of

KENNER COUNTY CRIME UNIT

[illegible]

[illegible]

Secrets in Four Corners

by

Debra Webb

Sabrina Hunter fastened her utility belt around her hips. "Eat up, Peter, or we're gonna be late."

Peter Hunter peered up at his mom, a spoonful of Cheerios halfway to his mouth. "We're always late."

This was definitely nothing to brag about. "But," his mother reminded him, "our New Year's resolution was to make it a point *not* to be late anymore." It was only January twelfth. Surely, they weren't going to break their resolution already.

Chewing his cereal thoughtfully, Peter tilted his dark head and studied her again. "Truth or dare?"

Bree took a deep breath, reached for patience. "Eat. There's no time for games." She tucked her cell phone into her belt. Mondays were always difficult. Especially when Bree had worked the weekend and her son had spent most of that time with his aunt Tabitha. She spoiled the boy outrageously, as did her teenage daughter, Layla. Even so, Bree was glad to have her family support system when duty called, as it had this weekend. She grabbed her mug and downed the last of the coffee that had grown cold during her rush to prepare for the day.

Peter swallowed, then insisted, "Truth. Is my real daddy a jerk just like Big Jack?"

Bree choked. Coughed. She plopped her mug on the counter and stared at her son. "Where did you hear something like that?"

"Cousin Layla said so." He nodded resolutely. "Aunt Tabitha told her to hush 'cause I might hear. Is it true? Is my real daddy a jerk?"

"You must've misunderstood, Peter." *Breathe.* Bree moistened her lips and mentally scrambled for a way to change the subject. "Grab your coat and let's get you to school." Memories tumbled one over the other in her head. Memories she had sworn she would never allow back into her thoughts. That was her other New Year's resolution. After eight years it was past time she'd put *him* out of her head and her heart once and for all.

What the hell was her niece thinking, bringing *him* up? Particularly with Peter anywhere in the vicinity. The kid loved playing hide and seek, loved sneaking up on his mother and aunt even more. His curious nature ensured he missed very little. Tabitha and Layla knew this!

Bree ordered herself to calm down.

"Nope. I didn't misunderstand." Peter pushed back his chair, carefully picked up his cereal bowl and headed for the sink. He rinsed the bowl and placed it just as carefully into the dishwasher. "I heard her."

Bree's pulse rate increased. "Layla was probably talking about..." Bree racked her brain for a name, someone they all knew—anyone besides *him*.

Before she could come up with a name or a logical explanation for her niece's slip, Peter turned to his mother once more, his big blue eyes—the ones so much like his father's and so unlike her brown ones—resolute. "Layla said my real daddy—"

"Okay, okay." Bree held up her hands. "I got that part." How on earth was she supposed to respond? "We can talk on the way to school." Maybe that would at least buy her some time. And if she were really lucky Peter would get distracted and forget all about the subject of his father.

Something Bree herself would very much like to do.

She would be having a serious talk with her sister and niece.

Thankfully her son didn't argue. He tugged on his coat and picked up his backpack. So far, so good. She might just get out of this one after all. Was that selfish of her? Was Peter the one being cheated by her decision to keep the past in the past? Including his father?

Bree pushed the questions aside and shouldered into the navy uniform jacket that sported the logo of the Towaoc Police Department. At the coat closet near her front door, she removed the lockbox from the top shelf, retrieved her service weapon and holstered it. After high school she'd gotten her associate's degree in criminal justice. She hadn't looked back since, spending a decade working in reservation law enforcement. The invitation to join the special homicide task force formed by the Bureau of Indian Affairs and the Ute Mountain Reservation tribal officials had been exactly the opportunity she had been looking for to further her career.

Besides her son and family, her career was primary in her life. Not merely because she was a single parent, either, although that was a compelling enough motive. She wanted to be a part of changing the reservation's unofficial reputation as the murder capital of Colorado. This was her home. Making a difference was important to her. She wanted to do her part for her people.

Not to mention work kept her busy. Kept her head on straight and out of that past she did not want to think about, much less talk about. An idle mind was like idle hands, it got one into trouble more often than not.

Enough trouble had come Bree's way the last few years.

No sooner had she slid behind the wheel of her SUV and closed the door had Peter demanded, "Truth, Mommy." He snapped his safety belt into place.

So much for any hopes of him letting the subject go. Bree glanced over her shoulder to the backseat where her son waited. She could take the easy way out and say his aunt and cousin were right. His curiosity would be satisfied and that would be the end of that—for now anyway. But that would be a lie. There were a lot of things she could say about the man who'd fathered her child, but that he was bad or the kind of jerk her ex, Jack, had turned out to be definitely wasn't one of them.

"Your father was never anything like Big Jack." Even as she said the words, her heart stumbled traitorously.

"So he was a good guy?"

Another question that required a cautiously worded response. "A really good guy."

"Like a superhero?"

Maybe that was a stretch. But her son was into comics lately. "I guess you could say that." Guilt pricked her again for allowing the conversation to remain in past tense...as if his father were deceased. Another selfish gesture on her part.

But life was so much easier that way.

"Am I named after him?"

Tension whipped through Bree. That was a place

she definitely didn't want to go. Her cell phone vibrated. Relief flared. Talk about being saved by the bell, or, in this case, the vibration. "Hold on, honey." Bree withdrew the phone from the case on her belt and opened it. "Hunter."

"Detective Hunter, this is Officer Danny Brewer."

Though she was acquainted with a fair number of local law enforcement members, particularly those on the reservation, the name didn't strike a chord. She couldn't readily associate the name with one department or the other, making it hard to anticipate whether his call was something or nothing. That didn't prevent a new kind of tension from sending her instincts to the next level. "What can I do for you, Officer Brewer?"

"Well, ma'am, we have a situation."

His tone told her far more than his words. *Something.*

When she would have asked for an explanation, he went on, "We have a one eighty-seven."

Adrenaline fired in Bree's veins. Before she could launch the barrage of homicide-related questions that instantly sprang to mind, Brewer tacked on, "My partner said I should call you. He would've called himself but he's been busy puking his guts out ever since we took a look at the…vic."

Damn. Another victim.

Bree blinked, focused on the details she knew so

far. Puking? Had to be Officer Steve Cyrus. She knew him well. Poor Cyrus lost his last meal at every scene involving a body.

One eighty-seven.

Damn.

Another murder.

"Location?" Bree glanced at her son. She would drop him off at school and head straight to the scene. Hell of a way to start a Monday morning. Frustration hit on the heels of the adrenaline. She'd worked a case of rape and attempted murder just this weekend. As hard as her team toiled to prevent as well as solve violent crimes it never seemed to be enough.

"The Tribal Park." Brewer cleared his throat. "In the canyon close to the Two-Story House. One of the guides who checks the trails a couple of times a week during the off-season found the victim."

"Don't let him out of your sight," Bree reminded. She would need to question the guide at length. Chances were he would be the closest thing to a witness, albeit after the fact, she would get. "Did you ID the victim?" She hoped this wasn't another rape as well. Twelve days into the New Year and they'd had two of those already. Both related to drug use.

Bree frowned at the muffled conversation taking place on the other end of the line. It sounded like Brewer was asking his partner what he should say in answer to her question. Weird.

"Ma'am," Brewer said, something different in his voice now, "Steve said just get here as fast as you can. He'll explain the details then."

When the call ended Bree stared at her phone then shook her head.

Damned weird.

"M-o-o-m," Peter said, drawing out the single syllable, "you didn't answer my question."

She definitely didn't have time for that now. More of that guilt heaped on her shoulders at just how relieved she was to have an excuse not to go there. "We'll have to talk about it later. That was another police officer who called. I have to get to work."

Peter groaned, but didn't argue with her. He knew that for his mom work meant something bad had happened to someone.

As Bree guided her vehicle into the school's drop-off lane, she considered her little boy. She wanted life on the reservation to continue to improve. For him. For the next generation, period. As hard as she worked, at times it never seemed to be enough.

"Have a good day, sweetie." She smoothed his hair and kissed the top of his head.

His cheeks instantly reddened. "Mom."

Bree smiled as he hopped out of the SUV and headed for Towaoc Elementary's front entrance. Her baby was growing up. Her smile faded. There would be more questions about his father.